THE FOUNTAIN OF ESSOMUAI

JH Tomen

To you, Dear Reader, once again. I will never be able to thank you enough for taking this journey with me. We made a world exist together, plucking magic from the air, and that is something special.

Wherever life takes you, I hope you live with joy, and remember that you have **been**. Kindness and love fear no erasure, for they are not of us, but rather, we are of them — eternal fragments of stars, forever expanding, the stuff of time itself, woven into an ever-blossoming array.

Cover by Karl Nilsson (@sigvardnilsson)
Map of Ekosinar, the Isles of Dawn, and Berill Detail by Matt Dye (@mattdyedraws)
Map of Wellonai & The Three Sisters by Jeremy DeBor (@jeremydeerboar)
Stone diagram by Shawn Russell (@shawnerussell)
Editing by A.K. Edits (@AdotKEdits)

et tui amóris in eis ignem accénde
renovábis fáciem terræ

Maps

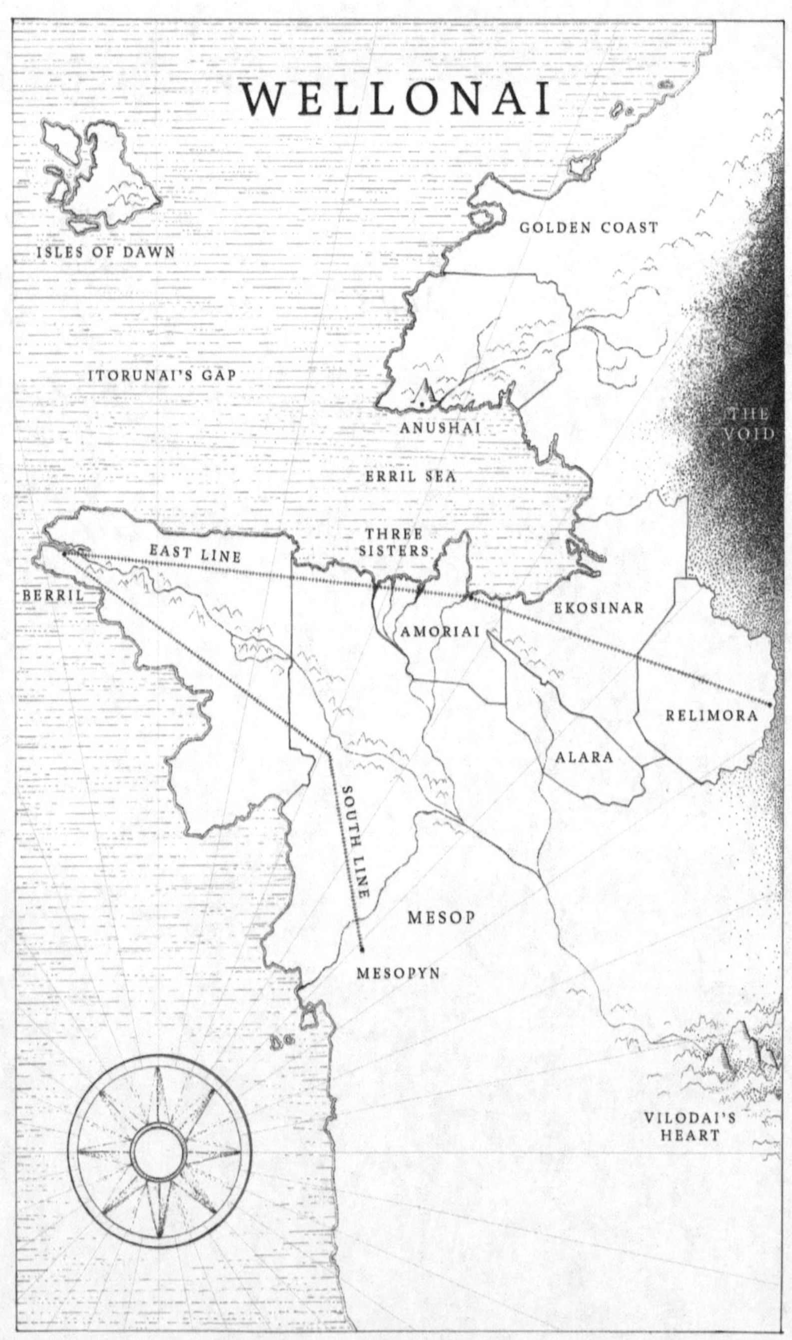

WELLONAI
ISLES OF DAWN
GOLDEN COAST
ITORUNAI'S GAP
ANUSHAI
THE VOID
ERRIL SEA
THREE SISTERS
EAST LINE
BERRIL
EKOSINAR
AMORIAI
RELIMORA
ALARA
SOUTH LINE
MESOP
MESOPYN
VILODAI'S HEART

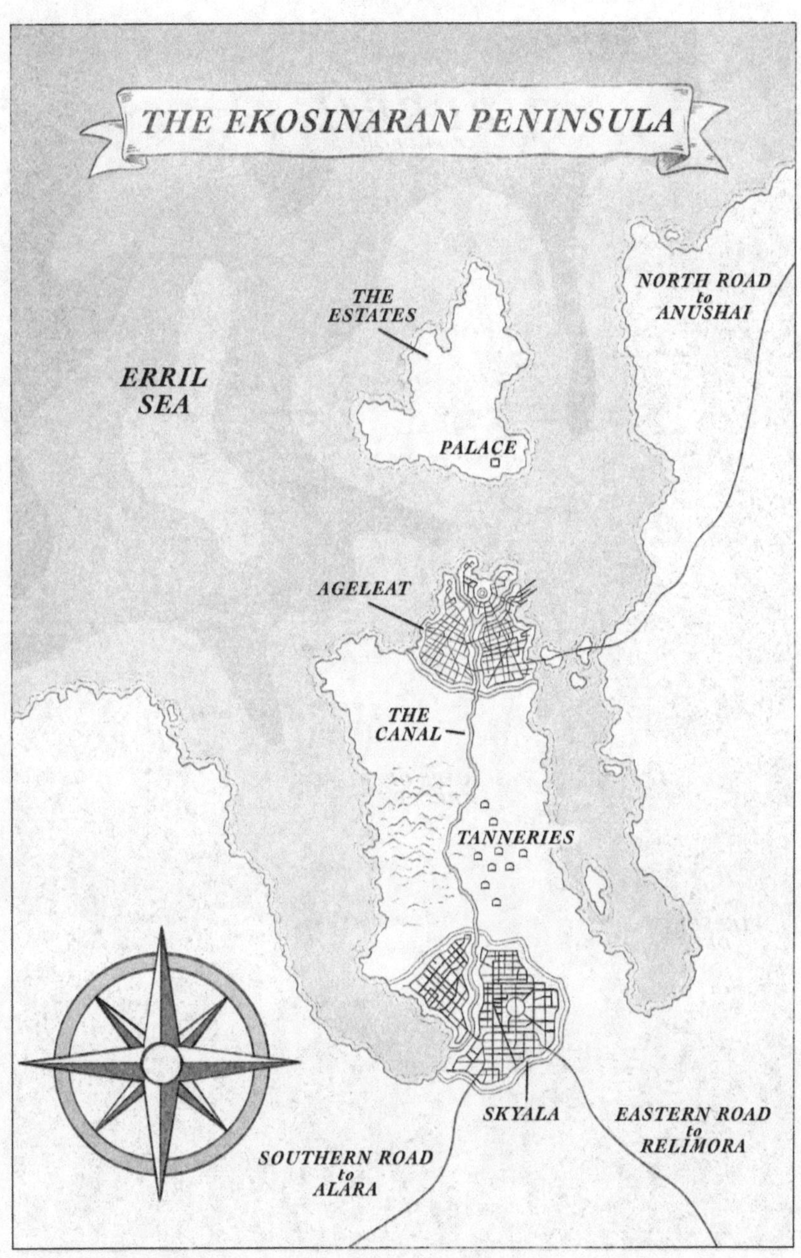
THE EKOSINARAN PENINSULA
THE
ESTATES
ERRIL
SEA
PALACE
NORTH ROAD
to
ANUSHAI
AGELEAT
THE
CANAL
TANNERIES
SKYALA
EASTERN ROAD
to
RELIMORA
SOUTHERN ROAD
to
ALARA

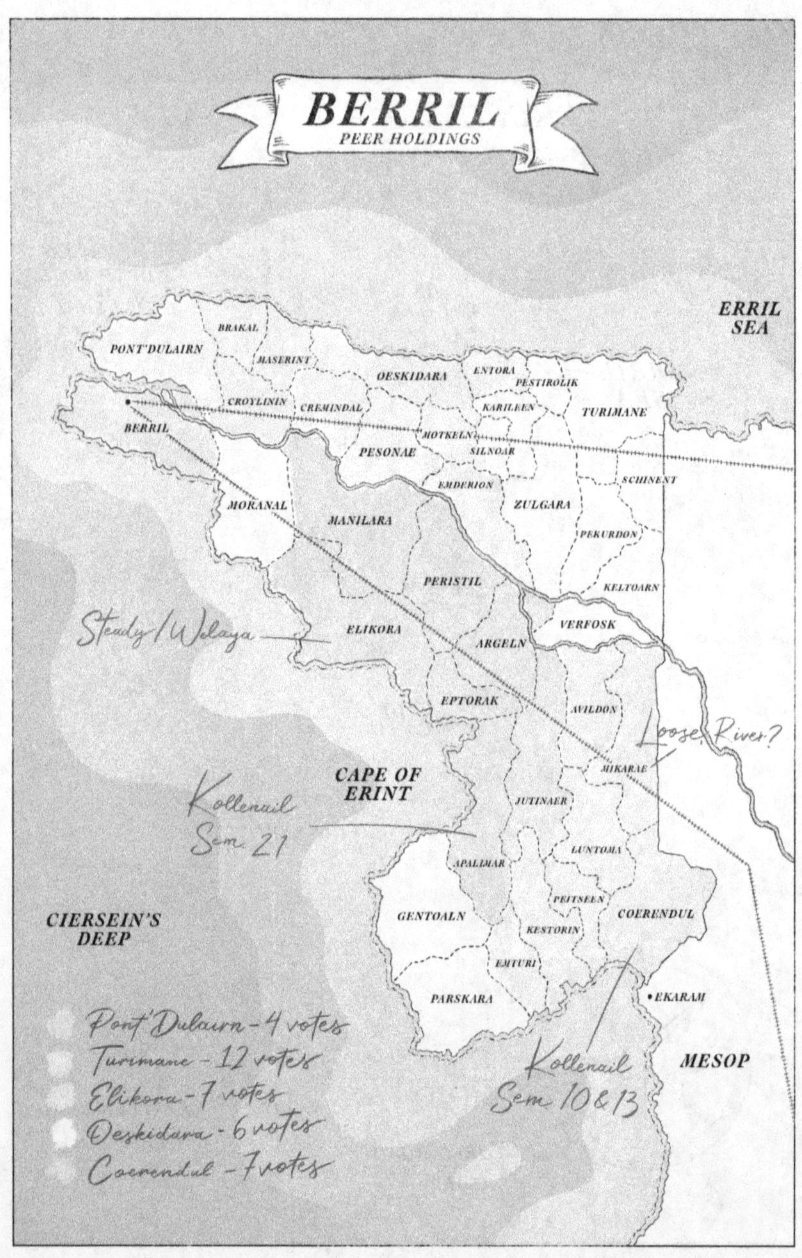
BERRIL
PEER HOLDINGS
ERRIL SEA
BRAKAL
PONT'DULAIRN
MASERINT
OESKIDARA
ENTORA
PESTIROLIK
CROYLININ
CREMINDAL
KARILEEN
TURIMANE
BERRIL
MOTKELN
PESONAE
SILNOAR
EMDERION
SCHINENT
MORANAL
ZULGARA
MANILARA
PEKURDON
PERISTIL
KELTOARN
Steady / Welaya
ELIKORA
VERFOSK
ARGELN
EPTORAK
AVILDON
Loose River?
MIKARAE
CAPE OF ERINT
JUTINAER
Kollenail
Sem 21
LUNTOMA
APALIMAR
PEITSEEN
CIERSEIN'S DEEP
GENTOALN
KESTORIN
COERENDUL
EMTURI
PARSKARA
EKARAM
Pont'Dulairn – 4 votes
Turimane – 12 votes
Kollenail
Sem 10 & 13
MESOP
Elikora – 7 votes
Oeskidara – 6 votes
Coerendul – 7 votes

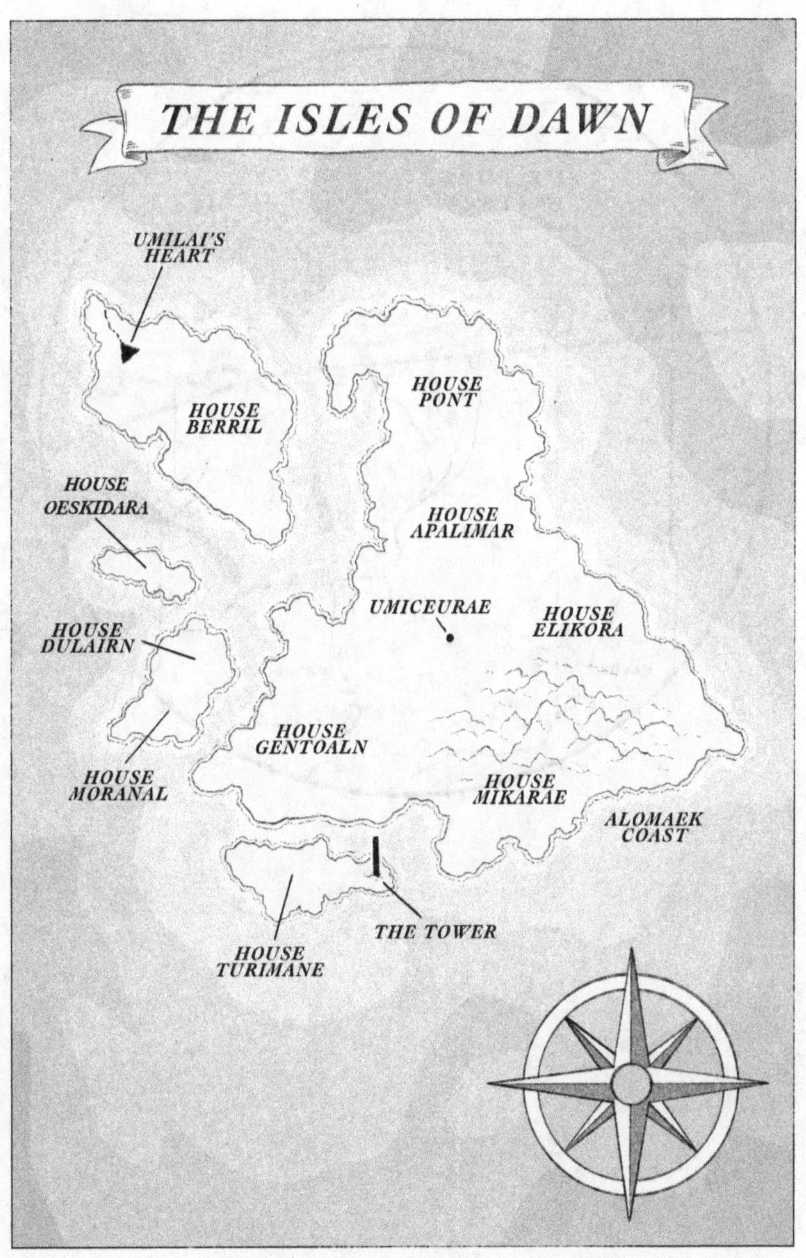

THE ISLES OF DAWN
UMILAI'S HEART
HOUSE BERRIL
HOUSE PONT
HOUSE OESKIDARA
HOUSE APALIMAR
UMICEURAE
HOUSE ELIKORA
HOUSE DULAIRN
HOUSE GENTOALN
HOUSE MORANAL
HOUSE MIKARAE
ALOMAEK COAST
THE TOWER
HOUSE TURIMANE

THE THREE SISTERS
VOLNEERAN PENINSULA
CÖTTHURN
HAFANELLE
STRUSSFARAN
CAPE OF V'INIEL
BERRIL
LUTERRIN
KASELDA
ENOZEIRA
KOLBENZ
AMORIAI
KO'LESTA
ELTIMEIR
MESOP
MALDEGURN
MIEDARAL

Partaking of the land and its awesome power, these pieces of Wellonai became her Daughters. Her blood became Essomuai, her breath, Itorunai, and her voice, Vilodai.

-Verses 4-5 of the Anushgiar Leyosil

Sing of the forgotten daughters, you lost and weary creatures!
You who sail the world, seeking refuge in the storm.
It is our mother who you seek beyond the realms of men.
No kingdom awaits you in the sea, only sacred breath upon the waves.
She comes! The one who knows beginnings as surely as she does ends.
She has seen the air before it filled your lungs, counting the days it would be lent to you.
The stones shall quake with voices, the blood aglow like fire.
But to you, she brings tomorrow. To you, she speaks forever.

-Song of Itorunai, Poet Unnamed
Ekosinar, 207 NE

PART ONE

1

One of the peers brought some personal ephemera to the library today for cataloging. While I was sifting through it, I had an interesting idea about the genealogies, making me wonder how far back the records go on the Isles of Dawn. I'll make sure to write my findings here.

-Excerpts from the personal journals of Peloris Domelgaine
Red Notebook, Age 35

—:—

Vice Peer Kemarin Pont'dulairn crumpled up the telegram in his hand and threw it in the fire. It was from Yeilorn, sealed by the foreign office in Anushai. It appeared that the rumors were true — the Queen was chasing after some Shapewalker on the run and using Detective Parimu to do it. He leaned against the mantel on the fireplace and watched as its edges caught fire, the paper crinkling as it slowly lit and turned to ash.

He ran his hand through his beard as he watched, his mind racing, trying to do all the calculations of what this would mean for his plans. Some liked to call politics a game of towers, but that had never seemed right to him. In towers, you could at least see the other player's pieces, and all the moves were prescribed. In this game, there was really no way of knowing *anything* until the end. You made as many moves as you could, tried to ascribe motives to your enemy, but the results only became clear when the knife slipped in. If only it could be so simple…

This had to be some kind of counterstroke from Welaya. She couldn't know about his upcoming bill yet, though, could she? Perhaps he'd pushed too quickly after the Shapewalker's escape… You never wanted to make a strong enemy truly desperate until you were ready to finish them. Not that he was even out to finish Welaya, though she was unlikely to see it that way. He just wanted to change things. Was that so

12

much to ask? Perhaps it was… It seemed the only thing she truly wanted was to keep Berill exactly how it was when her father died.

Though the Thorns were an entirely different story. There was no telling what they wanted half the time, although control of the military seemed to be a start, by the looks of things. If his informants were right — and any of them could very well be in Kollenail's pocket if he weren't careful — the Thorns were taking more meetings than usual with key admirals. Hopefully, he still had the upper hand. Even knowing that their leader was Kollenail was a truly clever bit of reconnaissance…

He shook his head, turning back to his desk and his personal map of Berill. The Thorns were like rats, but for now, they were just a distraction. The Peerage should have the votes for his next reform bill, but was it time? What if the Queen did find her Shapewalker? He did the math in his head again, tallying the peers that were still firmly his. Out of thirty-six, Oeskidara's last two should give him a majority to pass almost anything. He'd always had Turimane's twelve votes plus his usual four from his father's coalition. With Oeskidara's full six, he was bloody swimming in votes. Still, votes were only part of the game.

The Queen had let his policing bills pass easily enough, but when it came to his plans for the Navy, he would be shocked if she didn't use a royal stay — and keeping enough votes to overturn that would be no easy feat. More importantly, he needed true believers. The other peers only went along with him to line their pockets, but what if a reform actually cost them something someday? He wasn't foolish enough to want to do away with the house system — that kind of power could be well-used in the right hands, obviously — but he'd also just about had his fill of all these coddled barons and dukes.

He took a deep breath, stepping away from his desk and looking up at the portrait of his father over the mantel. If only he were still alive. It had been his dream to bring the Continent together, and his savvy investments had left them with trains, factories, and shipping yards dotting the kingdom. But the phase he'd left to his son, turning all of that into fundamental change, sometimes felt all too impossible. His father hadn't even had more than a vague idea of that last step — take the military from the Queen, make a durable peace between the kingdoms, and finally honor the Continental bloodline of the Pont'dulairns.

Kemarin went back to his desk and took out a fresh piece of paper. Beneath his ink blotter, he reached into the hidden panel and pulled out his cipher. He would need to get something back to Anushai immediately. It was probably too late to save the girl — it usually was by the time the crown sent out the hounds — but he needed to get a handle on it. It was bad enough to see needless blood spilt, but he couldn't let them drag the girl back to Berill if there was something in it for the Thorns.

A short while later, he emerged from his study to find his wife, Elisal, coming down the hallway toward him. She wore scarlet, of course, as she did almost every day. Even after a quarter-century, she still looked positively stunning, quite the contrast to the haggard old politician he'd become. Even with her brows furrowed in worry, she managed to be angelic. How did she do it? Other women in the Three Sisters certainly didn't age so well.

"What has happened?" she asked, taking his arm as he locked the study door. Her accent was thick today, always deepening by a few shades when she was worried. "I saw Terosan leaving."

He turned, cupping her face.

"More of the Anushai business, I'm afraid."

Her frown turned into a scowl as Detective Parimu no doubt entered her mind. They were aligned on police reform, of course, but after that incident in the market the year before, she'd taken a somewhat more...personal stance on the issue.

"Do you need me to write you something for Yeilorn?" she asked.

"I have it here," he said, holding up the letter he'd already sealed. "I'm taking it to Terosan now so he can send it from the Peerage telegraph."

She nodded.

"Alright, just don't stay at the office too long. We have Oeskidara for dinner tonight."

"Of course," he said, though he'd completely forgotten in his rush. This woman! He'd be absolutely lost without her. Just another thing his father had been right about... It wasn't just remembering little details, though — she was as good at politics as he was. She hated Lady Oeskidara with a burning passion, and yet, she entertained the woman twice a month to keep his alliances strong, all without being asked. He leaned in and kissed her cheek, relishing the smell of her perfume for just a moment.

"I won't be long," he said, squeezing her shoulder before heading down the hall where a valet was already waiting with his cloak. At least he'd had one moment of domestic bliss before leaving again... Outside these walls, there was only politics, where lives were squandered chasing after nothing more than a coin toss — a moment of glory or a knife in the gut.

2

The Vice Peer died today after a terrible bout of sickness. He was a good friend and ally, and I will miss him dearly. His replacement from House Croylinin doesn't seem anywhere near as amenable to our plans, but perhaps if we wait for his son, Kemarin...

-Excerpts from the personal journals of Peloris Domelgaine
Yellow Notebook, Age 63

—:—

Sumi sat on a rock in the woods with her legs pulled up under her. Erso and Parimu were breaking down their campsite, though the sounds seemed distant. Instead, with her eyes closed, she was focusing on the jumble of songs around her. There seemed to be thousands of them coming from every living thing — and every non-living thing, for that matter. Ever since she touched Essomuai directly, it seemed she could hear them all the time. Her sleep was still filled with strange dreams, too, though they were hard to remember most mornings.

She tried to focus on just one, the song of the rock she was sitting on. It still felt strange to refer to them as songs, but that was the only word that even remotely did them justice. Sometimes they really did sound like songs as you'd normally think of them — especially birds. Others, though, were more like feelings or heartbeats, a rhythm that reverberated against her core. The rock beneath her sang a deep bass, a pulsing sound as if a wide drum were being struck. It had a rhythm, but it was almost undetectable for its slow pace.

Images began to flash through her mind like when she'd merged with Parimu, snippets of the rock's 'life' whirring by. She could see them as if through a thin golden barrier, the part of Essomuai in her heart reaching out, yearning to be the rock. Sometimes it was hard to decide if it was her that wanted to be the rock or Essomuai… She still seemed to be in control, free to step through that golden barrier like a door in Mu'lalat, but the songs were nearly impossible to avoid. She heard them more easily when she reached out to Essomuai, but some days, they came barging in whether she wanted them or not.

Still, with songs so beautiful, it was hard not to *want* to stop and listen to them all… Like this rock, its steady drumbeat holding her in rapture. It could remember being born, cleft from a mountain during a great quake. It had rolled for some time before landing in this field. There hadn't even been a forest then. Suddenly, the memories quickened, thousands of years passing in an eye-blink. The rock was a fraction of its original size now, but its memories were long and rich. The sun warming its face, the forest growing around it. She could almost taste its minerals on her tongue. If she could only reach out—

"We're ready now," Erso said, touching her shoulder. She nearly jumped, blinking hard as if she'd just come up from underwater. She stared at him for a second, almost unknowing, like waking from a dream and not recognizing the room you'd gone to sleep in. But the songs receded from her mind, and luckily, the love she felt for Erso came rushing back in. She smiled.

"Sorry," she said, fixing her hair, "I should have helped. I just…"

"It's alright," he said, taking her hand and lifting her up. "We all have jobs to do. Some of us are rolling up tents, others are communing with goddesses or something strange like that. All jobs are equally important, though my pay is better."

She cocked an eyebrow at him.

"Your pay? I don't think we discussed any wages for your service."

"Funny," he said, leaning in and kissing her gently. "You've been paying me for weeks. In fact, you just paid me again." She still felt the tingle of his mustache after he pulled away. She almost heard his song, but she shook her head, focusing on the feeling of her own lips. She knew enough of his past already, knew almost every note of his song by now. What she needed now was to be here with him in the present as the rest of his song was being written. She squeezed his hand, and he turned away, heading toward where Parimu was saddling the horses.

She approached Parimu, touching his shoulder gently.

"Thank you, Relsenair," she said, smiling. "How did you sleep?"

"Not too poorly, thank you, Miss Elerair," he said, nodding. He was still being too formal by half, though he was probably desperate for some structure, going from the police to wandering around with two Shapewalkers… He had even been on the orders of the Queen before he'd found them! She was a poor substitute for royalty, but they'd need him if they were to have any chance of reaching the Fountain of Essomuai in the southern mountains. At least he wasn't calling her princess anymore… They had told him of her loose connection to Grass House, and he'd been trying to cling to that at first.

"You can call me Sumi, you know," she said, smiling as warmly as she could.

Parimu nodded gratefully, turning back to his horse. She shot a glance at Erso, where he was sulking by his horse in the rear of the line. He looked away as soon as he saw her, pretending to tighten one of his stirrups. He'd just as soon have put a knife in the detective, but she was trying to keep them at least civil for now. She couldn't blame Erso, of course. The two men had crossed swords just weeks earlier, and he hadn't had the opportunity to hear Parimu's song.

It was a funny thing, what Essomuai could do, replaying a person's life like that. It was like the rock's story, only living it instead of watching it, seeing all the more easily how they'd been shaped like the rock whittled away by rain. There was a great deal of pain in Parimu's life, and a lot more goodness than you'd suspect at first glance. He'd always wanted to help people, he just hadn't known how. She was still working that part out herself, but they would need his loyalty in the days ahead.

Erso at least seemed to respect Parimu's experience with everything they were up against — staying in the woods, protecting their camp, avoiding the Thorns... None of those were things *she* was particularly qualified for, even if she had accidentally touched a goddess. Not that she was even remotely sure what she'd do once they reached the Fountain… Still, she could feel Essomuai in the south, her song the backdrop to all the others, hiding in her mind all along. Even in Amoriai, those phantom keyholes — the goddess had been reaching for her, for all her children.

They would go back to Berill eventually; she refused to let go of that promise to herself. There had to be a way to change her people, to get herself back home. If anything, it was her love for Berill pushing her to reach out to the goddess in the first place. Had no one else ever tried as much? For whatever reason, though, when she called on Essomuai, the goddess had answered. She had changed everything, opening her to a light she hadn't even realized was shining. If there were answers anywhere, they would be at the Fountain.

With everything packed, she pulled herself into the saddle. At least she'd have plenty of time to plan… Until they reached Erso's friends in

Ekosinar, they'd be on horseback, and even then, if they found a boat to take them up the Nyfatsi River to Vilodai's Heart, they had hundreds of miles to go. Luckily, the others had given her the nicest horse, a beautiful mare with a chestnut coat, a bright white splash on her chest.

"Morning, Eto," she said, stroking the horse's mane. She turned a giant hazel eye on her before snorting and turning back around. That was a happy sound, right? Hopefully it wasn't the new name…

She'd had a name when they bought her from the livery, but she'd given her a new one — *etoseram*. Or perhaps 'giving' wasn't the right way to put it since she had no idea what it meant or what language it was in… Still, the moment she'd touched the horse, its song had come rushing in, the name bubbling up with it. It put an image in her mind of a horse running across a field — *freedom*, it seemed to say. There had been a few times when the songs turned into words, the images leaving a strong sort of meaning in their wake. Was that how the goddesses spoke?

Whatever it meant, Eto had better like it because she was hopeless in the saddle. Luckily, Eto was about as docile a creature as was likely to exist, though she offered little help. Grandpa had taught her the basics as a girl, but it wasn't like she'd had much opportunity to practice. She was probably letting down her royal heritage, though Nela hadn't seemed particularly taken with the animals. At least she was no worse than Erso. He almost seemed offended the forest wasn't paved.

Once they were all mounted, Parimu took the lead, nudging his horse out of camp and back toward the road. Sumi clucked her tongue, and Eto followed the other horse, Erso behind them. The boys pretended they liked roughing it, but she was glad they'd picked up the road again. They'd been opting for speed — and secrecy — more than convenience, bushwhacking their way across steep hills covered in thickets. Now that they'd finally come around the cape, though, it was a straight shot to Ekosinar, and they were picking up the Northern Road again.

After a few minutes of riding, they finally reached the steep berm that edged the road, the horses' hooves shuffling through the yellowing grass. It was jarring how quickly the forest had changed. Near Anushai, it had been raining constantly, the woods choking with ferns and thick knots of pines. Now, though, they were close to the Void, and the lush greenery had given way to thickets of grass and towering aspens.

Most of their gear was tied behind Parimu's saddle, and as his horse climbed the hill ahead of hers, she looked at their little stack of tents, smiling. Though, admittedly, she did have just a *brief* moment of panic when Erso had gone to buy them… They had kissed, and he was so experienced with the world and— Well, he had come back with three, so she hadn't been forced to cross that bridge just yet. Not that she'd be opposed to sharing a bed with him someday… Still, the tents may not be as solid as a cottage, but they were starting to feel like home.

When she was drifting off to sleep, she liked to imagine what it would be like to share a real home with him someday. Though all of that also depended on her not getting him killed with her foolish plans first… And that usually got her thinking about sending him away before he got hurt. Needless to say, picturing your beloved on the gallows wasn't a very romantic train of thought.

And yet, Erso was managing to make each day special. Even though they were on the run, eating beans, he managed to nurture the tiny seed of love they'd planted together. He had a knack for carving out tiny slivers of time where everything seemed like magic, and anything seemed possible. He never did anything that would make Parimu feel left out — they were only three, after all — but he always found something they could do together. Looking for mushrooms, getting water from a creek, taking just enough time to hold her hand and kiss her softly. She could still hardly believe she had someone in this world that was truly hers, someone as incredible as Erso.

They crested the hill, turning south again. They stayed in their single-file line like always, clomping along the hard-packed dirt in silence. Sometimes Erso would whistle something, but mostly they just kept to their own thoughts. The others said a single line was safe, but she did worry about getting lost in thought, especially with the songs pulling at her… If they were attacked, she'd be basically useless.

There had to be some way her powers could protect them, right? Something useful in the songs only she could find? She couldn't just wait on Erso and Parimu to do everything with their swords. Besides, she had a feeling Essomuai would want more from them than fighting. Even tiny deaths, like animals they found along the road, seemed to fill the goddess with sadness, the feeling seeping into the songs of the dead.

She shook her head, trying to stay present, forcing her eyes on their surroundings. As she'd taken to doing since leaving Anushai, she looked out toward the east. She couldn't see anything beyond the tree line, of course, but knowing the Void was out there somewhere made her wish she could see it. What was it like? A desert wider than any sea, completely *empty*. She hadn't thought about it much during geography growing up, Anushai always seeming more interesting, but now that she knew Essomuai was real… She thought back to the house histories she'd read in Anushai, every legend now potentially true for all she knew.

Wellonai both was and was not. In the Void, there was nothing, and there was everything. Wellonai desired to become, and so became the land. This land was blank, but in it was her blood, her breath, and her voice.

So where was Wellonai? Was she the Void itself, the part of the world where her daughters were not? Or was she broken up into all things now? Was there anything in that desert, or was this land all there was to life? She shook her head. It was almost too much for one mind to hold. Everything she had ever learned, if not coming undone exactly, was only growing more mysterious each day. She had enough problems trying to understand the Continent, let alone what lay beyond the edge of the world.

She turned to look at Erso, and he smiled, tipping his hat. He had taken to wearing a wide-brimmed Relimoran thing he'd shaped for himself, claiming he wanted some local fashion, even in the woods. Across his lap, he held a musket, his eyes darting between the trees. He said he wasn't a very good shot, but Parimu didn't much like muskets, and he'd wanted more protection than their swords and bow.

"Hey, Parimu," she asked, turning back to the front, "why is it you don't like muskets again?" It was something about the…navy?

He turned to her, smiling shyly. She'd need to file that away — he seemed to like being asked about the navy. From his memories, those seemed like happy times for him. Perhaps because that was before he'd lost Jalicyne…

"Don't know a lot of navy men who like them, to be honest," he said, turning back around in his saddle. He always tried to face forward when he was in the lead, but he continued to turn his head just a bit to talk to her out of the side of his mouth. "They're pretty hard to use at sea, and you might as well use a cannon if you're going to waste the gunpowder. I grew up around bows, though, so I guess they work for me."

"Well, they certainly do that, mate," Erso said, nodding respectfully. They could only pack so much meat into their saddlebags, and Parimu had managed to hunt something in the woods every night to add to dinner. Maybe they'd get along after all…

They kept on in that way for a while, chatting only occasionally as they let the horses clop along at an easy pace. Now that they were only two or three days out of the capital, Ageleat, the terrain seemed to be getting easier, which the horses didn't seem to mind. They were coming around a bend in the road when they found a merchant caravan by a stream, watering their horses and filling up jugs. There were only three or four wagons, but a whole mess of workers dashed about, looking things over.

"There we are," Erso said, winking at her as he kicked his horse up from the back of the line, "knew our luck would turn."

He'd been talking about running into merchants all week, desperate for something other than beans and sparrows, if only for a night. Still, there hadn't been anywhere near as many people on the road as she'd expected. They had camped near the water a few nights along the coast, and she hadn't seen all that many boats either. They could be sailing straight across the Erril Sea, but it still felt quiet for how bustling Ekosinaran trade was supposed to be.

Erso shot ahead at a trot, and by the time she and Parimu reached the bridge over the stream, he was already off his horse and slapping a large man on the back behind the wagons.

"He's from Amoriai," Erso said, jerking a thumb at the man as he grinned. "Told him I'd trade your horse for some decent grain."

She shot him a look, putting a protective hand on Eto's mane.

"How d'ya do, ma'am?" the man said, nodding. "I'm Hilsan, and I couldn't dream of taking such a fine horse." He seemed to be a foreman of sorts, especially since he was just watching while the other men worked on the horses.

She turned to smile at him when his song hit her mind, the powerful rhythm making her blink. That must mean he was a Shapewalker, then… Everything, even humans, seemed to have a song, but Shapewalkers were much louder, like their keyholes, almost insistent as they reached out for Essomuai. As she looked again, she noticed the faint golden glow around him, more subtle than the song. She was tempted to listen, but she shook her head, focusing on not being rude instead.

"Lovely to meet you," she said. "I'm Sumi, and this is Relsenair." Parimu nodded quickly before he went back to watching the road. Even surrounded by a dozen wagon drivers, he was still watching for an ambush. He could probably use a lesson from Erso on enjoying himself, though she'd have to get them talking first…

"All jokes aside," Erso said, "Hilsan here has a few extra bags of grain, and he can give us a decent price if you think we can spare the coin."

Sumi nodded, staring into space as she tried to count in her head. They had pooled their money together when they left Anushai, though the purse hidden in her saddlebags wasn't quite as full as she'd like. Still, Erso's pretzels would do a lot for morale… She glanced at Parimu, though he kept his eyes on the road. He'd clearly struggled when he bought them horses with the Queen's coin, holding the money in his hand for a full minute before handing it over.

"Well, it really is for Berill, after all," he'd mumbled, "maybe just not how the Queen had planned…"

Still, even if he'd only wanted it off his conscience, it seemed he'd stopped worrying about the money the moment he handed it to her. It was a mystery why a police officer would follow a mousey shopkeeper, but he hadn't raised a single objection to how she spent the coin.

Queen Welaya had given him nearly eight hundred crowns when he left to hunt them. It was a staggering amount of money — nearly seven times Grandpa's pension — but he'd still had around a hundred left after all his traveling and buying the horses. That, added with Erso's mishmash of money, did give them some wiggle room. It was just hard to know when to spend it with a long way to go and no end in sight… Parimu technically still had those royal bank writs for another four thousand crowns — her eyes had nearly popped out of her head when she'd heard that — but the Berillai treasury would know as soon as they withdrew the money.

"Don't want to get between you and your wife," Hilsan said to Erso, a nervous look in his eye. If anything, she was flattered she could be mistaken for his wife, though Hilsan was probably mistaking her pause for anger. If they ever did get married, though, she'd probably have to get in the habit of watching their money a bit more carefully… Not that Erso was profligate, but he did have a tendency to steal whatever he couldn't afford.

"I'm sure we could work something out," Hilsan continued, "spare musket balls maybe— "

"That's alright," Sumi said, smiling. The pretzels felt right. She could probably eat beans forever — it wasn't much worse than what she'd lived on after Nela died — but they really should enjoy themselves once in a while. They'd never be able to face what was ahead of them if they couldn't keep their spirits up.

"How much did you say for the flour?"

"Well," Hilsan said, smiling as his shrewd merchant face slid back on, "that would depend on the coin, of course. Certain crowns aren't what they used to be. I suppose a half-sovereign Berillai would work for a five-pound bag."

She thought through the coins in her purse again. She almost wanted to laugh, thinking of how much she'd hated the haggling at Wembly back home. She still hated it, of course, but now that she was the 'keeper of the coin,' as it were, she felt compelled to get every last ounce out of their purse. She tried to picture the pile of Anushai coins they had from Erso's savings. Those would only get harder to spend the further south they went.

"Well, it seems you're going north," she said slowly. Nela had always said that good haggling was about knowing when to walk away, but she wanted the flour. "Do you think you could do it for an Anushai bronze?"

"You were right," Hilsan said to Erso, laughing, "she's much tougher than you. Seems fair, though." He called out to one of his workers. "Perrik! Get 'em a bag of flour, eh?"

"Coming!" one of the workers called out, heading to the back of the first wagon in the train.

"So, where you headed?" Hilsan asked, seeming to relax once the deal was struck. She was still trying to discreetly dig out the money, but Erso thankfully jumped in.

"Ageleat," he said casually, "we raise horses, and we're meeting a buyer. Good bit cheaper to ride 'em down, of course."

She'd thought it a strange cover story, seeing how little they knew about horses, but Hilsan seemed to take it in stride.

"Now that's interesting," he said, rubbing his chin. "Not a lot of horse flesh up north anymore. It's all Mesop stock at the markets these days with the trains and all."

Erso nodded sagely, an artisan at bluffing if she'd ever seen one.

"Surely is," he said. "We do what we can with our little herd. Bit of a niche market these days, to be honest. But we haven't been down south in a while. Is the road always this quiet these days?"

"Afraid so," Hilsan said, nodding in thanks as she finally fished out her coin and handed it to him. "Used to be everyone in Ekosinar went north twice a season, but it's definitely slower these days. We'd be taking a boat too if the captains weren't all tripping over themselves to head west for the steel mills."

"Fair enough," Erso said, meeting Sumi's eyes. He'd been the first one to bring up the slow traffic heading north. It seemed the Berillai really were on the brink of winning over the whole basin... If they were going to change things, they'd need to do it quickly before Berillai trade — and its requisite hatred of Shapewalkers — became the law of the land everywhere.

Hilsan's man came up with a large bag of flour in his hands. Erso took it in one arm, extending the other to shake hands with the merchant.

"Well, thank you, friend," he said. "Safe journey to you. We better be on our way if we're gonna make a decent camp by nightfall."

"A pleasure," Hilsan said, smiling broadly. "Maybe I'll see you on your way back north. If you've eaten all that flour, we could do a bit more business."

He laughed, clutching his belly as Erso slapped him on the back, stowing the flour. As soon as he was in the saddle, Parimu nodded at the merchant, nudging his horse over the bridge. Just when she thought he hadn't been paying attention to their conversation... They continued down the road, moving at a quick walk as they wound through the forest.

———

They passed the rest of the day in the same way, only stopping to water the horses and sneak behind the trees to use the facilities, such that they were... They ate lunch on horseback too, chewing on some jerky, all in the service of covering as much ground as they could while the sun was out. And they really were making good progress. Each time they stopped, she pulled out her map, the matching curves of the road and the coast telling her roughly how far they'd gone.

Finally, the sun arced lower until it touched the tops of the trees. Parimu pulled his horse to the west side of the road, looking into the trees for a campsite. After a minute or two, he waved for them to follow, nudging his mount into the underbrush. He seemed to have a knack for finding a comfortable clearing, even when nothing was visible through the canopy. He'd said he picked it up hunting with his father growing up, another thing she and Erso knew nothing about...

They picked their way down a gentle slope, emerging into a beautiful little clearing, a babbling stream winding through a tall ring of trees. Eto whinnied happily, bending her head to pull off big clumps of yarrow and chamomile from the tree line. The others were stricter with their horses, but she never had the heart to yank on the bridle. Besides, Eto was good when they were on the road. After a few more mouthfuls, she gently nudged her sides, goading the horse toward where the others were unpacking.

"How *do* you find these spots?" she asked Parimu, swinging out of her saddle. "This is lovely."

"The wind," he said, pausing with his tent under his arm to point at the treetops. "I guess I don't know they'll be *lovely*, but you can feel from the breeze that there's a clearing."

She looked up, watching as the branches waved in the wind. It was breezier than she'd realized, and the wind did sort of swirl over the clearing, rustling through her dress as it ran back out to the woods. There were stories of Berillai sailors reading the wind, but she'd thought it was a metaphor... Not that she was much different listening to the songs of a goddess. Maybe it had something to do with Itorunai?

She jumped again as Erso came up behind her and tapped her on the shoulder. He chuckled, handing her one of the rolled-up tents.

"Why don't you go pick out a spot you like, and I'll get it set up for you before dinner?"

She opened her mouth to protest but remembered what a poor showing she'd made of pitching her own tent the first night… Besides, she *had* promised Parimu they'd do another lesson before dinner, and if she really wanted to marry Erso, she'd have to stop being so shy about everything. She chuckled to herself, turning to look for a spot. With both of those big louts snoring, she'd need the perfect place, far enough to sleep without being so close to the forest that the darkness kept her awake…

3

*The expedition to the Isles has been a resounding success so far. I'll
need to thank Estoras again for securing that meeting with the King.
If I had known what it would be like, I would have come years ago!*

**-Excerpts from the personal journals of Peloris Domelgaine
Blue Notebook, Age 52**

—:—

An hour later, with camp all set up, Erso squatted by the fire, stirring
their dinner. He had his pipe in his mouth, only paying half a mind to
the hot slop in the pot. He'd become head chef while Sumi trained
Parimu — if you could call boiling things cooking. Whatever it was, it
didn't take much focus, though it was still better than having him teach
the detective. And at least now he had his pretzels to occupy him...

He glanced at the others. They were a little ways out of camp, both
sitting on good-sized rocks as they faced each other. Sumi was talking
quickly, her hands flying as she tried to explain everything to Parimu.
Another reason for her to do the training — now that she understood
magic better than anyone else on Wellonai. He hadn't ever heard of
anyone communing with Essomuai — hadn't even thought the gods
were real, for that matter. But it seemed everything they'd practiced, the
art of letting go, was just letting the goddess pull you through the halls.
It was enough to make your head spin. At least the bloody god of the sea
wasn't real...right?

He watched her for another moment to make sure she was busy before
checking on the pretzels. They probably weren't going to turn out, but
he still wanted to surprise her, anything to keep her in the here and now.
That Hilsan bloke hadn't had any ale, but he did have a bit of dry yeast.
The grain wasn't Amoriai either, the good stuff probably going west.

Still, the fire was hot, and hopefully, they'd have a nice shell on them. He'd twisted them up on his little iron pan, putting them right in the hot coals.

What would Ma think of these pretzels? It was strange, but now that he was — what, madly in love? — he was remembering his family all the time, as if unburying his heart had forced him to dig up the past too. He shook his head. Him, a lovebird. It seemed so…normal. Not that he'd fallen in love for his own sake, to be a bloody family man like Beysal. He had fallen in love because an angel burst into his halls, and there was just no running from things like that.

Still, the more he found himself thinking of his mother, the more he wished Sumi could have met her. There was no question his parents would have loved Sumi — that feeling was almost universal. Even Parimu, who'd been hunting them just a couple of weeks ago, was already becoming her lapdog. But the thought of taking Sumi home to his parents' house, before the coup, before the fires... The daydream pulled at him. Ma giving him a hard time, dragging Sumi around the theater, showing her off. Maybe he really did want a family, so long as he could have it with her.

He glanced back at her. They may be marching toward their deaths — by goddess or Thorns, it was too soon to tell — but this was where he belonged. Sumi was his family now. Maybe they hadn't said any vows or shared a bed, but he was firmly hers as long as she'd have him, and he was going to see her through this. They may not be in a lovely little cottage, but they had tents and a fire, and that was home enough. Besides, he could use some practice after all those years on the road, and cooking gruel in the woods with no ale was probably all the training he was gonna get…

_____

Parimu sat on a rock with his eyes closed, listening to Sumi's voice. It was difficult to sit there like that, like a sheep in the dark. He had spent his whole life looking around every corner for a threat, and now he was just supposed to…let go? Even with his eyes closed, he could feel the woods around him, hundreds of unseen eyes lurking in the dusk. Not to mention Erso… The man had such a casual way about him, but he saw everything, and it made him feel even more self-conscious. Not just for his weak Shapewalking but for crossing swords with the man when he'd only been protecting Sumi… It made his guilt come roaring back that much more.

"Parimu," Sumi said gently, touching his shoulder, "are you still there?"

He opened his eyes, scratching his head in embarrassment.

"Sorry," he said, "yes. Just trying to…absorb the lesson, I guess."

She gave him a knowing smile. She knew letting go of his guilt was easier said than done. From where he sat now, it felt like a boulder he'd be carrying for the rest of his life. She said Essomuai accepted him for what he was, to just put his memories into the pool and exist as Essomuai knew him. But what if the version of himself Essomuai knew was just a monster? It made him want to hold that guilt, if only to keep himself from becoming that again.

"You're here now," she said as if reading his mind. And maybe she could, the way she listened to the songs… "That's all that matters. You *are* good, Relsenair, and we need you. I know you're trying to keep us safe, but you still have to know when to let go, alright?"

He nodded. Letting go… That must be why he hadn't heard the songs yet. Although, Erso still couldn't hear them either. For all they knew, Sumi might be the first person who'd ever heard them, which was strange with all those Anushai up north. Though he might have never even heard the keyholes if he hadn't forced himself… He could still hear the buzzing from Sumi, though it wasn't exactly a song, not like that strange day when they had merged. He still didn't know how to process that memory. It felt more like a dream, like something he'd seen with his own eyes but forgotten when he woke. For now, she was just trying to teach him the way she'd been taught — with an extra dose of Essomuai thrown in.

"Alright," she said, "this time, let's focus on sound. Put all your worries in the pool and listen to the world around you." She took a deep breath, closing her eyes. "I can hear the wind rustling through the trees, like breath, coming from somewhere, going nowhere. In and out. Picture your pool—"

He closed his eyes too, picturing his pool. He wasn't sure if it looked right, though Sumi said it didn't matter, as long as it was truly his. Hers didn't have an exact location, but he had used a real one, jumping on the first thing that had come to mind. There had been a cave just outside of Emillon where he and Jalicyne spent their days in the summer. It hadn't been a dangerous chasm or anything, just a place where the land opened up, a rocky vault covered in moss and a tall, broken ceiling where the light came through.

He pictured his pool there. It was a bit misshapen, but there had always been a large dip in the floor of their cave where he and Jalicyne would poke sticks in the puddles, looking for frogs. If there was any place that could hold magic for him, it would be there. In fact, he always pictured Jalicyne next to him, crouching down and smiling as she stared into the pool. It probably wasn't necessary, but it made him feel like he belonged there, like he was home again.

He opened his eyes to tell Sumi he was ready, but she was gone. He had been so wrapped up in picturing his cave, he had stopped listening to her voice. He frowned. That was unlike her to walk off during a lesson. She was so considerate, so thoughtful — really one of the best leaders he'd ever had. He turned toward the fire where Erso was cooking, but she wasn't there either.

"Um…Erso?" he called out. "Did you see where Sumi got off to? She was just here giving me a lesson, and now she's…not."

Erso looked up, a frown on his face. He turned toward the woods, and Parimu looked too. Had she just gone to relieve herself?

"Sumi!" Erso called out, but there was no reply.

Erso looked back at him with wide eyes, walking quickly toward the trees. Parimu followed, dashing back to the fire to grab his bow first. They had made camp in a clearing about a half-mile west of the road. There were tall trees all around them, and it was starting to get dark. His mind raced; where could she have gone? She couldn't have been taken, not all the way out here, right?

They wandered into the scrubby thickets growing under the trees, pushing quickly through the branches. They both began to call out her name.

"Sumi!" Parimu yelled as loudly as he could. Without needing to discuss it, they both waited a few seconds after each shout, straining their ears. Still, the only thing they heard was the wind. It was still blowing strongly, rocking the canopy back and forth in waves.

"You said she was just sitting there?" Erso asked, turning around. A momentary suspicion came over his face, but just as quickly, it was gone, his eyes tight with worry as he turned back to the woods.

"Yes," Parimu said. "She had me close my eyes to meditate, and when I opened them, she was gone."

Erso took a deep breath, turning in a circle.

"Should we split up?" he asked. "I don't know what could have happened, but there's a lot of woods to cover… You any good at tracking?"

"I know a bit," Parimu said doubtfully. He'd learned that from his father as well, of course, but that was different… He turned to look back at the crushed bushes and grass they had left in their wake. If she had walked out of camp, hopefully they hadn't already destroyed her tracks. An owl hooted somewhere in the trees above them.

"If there is a trail," he continued," I don't think we'll be able to find it in the dark." He lifted his bow. "Let's stick together in case she didn't leave…on her own."

"Right," Erso said, squaring his jaw. He looked back to the camp, probably thinking to grab his musket, but he just shook his head. "Let's get moving, cover as much ground as we can."

Parimu nodded, following him forward. They went a bit deeper into the woods and then started to the right, walking in a wide circle around the camp. They continued to call out her name, yelling louder each time, struggling to raise their voices over the wind. They were starting to get hoarse, but they kept taking turns, each man calling out at the top of his lungs. They eventually reached the spot where they'd first entered the clearing on their horses, but otherwise, the ring of grass was unbroken. They kept moving, completing a full circle around the camp until they stopped back at the first thicket.

"Should we go back to the road?" Parimu asked. "If she isn't anywhere around here, maybe she left that way? We just have to hope there's some new tracks from when we arrived this afternoon."

Erso nodded. They started to head that way when a giant burst of wind ripped through the trees, kicking up leaves and dust. He went to cover his eyes when the air seemed to burst with light. He blinked, and suddenly Sumi was there, sitting on the ground in a daze, looking up at them.

"Sumi!" Erso yelled, running up and falling to his knees by her side. She smiled, blinking as she reached out and gripped his shoulder. She turned to Parimu.

"I heard you calling me," she said, shaking her head. "I was…training Relsenair, and the wind was blowing. I must have listened to its song a bit too long and… It's the strangest thing; I think I changed into the wind?"

Parimu looked at the woods around him again, his brow furrowed.

"How do you…become the wind?" he asked.

"Oh, um…." Sumi said, her eyes blinking heavily. "Well, now it's like anything else, I guess. I was listening to the song and accidentally…stepped through? It was beautiful, though." She closed her eyes, her lips parting as she heard something they couldn't. "The wind sings about everything, where it came from, what it sees from the sky, where it's going. It's a strange feeling — like someone's trying to tell you something, like Essomuai's song, but further away? I don't think

I went far, but it's hard to tell when you're going that fast, and then I heard you calling my name."

She opened her eyes and looked at Erso's face. He was still breathing hard, clinging to her shoulder as if she were the edge of a cliff he was hanging off of.

"Oh gods above, I'm so sorry!" she said, her eyes darting between them. "I didn't mean to scare you like that." She shook her head. "I have to be more careful. I hadn't even realized the wind had a song, and then…"

"It's alright," Erso said quickly, patting her shoulder as he let go of her dress. "You're safe now." He stood, letting out a deep breath as he lifted Sumi up. "Why don't we go back to dinner, eh?" He grinned. "Assuming it's not all burnt to ash."

The three of them walked back toward the campsite, tromping through the woods. Erso started telling jokes, and Parimu finally felt the tension ease just a bit from his shoulders. Sumi was *safe*. Perhaps he couldn't admit it until now, but his world had fallen into pieces over the past few weeks, and she was the only thread still holding it all together.

He bit his lip, suddenly thinking of Queen Welaya. Her face still haunted his dreams, those sharp eyes accusing him, calling him a traitor. He needed to get back to Berill, needed to show them the truth about Shapewalkers. But if they lost Sumi… He could never do all that on his own. Who was he to tell the Berillai anything? He couldn't even hear the goddess.

He shook his head. He had to protect Sumi at any cost. He watched her speeding ahead, walking quickly toward the campsite as she talked about dinner. Erso walked beside him, both of them stepping carefully through the grass they'd just trampled. The other man had a smile now, but he still looked like a coiled spring. He glanced at Parimu for just a moment before nodding firmly. Yes, they would both protect her. She was the most important thing they had, and at least he wasn't alone in that.

4

I have been asked by a very important friend of mine to keep this research secret. Of course, I can only promise that I'll comply during my lifetime, but if you should inherit these notebooks, I ask that you treat them with care. If the truth is a tidal wave, you'd best ensure the beach is prepared before you let it come crashing down.

-Excerpts from the personal journals of Peloris Domelgaine
Green Notebook, Age 42

—:—

After dinner, Erso carefully buried the scraps before washing out his pot in the stream. Apparently, there were loads of bears around Anushai, and Parimu said if you don't wash up well enough, a bear might just walk into camp to root around. He'd laughed at the thought of it the first night, but then he'd found himself waking up every five minutes, hearing a horse's whinny or the wind against his tent. He'd even had a dream or two of a bear ripping through his tent, ready to devour him. And he'd thought cities were dangerous…

He wandered back over to the campsite, stepping carefully through the grass in the dark. They'd only lit the fire, but it wasn't terribly hard to see. There was an almost ridiculous bevy of stars this far out, and the moon was bright. He made it over to where the horses were hobbled, setting down his pot.

"No bears tonight," he said to his horse as he patted its shoulder. Though what a bear would want with a bunch of nasty burnt remains was beyond him. Unfortunately, the beans had been mostly unscathed, returning to their position as the main course. His poor pretzels, on the other hand, had been like charcoal sticks. There'd been a bit of salvageable dough on the inside, though that had been pretty dry. Sumi had forced herself to eat one, saint that she was, but he'd still caught a grimace or two slipping through her smile. At least they'd bought five pounds of that flour…

Erso moved back across the campsite, taking a seat on a log he'd dragged over to the fire. Sumi had gone to bed early, understandably exhausted. Parimu, however, was still up, sitting on a log of his own and staring into the flames. Erso glanced at him for a moment before doing the same. They hadn't talked much for obvious reasons, though he had to admit…the look on the man's face when Sumi disappeared had been worth a thousand oaths. You could force yourself to follow anybody when the chips were down, but you couldn't force yourself to care. The man was a bit of a blowhard still, but he had to respect that, especially if it meant keeping Sumi safe.

Erso pulled out his polis leaves, carefully packing his pipe before reaching a stick into the fire to light it. He was almost out of matches anyway, and it'd be better to save them up before the next town. At least he and Parimu had that in common. Both of them would almost always pack a pipe in the evenings, though they usually had Sumi's bright, beautiful voice to fill the silence. Erso glanced over, noticing that the man wasn't smoking.

"No pipe tonight?" Erso asked, forcing the words past his awkwardness.

Parimu looked up as if he were startled. During the day, the man prowled like a bloody tiger, but now he looked like a lost boy. He shook his head, scratching his chin.

"Not tonight," he said. "Ran out of leaves. Sounds like we'll pass through a town in a day or two, though."

"Well, I don't know if you take polis," Erso said, "but I'd gladly pack you one after the day we had."

He seemed to smile in spite of himself, pulling out his pipe.

"I'd appreciate that," he said, "thank you."

He reached across from his log, handing it over. It had a Royal Navy emblem on the bulb and looked cared for. Erso carefully packed it, taking the time to tamp it properly. It wasn't much of a thank you, but he owed the man at least that much. He lit the pipe and handed it back, letting Parimu take his own starting drags. Before long, there were two columns of blue smoke rising in the air. He'd never understand why the Berillai smoked the grey stuff, couldn't be good for you. After a drag or two, Parimu nodded in appreciation.

"It's good," he said, "thank you. Haven't had it before, but it's smooth."

Erso nodded. "They say polis can only grow on a hillside, plenty of shade. Mellow ground, mellow leaf — or something like that, anyway."

He left out the part about a mellow person. Didn't seem like something the Detective would appreciate. Besides, the Berillai were probably proud of how ornery their tobacco made them. The two of them smoked in silence for a few minutes, though with a pipe in hand, the silence didn't feel anywhere near as heavy. Finally, Parimu spoke in a quiet voice.

"So…what do you make of that today? You think she's alright?" He glanced over at Sumi's tent, though it was too dark to tell if she was asleep or awake.

"Well…" Erso said. "If anybody can figure all this out, it's Sumi. But that did give me a scare." He stared out at the darkness of the woods. "I worry about this whole goddess thing. I don't want her to give so much to this she's got nothing left, you know?"

Parimu nodded firmly. Erso looked back to the fire but kept watching the other man out of the corner of his eye. There was a lot more to trust than liking somebody. To keep Sumi safe, he needed dedication.

"Would you try to keep her present with me?" Erso asked, barely more than a whisper. "Keep her talking, keep her from disappearing?"

"Of course," Parimu said without hesitation.

They both went back to their pipes. Perhaps he could be friendlier to the man… Still, this seemed like a start. They went on in silence after that, sending their smoke toward the stars with a world full of worries on their minds.

———

Sumi sat in her tent in her nightgown, her legs crossed under the thick bedroll Erso had bought her. It was a little lumpy, but it was warm, which mattered more than looks when you were sleeping on the ground. Spring was creeping back into the world, though the nights were still awfully chilly. Tonight, though, she needed the cold, anything to clear her mind. She'd slipped off to bed early, still trying to make sense of what had happened. She'd become…the wind.

She couldn't let that happen again — not with Erso and Parimu relying on her — but a part of her also yearned to relive it. She had never been anything so incredible, hadn't even imagined a shape like that was possible. Even with her consciousness more or less intact, flying with the wind was unlike anything she'd done, like breathing, soaring from the goddess's lungs with no effort at all. It was like becoming part of a river, rushing off to see what secrets the future held.

Not that the others were wrong to be scared… The transformation *hadn't* been intentional. Transforming used to take effort, but now it seemed the other way around. How was she supposed to contain something as powerful as Essomuai? And even more frightening, what kind of power was waiting for them in the mountains? In the house histories, Vilodai had ridiculed Essomuai for her weakness, a goddess who could turn into the wind on a dime. How did you prepare for something like that? There was just so much she didn't know.

"Essomuai," she prayed in a quiet voice, "I need you to guide me. My powers, our future, all of it. I'm not sure how much you can control these dreams I'm having, but please show me whatever you can."

She laid down, closing her eyes as she pulled the blanket over her chest. She breathed slowly in and out, picturing the cave in her mind. She wanted to be close to Essomuai when she fell asleep, and the pool was the best way she knew how. She listened to the songs floating through the night, letting them filter into her mind. There were hundreds around her, maybe thousands, but she focused on the one beneath them, Essomuai's song, thrumming in the distance to the south.

"*Essomuai siom leyon, guyang siom teyal,*" she prayed, taking the line from the poem that felt most relevant. *Essomuai is the prism, but yours is the light.* "*Relang woyel kelm,*" she added, '*let me see.*' Then, she simply breathed, lying there as the songs floated around her. The pool was still held firmly in her mind, and it began to glow with golden light, just like when she'd joined with Parimu. For some reason, she got into the pool, imagining herself crawling over the edge and slipping into the water. It was warm, like liquid gold. There was no bottom, but floating there was so easy. She lay there, in the tent and in her mind, floating until, finally, she fell asleep.

5

The tower was full of records that no one in our party had ever seen before. We've taken to calling them the 'sea scrolls.' They name the place 'Tor Vilnosara,' and they seem to hold the records of some kind of priestess, though very much unlike any of the priests we have in Berill now.

-Excerpts from the personal journals of Peloris Domelgaine
Blue Notebook, Age 52

—:—

Sumi opened her eyes, finding herself in a strange place. It was evening instead of night, and she was sitting outside. She blinked, shaking her head, but then...no... He knew who he was — he was Elomikarus, the true emperor of Wellonai. He must have drifted off in his chair, which made sense, given how poorly he'd been sleeping... There was just too much to worry about these days. It was laughable how little ease power brought you. You certainly didn't build a palace so you could enjoy it!

Most of his nights were lost to nightmares about bloody goddesses, though he had far more important things to do, feeding his people chief among them. He sat on the veranda of his palace, staring out at the Erril Sea as he considered the reports in front of him. The palace may be new — he'd built it in the years after the failed attack on Anushai — but these problems, unfortunately, were not. It had been a bloody few years, forcing him to reassert his authority as news of his failure sent waves through the kingdoms of the south.

He had left no question as to who controlled the empire, though the campaigns had drained him of a good amount of coin and grain. Now that peace had returned, his people were working as hard as they could to replant the fields of Amoriai, but it would take time. Until then, the sword was still his best way to feed them. He put down the reports, looking over the maps in front of him again. They would need to raid in the west again soon. The Mesop could be tricky when they struck on their horses, though he'd easily take the lot of them if they ever found the courage to face him outright.

Still, the Mesop were said to have powerful shamans that could control snakes... Did that mean they served one of the sisters? Elomikarus laughed joylessly. It seemed that even with a kingdom to save, the goddesses would never stray far from his mind. Even the name his rivals used for him — the Southern Emperor — only grated at him, reminding him of his failure in the north, a defeat caused by yet another goddess. The things he had seen in the sky were still locked in his mind: horrible serpents, giant waves looming over his ship, ghostly faces larger than any city.

He understood now that it was Essomuai, the sister Vilodai had spoken of. Had everything he'd seen in Anushai been an illusion then, or could Essomuai truly field such monsters? Vilodai had seemed so dismissive of her sister, so sure she was the softest of the three. Though even that thought was laughable. Even the weakest wolf had teeth, no? He did toy with the idea of heading north again, but after the first failure, his liege lords would never back it. He could force them, of course, but there wouldn't *be* a southern kingdom if he failed again.

Staying in Volnera was the right choice, the rational choice. And yet, somehow, as he lay awake every night, he found himself planning: ships, swords, supplies, everything it would take to roll the dice one last time. Not that any of it compared to his previous power... He glanced to his side where his scepter sat. The top of it was capped in a strange, glowing blue metal. It served as a reminder of the power he'd once known, though that was as good as gone to him now, lest he risk Vilodai's wrath even more. The top of his scepter was but a fragment of the true stone, the giant rock he'd carried from Vilodai's Heart. It was buried now, though he still dreamt of it sometimes.

His generals said that when he touched it, his eyes would go completely white, filling his vision with Vilodai's sight. It was as if she could read the earth, knowing every stone and metal. It was like turning the soil into water, and he was the wave cutting through it. Even from her prison, she had been able to connect the tiny fragments of Wellonai, understanding how the metals and minerals would interact, like lighting a fuse. He still remembered the first time, the earth exploding around him, bursts of power that turned his enemies to dust.

He rubbed his eyes and tried to look at his maps again. Those things were better off forgotten, lest he give himself even more nightmares... It was one thing to be tormented by failure, but what truly kept him up at night was *who* he had failed. Vilodai. She had sent him north to destroy the Essom, given him the silver that filled his swords and paid his men. She had summoned him to her mountain and spoken to him through the stones. How could you hide from such a god? Even trapped in the mountains as she was, she could find any man at any time. So why hadn't she come for him? More than a decade had passed, his temples were starting to grey, and still, she had not come.

He sighed, tossing the map back down on the table. The sun was already setting, so he left the veranda to see about dinner. Some of his liege lords were coming to dine, and as much as he liked to keep them waiting, he wouldn't let his food grow cold just to make a point. As one of his servants opened the door for him, he turned back to face the water one last time. He froze, a black dot on the horizon. Ships? His pulse quickened for a moment, the memory of those monsters in his mind. But no, just like Vilodai, the Essom had never faced him. By all reports, they were as peaceful as they'd always been, content to stay in the north. Those had to be merchants — he had sent out a good number of those to search for food. He shook his head, heading in to dinner.

In the night, Elomikarus woke to a banging. Even before he rose from the bed, his hand was on his sword, crossing to the door in the span of a heartbeat. His head seared a bit from the wine, but it wasn't the first time he'd have to fight with a fog. His wife began to rouse herself as he unlatched the door.

"My lord," his servant said the moment the door was cracked, "we're under attack. They think the Anushai. The keep is holding for now, but they've breached the walls."

"Where was the bloody alarm?" he snarled, wrenching open the door and storming into the hallway as he pulled his sword from its sheath. He felt the cold night air bite his bare skin, but that wasn't important. He needed to be with his men immediately. But...an attack by the Essom? How could that be? The servant scurried behind him.

"I don't know, my lord," the servant said, his voice shaking. "When they woke me, the walls were already breached. And the alarm bells, they're on the walls, so—"

"Fine," Elomikarus said, raising a hand to stop the man. "Get my wife's servants, have them ready her to leave through the tunnel. Now!"

The man took off at a run just as they reached the end of the corridor.

There was a knot of guards there, protecting the entrance into his wing of the palace, all of them eyeing the door warily. It was barred with thick timber, and they all had swords drawn as he did. He locked eyes with one of them, a captain in the king's guard named Povesek.

"What's happening?" he asked.

"My lord," the captain said, his voice at least firmer than the servant's. "Something came over the walls — birds, some said. Before we knew it, we were overrun. The inner gates still hold for now, but I'm not sure how many made it."

Birds… Then this *was* the work of the northern goddess. She'd somehow made those men into birds. That, or their sister Itorunai had finally decided to join the fight. His memory was still fuzzy from his time with Vilodai, the way a goddess entered your mind…but the third sister, Itorunai, had made all the animals. Although Vilodai had warned that Essomuai's children could become anything… Never mind. He'd fought thousands of men, he could fight a few bloody birds!

"The gates won't hold for long if we're fighting the gods," he said, pointing to the thick piece of wood barring the door. "Open it, we're going to rally the men."

The captain's face fell, but the soldiers obeyed without the captain needing to repeat the order. Elomikarus took a deep breath, bracing himself, the familiar call of battle filling his veins with fire. He flexed his hand on his sword, eager to begin. He had failed Vilodai once before, but he would honor her now.

"For Vilodai!" he shouted as the men opened the door. He rushed out into the screams and clangs of battle. It seemed the gates hadn't held after all. It was time to fight or die.

An hour later, Elomikarus knelt in the sand by the water. He still had no shirt, and he felt the bite of the gusts off the sea. He had felt hot blood on his chest earlier, but even that had dried in the never-ending wind. Was it windier than usual, or had he been softened by life in the palace? His hands were bound, and around him, his liege lords were much the same. The rest of his men were routed, all of them either dead, captured, or fleeing through the woods to the south.

He looked at the knot of Anushai that stood between him and the water. They were all centered around one man, the one they kept calling Father. The Anushai seemed far more organized than when he last saw them, and he appeared to be their leader. He had been a fool to dismiss those ships on the horizon… He had thought any enemy ship would have a hard time docking in his city, but a flock of birds wouldn't need a bloody dock.

The Anushai all wore swords, rough iron things but swords all the same. They had mostly black uniforms with different sigils on the arms, a few of the older ones wearing colors. The one called Father wore a grey tunic, while another man near him had a blue one. It was useless to keep taking in details like this, but the soldier in him couldn't seem to help it. Even with no hope left, the longer they delayed, the more he yearned to fight. So why all this talking? Why not just be done with it?

Two Anushai soldiers to either side of this 'Father' held a long sheaf of parchment rolled out and lit by torches. All the men in the circle kept referring back to it, pointing to the captured soldiers and other things around the castle as they murmured in low voices. He couldn't make out what it said, but by the torchlight, he could at least see the outline of words on the other side. So…not a map then, but what? He strained his ears to listen, a few snippets drifting over the wind.

"Will it work? Do you—" one of the voices said.

"It has to, we've already—" another said.

He ground his teeth; it was no use.

"*Foremosara*," the Anushai leader said in a loud voice, making him look up quickly. His Anushai was spotty, but that had been Vilodai's tongue. His mind could still perceive it, apparently, and in the way of the spirit tongue, it put an image in his mind, a hammer driving home a nail. Even single words in their language carried the meaning of sentences in the human mind. It meant to finish things, to reach the end. The 'Father' batted away the parchment and stepped up to the front of the group. His eyes were like ice as he stood staring at him. He actually seemed like a king standing like that.

"Elomikarus," the *king* said, "we regret the blood that had to be shed this night." He spoke in Elomikarus's own mother tongue, the tongue of the eastern tribes where he had grown up. Odd that. He wasn't sure whether to be reassured or offended. No matter. Like the man said, it was time to finish this, whatever it was.

"However," the man continued, "due to your crimes of war and the threat you pose to our kingdom in the north, we have no choice but to banish you and your people, to erase your menace from Wellonai."

Banish? To where? What would be the bloody point of that? He thought momentarily of his wife, his children. But no — he'd still rather have the sword. He felt his anger welling up.

"And who are you to banish the Southern Emperor?" Elomikarus asked. Tonight, even he would use the wretched title if it served.

"I am Lelman Geomongiar," the man said, "son of the First Father, Geomon, and heir of Stone House. I come here at the behest of the Houses of Anushai to see that justice is done." He motioned to the large sheaf of parchment behind him where his soldiers still held it unfurled, looking unsure. "We come to complete a goddess pact."

A goddess pact? This didn't seem like Essomuai's style, not that he really understood the goddesses, infinite as they were. Still, Vilodai had thought Essomuai and her people soft, and all his campaigns against them had made them seem so…

"After all this time, Essomuai still wants revenge for my campaign?" Elomikarus asked.

Lelman winced. "No," he said, his voice even icier than before, his mouth a thin line. "We serve a pact with Itorunai."

Elomikarus narrowed his eyes despite himself. He had feared Vilodai had chosen his enemies for her revenge, but…Itorunai? The goddess of wind and animals? What did she care for the realm of humans and Essom? Seeming to sense his confusion, the man stepped closer and spoke for the whole beach to hear.

"Itorunai wants an end to war," Lelman said. "As do we. During your brutal campaign to conquer this world, you killed many of her children, stripping the forests bare of animals and clogging her sky with smoke. We have made a home in the north that pleases her, a home for all peaceful peoples. You will not be satisfied to sit by the sea forever, and so we must fight to protect that peace."

He beckoned to a few more of his soldiers, and they scurried over, dragging a huge wooden chest, at least a head longer than a man and just as wide. They dragged it onto the sand between them, prying open the lid.

In the middle of the box, nestled in a pile of hay, was a strange object. It wasn't metal, though it shined in the torchlight. It was shaped like a large triangle with a blunt platform at the top that ended in a large crystal sphere. It had a stone inside, held in a wire of aged copper and surrounded by sparkling gems.

"What…is that?" Elomikarus asked, fear finally entering his voice. If he had learned anything from Vilodai, it was that the power of this world came from the earth. Vilodai had power over many metals, but this… What could a device like that do?

"This is Itorunai's promise," Lelman said. "With it, we will banish you deep into the western seas, never to return."

The western seas? There was nothing out there. None of his soldiers had ever ventured further west than the tip of the cape, and there was reportedly little life there at that.

"Why tell me all this?" Elomikarus asked. "If I'm so dangerous, why not just finish things?"

"Itorunai would have you know of her bargain with us," Geomongiar said simply as if it were obvious. *Gerotusanayil,* he thought, a word Vilodai had used once. *A choosing. A knowing.* He almost wanted to laugh. So the wind goddess wanted to give him a choice, did she? Not much to choose from when you were forced to kneel on a beach, everything you loved scattered around you. Or was it not about *his* choice? The image in his mind was of a man on a beach, spreading out seashells before a group of children. The man in the vision spoke, though he couldn't hear the words. Eventually, each child picked a different shell. A complicated vision…

The Anushai king turned behind him and motioned to the dark ships looming in the water. They had sailed closer after the attack, dozens of them in the fleet.

"We have brought you sturdy ships to ensure your safety," Geomongiar said. "Though you still have choices to make. You will be banished, along with all your heirs and liege lords. You are also to choose a third of your people to join you. You may take grain and cloth, but no weapons or animals. Itorunai has promised that your new home will have animals enough. But," he said, raising a finger, "if you break the pact, you will suffer. You will care for her animals as if they are your children. You will raise no armies, and you will never seek to leave your new home."

"No," Elomikarus said, spitting out the word the moment the man was done.

"No?" Lelman asked. "You are being given a fine bargain. A new home and your own choice of retainers. To what do you object?"

"All of it," Elomikarus said. "I demand the sword."

Lelman grimaced again, his hand pinching his brow.

"That is your right," he finally replied. "As written in the pact, we will choose for you." He turned to the men behind him. "Load the boats as you see fit, exactly to the letter of the treaty. When you are done, we will summon the winds."

He drew his sword, looking Elomikarus in the eye.

"You will have your wish, brother," Lelman said. He raised his sword, and Elomikarus smiled.

———

Sumi snapped awake in her tent, her hand clutching at her throat, sure she'd find herself bleeding… She slowly calmed her breath, blinking in the dark as she listened to the snoring on either side of her. That would be Erso and Parimu… She was herself, she was in a tent, she was safe. So that was what, a dream? It had been so vivid, though, more than anything she'd seen before from Essomuai. In a dream, even if you were somehow someone other than yourself, you still sort of knew who you were. But she had fully believed herself to be Elomikarus, right up until the moment they'd taken off her head…

She reached out to Essomuai, a sort of sadness flowing through the songs like when she saw a creature that had died. Were they…memories? She remembered the name Lelman Geomongiar from the house histories, the second Emperor Father of the kingdom. And, of course, she knew Elomikarus by now, the great Southern Emperor. Perhaps that was Essomuai's answer to her prayer, showing her something she needed to know. But what was she supposed to make of that?

She thought of the strange device the Anushai had brought. A *pact* with Itorunai, something to summon the winds… When she rode the wind earlier, it had remembered its mother, her breath pushing it across the land. So that meant the other goddesses were real, too, not just Essomuai. The three sisters, the daughters of Wellonai. It did little to solve them, though it sure made her problems seem bigger.

She took a deep breath, forcing herself to lie back onto her bedroll. She just had to trust Essomuai. She had brought them this far, and even in the songs, all she could feel from the goddess was love. If she wanted Sumi to know this, then it must serve some purpose. She closed her eyes, trying to leave the songs behind her as she focused on the gentle rhythm of Erso's snoring. It was soft, drifting over the camp like snow. She held onto that, her own breath growing heavy until she finally fell asleep.

6

I finally got the royal chemists to test the knife I brought back from the tower. Unlike the sea blades, it seems to be made of the same type of steel they found on the Volneran Peninsula. It makes me wonder, where did our people truly come from?

-Excerpts from the personal journals of Peloris Domelgaine
Yellow Notebook, Age 60

—:—

A day later, Sumi woke up in her tent, her whole body feeling dry. She blinked, rubbing away the silty crust that had formed around her eyes. She wriggled her nose and coughed, feeling like a roll that'd been in the oven too long. She rolled over, fumbling for her water skin and drinking greedily. The day before, they'd finally reached the end of the forest, emerging into the highlands of Ekosinar. They were only a day or two from Ageleat now, and the dry air made it seem like the Void was just over the next hill.

She poured a bit of water on her hand, rubbing it over her face. She'd slept like the dead, which probably hadn't helped keep her mouth closed... She'd been absolutely exhausted the day before, her dreams making her feel like she hadn't slept a wink — which she probably hadn't, seeing as she'd fought a battle and been beheaded all in a single night. Erso had looked worried all day, probably thinking she was losing her grip again. In truth, though, she'd hardly listened to the songs at all, completely focused on the dream — and not falling off her horse.

Her mind kept circling around one thing — Geomongiar banishing Elomikarus's people to the western sea. She could still feel his confusion from the dream. Elomikarus hadn't known what was out there, though she did — the Isles of Dawn, the homeland of the Berillai. And if that's where his people had been sent… She shook her head, trying to understand. What did it mean? And what was she meant to do with a secret that could undo…everything she understood about the world?

She wished she could go back to sleep in search of more answers, but instead, she wormed her way into her dress, rolling onto her knees to tie her bedroll. The others would be waiting for her before long, and she still needed to find a time to tell them about her dream. Would they think her silly, rambling about dreams? Would they even believe her? It was almost too much for her to take.

She scrambled out of the tent, finding breakfast already cooking by the fire, the other tents taken down. They had made camp in a little valley east of the road, the hills around them hiding their fire. The valley was little more than dirt, the chalky Ekosinaran soil interspersed with thickets of yellow grass and little groves of their famous olive trees.

She grimaced, remembering the night before. She'd only had olives once with Nela, but they'd been delightful — salty and soft. But when she tried to take one off a tree, she'd immediately spat it out, the bitterness still on her tongue. She shivered at the memory, rolling up her tent before walking toward the fire. Erso was there, still trying to make something of his bag of flour.

"How is it that you two stay up smoking half the night and still beat me out of bed in the morning?" she asked.

"Probably the beauty sleep," Erso said, shrugging as he poked at his pan of dough. "Detective and I don't need it, seeing as how we're not anywhere near as beautiful."

"Har-har," she said, sitting on the lumpy rock that had served as her stool the night before.

"Really, though," he said, scratching his chin, "I'm afraid you're making a decent man out of me. I used to be able to sleep until noon, but now, without a pub in sight, I wake the moment the sun hits my tent."

"We'll see how your virtue holds up in town," she said, sticking her tongue out at him before looking back down. She'd pulled out her map and was tracing her finger along the road, trying to judge how far they'd traveled the day before. "We'll probably make that town today — Simanafor."

"Oh, thank the halls," Erso said, raising his hands to the sky. "I keep dreaming I'm sleeping on a big feather bed, only to wake up with an especially pointy rock in my back…"

"I can't imagine what a good night's sleep will do for your winning personality," she said, rolling her eyes.

"Wow," Erso said, making a face, "you're getting pretty good. I'd better watch out."

She flashed him a grin.

"Not bad, right? I'm practicing so Beysal and I can team up on you next time we see him."

Unfortunately, thinking of Beysal pulled the grin right back off her face. She still worried about them back in Amoriai, was still desperate to apologize. And now that she was with Erso, they were her…what, in-laws?

"They'll be alright," Erso said, noticing the look on her face.

"You're right," she said, nodding. She had to believe him. Besides, now that Parimu had switched sides, the Fida'lalean should have no reason to come sniffing around again. She glanced over her shoulder where Relsenair was packing up the horses. She didn't want him hearing them talk about Beysal — the man had enough guilt to deal with already.

"You're still trying to send him letters, right?" she asked. He'd sent one to Beysal before they left Anushai, though how long it took to get to a different country was anyone's guess.

"Sure," Erso said. "Of course, we've been in the woods for a few weeks. I'll probably try again in the village today, though."

"I have one for him too," she said, digging into her bag. "Could you mail it for me?"

He took the folded piece of paper, turning it over in his hands.

"Nothing bad about me in here, right?" he asked, quirking an eyebrow at her.

"Just the usual," she said, her grin finally coming back.

"Alright," he said, stowing the letter in his saddlebag. "But you're paying the postage. I'm a kept man now, you know."

She pushed him on the arm before walking toward Parimu. He was loading up Eto, having picked up her tent and bedroll. That came with another twinge of guilt, though he did seem to have a knack for it. Everything went just where it was supposed to and didn't seem to weigh the horse down at all. Knowing her, if she packed the saddle, Eto would be bucking before lunchtime…

"Thanks, Relsenair," she said to Parimu, patting Eto's flank. The mare turned to look at her and nickered. Still, the horse didn't budge, always seemingly happy to stand still for Parimu.

"See?" she asked. "You know you're a good man if horses like you. They can sense these things."

"Maybe," he said, chuckling as he pulled a paper bag from his pocket. "I don't think I deserve all the credit, though." Eto turned her head as he reached inside, pulling out a sugar cube.

"You had these the whole time?" Sumi asked, her eyes widening.

"Got them at the stable," he said. "Bribery, plain and simple. Why don't you do the honors today?"

He handed her the cube, and she eagerly held it up, the horse slobbering on her as she snapped it up. She giggled, wiping her hand on her dress. It was just like Mr. Feirshin's horse back home. Parimu moved down the line, bribing the others before they headed to the fire for their own breakfasts. She was hungry enough to slobber herself, though a sugar lump sounded a good deal better than another day of beans…

An hour later, the sun already warming their faces, they were well on their way to the south. According to the map, once they reached Simanafor, they'd only be about a half day's ride from Ageleat. They'd all agreed to push for town before sunset, more than willing to trade a hard day of riding for a chance at sleeping in an inn. No one was quite as desperate for civilization as Erso, but she certainly wouldn't object to sleeping in a bed either…

The woods had been lovely, of course, full of life and songs, but she was still a city girl at heart. No matter how beautiful its song was, a spider was still a spider, and they seemed rather fond of her tent… She could probably use a proper bath as well. She wasn't the vain type — she'd look just as plain with or without a week's worth of dirt on her face — but now that she had Erso to think of… Well, he did like to stand close during their little evening rendezvous, and she probably didn't smell of daisies.

She was thinking silly thoughts like that, hardly paying attention to the road, when Parimu pulled his horse alongside hers. She blinked in surprise, her eyes darting ahead, thinking she'd missed some kind of danger.

"Er…if you don't mind," he said, "I wanted to chat with you about something."

He glanced over his shoulder nervously, but Erso had already started whistling something, pulling his horse back to give them some privacy. Bless that man; you never had to tell him anything. Just another reason he was too good for her. Though, like Nela used to say — "Your Grandpa, Sumi, his good things, also his bad things." She could only hope to love Erso so long that his virtues became flaws. Not that she was getting ahead of herself…

"Of course," she said, turning back to Parimu. "What is it?"

"Well," he said, chewing on his lip. His eyes were back on the road ahead, his hands tight on his pommel. "I guess I wanted to apologize. For that last conversation we had in Berill…at the jail." He chuckled nervously. "It's strange to think about it now, the way we came together in Anushai. But…I suppose I also wanted to hear your ideas again. That night, you were trying to tell me about Essomuai. But you were also talking about what Berill needs, and I feel like I need answers in that department more than ever."

She smiled, nodding. "It is strange, isn't it? It certainly doesn't feel like you're the same person I had that conversation with." She reached out and touched his shoulder. "But you don't need to be sorry; it's in the past now."

His grip on the saddle softened a bit, and he nodded. It would take him a while yet to believe it, but she had to keep trying. They weren't all that different in that respect… Erso said it was impossible to get her to take a compliment, and she would struggle just as much getting Parimu to realize he'd been forgiven. But that's what love was, wasn't it? Everyone you loved was like a mirror, trying to show you wonderful things about yourself until you believed them.

"Anyway," she said, chuckling, "I still don't know what came over me. I certainly hadn't ever stood up to anyone like that before. You must have thought me a bit silly, eh?"

"Not at all," he said, shaking his head vigorously. "I thought you were *right*. Though I couldn't admit it at the time, of course… I thought you were trying to manipulate me, but what you said bothered me the whole way to Anushai. I guess it just wormed its way into my heart. Like you said, the Berillai need each other, a…community, and we won't find it hunting each other down."

He looked off in the distance and sighed.

"I know now how right you were, but we never got to finish that conversation. How do we fix it? Not just the Shapewalkers, but…all of it — the factory workers, the sick and dying, the orphans. Where do we even begin?"

"It's a big question, isn't it?" she asked in a small voice, looking out at the dusty road.

She thought of Nela's letters, hidden safely in her saddlebags. It seemed she'd thought that same question almost every day. She'd actually started her charity network when she came across a beggar who had lost an arm in one of the factories. But while she'd wanted to help every person in Berill, she had also wanted *more*, even if she wasn't entirely sure how to realize it.

'The world is like a Shapewalker,' she had written to Hiyelleom when the rail lines were going in. 'This is the moment of change, when the light begins to glow and anything can happen.'

Nela had envisioned a world where they used commerce to bring people together, where the poor were valued — and the sick, and the Shapewalkers — where the kingdoms saw their problems as one. 'There can be abundance in the world, or there can be famine,' she'd written, 'and the only difference is how we till the soil.'

She blushed, realizing that Parimu was still listening, waiting for her to say more.

"I think you'd like reading my Nela's letters," she said. "They're in Anushai, but I could translate them for you." She patted her saddlebag and smiled. "She believed that the whole world could change, just like a Shapewalker. I guess I have to believe that Essomuai can help us. That if we show our people who we really are, we can change them. Maybe it's naïve, but it's a start."

Parimu nodded, looking wistfully at the hills in the distance. Was he thinking of Jalicyne? She pictured the woman in her mind, wishing she could have met her, though she supposed she had, in Parimu's memories anyway. She didn't want to ramble, but he looked like he needed something more.

"It's a bit like your memories of Emillon, right? Not everyone was perfect, but everyone knew each other, treated each other like flowers in Essomuai's field. If you can see a Shapewalker as human, then you'd have to do the same for a beggar. I don't know if it'll happen in our lifetimes, but I know we can try. My Nela still got up in the morning and decided to help someone, anyone, every single day, and we'll just have to do the same. If we make it through this, I'll take you on the rounds with me, show you what I mean."

"I'd like that," he said, turning back to her and smiling sadly. "I spent all this time as a police officer, thinking I was chasing after the thing that took…Jalicyne from me." He still paused sometimes when he said her name as if he'd gotten used to no one else on Wellonai knowing it but him. Still, when she met his eyes and smiled, he nodded. It helped him that she already knew, that he was free to remember.

"But," he continued, "I was chasing after the wrong thing. I should have been with the sick, the Jalicynes that were still alive, still working in those factories. They should have seen my face, seen me fighting for them. Instead, I was chasing the good out of the kingdom, thinking I was saving it."

"There's still time," she said. "Jalicyne would be proud of you,

Relsenair."

He smiled — *really* smiled.

"Thank you," he said, nodding as he nudged his horse, riding back up to the front of the line.

He seemed to sit a little taller in the saddle, turning his attention back to the hills, the mask of the soldier returned. They all had people they needed to do right by, ghosts from their past. But their loved ones weren't gone — they were riding with them, glowing in Essomuai's light. Even Elomikarus remained, no further away than a dream, hiding right around the corner in Mu'na'sokar. That light was with them, and one way or another, they were going to carry it home.

_7_

Surprisingly, I was able to secure funding for my research. After what happened to the temple in Colein, you'd think there wouldn't be much room for antiquities of any kind, but it seems the crown can still surprise, even at my age.

-Excerpts from the personal journals of Peloris Domelgaine
Green Notebook, Age 43

—:—

They rode the rest of the day, winding through the dusty hills until the sun tilted low in the sky. They'd occasionally passed a farm or a herd of goats, but there hadn't been much sign of anything else right up until Simanafor appeared. They crossed over the top of a particularly tall rise, finding the village in the center of a thick clump of farms, a large stream running lazily nearby.

The village wasn't a large one, though it seemed like a massive city after so many days in the wilderness. There were maybe two dozen buildings crisscrossed by three or four streets before the fields took over again. Still, they were paved, and one large stone building stuck up above the rest, which would hopefully be a halfway decent inn…

They eagerly rode down the last stretch of road, dismounting just as they reached the village. There was a stone bridge that arced over the stream, joining the village streets with the northern road. They crossed over it, leading their horses as the three of them walked side by side. There weren't many people out and about, though a few faces appeared in windows and doorways to watch them pass. At least some of them smiled before ducking their heads back in.

Sumi found herself unconsciously reaching for Essomuai, the music flooding her mind in a staggering burst. The forest was just as full of life, but the trees all sang songs that were at least in the same…key. Here the songs of civilization seemed to crowd in on each other, competing for space in her mind. The cobblestones all thumped with the heavy richness of stone while the houses blurred together, torn between what they were and what they had been. The wood of the houses seemed to remember being trees and the bricks chattered like birds as the clay sang a mishmash of stories about the quarries they came from.

She blinked, putting a hand to her forehead. She focused on her breath, bringing the symphony down to a more manageable hum. That seemed to help. She could have tried to close herself off entirely, but she still wanted quick access to Essomuai in case something happened. She looked up and caught Erso watching her. She smiled at him, trying to look like she had it together.

They finally reached the center of town, staring up at the tall building. It had been built with the same mix of timber and brick, but it looked far grander, with diamond patterns laid into the masonry and interspersed with thick splashes of stone. She couldn't read the Narala on the sign out front, but it was carved in the shape of a crescent moon, which was hopefully a universal sign for a place to sleep.

They tied off the horses and crossed the street, coming under a long cloth awning on the side of the inn. There were a handful of wooden tables in the shade, and two men sat there, smoking pipes with their backs to the inn. They were both older, though one had about two decades on the other, with a white, wispy beard. Their songs began to echo in the back of her mind. They were decidedly human, their rhythms having that strange…stillness compared to a Shapewalker's.

"Looking for a place to stay?" the one with the beard asked.

They had agreed that Erso would do the talking since he knew more Narala, but when she understood him, she spoke without thinking.

"Yes," she said, smiling. "Is this an inn?"

"Why, it is, miss," he said, smiling widely. "We don't get many guests anymore with how slow the road is, but we certainly don't get any as pretty as you."

"Oh, please," she said, waving him off, "you flatter me. Should we just go inside, then? Is the owner in?"

"I'm the owner," he said, standing with a little bow, "and this is my son, Tobarin." He turned toward his son, who had also stood. "Toba, if you wouldn't mind taking the horses around to the stable?"

"Of course," Tobarin said, heading toward the horses. "I'll bring your saddlebags to your rooms."

The older man held the door open for them, waving them in. She looked to Erso and Parimu, both of them staring at her with eyebrows raised. She shrugged, nodding to the innkeeper as she slipped through the doorway.

The inside was just as well-appointed, with rich dark wood covering every surface. It still felt bright, though, the large windows out front letting in plenty of light. To the left of the front desk was a narrow staircase, and to the right was a sitting room. All of the furniture looked to be about as old as the proprietor, but it was clearly well cared for.

"Let me see here," the owner said, slipping behind the counter and opening a guest book.

"Sumi," Erso whispered, motioning for her to come closer. "I didn't know you spoke Narala," he said.

"What?" she asked, cocking an eyebrow. "He's speaking Berillai, that's why I jumped in."

The songs suddenly flooded from the back of her mind, crashing about like cymbals. She put a hand to her temple, shaking her head as she forced the songs away.

"Are you alright?" Parimu asked, putting a hand on her shoulder.

"Fine, fine," she said, shaking her head again. They'd never get a room if she looked…unreliable. She turned around, the innkeeper speaking again.

"—*eptokes demota terane?*" he asked in Narala.

"Excuse me?" she asked, cocking her head. "I'm sorry, I don't understand."

The man scrunched up his face, looking at her strangely. He spoke again in heavily accented Berillai.

"You are…alright?" he asked. "You are…Berill?"

Suddenly feeling dizzy, she put a hand down on the counter and took a deep breath. Maybe she was more nervous than she thought? She opened herself to Essomuai again. As confusing as that could be, it also seemed to steady her. She opened her eyes again and smiled at the man, his song filling her mind. It sounded deep, like a baying cow, though it had a certain sadness to it. She stepped up to the counter, reaching for the pen he had placed there.

"Sorry, yes," she said. "I'm alright, just a little dizzy. Probably too much time on the road."

He smiled warmly again.

"I thought you were a local girl at first," he said, "your accent is so good."

She raised an eyebrow at him. Where had *his* accent gone? Had he been playing a joke on her? They had been speaking Berillai the whole time, and his was nearly perfect!

"Anyway," he said, "we're glad to have guests from anywhere. It's just unusual to have one from so far west!"

"Yes," she said, chuckling, "we've come a long way. Thank you for having us." She finished signing for the rooms, and he handed her a set of keys.

"The rooms are on the top floor," the innkeeper said. "There's a common room there, too, so please relax, and feel free to come down for dinner in three hours."

"Thank you," she said. "I hope we'll get to eat with you."

"I should be so lucky," he said, laughing. "It would be an honor, Miss—" he looked down at the guest book, "—Elerair."

She shot the others a look before leading the way up the stairs. The narrow steps were covered in a thick, dusty carpet, though it had a beautiful moss color with acorns and squirrels stitched into the weave. This inn really was a lucky find! She quickly climbed to the third floor, feeling lighter, the whisper of the songs humming to her from the old building.

As she reached the top, Erso and Parimu were right behind her, both of them still giving her strange looks.

"What?" she asked. "You don't like the place?"

"No, it's…fine," Erso said, cocking his head at her, "but you do realize you were just speaking fluent Narala, right?"

"No, I just…" she said, scrunching her face up. "You two weren't just messing with me?"

"Nope," Erso said. "You were chatting with the innkeeper like it was nothing." Parimu nodded next to him.

"No accent or anything," Parimu agreed. "If my eyes had been closed, I'd have said you were born here."

"Well," she said, biting her lip, "I suppose that's just one more of Essomuai's little gifts, eh?"

She turned toward the rooms, trying to match the keys to the doors. But as she unlocked the first one and moved to give Erso the key, they were still frozen on the landing, gaping at her.

"Oh, come on," she said, waving them off. "You'll worry yourselves sick. We didn't know I could do that, and now we do. If anything, I'll make sure to order you something extra special for dinner."

She stuck her tongue out at them, moving on to the next door. Although, maybe there was such a thing as taking surprises too well? It was understandable that the others would worry more than her, but if she could speak any language she wanted, what else didn't she know about these powers? She shook her head, unlocking the door and motioning for Parimu to take his key. Maybe she should be worried, but with strange dreams and two other goddesses to smite them, there was plenty else to lose sleep over. Besides, like Erso always said, if the cat was on the prowl, there was nothing she could do but enjoy her cheese.

Several hours and a massive dinner later, Sumi found herself back in the upstairs sitting room, struggling to stay afloat in an overstuffed armchair. After so many nights of beans, the dinner had been downright opulent. There had been baked trout from the stream, huge roasted eggplants, and something called lentils, too — which had seemed dangerously similar to beans but were covered in a rich sauce with a countryside's worth of vegetables and spices in it.

She'd also gotten to know the innkeeper better, pushing herself to speak in Narala the whole dinner. It felt strange to keep herself open to the songs for so many hours, but it had helped to have the innkeeper to focus on. He'd lost his wife young, confirming the sadness she'd heard in his song. But he'd also had a beautiful life with Tobarin, the two of them building the inn together back when trade was bustling along the Northern Road.

It had been a lovely night, but now, she just felt wrung out, wanting nothing more than the armchair she was in. There was still a small fire crackling in the grate, but otherwise, it was quiet, Parimu long since gone to bed. Erso was somewhere downstairs, trying to rustle up a bottle of wine for them to share. She yawned, her mouth stretching as wide as it could go as she tried futilely to cover it with her hand. She blinked hard. She was exhausted, but the brief moments with Erso before bed were too precious to skip.

And, if she were being completely honest…there was another reason she liked the nights. Once the sun was gone, the songs seemed to grow quieter, making it easier to stay inside herself, to stay with the others. It could be the gold of the sun reflecting Essomuai, or maybe it was just that most of the world was asleep, but the songs at night were quiet things, like chimes in the wind. The days may be full of songs, and the nights may be full of dreams, but this time was truly hers.

She heard a creak on the stairs and turned to find Erso on the landing, a sneaky grin on his face and a dark green wine bottle in hand.

"Bad luck," he said, "I think it's strawberry. There weren't any glasses either, but I figured we could share." He winked, leaning in to give her a kiss. She sighed out with a smile, feeling a warmth she hadn't gotten from the fire. He sat on the floor next to her armchair before pulling the cork and taking a swig.

"Oof," he said, blowing out his mustache before handing it to her, "not very good, but I'll take what I can get."

She held up the bottle, looking at the label. It was handwritten, with a tiny drawing of a strawberry above the name of the farm it had come from.

"Well," she said, shrugging, "you're the snob, not me." She took a sip, and unsurprisingly, it was delightful. It tasted like jam, almost a liqueur, though Erso didn't seem to like anything sweet. Even on the boat to Anushai, he'd only eaten the herb pastries.

"Yes, yes, I know," he said, "I fell in love with an awfully simple girl."

She smacked the top of his head, and he laughed. It seemed she had been forced to hit him more lately, albeit fondly. She smiled, thinking of how much Nela had loved it when Grandpa picked on her. She wasn't sick of being a coddled princess like Nela, but there was still something wonderful about Erso's constant teasing. You could count on a love like that. Flowers wilted, and chocolate melted, but badgering was forever.

"Even if I get smacked," Erso said, "it's nice being with you like this." He reached up and patted her knee, running his hand along the fabric of her dress. "I do worry about you in the daytime, though. You seem so…lost sometimes."

"I'm sorry," she said, running her fingers through the hair on the back of his head. "I know I make you worry. There's just…so much to learn, so many things I don't know. I just feel so *small*, and now that I can finally be useful, it's hard to know when to stop."

"You're more than that, and you know it," he said, turning to look her in the eye. "As much as I hate to admit how similar I am to the old bloke, you already changed both me and Parimu, just by being yourself."

He grinned, though his eyes were still intense.

"Your *life* is useful, Sumi, because only you can live it. Whether we win or lose, most of us will be forgotten. But that doesn't mean we should just forget to live."

He paused, looking into the fire, taking another pull of the wine with a grimace.

"I feel like that's why I'm here, to keep you whole. Parimu could probably protect you on his own, but this time we have together matters — *you* matter, and I won't let that goddess use you until you're all used up."

She reached out, cupping his face in her hand.

"You're right," she said. "This time *is* precious. And if you're an expert in anything, it's living. It's just…"

She broke her eyes away, staring into the fire. What were the right words? If she was going to risk his life, she needed him to understand why it was all worth it. They were probably going to fail — it had already been two thousand years of war, after all. Still, they had to press on. She'd love nothing more than to run away with Erso and live out her days, but she already knew she couldn't. She just needed him to understand that the choice had never come lightly.

"I don't know why I can hear her," she finally said, "but I can. And if she can speak to someone like me, then there's still hope. Even if we fail, I have to believe that it matters if we tried. It has to matter that someone tells our people that they're loved, that Essomuai is there, calling to us. Even if they get every last Shapewalker, we have to die knowing we mattered."

She felt a tear forming in the corner of her eye, but she kept going.

"You matter to me so much, Erso. I've never felt a love like this, never felt this kind of love at all. But that's all the more reason to go. Like Nela said in one of her letters, 'love is not a cold pool where you quench the heat of life. It's a fire that has to light more fires.' I know that sounds vague, but I hope you understand."

He got up from the floor, folding her in his arms.

"I understand," he said, his breath warm on her neck. "We have to try. Just don't forget that you have a song too, alright? If Essomuai can love every bloody bug and rock, then she can love you too. She put a song in you because you *exist*, not because you have a job to do. So if we do this, do it as yourself, not just a vessel for some god. We're our own bonfire now, remember? I want you burning bright, even if it's only for a little while."

"Okay," she murmured into his neck, sniffling as she felt her tears wet his collar. Maybe it was easier to face this as a vessel, but they had to live and die as themselves, together. She could still hear Essomuai's song, but she could hear Erso's too. And faintly, if she really listened, she could hear her own. It was quiet, but it was beautiful, and it deserved to be sung.

8

Today we took our ship around the southern coast and found a strange black tower on the southernmost island. I believe those used to be House Turimane lands, though the records are vague. It's easily the tallest thing here outside of the Umi'ceurae, and I've demanded that our captain let us off to search it at first light.

-Excerpts from the personal journals of Peloris Domelgaine
Blue Notebook, Age 52

—:—

Commissioner Kollenail stepped down from his carriage in the west side of Berill, finding himself outside a large cottage beyond the city walls. Similar pretend mansions dotted the street as far as he could see, identical to all the other upstart neighborhoods for the newly rich. It surely galled the peers that so much new wealth was printed in the factories every day, but it mattered little to him. The age of a mansion didn't determine the strength of its inhabitants. Besides, he wasn't nearly as welcome in the more *traditional* parts of the city…

He stepped up to the gated drive, where two guards raised crisp salutes before showing him through. At this house, at least, he was a regular guest. Not just anyone could visit the Chief Admiral of the Berillai Navy at his home, but fortunately, his cover as Vice Commissioner of the Crown gave him the pretext to visit Admiral Heller at all hours. His commission, in name anyway, was tasked with all manner of procurement for the royal forces, so it would appear that he had been summoned here when, in fact, it was the other way around. They certainly wouldn't be talking about mutton and sailcloth.

Luckily, the oath that bound them together was strong enough for what they had to discuss. It was the same one that all officers had sworn since the time of King Rummon: *"By the gods of our fathers and the light of the stone, I promise strength beyond that of any man. I pledge my sword to the true crown, the silver blade of Umilai's heart, to become the fist of the gods."*

Not many thought about what they were actually swearing to, but Kollenail was a man of precision. It may sound like some vague oath to uphold the crown, but in reality, it was a promise to prize the strength of the Berillai above all else. Their forefathers hadn't chosen Rummon because of his house — they had chosen the might of his sword.

He walked up the gravel walkway, lined on either side by tall hedges. Perhaps cottage wasn't the right word — the place was enormous. Clearly, the Chief Admiral's salary was to Heller's liking. Placing him as head of the navy had been a stroke of genius on his predecessor's part. It was the first promotion Welaya granted after taking the throne, giving Heller nearly ten years to solidify his grip on the navy.

What she'd failed to realize was that the Thorns had cultivated Heller nearly twice as long. They'd found him in officer's school after he wrote a treatise on the history of Berill's greatest battles. Even as a youth, he had reached the same conclusion as the Thorns — the Battle of Strussfaran had not gone nearly far enough. Train lines were well and good, but the Continent would be a threat until the Berillai dominated every inch of it.

That wasn't the kind of goal you accomplished in a single lifetime, of course, but what mattered most was always having someone at the helm who understood the threat of the Continent. The Queen seemed to know it on an emotional level — she was as radical as they came — and yet…the crown was weakening. Even if she had the stomach for it, she was letting Pont'dulairn dance circles around her. But he would protect the crown, whichever head it ended up sitting on.

Heller's wife greeted him at the door, bowing slightly as she waved him in. He nodded to her, stepping through into the gaudy front hall. Somehow, the place looked even larger from the inside, not a cottage indeed. There was a wide staircase with formal dining and sitting rooms to either side, both of which could easily seat twenty or more.

"Commissioner," she said, "nice to see you."

Even after dozens of visits, it was hard to tell where the woman stood. Was she all smiles because she knew her husband's true ambitions? Or did she simply enjoy getting to open the door for important guests? They didn't have a butler yet, though they'd followed basically every other fashion from the peerage. He'd studied her background — born on a farm, her father doing well enough to land some military contracts, sending her to a fancy boarding school where she met Heller. Not much of a story at all, though he knew all too well that snakes liked to hide in surprising holes.

"A pleasure," he said, nodding without a bow.

As she led him to Heller's study, he noted a few new decorations she'd jammed in between visits. Unfortunately, she had no sense of style beyond aping the Lournoy District — brocaded carpets, pine paneling with silk hangings. There was even a boar's head hanging above a doorway, even though he was almost certain Heller had never hunted — least of all since his last visit. One day, he'd have to get these fools to realize there was more for them than copying a bunch of spineless peers. When they were done, he'd make sure there was a stuffed bear in every home, a proper trophy for burning the Anushai heartland.

They followed another long hallway before she bowed again, leaving him by the door to the study. Another oddity — she always insisted on escorting guests but never stayed long enough to see them into the rooms she took them to. He shook his head, letting himself in. At least here, he had no need to knock.

The door opened onto a brightly lit room, revealing a table covered with a giant map of the Continent, not really a study so much as a war room. Heller was standing opposite the door, a stack of reports in one hand while the other moved small painted ships around the map. Kollenail eyed them, the various colors and sizes hiding a world of meaning. There were far more ships along the northern half of the map, dotting the coastline of Anushai — and more than a few of them steel-bottomed. More importantly, they confirmed his intelligence on the Queen's latest orders.

"Kollenail," the Admiral said with a nod before going back to his map. "Quite a bee's nest Her Highness is stirring up. What do you make of it?"

In a year, maybe two, this map would've been a delight to behold. But they just weren't ready. Ekosinar was almost in their pocket, and they were just beginning to plan their first naval base on the coast in Amoriai.

"It's too soon," Kollenail said. "What are the chances the Anushai don't notice this many ships moving around?"

"I'm pretty sure they're meant to," Heller said, sighing. He pointed two fingers at the tip of the Anushai coast, where it stuck out toward Itorunai's Gap. "They have a station here with long-range scopes. One of my instructions is to sail past it every two days with a different galleon."

Kollenail ground his teeth. It was far too much trouble to stir up over one measly Shapewalker. But ever since Parimu disappeared, Welaya was apoplectic, not even seeming to care if war broke out tomorrow.

"I'll see what I can drum up in Ekosinar," Kollenail said, running through the list of agents in his mind he had stationed in Ageleat. "It'd be a godsend if we actually found the damned detective, but I think we'd better prepare a few contingencies."

The Admiral glanced up from the map, his eyes narrowing. There were times that the man seemed to think the Thorns as magical as everyone else did. He wasn't much for 'land operations,' as he so often called their spycraft, but at times, it seemed the man didn't understand anything that couldn't float. At least he was reliable…

"What did you have in mind?" Heller asked. "The more ships I move, the more my hands are tied."

For years now, they'd been planning the exact opposite of this. Their plans had been simple, elegant, not the mad rush of an angry queen.

"I intend to get back to our project," Kollenail said. He looked at the northern edge of the map, where thankfully, Heller still had three ships stationed past the cape of the Golden Coast. There was still time to salvage this. They very nearly had the northern mines, and once they had Ekosinar…

"If we move too soon, we'll have the Three Kingdoms War all over again, with all the old alliances against us to boot. If I can't find the Shapewalker, I think it's time Ekosinar got less of a push and more of a shove — albeit with spies instead of ships. Though we'll still have Pont'dulairn to worry about. Do what you can to keep the ship movements out of the peerage reports."

"Alright," Admiral Heller said. "But if your first two plans fail?" He set his jaw, boring his eyes into Kollenail. Maybe the man wasn't so oblivious after all…

"If they fail," Kollenail said, "I'd better hope you're as reliable as you say you are."

The man nodded, taking a black ship from his pocket and placing it on the western edge of the map, just outside Berill. It wasn't a promise, not yet, but as far as signs went, it was a good one.

"Well," Kollenail said, extending his hand, which the Admiral shook. "I'll be in touch."

With that, he left the study, eager to be on his way. There would be a dozen more meetings like this before the day was up, but at least the first had gone well.

9

The new trains going in are truly a marvel. Though, it seems to me that everyone is lining up with their hands out, eager to make money off the blasted contraptions. The only thing I could think was how easy it will be to transport our findings back safely from the new dig!

-Excerpts from the personal journals of Peloris Domelgaine
Purple Notebook, Age 73

—:—

The next morning, Erso was on his horse again, taking the rear behind Sumi. Despite riding the same horse, on the same saddle, at the same ungodly hour, he felt like a new man. It was a bit disconcerting that drinking half a bottle of awful strawberry wine deserved most of the credit… But for now, at least, he could pretend it was the soft feather bed where he'd slept like a dead man. In fact, this was the first morning since they left Anushai that Sumi had woken *him* up.

Oh sweet, wonderful Sumi… He watched her as she rode ahead, greedily taking in everything about her. He was a besotted fool, of course, but at least now he understood how his parents had felt when they would moon at each other. His father, such a cold, practical man, would stare at his mother on stage like she was the bloody goddess Pe'ritrine, draping the world in flowers. Sumi's beautifully long neck, the square of her shoulders, even the messy bun sticking out from under her hat… He wanted to breathe it all in. Yes, he'd have no problem loving her; the issue would be deserving her.

He grimaced, the taste of strawberry wine forcing its way back into his mouth. He'd never really thought of himself as having a problem with drink. He spent most of his time in pubs, sure, but who didn't in his line of work? Besides, he could always get up in the morning, always

62

show up where he was meant to. If the drink made him a bit more likable, a bit more sure of his sword, let him forget the Hardness for five bloody seconds, that was all to the good, no? Until, of course, it wasn't…

Ever since Sumi had come into his life, every problem he'd ever ignored suddenly begged to be dealt with like she'd dug a well in his heart, the good and the bad flowing wherever they wanted. Being a drunk fool had suited the old Erso, but what about the new? What about the Erso who didn't want to run anymore, the one he hoped to become if they survived this mess? What if — gods strike him down for even thinking it — he had children with this goddess of a woman? He wanted to be there for them always, grinning like a fool in some cottage, the pub be damned.

He laughed to himself, earning a look from Sumi. 'What's so funny?' her eyes seemed to ask. Oh, nothing, of course. Just a man with half a soul stumbling drunkenly into the greatest woman in the world. He shook his head, waving her off, forcing himself to focus. They were close to Ageleat, and soon, they'd be trading bears for humans, a far more dangerous beast. At least he was used to dealing with those. He looked off to the right, trying to catch a glimpse of the sea. You could smell it already, the salt on the breeze pushing back the dust.

It took another hour of riding, but finally, they came over the top of the last hill, and the capital came into view. Ageleat was sprawling, gobbling up the tip of the Ekosinaran peninsula as it stretched along the coast. Even that didn't seem to satisfy the place, though, more buildings dotting the islands that stuck out into the Erril Sea. It was big enough to be its own country, which, of course, it had been once…

It may have been three hundred years ago, but the Ekosinarans seemed to like their grudges well enough, every other bloke and his uncle talking your ear off about the time their ancestors had duked it out with Sykala for this field or that. And hey, maybe they'd go at it again. The things that had bound up the world no longer seemed to hold these days, every place just a nudge away from becoming a powder keg.

They followed the last stretch of road down the hill, the wide sweep of water drawing closer as they approached the channel. Boats rolled through the waves as far as he could see, and off the western coast, he could just make out the palace on its private island. Bloody Anushai. When they forced Ageleat and Sykala together, they'd built the new palace, supposedly to appease the southerners — as if they'd forget being stripped of their capital. He also seemed to recall the colonial governor taking a wife from each royal house…lecherous bastard. Those

Anushai sure loved the 'greater good' when it suited them — not that they bloody came to his rescue in the Hardness.

He reached into his saddlebag for his leaves, letting his horse follow the others while he stuffed his pipe. This would probably be his last chance, the dirt road merging at the bottom of the hill with a stone one from the city. Soon, they'd be surrounded by people, and he'd be gripping his reins like a bloody Alaran. Much better to have a smoke now, keep his head clear. As he lit the leaves, the blue smoke drifting behind him, his eyes landed on Parimu.

"Oy, Parimu," he called ahead, "toss me your pipe, eh?"

Of course, the man chose not to toss it, proper as he was. Still, he turned, giving Erso a nod as he handed it to Sumi. She pulled her horse back alongside his, giving him the pipe as she flashed him that big smile of hers. He smiled like a child, barely keeping his own pipe in his mouth as he packed Parimu's. The detective might not be his first choice for a friend, but he wasn't so bad once he loosened up a bit. Still, he'd have tea with bloody Queen Welaya if it earned him one of those smiles. Maybe Beysal was right after all...

More importantly, if Sumi was smiling, that meant she was still there. When she'd used her songs to say goodbye to the innkeeper, he was worried they'd lose her again. It was a hell of an ability, of course, but things like that never came for free. Reminded him of that bloke from Mesopyn, actually, hadn't been in his own bloody form for five years. You could get proper addicted to magic if you weren't careful, and that was just regular old Shapewalking, not Continent-forming goddess magic... He wasn't quite convinced about the goddess yet, but he believed in Sumi, and he'd bloody well keep her here.

They finally reached the bottom of the hill, coming onto the paving stones. The horses seemed skittish at first, the clopping of the horseshoes jarring them after so much time in the woods. Even on the north side of the bay, the city already seemed to be surrounding them, buildings rising up in every direction. Somehow, the village they'd stayed in the night before hadn't been anywhere near as shocking. Already there were clumps of people walking about, and the slate roofs spoke of money the villagers could only dream of.

Ahead of them, the bay narrowed into the channel, and there was a long bridge crisscrossing between a clump of islands into the city proper. He'd always come by boat in the past, though this seemed like the safer option. You never knew who was watching the ports these days. And while the Thorns Parimu kept talking about could be imagined, knowing the Berillai, he wasn't in a hurry to find out. They were only going to stay a day or two — long enough to find passage to the river — and hopefully, they'd be well on their way to Sumi's mountains before anyone realized they were here.

Still, it'd be a shame if they didn't enjoy the city at all. The whole reason they'd traveled east in the first place was to avoid Berillai influence. Ekosinar wasn't Amoriai, after all. If you couldn't enjoy yourself here without feeling like a criminal, where could you? Sykala seemed a bit more aligned with Berill, but both cities had managed to keep the trains far to the south from the capital, which would hopefully keep them from falling headfirst into the bloody honey pot...

Besides, the Ekosinarans had their little canal to connect their cities. The thing was always clogged with boats and trash, stinking worse than a kellor tree in spring, but they didn't seem to mind. Beyond that, they had those rickety little wagons that crossed the Continent, easily bridging the gap between the cities and the train. With any luck, they could worm their way onto one of those caravans. If he never saw the inside of a train station again, it'd be too soon.

As they approached the water, they reshuffled the horses, putting Erso in the lead. Having Parimu in the front with his bow was fine and well in the woods, but he'd have no idea where to go in the city, not to mention that brandishing weapons was frowned upon in polite society... They rode onto the first bridge, the traffic surprisingly dense despite the early hour. Even at forty feet wide, the bridge was a jumble of humanity going in both directions, wagons crowding against knots of people on foot.

With the sea breeze, it was colder than it had been inland, and most of the people were wearing those odd knee-length leather coats the Ekosinarans were so fond of. They were a bit rigid for his taste, though you'd probably start a bar fight if you told a local that. In all honesty, the poor blokes probably didn't have much choice. Their canal was littered with tanneries processing all that Relimoran leather, and once you were awash in the stuff, of course, you'd have no choice but to wear it.

As they reached the peak of the first bridge, the city suddenly spread before them, and he heard Sumi suck in a breath. He smiled to himself; at least he'd fallen in love with a woman who was easy to please. All she seemed to want in life was to take walks and look around — much easier than the stunts Pa had pulled to please his mother...

From where they were, he could just make out the canal, the tops of boats poking out from where they glided below street level. Around the middle of the city, the canal split into a wide V, wrapping around the capital building. Luckily, their inn was in the eastern third of the city, so they didn't have much further to go. He didn't mind staring at the view with Sumi, of course, but he'd had enough of the wilderness for one lifetime — and he'd certainly had enough of those bloody beans! He was planning his next meal in his head when Sumi spoke up behind him.

"It's beautiful," she said, "so much water!" He looked around again; there *was* a lot of water. It may seem like an obvious thing to say to the uninitiated, but he'd learned the importance of looking again when Sumi was around. Almost every city sat on the Erril Sea in some shape or form, but here on the peninsula, Ageleat was smack dab in the water. And still not satisfied, the bloody Ekosinarans had built the canal to make sure brackish water would soak into every nook and cranny, too.

"Bit wet for my tastes," he said, chuckling as he turned his eyes back to the crowd, half looking for danger and half trying to take stock of the city.

Everything looked pretty much as he remembered, but it was important to keep a finger on the pulse of a place. The last time he was in town, the hubbub had been all about the trains — who wanted 'em, who didn't, and who didn't much care so long as the bills were paid on time. It didn't seem like the kind of argument that just went away, though it was hard to tell now with everyone tripping over themselves to get to work. The Ekosinarans were disgustingly mercantile, loving work in a way that was utter anathema to his way of life.

Still, he had to keep his eyes peeled. This was the job that only he could do. In the woods, Parimu was always finding a campsite or hunting dinner, but Erso knew cities and people. If you knew what to look for, there were always warning signs, something out of place. Sometimes it took asking around, worming your way into the pubs until you could get folks talking, but like finding a lion's footprint in the forest, you bloody well didn't want it smelling you first.

Lo and behold, as soon as they crossed the last bridge and entered the city, he found what he was looking for. It seemed like on every other shop, there was a new sort of banner hung over the door, waving in the wind. There were only two kinds, as far as he could tell, and they weren't all that different. Each one had the Ekosinaran seal in the middle and a different color background, green or blue. Those definitely hadn't been here last time he was in town...

"Hey, Parimu," he asked, turning over his shoulder, "you ever dock here in the navy?"

The man snapped to attention, pulling his gaze from where his eyes had been darting around. At least the man was keeping a good watch, but did he need to be so damned skittish?

"Once or twice," he said. "Seems different."

"That's what I'm thinkin'," Erso said, nodding. If someone hung something on the outside of their shop, it was likely to be important, so he lowered his voice to not offend the passersby. "Banners seem new, eh?"

Parimu nodded, and Sumi stared extra hard at a nearby blue banner, this one hanging in the window of a townhome.

"Songs are different," she said. "I tried a green one and a blue one."

Erso needed to keep his eyes on the traffic ahead of him, but he spared a glance at the banner she'd been looking at. Looked pretty much the same as the others.

"How do you mean?" Parimu asked.

She was quiet for a spell before answering.

"Intent?" she said hesitantly. "There's…three parts to a song. The memory of a thing, the…type of a thing, and its purpose. Like our horses. They all have a song that's part horse song, part what that horse remembers — its name, whatever else — and its purpose. For example, a horse with a saddle and a horse on a cart sound different."

Erso blinked hard from where he sat at the front of the line. Every time he thought he had a handle on the whole goddess thing, it only seemed to get stranger… Best not to think about that now. If he broke his fragile brain on something only Sumi was qualified for, he'd be even more useless. Although, he did store away that little bit of information for later, preferably to ponder over a glass of ale. It was best not to get too philosophical without the proper lubricant…

Luckily, just then, their inn appeared on the horizon. It had a high-pitched roof and clean clapboard sides. The sign on the front, which rocked in the breeze, read *Minkhop's*. He gulped. He'd promised himself he'd never come back to this place, but it was the best inn in the city. He was fine sleeping in pubs and alleyways, but he had Sumi in tow now, and she was worth any risk. Even Mrs. Minkhop putting a knife in him while he slept…

He shook his head, swinging his leg off his horse and handing the reins to a stable boy. Best to face your fate with your head high. Or run for it… He'd decide which soon enough.

10

The things they left behind here! All of the roofs are gone after eight hundred years, but the number of stone structures left, just abandoned... It's astonishing to think we just walked away from all this. It seems a most pleasant place now in summer, though the winters must truly be as harsh as they say if they were willing to leave such glory behind.

-Excerpts from the personal journals of Peloris Domelgaine
Blue Notebook, Age 52

—:—

They walked into the inn, Erso's eyes adjusting to the dim interior. Surprisingly, it felt nice to be back. Probably how a fly felt as it floated into the spider's web... Still, the stained glass on the windows dappled the waxed floor with colored light, and the dark paneling seemed to envelop them in its warmth. This was the kind of place you came to relax. No one of note ever stayed here, and nothing remarkable ever happened — you wouldn't even get roped into a knife fight like you might at the pubs. Only in Ekosinar could you find a gem like this. If only he hadn't poisoned the well after his second stay...

He was still looking around the lobby when he heard the door behind the front desk swing open.

"Well, well," an older woman's voice said. He turned to find the innkeeper, Lulsara Minkhop, looking at him from behind wiry half-moon spectacles, her eyes no less terrifying with the passing of the years.

"If it isn't Erso Milak'erat," she continued, her eyes running over the rest of his party, "with friends no less." Anger seemed to ruffle her face for just a moment as her eyes passed over Sumi — there had been that...misunderstanding with a niece — before the merchant in her took over, smiling as she realized that more people would mean more money. "I didn't think I'd have the…pleasure of seeing you again."

"Well," he said, sidling up to the front desk, "I hope there's no hard feelings from last time." Perhaps the entanglement with her niece had been more…entangling than he remembered? "But I was in town, and there's not many inns where the proprietors remember your name. Always feels like home."

Lulsara snorted, opening her ledger.

"Yes, well, all is forgiven, of course. Misunderstandings happen from time to time when family's involved." She flipped through the pages quickly, her finger running along lines of rooms. She stopped about halfway through, her smile taking on a particularly wicked curve. "Your luck is as good as always," she said. "The top floor suite is open, lovely sea views — three beds as well."

"Lovely," Erso said, smiling back at her, trying to keep himself from gulping. Well, it wasn't his gold anymore. "Any chance we can get that famous Minkhop family discount?"

She laughed a bit too heartily at that, flipping over the register to have him sign before she even answered.

"You know," she said, "I met my husband when he came into this inn to sell my father a barrel of salted fish. I caught his eye, and even though he gouged my father on the price, he still had the gall to come back the next day and ask for my hand. So, I wouldn't say the Minkhops are known for discounts."

"He was a great man," Erso said, signing his name with a flourish, "may we all follow in his footsteps."

She handed him the key, and he smiled again, nodding as he turned back to the others. They were both watching him carefully, and Sumi looked like she was holding in a laugh. He shot her a warning glare, grinning to himself as he grabbed the luggage and turned toward the stairs.

The inn had a split staircase, running straight before dividing into two sides that wound their way to the top floor. They had a bit of a climb, if he remembered correctly, but at least there was a wide picture window on each landing that looked out at the sea. He should probably feel grateful. Having his purse bled was hardly the worst thing that had ever happened. His last run-in with Mrs. Minkhop hadn't even involved any chasing or stabbing, which was more than he could say for most towns he stayed in…

"So," Sumi said as they reached the second floor, unable to contain her mirth any longer, "what on Wellonai did you do to poor Mrs. Minkhop?"

"Well, I—" he began, but Sumi cut him off.

"You know what, better if I don't know," she said, chuckling. "It'll be more fun to watch you squirm if I'm unaware."

He shook his head, rolling his eyes. This was definitely the right inn. If all he had to do to keep Sumi present was look like a fool, his job would be a piece of cake. They finally reached the top floor, turning down a short hallway. There were only two doors on the suite level, and as promised, the one that matched their room number was facing the water. He unlocked it, pushing the door open to oohs and aahs from Sumi.

The suite had a bright, tiled central room that let out onto a little veranda with a view of the sea that was actually quite lovely. There was a little kitchen area to the left and doors to bedrooms along the walls. Sumi dropped her bag on the floor and walked straight out onto the balcony, leaning against the railing. There were huge sheets of cloud sweeping over the sea, their bottoms dark with rain. The afternoon sun cut through them, golden bars glittering off the water that made her look even more angelic than usual. He smiled, picking up her bag for her and putting it in the largest room.

He came out to find Parimu exiting the room across from him. The detective nodded, moving to sit in one of the many chairs at the end of the room. Good of him to let him have the room next to Sumi's. She had sunk into a metal chair outside, still staring at the view. Poor thing. She'd seemed remarkably present all day, but that was probably just as draining. Ignoring that much magic must be like trying not to smoke for a day, all the while thinking about the leaves sitting in your pocket...

Well, he could take charge for now. It was time to start scouting for their next move. They needed a way south that was faster than horses, and they should find it sooner rather than later. He hadn't expected Ekosinar to be so…different. He needed to find out a bit more about that — it wasn't wise to dance on a powder keg without knowing what was inside. He did speak a bit of Narala, albeit not very well. Still, it shouldn't matter with how many merchants there were in the city. There was always somebody who spoke Amoriai this far east.

Besides, it was his old buddy Arkesht he really needed to find. The bloke had his own boat, and if he couldn't take them south, he'd know someone that could. It'd be safer if he scouted on his own, too. The Thorns shouldn't be expecting them here, but if they were, they wouldn't know his face as well as Sumi's or Parimu's. He walked over to Parimu, speaking in a low voice.

"Why don't you two do some training?" he said. "I'm gonna take a look around, see if I can find my friend while I'm at it."

Parimu stood, looking out at Sumi.

"I could use the practice," he said, nodding. "You sure you'll be alright?"

"Should be," Erso said, grinning. Funny the man should worry about his safety, seeing as he'd been trying to kill them a month ago. Still, the man really was loyal, and his sword wasn't half-bad. He'd feel better knowing Parimu was with her, strange as it was to admit.

"Just look out for her, yeah?" Erso asked in a low voice. The man would know what he meant. They weren't friends, not yet, but they'd at least come to an understanding over the past few nights around the fire. Like his father had always said, 'it only rains twice a year in Amoriai, but a man still owns a pair of boots.'

"I will," he said, nodding firmly.

Erso let out a breath, grinning again as he left the suite.

———

Parimu stepped onto the veranda, sucking in the lovely salt air. This was the smell of home. No matter where he was — Emillon, Berill, on a ship — the sea had always been there. Of course, they hadn't been far from the sea in the woods, but here, it actually smelled like it was supposed to. In Anushai, the water had smelled…colder somehow. Not to mention that for the past few days, all he could smell was dust blowing in from the Void. Sumi heard the click of his shoe on the tile and looked up, shaking her head.

"Sorry," she said. "Have you been there long? I'm getting better at ignoring the songs, but when I saw the view…"

She gestured out at the water before turning to look back into the room. She narrowed her eyes as if she'd forgotten they were at an inn altogether.

"What happened to Erso?" she asked.

"Said he wanted to have a look around," he said. "I think maybe find that friend he mentioned. But…I thought we could do some training while we wait?"

"Great idea," she said, smiling. "Have a seat."

He'd actually had some success the last two days, but he'd need to get a lot more comfortable if he was going to shape in an emergency. The way he had to get everything just right still made the magic feel too much like luck. At least he didn't need to worry about setting off a ripple…

For him, it seemed he could either transform properly or not at all. When he was truly focused on the thing he wanted to be, getting himself in that place of listening — like he had when he'd first discovered the keyholes — he could usually manage it. But if his mind filled with his regrets, the sheer weight of the guilt was just too much to lift.

At any rate, he took the seat opposite Sumi and tried to relax, following her instructions as they started with the usual meditations. He took a deep breath, sitting a bit taller as he closed his eyes.

"Wait," he said, cracking one eye open, "you're not going to fly away on the wind, are you?" Erso had asked him to watch out for her, not close his eyes while she disappeared again, this time in a city of thousands.

"No," she said, chuckling, though as she glanced back out the window, it still seemed like she was seeing something he couldn't. She shook her head. "Nope, just a regular old sea breeze, nothing to worry about."

"And that's better?" he asked, raising an eyebrow.

"Oh, definitely," she said, nodding firmly. "The wind in the forest was such a pure song, like Itorunai was singing herself. I'd never heard anything like it, and it was hard to ignore. But here... This breeze is actually a bunch of different songs."

She narrowed her eyes, listening.

"I can hear her — Itorunai — but she's just an undercurrent, and the wind seems to be coming from all over — all across the peninsula, I guess. Anyway, it's more like the hundreds of songs I hear around me all the time. Strangely, they're easier to ignore that way."

"Alright..." he said slowly, finally closing his eyes as he tried to relax his hands on his lap.

"So," Sumi said in a quiet voice, "what do you want to practice today?"

"My disguise," he said without hesitation. The closer they got to Berill, the more important it would be for him to hide like the others. Not that he thought himself particularly recognizable, though he'd had more than one nightmare of finding his own face on a wanted poster...

"Alright," Sumi said, "let's start by breathing."

Parimu squeezed his eyes shut tight, trying to banish the nightmare as he focused back in on his breath. Wait, no, she'd said to have soft eyes, right? He stopped squeezing so hard, though it didn't come naturally.

"In..." Sumi's voice said soothingly, "and out..."

He followed her voice, trying to think of nothing, watching the breath as she'd taught him to, filling his lungs before rushing back out. It was strangely effective. You'd think it'd be utter foolishness to watch your own breath, but even in his first lessons, his breath had shown him otherwise. In almost no time, it took on a life of its own as if it were something that existed without him, a wind that didn't even need his lungs.

"Now picture your cave," she said gently. "Picture the moss, the light, the frogs stirring in the pool."

Every word she said brought his attention more deeply into the cave, allowing him to picture things so much more clearly than he could on his own. Even though his cave was real, he had trouble thinking of it like that. If it was a memory, how could it be right there in front of him? Still, leave it to Sumi to somehow know just how to describe it. She'd probably seen the cave in his memories, of course, but even if she hadn't, that seemed to be her greatest power — noticing every detail, getting to the heart of things. The same power that had allowed her to see the potential in a fool like him…

"Now picture him across from you, sitting at the pool," she said, her voice breaking back through his jumble of thoughts.

His father. That's who he'd chosen for his disguise, a man who was fifteen years gone from the world with no risk of being recognized by the Thorns. A man who was strong, who could carry the weight of this task. Most importantly, it was a man he knew well, whose form should be no mystery to him. And yet, when he pictured his father by the pool, it felt like looking at a stranger… Or rather, something worse than a stranger, someone you felt you should know but didn't. There was no one he respected more than his father, but it was like respecting a fortress, the thick walls hiding whatever treasures were inside.

He had chosen a younger version of his father with no grey in his beard, the man he'd spent so many afternoons with as a child by the forge. That was before the walls had grown up between them, before he had become so shy he could barely speak. How had they come to that? His father was a *good* man, never drinking more than a swallow of whiskey, always faithful to his family. But had he been too good, too much to live up to? He'd started questioning everything he wanted to say to his father before he said it. And then, silence seemed preferable, the only way to not say the wrong thing.

"Relsenair," Sumi said, her voice quiet, "your father loved you."

"What?" he asked, opening his eyes. Her eyes were sad, and she gave him a tiny smile. How did she know what he was thinking? Could…the songs really tell her that much?

"He loved you," she said again. "I know it doesn't feel that way, but he did." She tapped the side of her head. "In your memories, I can see it in his eyes." Her smile grew brighter like it was warming the room more than the sun outside. "Like the day you and Jalicyne caught that fish, he was so proud. Just think about that day."

Parimu smiled in spite of himself, thinking back to that summer day so long ago.

"Alright," he said, closing his eyes again. He took a deep breath, bringing himself back to the cave. He and Jalicyne had still been so young then — ten, maybe? But they'd taken some of the iron tackle from the shop, determined to catch their own dinner. Jalicyne's mother had taught her how to spin the silk fishing lines that summer, and they'd spent hours looking for branches to use as poles.

It'd taken them the whole day up at Trout Lake, but they'd made it home just before dinner, each of them carrying a fish the size of their arms. That was the only time he could remember seeing his father genuinely surprised. His eyes had nearly popped out of his head at the size of the fish. Before long, his father had run over to Jalicyne's to invite her parents over, and they'd cooked the fish over a huge bonfire.

He imagined his father again, sitting on the opposite side of the pool. He pictured Jalicyne there too, standing to the side, at the age she'd been when she died. She had a fish in her hands, and she handed it to his father. He smiled the most genuine smile, laughing as he hefted the huge fish in his hands like a bar of iron.

Parimu smiled too. Maybe there *was* pride in those sparkling eyes… His father had always told him to do his duty, and now he finally had a chance to. If he could serve Sumi, maybe he could really finally help Berill. And maybe it would be enough…*he* would be enough. He closed his eyes in the cave, breathing out as a gentle glow filled the darkness.

11

Ever since the expedition, I can't stop thinking about the speaking stones in the library. The scrolls we found at Vilnosara seem to talk of nothing else. I've grown attached to their peaceful glow over the years, of course, but why had our ancestors collected so many? What ceremonies were lost when we left the Isles that rendered them a mere decoration?

-Excerpts from the personal journals of Peloris Domelgaine
Blue Notebook, Age 54

—:—

Kemarin Pont'dulairn sat in his chair in the voting hall of the Peerage, fondling the clasp of his cloak. Kestorin was speaking, blathering on about shipping traffic through his tiny sliver of sea holdings, which absolutely no one cared about. He was in Coerendul's pocket, which, while making him an enemy, didn't make him any more of a threat. At least it gave him time to prepare for his own speech. It would likely be the most important of his career, but he didn't feel even a twinge of nerves, only an…eagerness.

Of course, he was getting a bit old to be afraid of the peerage anyway. He'd held his seat for more than twenty years and the vice chair for five. Still, when it came to his father's plans, there had always been a tremor of fear, the weight of his family's legacy hanging over him. Why now, at the end, was he so ready? Was this the bloodlust their ancestors described, the itch to rush the field and vanquish his enemies? After so many years, he finally had Welaya on her back foot, today's speech marking the beginning of the end. He had held the meetings, he had secured the votes, and now, all he wanted to do was light the match.

Finally, the bondsman struck the gavel. A few peers called out their

75

votes on Kestorin's sea traffic measure, but Kemarin simply kept his hand at his side. Abstention was acceptable on trivial matters, of course, and it was best that Kestorin knew just how trivial this vote was, especially before the speech he was about to give.

"Seven votes aye!" the bondsman called out. "Twelve votes nay! The proposal has failed!"

It was hard not to laugh as Kestorin came down from the podium, his face turning purple in rage. Even if Turimane's twelve votes against hadn't already slid the dagger in, seventeen abstaining out of thirty-six was nothing short of a slap in the face. It probably wouldn't do to embitter small peers out of spite, but he had never said his coalition wasn't petty, only reliable.

"Vice Peer Pont'dulairn will take the podium!" the bondsman called out. "All rise for the Vice Peer!"

He stood from his chair, sweeping his cloak behind him. He hated the damned thing, but he'd need it today. Few peers wore the cloak of office anymore — the wool was cursedly warm in the summer and scratched something awful — but his was original. Only nine families had cloaks from the Isles of Dawn, the brilliant blue of the speaking stones unparalleled by any modern dye. He preferred his suit, of course, but on a day like today, that history was essential.

He took the podium and stood silently for a moment, looking out at the voting hall. Just a sliver of light filtered through the arrow slits, and the braziers glowed red against the stone of the keep. There were a few smiles, all from men as eager for change as he was, though more than a few of the faces looking back at him were decidedly...hawk-like. Regardless of which side they were on, though, every eye was on him. The most important lesson he'd learned in life was that having the upper hand never lasted as long as you'd like, so you damned well better use it.

"We the *Peers*," he finally began, "are here today to discuss the Queen."

The rabble started immediately, and the bondsman had to strike his gavel like a blacksmith flattening a nail. As the din began to reduce just a fraction, he put up a hand.

"I know that many of you fear change," he went on in a loud voice, "but what I represent need not be so terrifying. I only propose reforms that would bring us closer to who we were when we came to these lands some eight hundred years ago."

"Hear, hear!" Oeskidara yelled. The thick man barely fit into his seat anymore, but he was made of iron. Pont'dulairn gave him a nod before continuing.

"The Queen has caused us a great embarrassment. She is a chaser of *fairytales*, and she sent a sovereign agent of this kingdom after a single fugitive, disrupting commerce and vital diplomatic ties with the preposterous allegation of a Shapewalking plot!"

Laughter rang out from his side of the hall. The effect was good, though he knew at least three of them were Shapewalkers themselves. Very good indeed. There was still some rabbling from the other side, but it only took a few hits of the gavel to quiet them now. Once they'd realized the topic of his speech, there was nowhere to hide. They'd all seen the Foreign Office reports out of Anushai, and they were as embarrassed as anyone else.

"I bring to you today a most essential reform bill," he continued, brandishing the long scroll the bondsman had laid out for him. "The Queen has proved unreliable in handling delicate matters of state. She has in her hands the sword of Berill, the most powerful weapon on Wellonai. However, since time immemorial, it was the Peers — I say, the Peers! — who held that sword and threw their lot behind King Rummon. Before there was any Berillai army, there was the peerage. And so, I propose today that all war powers should filter through *this* hall, with no future military action taken without our express vote."

The hall exploded then. They had grown too used to his incremental reforms, it seemed. They were all fine with him tinkering with the police to a point, though it was this exact moment he'd spent so many years lulling them for. As the old saying went, *'first the needle, then the knife.'* There was shouting from all sides, and not a few Peers actually stood from their chairs, gesticulating at each other. It wouldn't do to have a brawl break out before the vote began, though it would certainly suit the mood these days.

"Now!" he yelled, refusing to wait for order as the gavel pounded away. With this kind of uproar, the bondsman would break the desk before he got control, anyway. "I do not propose taking the running of our incredible navy away from the Admirals, no! Only they know best how to deploy our brave sailors across dangerous waters. Neither do I strip the crown of its full authority. The Queen will remain the head of state and the Crown Admiral. I only seek to offer a guiding hand to Welaya, to filter her zeal through the wisdom of this hall. She will still propose war, consistent with her powers, but *we* will have the approval to launch those ships. What say you?!"

The voting began, and he stepped back, hands on his hips. As he stood there, he noticed Elikora slipping out with one of his aides. Off to

Welaya, no doubt, or maybe the Thorns… Well, she would know soon enough regardless. What mattered now were the votes, and the real work would come after. Welaya could stop him with a royal stay — if only temporarily — but more than that, the men of this hall hadn't held swords in over two hundred years. It would be one thing to get the motion in writing and another entirely to actually tame the Admirals. But it was a start, and he was ready for the rest.

12

I find no references of Shapewalkers on the Isles of Dawn. It stands to reason that our bloodline was pure before our arrival on the shores of the Continent, so my investigation will begin with the marriages immediately after the first treaty with the Mesop.

-Excerpts from the personal journals of Peloris Domelgaine
Green Notebook, Age 38

—:—

Erso paused in the stairwell of the inn, flashing his coat into one of those local leather numbers. As stiff as they were, the more inconspicuous he could be, the better. He'd actually seen this one on old man Minkhop once — the leather was dark, nearly black, with a high collar and sides that went down to his knees. It still felt semi-fashionable compared to most of the ones he saw, and besides, the innkeeper's husband had been a proper brawler, so hopefully it would scare away trouble. He'd already shaped his hat in the woods, of course, but he kept his fancy shoes — a man couldn't rightly sacrifice everything for the cause…

As he came down the main stairwell, Mrs. Minkhop looked up from her ledger.

"Well," she said, "at least you look like a man now. If you wanna dump the rest of those foppish clothes, I have a niece who's a seamstress."

"I don't think that'll be necessary," he said, chuckling. "I've sworn off nieces for a while, realized it's bad for my health."

She shrugged, giving him a 'suit yourself' look before going back to her ledger.

"Say," he said, sidling up to the front desk and leaning on it with one elbow. "I was curious, what's the story with all those flags?"

She didn't need to look, of course, they were everywhere. Without taking her eyes off her ledger, she scoffed, shaking her head.

"Politics," she said.

"Right…" Erso said, nodding, but apparently, that was all he'd be getting out of her. He couldn't disagree with her on that point, at least. All politics was good for was putting pretty words around other people wanting to either take your stuff or kill you and *then* take your stuff. Might as well be a curse word.

"Well, cheers," he said, tipping his hat as he left the inn.

He moved carefully along the wide stone avenue, doing his best to avoid looking like either a green flag man or a blue flag man — whatever that bloody meant… He noticed a few people on the street openly glaring at one flag or the other. No one tried to tear them down or anything, but that might not apply to picking fights if somebody thought he had the wrong look about him.

The flags were only on about a third of the buildings, but there seemed to be no rhyme or reason to where they were hung. Maybe there were more blue? But likely only just, and there was nothing particularly blue or green about the buildings they hung on. He did see a few people with blue or green feathers in their hats, which was unlikely to be a coincidence.

How deep does this bloody thing go? he thought, shaking his head.

After a few blocks, he came across one of the open-air taverns that were so popular in the city. They were all on wheels, though the owners seemed to take the same spot every day. The sides opened on hinges, turning the wagon into a bar, and little stools were set up alongside. It was always easier to ask questions over a drink, of course, and luckily, this one had a blue flag hanging from the back corner of the roof.

He slid onto one of the stools, sitting sideways so he could keep an eye on the other patrons and the street. He leaned forward with one elbow, catching the eye of the barman.

"*Mu'shrikal*," he said, greeting the man in Amoriai. His Narala probably wasn't good enough for delicate questioning, and Berillai didn't seem like a safe choice either — especially if the blue flag blokes were on the 'We Hate Berill' Committee… Luckily, most of the traveling barmen spoke enough of everything, given how much trade passed through the canal.

"Welcome," the man answered in Amoriai. "Not too many grain barges these days, eh?"

"Not nearly enough for my wife's shopping!" Erso bellowed, sliding into one of his favorite drunken grain merchant roles. The man laughed, dropping a glass in front of him.

"What'll it be?" he asked.

"Whatever's local," Erso said, nodding to the row of liquor bottles lined up behind the barman. He grimaced as he saw a bottle of hartisuan on the top shelf. It was ghastly, a kind of olive-flavored rum the locals loved. He absolutely despised olives and didn't like the slimy liquor much better, but these barmen loved it when somebody took their bloody national drink.

"Well, you're in luck," the man said, turning around with that exact bottle in hand. "Got some fresh hartisuan, about as local as it gets. My own brother makes it."

"Lucky indeed!" Erso said, slapping a big coin down on the counter. He shot the first drink back in one go as his insides squirmed, but he kept the smile firmly on his face as if he'd nailed it in place.

Another patron at the other end of the bar toasted him, cheering him on as he drank the vile filth, so he bought that guy a round and had to drink again. Seeing as he might not survive a third, he decided to go headlong into his questions.

"So," he said quietly to the barman, nodding his head toward the flag. "I've been gone a while, mind catching me up on the whole flag thing?"

The barman looked up from where he was polishing a glass, his eyes narrowing. But then he softened, letting out a sigh.

"Sure," he said, "I guess they have come up a bit quick if you've been gone a while." He looked over at the other patron quickly, speaking in Narala. "*Ipsetos umbleno maral?*" Something about blue...

The man nodded, raising his glass. Maybe the barman was double-checking the bloke's affiliation? Though why you'd drink at a blue-flagged pub when you were a...uh...*greener* was beyond him.

"So," the barman said, leaning forward and switching back to Amoriai. "You know about the princes, right?"

"Sure," Erso said, nodding. The king had two sons. He couldn't remember their names, what with him not giving a spit about royalty, but everybody here seemed to love them. "Remind me their names?"

"Basili and Feteris," the barman said. He said the first like it was candy in his mouth, spitting the other out like dirt. Probably a right proper clue in that!

"So anyway," the barman continued, "the King, gods bless him, is getting older, and it's getting time for him to step down."

"Ah," Erso said, starting to understand, though he didn't want to interrupt further. Ever since that first king came over from Anushai and took two wives, there had always been two royal lines. Each bastard after him had taken his own pair of wives, and when it came time to step down, the king would pick between one of the two firstborn sons on either side. If that son died, his half-brother on the other line would take the throne. Seemed a bit loony given how much royals like to assassinate each other, but whatever hulled their grain.

"Anyway," the barman continued, "we want the king to know who we support, and the blue flags are for Basili. Basili stands for tradition here — hence the blue for the sea — and he's the only one who'll protect our way of life and keep us free of those damned Berillai."

"Hear, hear," Erso said, raising his glass and forcing himself to drink more hartisuan. Good choice not using Berillai with the blue gents, then — noted. "So what's the…uh…over-under on numbers? You lot got more flags, I hope?"

"On this side, sure," the man said, his eyes darting around at the street, "in the true kingdom."

He leaned in, trying to be properly conspiratorial, let this bloke 'show him the truth' and all that.

"You mean Sykala?" Erso asked. "They got more green flags down south?"

"That's right," the barman said, shaking his head. "Ever since the Anushai forced us together, that lot's been dragging us down by the ankles. They don't know the sea like we do, and it's making 'em captive to Berill, selling off the kingdom for bloody trinkets and trains!"

The man took in a deep breath, shooting back his own shot of hartisuan.

"Well, at least we won't have to deal with that for much longer. You see, Basili can trace his line all the way back to Vikosana, the first Queen, the true heir to the throne in Ageleat."

That was absolute bullocks, obviously. Like any royal family, Erso was positive there had been far too much inbreeding to actually ferret out a bloodline. Unfortunately, he also knew just how dangerous that line of thinking could be… It was bloodlines, real or imagined, that had killed so many people in Amoriai, after all. And now that people were tripping over themselves to either serve or fight the Berillai…well, it seemed this pot really was about to boil over.

"Well, I hope the king makes the right choice, uh…in his wisdom," he said. "Appreciate the drinks, boys." He put another coin down for a fat tip and made a speedy exit. That was probably enough information for now, and it was time to preserve what few functioning parts of his brain he still had left after all that slime. He needed to find Arkesht and get out of town before the city became a bloodbath.

He walked east for a few minutes before finally reaching the northern leg of the canal. He paused, looking up and down at the full stretch of the city. It really was beautiful. Sure, the canal was full of trash and smelt something awful, but it made for a great view. It was still bustling with people and boats and little buildings, but nothing that blocked the skyline. He was only a few blocks from the capital on its giant square, and beyond that, he could just make out the palace across the water, its tiers looking like a copy of the one in Anushai. Hopefully, he'd have time to show Sumi around. Even if the place was ready to pop, she'd be heartbroken if she couldn't get a little tour...

He turned back to the canal, eyeing the outbuildings that ran along the edges. They were all lower than the street, built on a lower tier of the canal that ran along the edge of the water. The shipping companies all built warehouses down there where they could pull their goods straight off the boats. It had been a few years, but Arkesht's crew ought to be in one of those. He'd become quite the success since he'd trained him, and his last letter had mentioned building a new warehouse near the fork in the canal.

Unfortunately, all the bloody warehouses looked identical. They were made in little fin shapes, the flat end facing the canal as the roof tapered back toward the wall that fronted the street, all made of tin with little chimneys puffing smoke out the top. The only difference seemed to be the uniforms the workers wore as they scrambled on and off the barges. They were a bit fanciful for a bunch of sweaty laborers, but no one seemed to fear the grime with bright blues, pinks, and greens dotting the canal.

Had Arkesht ever mentioned the uniform color in his letters? Erso shrugged, walking down a flight of stairs to the water's edge. He'd just do what he always did — stick his nose in other people's business until they gave him answers or chased him off with a stick. At least he was a quick runner — though that was just another reason to wear his own shoes...

An hour later, after asking directions at six different warehouses and surviving the stench of leather piles and fermenting olives, he finally got pointed in the right direction. He found the warehouse about five blocks away on the south side of the canal. Arkesht really had done well for himself! While the design was the same, his warehouse was twice as long as the others he'd seen, with two wide doors where barges were loading up leathers, all the men wearing sky blue shirts under their leather vests. There was a door facing the walkway too, where he spotted what he'd been looking for — a flat bronze eagle nailed above the door.

He took a deep breath, squaring his shoulders. He hadn't ever been one for taking favors. He'd gotten too used to his life on the road, never really needing much anyway. Pass in, pass out, easy to enjoy but even easier to forget. But he had Sumi now, and he'd cash in every favor he'd ever earned if it meant keeping her safe.

Besides, he'd never have an easier proposition to make — 'Come help the most pleasant woman on Wellonai save the world, won't you?' He chuckled, finally forcing himself to walk toward the warehouse. He could stand there all day thinking about it if he wasn't careful, and like pa used to say — 'if you want the pearl, you're gonna have to get used to opening the clam.'

13

It took us three days by horse to reach the Umi'ceurae. Even now, in my tent, I still find myself thinking of the building. To think that our primitive ancestors built something so tall is astounding! The dome has long since caved in, but the walls are still standing in a ring some five stories high. There seemed to be a raised area in the center, like an altar, though what it held is still a mystery.

-Excerpts from the personal journals of Peloris Domelgaine
Blue Notebook, Age 52

—:—

Her lesson with Parimu done, Sumi was still sitting on the veranda, looking through Nela's letters. Ever since her dream from Essomuai, she found herself reading them even more. Her mind kept circling around one fact — the Anushai had killed Elomikarus and banished the Berillai. But where did that leave *her*? She still desperately wanted peace between her peoples, of course, but this was so much…larger than she could have imagined. This was between the gods, a hatred between the sisters that came with millennia of death and revenge. And against all of that, what was she supposed to offer the Berillai exactly?

It all just felt so surreal, not that learning it through a dream helped… She believed in the gods now — she was letting one summon her to the southern mountains, after all — but she found herself wishing for something to confirm what she'd seen, to know it wasn't all in her head. She'd only heard of Elomikarus in passing, and the Berillai seemed to have no history before the Isles. So where *did* that leave her?

She returned to one of her favorite lines from the letters, from when she was four, a year before she'd gone to live with her grandparents: *I see hope in little Sumi*, Nela had written. *My little granddaughter, playing with her Berillai blocks, even as she babbles the Anushai I teach her behind her mother's back. She soaks up the words like a sponge, none of that wretched history keeping her from it. There must be a secret in that for the path we're meant to forge.*

Nela had still managed to hope. She had known what the Berillai were, knew what the war had cost her people, and she'd still wanted to live amongst them, start a family with one of them. And the Berillai *had* returned, against all odds, allowing her to be born without ever knowing what the Isles of Dawn were like. There *was* hope in that, perhaps even more than Nela had imagined.

Although, reading letters between Nela and Hiyelleom also made her wonder…did the Anushai know this secret? Did anyone? She couldn't imagine anyone knowing without the Berillai finding out… She shook her head. Every secret seemed to demand three more to explain the first. She would have to puzzle it all out, but for now, she just had to keep holding on to who Nela was and what she'd believed in. No matter what either side had done in the past, she had to believe peace was possible. Without it, she'd never even have been born in the first place.

She was just getting through her third letter when the door to their suite burst open, Erso and another man sweeping in like a storm. They carried a large jug of ale, laughing hysterically. The ale certainly seemed like his kind of reconnaissance… She put her letters down, chuckling as she walked back into the main room. The two men were still talking animatedly as Erso rooted around the small kitchenette for some glasses. Parimu appeared in the doorway of his room, blinking in surprise with shaving cream covering half of his face. It wasn't until Sumi cleared her throat that the two of them spun around. Erso looked like he'd been caught in the cookie jar, but the other man only smiled more widely.

He stepped up to shake Sumi's hand, pumping it up and down enthusiastically.

"Pleasure to meet you," he said, "name's Arkesht. Erso's told me all about you — a friend of his is a friend of mine, of course."

He was a giant man, easily a head taller than Erso and thick around the middle, a long beard hanging over his chest. He seemed to be about Erso's age but with thick lines around his eyes that made it hard to guess how old he really was.

Sumi blinked, smiling as she shook off her surprise.

"Very nice to meet you," she said, "I'm Sumi." She turned, gesturing toward Parimu. "This is Relsenair."

"Ah, of course," Arkesht said, stepping over and pumping Parimu's hand even more aggressively. "Sorry to interrupt your shave and all;

fancy a drink when you're done?" He slapped Parimu on the back before stepping back over to Erso. "Didn't think I'd ever see this one again, but I'm glad I did. Always hoped I'd get a chance to thank him properly."

Parimu slipped back into his room as Erso poured the ale into a hodgepodge of mismatched mugs and glasses.

"Arkesht is one of the first students I ever trained," he explained. "One of the least thieving of them all, too — outside of you, of course."

Arkesht looked at the floor, scratching the back of his head.

"Well, I did run one scam — sorry, Detective!" he added, calling to Parimu in his room. "Anyway, Erso here found me stealin' my first boat. Didn't have much, but I didn't feel safe on the farm anymore with all those Berillai crawlin' around to put in the trains."

He turned to take a mug from Erso, nodding his thanks before taking a long swig.

"But I swear on the wind, stealing that one boat is the only dirty thing I've ever done. Now I got a whole fleet of my own, even paid back the man I stole from double once I could afford it — anonymously, of course."

Sumi walked over, leaning against the small butcher's block as she took her own mug. She'd always wanted to meet another one of Erso's students. She squinted at Arkesht, his keyhole shimmering with his song, an oddly light melody for his size, like a flute. He just seemed...happy. She shook her head, taking a sip of her ale before she lost herself.

"This is wonderful," she said, staring down into her mug. It was unlike any other ale she'd had, almost spicy but still somehow floral. "What is it?"

"That's my own special brew," Arkesht said, proudly thumbing the edge of his coat. "Was savin' it for something special, and then this old rascal poked his head in."

Parimu re-emerged from his room, now fully shaven, though he still looked a bit thrown. She jerked her head to one side, calling him over, where she forced one of the glasses of ale into his hand. She smiled at him reassuringly, and he took a sip, though his hand was still tight around the glass.

"So," Arkesht said, "Erso tells me you all got in a bit of a scrape, need a ride south."

"That's right," she said. "We need to reach the Nyfatsi, and then I guess we need a boat to Vilodai's Heart. You wouldn't be able to take us, would you?"

"Sure," he said, tilting his head. "I could do the river. Not sure why anyone would wanna go to Vilodai's Heart, but I could use a bit of time on the road myself. I have a shipment of leathers going to Alara soon, assuming you don't mind roughing it. I don't have any boats on that stretch of the river right now, but I could probably set you up with a friend."

He took a long sip of his ale before putting the mug back down, pointing his thumb behind him in the direction of the city.

"Not sure if you all noticed, but it's getting a bit dicey down there."

What was going on with those banners? Erso seemed to catch the question on her face, speaking up.

"Asked around on my way to Arkesht's," he said. "Seems we got a couple rival princes vying for the throne, lookin' to pick sides on the Berillai and all that."

Arkesht nodded somberly into his drink.

"Which side you on again, mate?" Erso asked him with a grin. "I think you forgot to say."

Arkesht took a sly sip of his ale before raising his hands in surrender.

"Good merchants don't pick sides," he said. "We got both banners in the warehouse in case somebody comes with a pitchfork, but that's just between us. Like any sensible man, I support *the* prince, of course."

"That's a good oath," Erso said, chuckling. "Glad to see you haven't changed, you squirrelly bastard."

"Hard to change course when the wind only blows one way," Arkesht said, clinking his mug with Erso's. "Anyway, I always try to keep half my crew out of the city; nothing worse than idling inventory. But it wouldn't be a bad time to duck out myself. This next shipment should pretty well clear us out until I decide to come back."

"Do you really think it'll get violent?" she asked, a knot forming in her stomach. So much for taking the eastern route to avoid trouble… She glanced at Erso, his smile gone as he stared down into his mug. He knew all too well what happened when a city teetered on the brink, didn't he?

"Well," Arkesht said, shrugging, "there's twice as many flags this week as there were last. But a situation like this can be awful funny. Sometimes the storm doesn't roll in 'til well after you've seen the first cloud, eh?"

"How quickly do you think we could push off?" Erso asked.

"Tomorrow?" he offered. "Have to convince the wife of it, though she won't need too much convincing. The leather's set to ship this week anyway, only difference is us being on the boat. I'll just tell her we need to leave early to get a shipment of cloud wine, almost that time of year anyway."

"Thank you," she said, "really. But you're sure it's safe to leave your wife right now?"

"Oh, she'll be coming," he said, chuckling. "I stole the first boat, but it's her operation. But really, don't mention it, always a pleasure to have our kind around."

He drained the last of his ale, setting his mug down with a thunk.

"Well, I better scoot, lots to prepare. Besides, I think I'd better send some telegrams, tell my other captains to stay out a bit longer."

He nodded at all of them and left, bending his tall frame through the doorway. The three of them were left standing in a triangle that was too wide, ale still in their hands despite the festive feeling being gone. They wandered closer together, centering themselves around the butcher block.

"Well," Erso said, pouring more ale, "sightseeing and a drink or dinner and bed?"

She looked out the window of the veranda.

"I would like seeing the city a bit if we're leaving tomorrow. Do you think it's safe?"

"Sure," Erso said, nodding. "If anybody asks, just tell 'em you're too besotted with me to possibly choose a prince."

"Right," she said, rolling her eyes, "just let me grab my coat."

———

Sendinal Monderin looked at the piece of paper in his hands again, muttering to himself as he walked quickly through Ageleat. This was as strange an assignment as he'd ever received. So strange, in fact, that he'd almost thought his cipher was wrong when he first read it. He hadn't become one of the longest-serving Thorns on this side of the world by questioning orders, true, but still… He was used to spying on the crown, moving weapons — things of a much greater magnitude. If anything, these orders seemed…halfhearted. But supposedly, they were from Kollenail himself, not someone he was interested in crossing.

The first telegram had contained a vague description of three people he and his men were meant to watch for. Central command seemed to think they'd be crossing into Ekosinar over the northern bridges. They kept track of plenty of people in the city, so that wasn't strange, but the rest of the message…

Watch for three. Likely two men and a woman, two Berillai. Take prisoner if you can, but don't make a fuss. Use silver.

So he was to watch for three people and try to capture them, but don't try too hard? He knew well enough that Ekosinar was a sensitive post. The kingdom was about as on the fence between Berill and Anushai as a place could be, and they wouldn't want to upset that balance over nothing. But usually, once orders came down to his level, the thing was as good as done. You either captured people or you didn't, so why the hesitation?

Not to mention the silver bit — that would mean Shapewalkers. None of the men under his command currently had the ability, but why not send for one? And how exactly was he supposed to keep an eye out for something so vague?

Sendinal kept walking, heading east along the canal until he came to the main north-south street. He took a left, following it until he reached the alabaster bridge. He bought a newspaper, sitting on the stone railing. He only had to wait a few minutes until one of the eyes showed up. He glanced casually at the boy, recognizing him. He was a ruddy kid, local, but he usually kept a careful watch.

"Please, sir," the boy asked in Berillai, "a bit of coin? Perhaps a shoeshine?"

Sendinal made to shoo him away but then paused, acting as if he'd thought better of it.

"Fine," he said, "but be quick."

The boy smiled, pulling out a dirty rag and kneeling on the cobblestones, where he began to carefully run it along the top of his shoes.

"Two men and a woman," he whispered, "crossed the bridge this afternoon. Horses. Went to an inn in the north corner — Minkhop's."

"And they matched the description?" he asked quietly.

"I dunno," the boy said, freezing in place with the rag. "Speakin' Berillai, though."

"Alright, good," Sendinal said. He leaned back and opened his paper again. It may just be a cover, but the little urchin could at least finish the shoeshine while he was down there. It took another minute, but he tossed the boy a coin when he was done. That part was real, of course — they had to pay the children something for all the standing around they did. He'd at least made it a large coin since the information actually seemed good for once. Then he tossed his paper and set off to gather the rest of his men. The orders may be strange, but he'd carry them out now, or else it might be him hogtied in the next crate they sent to Berill.

14

Why me? And why now? It makes no sense.

-Excerpts from the personal journals of Peloris Domelgaine
Blue Notebook, Age 53

—:—

Sumi followed Erso and Parimu down the central canal. They were taking their time, enjoying the sunshine as they made their way toward the palace. Although, the alcohol probably wasn't helping them move very quickly... After the ale at the inn, Erso made them stop by one of the tiny taverns on wheels, insisting she try a strange olive liquor. Erso had almost gagged on his, but she'd actually kind of liked it... Unfortunately, she'd also ended up finishing both his and Parimu's, and now she felt like she was floating behind them on the cobblestones, the sharp spice of their pipes drifting with her through the air.

As evening approached, the world seemed to glow, and the alcohol made the songs swirl around her like her own private orchestra. It was a nice feeling, actually. Being tipsy meant she couldn't really force the songs out of her head, but she couldn't latch onto any single one either, allowing her to wade through them like birds lining the branches of the forest, creating a tapestry of indistinguishable, beautiful sound.

Ageleat really was incredible. There was just so much to look at, it was dizzying! Back home in Berill, the bay was in one direction, your eye always drawn in a single line along the coast. But here, the sea was visible on all sides, not to mention the dozens of boats zipping by on the canal surrounded by buildings. While the canal divided the city in a neat Y shape, almost nothing else about the place was even remotely symmetrical. The streets seemed to ricochet back and forth, the buildings almost like a coral reef, different colors sticking up in all

91

directions.

After walking along the right branch of the canal for a ways, they crossed over a bridge and into the central plaza where the capital building was. It sat on a giant square, made of dark stone easily twice as wide as the temple square in Anushai. It ran unobstructed all the way to the north, where it ended just before the beach. Thick knots of street vendors lined the perimeter, but there was nothing else built on the stone slabs, creating an impressive stretch of emptiness in a city that was otherwise bursting at the gills.

The capital itself was built in a perfect circle ringed with tall marble columns. There was a kind of mosaic at the top, the tiles sparkling before the roof rose in a steep cone, capped with some kind of shining stone. She stared at the building for a long time, losing herself in its swirling lines. She was so engrossed she didn't even realize Erso had stepped away until he tapped her on the shoulder.

"Here," he said, chuckling as he handed her a sandwich, "I think you could use it."

"That bad, eh?" she asked, grinning. "I guess I could use a bite to eat…"

She looked down at the sandwich, cocking her head. If you could call it a sandwich… It had a wide piece of flatbread folded in half and stuffed with half an ocean's worth of seafood. There were little silvery fishes lined up in a row, oysters and clams stuffed between them. The whole thing had been drizzled with olive oil and sprinkled with an odd, crumbly cheese. She took a big bite, her eyes widening.

"This is amazing!" she exclaimed, quickly taking another bite. "Where did you get this?"

Erso was taking a bite of his own sandwich, but he cocked his head behind him at one of the vendors that ringed the plaza.

"What do you think?" she asked Parimu. "Too much seafood?"

"No," he said, shaking his head. "It's salty, not bad at all."

She nodded eagerly, smiling. Why did salt taste so good right now? Was that the liquor too?

They wandered across the plaza toward the coast, inhaling their sandwiches. They passed more vendors, a few of them with the green or blue flags Erso had mentioned. It was hard to believe such a beautiful place was teetering on the edge of violence, but everything could change in an instant — it wasn't all that long ago she had to flee home herself, of course. Besides, after what she'd seen in the dream, it felt like violence was in the soil itself, a sickness that would spread across the Continent until it was cured…

They finally reached the end of the plaza, crossing the road that ringed the peninsula onto the beach. From there, only a narrow stretch of water, no more than a mile wide, separated the palace from the city. The water was a rich, dark blue, waves rocking lazily in the channel. The breeze was stronger by the beach, and it pushed against her face, blowing her hair about. Her head felt much clearer after the sandwich, and she dug her boots into the sand, luxuriating in the soft shifting of the grains.

"This is nice," Erso said from beside her. "I know we're off to save the world, and we'll probably, you know, die or something, but this has been quite the adventure."

Sumi hummed her agreement, reaching out and squeezing his shoulder. Erso always seemed to be teaching her that lesson again. No matter what lay ahead, there was this moment. There were sandwiches and the sea, and even potentially poisonous olive liquors to enjoy… But most importantly, they had each other.

"I agree," Parimu said, smiling. "I suppose I've traveled before, but this feels different. I didn't really have many friends in the navy, and well…thank you for having me along."

"We wouldn't have it any other way," she said. She squeezed his shoulder, too, and stood there between them, a link between two very different but very wonderful men. She finally let go, and they stood that way a while longer, staring at the water. The sun was slipping down behind the palace, the hills that circled it hiding where it would eventually disappear into the sea.

"Well," Erso finally said, "we'd better get back. It'll be dark before long, and I don't know these streets well enough to know which ones are safe at night."

She nodded, and they turned back toward the east, following the beach until they met the canal where they crossed a bridge back into their third of the city. They still took their time, strolling along as Erso pointed out a few famous landmarks. Despite not having visited in years, he knew a surprising amount. They even passed a strange tower where Erso said they made hartisuan. It was a narrow stone building, no more than twenty feet wide but built in a circle that soared straight up in the air. At the top, it had a wide roof that fanned over the sides with thick brass grates. It looked almost like somewhere you'd hide a princess in a fairy tale…

"The grates are to air the place out," Erso said with a grimace. "Let's the gas from the fermenting olives escape."

After a brief argument about whether or not they should go inside to sample the olives, they moved on. A few blocks later, as they were passing the naval docks on the northeastern side of the peninsula, Erso grabbed her by the elbow and leaned in close.

"Don't look," he whispered, "but I think we've picked up a tail."

Her pulse quickened, and she looked between him and Parimu. The two men simply nodded at each other.

"What do we do?" she asked. Could it be the Thorns? Of course, they couldn't avoid them forever!

"Let's see if we can lose 'em," Erso said. "Walk quickly, but don't look like you're running."

He took her by the elbow, and they picked up their pace by about a third. She struggled a bit to keep up, her boots clacking loudly on the cobblestones as she was forced to take two steps for every one of theirs. They started turning randomly down all the crooked streets of Ageleat. At least she'd always been good at directions, so she kept her mind focused on where they were in relation to the inn in case they got lost. Still, even with all that turning, it seemed it hadn't been enough. As soon as they made their third turn, Parimu cursed.

Another man had appeared on a corner ahead of them. He seemed normal enough, but it couldn't be a coincidence, just standing on a corner like that directly in their path.

"Spring trap," Parimu muttered, turning them down another street. "They're herding us."

"What's the play?" Erso asked.

"Have to find a narrowing," Parimu answered as he moved quickly ahead.

She thought about suggesting they fly out as birds, but Parimu may not be ready. Besides, if these men really were Thorns, they could have silver. She shook her head, focusing on keeping up, though they only made it another block before they were stopped in their tracks again. There was another man waiting for them in the street, his arms crossed and staring directly at them. She whipped her head around and found they hadn't lost their other tails after all, either. A few more men emerged from shops and pubs along the street until there were six in all. They still seemed oddly casual, but they were unmistakably of a group, their bearing and gaze all subtly oriented toward the three of them.

The one in the street ahead of them began walking closer, the others slowly closing in around them. It felt like her head was on a swivel, unsure where to look. For whatever reason, as the one in the lead approached, her mind tried to focus on his song. He was human, Berillai, his life beginning to paint itself in her mind. *No,* she thought, shaking her head, she had to stay focused.

"Like we discussed, then?" Parimu muttered under his breath.

"Yup," Erso said.

Like they'd discussed? What were they—

Parimu took her arm, yanking her into the nearest alley. Erso followed them in, the man on the street shouting behind them. They ran quickly down the alley, but halfway in, Erso stopped, turning as he glowed, his cane becoming a sword.

"What are you doing?" she asked, whipping back around. Erso didn't turn, facing the mouth of the alley where all six men had appeared. Parimu was pulling on her shoulder, forcing her further down the alley.

"It's alright," Parimu said, "we just have to stick to the plan."

She looked at Parimu, finding his eyes wide, begging her to come with him.

"But Erso," she said, looking back.

"He'll be alright," Parimu said, "trust me. I'll head back to help once we get you away."

She relented, Parimu pulling her around a corner in the alley, but she kept looking behind her. This didn't feel right. She'd told herself after Amoriai that she'd never let Erso run off on his own again. He was good with a sword, but what could he possibly do against six? They turned another corner, the alley stopping at a dead-end.

"Damn," Parimu muttered. He turned to her. "Turn into something that can climb a wall and get back to the inn. I'll head back to Erso."

Sumi shut her eyes. She couldn't do this, not again. She reached out to Essomuai, knowing she didn't have to speak but saying the word in her mind anyway. *Beyenjoel,* she thought in Anushai. *Help.*

For a moment, she was afraid help wouldn't come, but then, an image flashed in her mind, the man from the street, the one who had stepped toward them first. His song was still in her mind, and Essomuai knew it well, snippets of his life entering her mind in the span of a heartbeat. It wasn't like living his life like with Parimu, but she could see it all the same, like the story of the stones in the forest, time speeding up until it turned into dozens of tiny photographs.

Sendinal Monderin. He was a Thorn who had worked in Ekosinar for years, but beneath all that, he was just a man. He had a family, a life; dreams and hopes, fears and hurts. And just like with all her enemies — even Elomikarus — Essomuai couldn't bear to think of a sword going through him. There was an urgency infecting the songs that made her want to clench her teeth, the goddess's need threatening to overtake her. And yet, in all that need, there was somehow an answer, spoken in the strange goddess tongue. Before she could stop to think what it meant, it was just as Elomikarus described, a picture forcing its way into her mind.

Lesonekalinat, Essomuai said, an image of a leaf appearing, changing its color like in the fall, only instantly, within seconds. *A transformation.* Parimu began to turn, pulling out his own sword, when she stopped him, grabbing his arm.

"No, Relsenair," she said. "There is a better way."

She turned, charging back down the alley toward Erso, a plan already forming in her mind. She skidded around the corner and pulled up short, absolute chaos seeming to have poured down into the alley. Erso was gone, and in his place was a raging fire that leapt into the air, filling the narrow space between the buildings. Two of the thuggish-looking men were on the ground, bleeding from sword wounds, while the others held their weapons wardingly, hesitating before the flames.

The fire had to be Erso, but how long until they leapt over him or found a way to use their silver? He had been buying them time, but she would never abandon him again. She set her jaw, marching toward the flames. She saw Sendinal, still in the center of the group, the silvery gleam of a knife in his hand.

"Sendinal!" she yelled as she reached the flames. "Stop this, now!"

As she reached the center of the fire, she began to glow, taking a new form as Erso pulled back the flames just enough to let her through. She appeared as his mother, Neran, only twice her normal size, her eyes glowing with flame. Sendinal stared up at her with wide eyes, backing away, the other Thorns' eyes darting between them.

"How?" he asked. "You're— You're dead; this isn't real."

Still, she stepped closer, and he tripped and fell, slamming against the wet stones of the alley. The other men backed away too, their eyes now glued to her as they cowered.

"Your brother sent for me," she said, pressing her advantage. "He prayed to the old gods, the gods of the Shapewalkers. You must stop this violence. I command you to leave this place, to leave the Thorns. Live a better life, Sendinal."

He stared up at her, frozen on the spot.

"Go!" she roared, bursting into flames herself, transforming into a raging fire. He scrambled up from the ground and ran for his life, the other men behind him.

As soon as the alley was empty, she stumbled, the exhaustion rushing in. She reached out for the alley wall and closed her eyes, flashing back into her own form. Even though every form seemed easier with Essomuai, it was still difficult doubling her size like that. She whipped around, finding Erso alive and well, no longer a flame, and she rushed to him, pulling him into an embrace.

"I'm so glad you're okay," she said, mumbling into his neck.

"Me too," he said, clutching her tightly. She pulled away, holding onto his shoulders as she looked him over, terrified she'd find some horrible wound. Thank Essomuai, he was absolutely fine.

"I can't let you do that again," she said, meeting his eyes. "We have to do this together."

"Keeping you safe is the most—" he began to say.

"*Together,*" she said again, more firmly.

"Alright," he said, nodding.

"Thank you both," she said, turning to Parimu. "I can't tell you how much it means to have you looking out for me, but there has to be a better way. If we're here to stop the violence between our peoples, we can't rely on it to keep us safe. If we lose, we lose together, alright? "

Their chests were still heaving — their hearts probably pounding with the same adrenaline as hers — but after a second, they both nodded.

She looked back down the alley where the men had fled. This time, at least, it seemed there *had* been a better way. The Thorns were gone — for now, anyway. She motioned for the others to follow her out of the alley when she staggered, falling to her knees as a searing pain entered her mind.

She blinked, tears coming to her eyes as a painful song forced its way into her head. It was staccato, full of stabbing notes like breaking glass, fragments of what had once been a melody. She turned to the side where the two men lay dying, both of them unmoving in slowly oozing pools of blood. She scrambled on hands and knees to the first man, leaning over him. He stared up at the sky with glassy eyes, already gone. So what was this? The end of his song, the moment when his…soul left?

I'm sorry, Essomuai, she prayed in her mind. *Thank you for your help, I promise I'll find another way.*

"I'm sorry," Erso said, stepping up beside her.

"It's alright," she said, reaching out and grabbing a hold of his pant leg. "You did what you had to, but we should honor these men, for her." She turned around more fully, looking up at the others. "Can you help me?"

They helped her lift the men, lining them up next to each other. She gently closed their eyelids, covering them with one of their cloaks. She stood and held her hands in front of her for a moment, closing her eyes. She didn't know their names, the songs already too ruptured for that, but she wanted to say a prayer for them.

"*Essomuai siom leyon, guyang siom teyal,*" she said in Anushai.

Essomuai is the prism but yours is the light.

Erso stood beside her, putting his hands on his forehead in a triangle shape.

"Mu'amara, naimal quizen. Aydameen merkest," he said in Amoriai. Even Parimu joined in, muttering the Rites of the Sea. She wasn't sure what the right words were, but she felt like all of them could be, anything to honor these souls.

She reached out, holding both of their shoulders again. It was strangely similar to her gesture at the beach, though the meaning was so different now.

"Thank you both," she said quietly. "We'd better go."

They turned and left the alley. It was completely dark now, though some people were still out and about, and bright light filtered from the shops that were still open. A few passersby looked up at them as they left, but they quickly went back to whatever they had been doing, wanting nothing to do with whatever fight had just broken out in the alley. The three of them hurried away, tracing their way back to the inn.

———

Not long after, they all had their bags in hand, hastily hurrying down the stairs of the inn. Erso dropped a coin on the innkeeper's desk, paying her double what she was owed. They went out into the street and turned toward the canal. There was no telling how long her ruse with the Thorns would last, and they didn't want to be there when they finally rallied.

Erso was positive he hadn't picked up a tail earlier in the afternoon, so they headed for Arkesht's. Hopefully, they could sleep in the warehouse overnight and leave in the morning on the barge, disappearing into the dozens of boats moving up and down the canal each day. Erso had said that once they reached Sykala, Arkesht would take them by wagon to the south into Alara, where they could hopefully find a boat to take them to Vilodai's Heart.

It was a lot to juggle in her mind on top of everything else. She looked over her shoulder every few seconds as they slipped along side streets toward the canal. The buoyancy of their escape seemed to slip away, leaving them unsettled, their usual joking fading into a strange quiet, staring hard at every shadow they passed. Still, they had survived, and they had Essomuai to thank.

She looked up at the stars, forcing herself to hear their song. They were quieter here in the city, but she could hear their twinkling all the same. She had to keep her eyes on that light. It made her feel smaller, even more out of her depth, but it gave her hope too. No matter what had happened before in the long, bloody cycle of history, there was another way, a path where they could all live.

Thank you, she prayed, hoping those simple words would be enough for now. *Thank you.* They continued through the night, like ships slipping out of port, hoping for a warm bed and another tomorrow to see them through.

THE END OF PART ONE

PART TWO

15

There were two found this month, one on Elikora lands and one in the mountains north of Mikarae. I'm still curious how the one in the mountains came to be discovered, though the bounty seems to be helping give the people a certain amount of...ingenuity. The trouble will be getting it safely to the tower without anyone touching it. We cannot waste the message.

-Sea Scroll #132
*Estimated Date 383 PN**

**The documents are obviously Prenavigune given where we found them, though chemical analysis is the only method we have to gauge just how far before the Posdeven period they may be.*

—:—

Sumi entered another dream. She had laid awake in Arkesht's warehouse for a long time listening to the songs — as much for soothing as for guidance. She needed to feel the goddess near her, to feel like they weren't in this alone. Finally, without meaning to, she'd slipped under the weight of her exhaustion. Her thoughts began to drift, and she felt a golden light wash over her. For the briefest moment, she held onto herself as the visions took over.

The golden light faded away, and she found herself walking on a beach. She wore thick boots of fur or maybe wool, and she had a thick shawl hanging over her shoulders. The beach was rocky, covered in black stone, and the sky above was grey. The beach was only some forty feet wide before the stone gave way to limestone cliffs, climbing away from the water at a sharp angle before leveling off, the top covered in pines. She looked around her, wondering for a moment where she was before her mind disappeared.

What a silly thought, not knowing where she was! Ereilea shook her head and went back to her work. She must have been caught in a daydream, thinking she was someone else. A girl like herself, but with a strange name like…Sumi or something? Who'd ever even heard of a name like that? She chuckled to herself, trying to focus again. She'd be in trouble if she had nothing to show for her efforts when the elders came to check on her.

She looked off in the distance, catching a glimpse of the tower. It was made of the same black stone as the beach, and it loomed above her even so far off down the shoreline. *Tor Vilnosara*, the tallest structure on the Isles of Dawn. It had to be at least as tall as one of the spirit pines in the forest. Ever since she'd first heard of it, she had dreamt of this place. It still didn't seem real that she actually got to be here as an apprentice to the priestesses.

All the more reason to get back to work… House Turimane had taken a chance on her, and if she failed, she'd just be another poor village girl from — what had they called it? — the *frozen nothing* of House Berill. She certainly wouldn't squander her chance now by letting them find her idling on the beach, lost in some daydream!

She knelt on the stone, picking between the smaller rocks in search of what the priestesses wanted. Luckily, she had wool wound around her knees beneath her dress, making kneeling on the beach only slightly excruciating. She hoped she could find one of the stones today. She wasn't entirely sure why they were looking for them, to tell it true, but the priestesses probably didn't know either.

They were looking for special rocks called *goddess eyes* that could only be found on this beach, apparently. The example they showed her had looked like a pumice stone, but when she put her eye to it, it had been full of shimmering flecks of silver. They could bloody well use them in the bath for all she cared, but every time an apprentice found one, they got extra dinner for a week. The priestesses had built a big altar out of them and said prayers over them every night, but they kept asking for more.

Unfortunately, the eyes were black on the outside, just like the rest of the cursed beach. So every day, the apprentices were given a separate stretch of rocks to comb, crawling on hands and knees in hopes of finding something valuable. She could see at least three others like her along the water before the coast curved away, where the other two dozen or so were blocked by the thick forest on the cliffs.

She still found herself staring at the other apprentices during mealtimes, though she'd need to stop before they thought her daft... But why had they selected her out from the rest of the girls in her village? The priestesses had come through taking donations, and they had marched up to her mother, offering her a whole bag of coins to take her to the southern island. But they never said why they wanted her specifically. The other girls looked nothing like her. Some were short and stocky Oeskidarans, others tall beauties from House Pont lands. They weren't even all particularly young. She had worked up the courage to ask her teacher once, and she'd said it was her eyes...

Ereilea shook her head; they would be there soon to check on her, and she at least better get a decent pile going. Even if all you had done was move a bunch of the black rocks out of the way and into a pile, they wanted to see that you were working. She paused for just one more moment to look out at the water, reading the wind as High Priestess Moral had taught her.

As an apprentice, she didn't have access to the sacred calendar, of course, but wind reading was the first thing they taught you. The gusts were growing weaker and coming from the west, which would mean Middle-night was approaching. The seas were always calmer then — albeit still guided by the strange yearly cycles — and back home in the village, they'd be having a festival to celebrate being half through winter. It made her homesick, thinking of the lamb pies. Still, the bloody priestesses only ever ate fish, so why was the approach of the holiday putting such a thorn in their side?

She sighed, going back to work. There was no shortage of questions, but it wasn't as though the priestesses would suddenly start explaining themselves. She moved forward another pace, picking up one rock about the size of her hand and hefting it. You could always tell by the weight right away. The black stones were far heavier than the eyes, and it saved time from staring at each one. She had only held a real goddess eye once, though, so she usually hefted them more times than the older girls did...

She frowned, putting the stone to the side before picking up another. She went on like that for a long while until she started sweating despite the cold. Finally, she had a few dozen stones piled up next to her. She looked down, frowning as she realized she'd unearthed a large round stone. The other girls said you could sometimes find eyes buried under larger rocks, though how they got there was yet another mystery... The priestesses said they came from the sea, but then, how did they get buried? She'd never seen one floating in the water or anything, and no matter how many girls they had combing the beach, they always wanted more.

She set her jaw; there was nothing to it but to muscle it out. She stood up, squatting to get her hands under the rock. She heaved with all her might, but the stone flipped over as if it weighed nothing at all. Her mouth fell open, and she scrambled down onto her knees by the stone. Now that she ran her hand more carefully over it, she noticed the hundreds of little holes on its surface.

She unconsciously sat beside it, her heart beating like a drum in her throat. If this was a goddess eye, it would probably be the biggest one ever found... She wouldn't just get extra dinner for this, she might even make third rank. She pulled the stone onto her lap and lifted it up toward the sky, putting her eye against one of the larger holes. She squinted, and the inside sparkled. It was bloody chock-full of silver!

She hugged the stone to her chest as if it were an old friend. Her mind raced, trying to remember the instructions. She had listened well, but in the moment, her mind couldn't seem to dredge them up. Perhaps a part of her hadn't thought she'd ever really find one... Before you brought the stone back, you were meant to put it flat on the ground and say the prayer, but the lashing they gave you if you didn't do the prayer right would make you regret ever finding one in the first place.

She hastily put the stone back where she'd found it so it could lay flat. Rubbing her hands together, she placed them on the stone, her mind fumbling through the words of the prayer. They practiced it every night as a group, but it was hard to remember it perfectly with all the ancient words. Where did those strange words come from anyway? She'd never met anyone on the Isles who talked like that, but the priestesses said it was the only way to get the gods to hear them. Some help they were... The winters were always brutal, and the mutton was never enough. But still, they prayed, hoping for something.

The first word was Vilodai, which was...the old name for Umilai, right? The rest of the prayer was about bringing aid to lost children or something like that, but the priestesses didn't seem to know what it meant any more than the apprentices. She'd be switched if she ever said that out loud, though... She didn't really have a head for the old stories, which only made her wonder more why they chose her.

She started to say the words, her teeth chattering from cold and adrenaline.

"Vilodai," she started, closing her eyes, *"ke'loseya ashkarasan alomaekar, torunaru nafilyae."*

She opened her eyes, taking in a deep breath of the sea air. Her hands still flat on the stone, she looked around. Nothing had changed. She shrugged, standing up — just another random thing the priestesses did, then. She pulled her shawl closer, heading down the beach for help. The stone was deceptively light, but only a fool would carry it back on their own. The glory of her discovery would be ruined if she so much as nicked the thing on her way to the tower.

She had gone ten feet or so when the ground began to shake. Ereilea stumbled, falling hard on her side. Trees began to shake on the ridgeline, one or two of them popping loudly as they did when the trunks froze in the cold. She rolled over, scrambling across the rock to check on the stone. If it broke from some earthquake, they'd never bloody believe her!

Just as she reached the stone, the shaking reached a peak, popping sounds exploding all around her. Black stones flew in all different directions, filling the air as new stones rose out of the earth on their own. They were long, jagged crystals, about the length of her arm and glowing blue. She screamed, falling on her back as hundreds of them shot up into the air around where the goddess eye had been. She covered her head with her arms, but just as suddenly, the shaking stopped, and everything was still.

She shakily got to her feet, looking back down the beach toward the others. She heard yelling now that the tremors had stopped, but she could no longer see the other girls beyond the ring of blue stones encircling her. She looked at the center, breathing a sigh of relief as she found her goddess eye unharmed. She reached for it, holding onto one of the blue stones, but the moment she touched the glowing crystal, her eyes went black.

Ereilea was…nowhere. The ground beneath her feet was gone. She tried to scream, but there was no sound. Her eyes darted around but found only darkness like she had been swallowed by a cave. But wait… Something was there… She shook with fear. She opened her mouth to scream again when a voice suddenly shook inside her mind.

Daughter, the voice said. Or maybe it didn't say so much as rumble, images appearing in her mind, a woman with a girl behind her and one behind that. Suddenly she found a calm washing over her like a wave on the beach, and all her fear was gone. Another image implanted itself in her mind, of herself holding a blue stone, flying over the sea on some strange wooden contraption. *Return,* the voice urged, *return.*

Was this…Umilai? Had the…the prayer worked? Suddenly, she felt smaller than small; no more than a speck, a tiny slice of nothing. She'd never thought much of the gods, but she knew this was real. Whatever Umilai wanted, she would do it. Whatever that wooden contraption was supposed to be, she clearly had to return to the tower with one of the new stones right away.

"I will," she said hurriedly, "I promise. Thank you, Umilai, thank you."

Just as quickly, the image was gone, and she found herself back on the beach, sprawled out on the rocks. She hadn't felt herself falling over, but the image she'd seen was burned into her mind. She sprang to her feet, grabbing the same blue stone and yanking it toward her. It gave away easily, the crystal breaking clean and leaving her holding a long rod of glowing blue in her hand. She took it and ran, clambering through the forest of stones toward the tower.

16

There shall be no limitation upon the free exercise of orderly trade nor the movement of civilians. However, there will be a strict limitation on the military escort of mercantile vessels. Such escort shall not exceed two brigantines per four mercantile vessels or one galleon, unless those ships are requisitioned for military use and supplied with sufficient documentation. In that case, the previous rule of naval patrol numbers shall apply.

-Excerpts from the Treaty of Trilathdrei
Second Page, Third Paragraph

—:—

Sumi felt something licking her face and jerked awake, terrified she'd find a rat on her. But as her eyes focused, it was only a giant orange tabby perched squarely on her chest.

"Oh, hello," she said, her voice sounding hoarse as she scratched the cat's head. It looked nothing like Amis, but it made her think of him, all the same.

"Can you tell I have a cat?" she asked. "I'm sorry I don't have any treats."

She gently picked the cat up and put it next to her so she could sit up. Now that it was morning, she could properly see Arkesht's warehouse, where her makeshift pallet was nestled between the huge stacks of goods. It felt like sleeping in a cavern, the aisles only about as wide as she was, with tall crates rising up on either side. They'd slept in a lot of strange places so far on their journey, but this had to be the strangest — as if camping and being in the city had had a baby.

Arkesht's warehouse was bursting at the gills with merchandise — leathers, random stacks of furniture, even a few open crates of olives. Like all the other buildings along the canal, it was wedge-shaped, the tin ceiling sweeping overhead from the edge of the canal. Arkesht had opened the door in his nightgown, a lantern gripped tightly in one hand and a cudgel in the other. But the moment he'd recognized them, he'd rushed about in the dark to give them somewhere to sleep.

The tabby meowed at her, and she petted it again, chuckling as it nibbled at her finger. It felt good to laugh. The stress from their scrape with the Thorns was still lingering in her mind, not to mention that dream… She idly played with the cat as she thought through what she'd seen — Ereilea, the black stones, a strange tower. Essomuai's visions didn't fade like normal dreams, but unfortunately, that didn't mean she understood them…

She'd been on the Isles of Dawn, so those were her people — and Elomikarus's presumably — living out their exile. And Ereilea had been looking for something, the…goddess eyes, which had somehow summoned the blue stones? Those had looked just like the speaking stones in Berill, only gigantic, just like the one on Elomikarus's scepter. And Ereilea had said that prayer first…

"Vilodai!" she said loudly.

She slapped a hand over her mouth, looking sheepishly at Erso and Parimu, their pallets across the walkway from her but in the same row. Luckily, neither of them stirred. They did have cat companions of their own already, though, who would surely be getting them up soon. Besides, judging by the light, it was well after dawn, and Arkesht said the boat would be leaving as soon as it could be loaded up for the trip to Sykala.

She shook her head, turning back to the dream. Vilodai was clearly the common link between the dreams. But Ereilea had called her Umilai. And those stones… Had Vilodai summoned the Berillai back to the Continent? But if she could send those rocks hundreds of miles, why had she waited a thousand years? And if she *was* that powerful, they were just supposed to head to the mountains, where she would be at her strongest?

She wanted to keep puzzling out the dream, but she heard footsteps approaching down the center aisle. A moment later, a short woman appeared, turning into Sumi's little row and locking eyes with her. She wore the same tough-looking leathers as every other Ekosinaran, her hair up in a tight bun.

"Good," the woman said, "you're awake. Come get your breakfast before the men eat it all."

Sumi nodded, scrambling to her feet. She had slept in her clothes, which probably didn't do much for her overall appearance, but at least she was already dressed. She shoved her boots on without tying them and hurried behind the woman as she headed toward the back of the warehouse.

"I'm Yalkai," she said in thickly-accented Berillai, extending her hand as Sumi caught up. "Arkesht's wife." Yalkai couldn't be more than ten years older than her, but she still reminded her of the women's group back home. Her voice was deep, and there was something solid about her, some hidden strength that went beyond the gleaming leather outfit.

"Nice to meet you," she said, "I'm Sumi. Thank you for having us."

"Don't mention it," she said, waving her hand. "I didn't know him back then, but from the sound of it, I wouldn't even have a husband if it weren't for Erso — not that it's heaven running these godsforsaken boats." She played with a little metal rod hung around her neck, shaking her head. "My mother always warned me against marrying Ekosinarans, but I guess I got a decent enough husband, all things considered."

Sumi smiled, unsure of how to respond to that. Were you supposed to agree with someone when they were badmouthing their own husband? Luckily, Yalkai continued on her own, apparently satisfied by her silence.

"So you're Erso's girl, eh? Bit fancy for my taste, but he seems a good enough bloke."

"Um...I guess so," she said, her cheeks growing hot.

Was she Erso's girl? She loved him madly, obviously, but did that mean they had a future? She knew him well enough to know he meant it when he said he loved her back, but should she really hope for more?

"Anyway, he hasn't really...um..."

"You mean the eel hasn't proposed?!" Yalkai hissed, her head whipping back to the front of the warehouse as if she meant to go yank the man out of bed for a beating.

"Well, no. I mean, there hasn't really been time," she said quickly. Traveling the world for Essomuai did seem to get in the way of frivolous things like weddings, but how to explain that without sounding daft?

"Well, we'll turn the screws on him," Yalkai said, winking. "Just keep looking as pretty as you do, and we'll shove the rat in his hole."

Sorry, Erso, she thought, smiling awkwardly.

They reached the back of the warehouse, where there was a sort of house built inside the larger building. It had two floors, the bottom filled with tables like a mess hall, while the second story looked like a cottage with shutters on the windows and everything. Erso had said most of the warehouse owners lived with their merchandise, but she hadn't expected it to be so…cozy.

They stepped through the mess hall door where Arkesht was working away at a stovetop in the corner. There were two men already at a table with full plates, and they lifted hands in greeting. Along the far wall, a table was covered with an Ekosinaran feast — seafood, rice, a dozen different types of olives — not to mention more familiar breakfast foods like eggs and bacon.

"Sumi!" Arkesht said, smiling as he turned from the griddle with another bowl of scrambled eggs. "Nice to see you in the daylight," he added with a chuckle. "Hope you slept alright."

"Oh, yes," she said, stopping to bow formally. "Thank you so much for helping us."

"Please," he said, waving her off like Yalkai had. "We don't bow here, just eat and be part of the family, eh?" He handed her a plate, gesturing toward the buffet. "We always do a big breakfast before shipments, thank the team and all that. It might look like a lot, but you're lucky you're up early. The crew'll wipe this out before long."

"I should thank your cat then," she said, chuckling. "I'd still be sleeping if it weren't for her. She was very friendly."

"That's one word for it," he said, laughing, a deep, rich sound that matched his height. "Which one'd ya get this morning?"

"Big orange tabby?" she offered.

"Ah, Seberine," he said, nodding knowingly. "She *is* a sweet one, but she's lived here the longest, so she can be a bit pushy. The crew has spoiled her rotten over the years."

"You know them all?" she asked, pausing with a spoon of rice in her hand. "There's dozens of them!"

"Of course," Arkesht said, "interviewed 'em myself." He came over, taking the spoon from her hand and doubling her rice with a wink.

"Interview, eh?" she asked, moving toward the platters of roasted fish.

"Sure," he said, "can't just trust any old cat. When we need a new one, I go out as a cat and play around 'til I find one I get on with, bring 'em back, show 'em the place. If they like it, they usually stay."

She glanced towards the men at the table, worried they'd overhear, but Arkesht caught her eye, waving a hand in the air.

"Don't worry," he said, "like I said, we're family here. You can talk freely — crew's about half and half, anyway. Besides, we split the profits, so I figure they like me picking out our cats. You get rats in the olives out here, you're finished."

That was…beautiful, though it'd take some getting used to. She could be herself in Anushai, of course, but it felt like they hadn't stayed long enough for it to sink in.

She took a fork from a giant bucket at the end of the buffet before joining the two men at the table. They smiled, nodding at her before returning to their own conversation in Narala. She could probably use the songs to eavesdrop but thought better of it. Neither of them had keyholes, and it felt wrong to use her powers on them like that. Still, they really did seem like family. They apparently had no problem with three random strangers sleeping on the floor and didn't seem bothered by her heaping breakfast.

Yalkai sat across from Sumi, her own mound of seafood threatening to tip off her plate. The workers tensed up a bit, their conversation suddenly stopping as Yalkai glanced at them with narrowed eyes.

"I need you two sharp today," Yalkai said in Berillai, presumably for her sake. "When the others arrive, get lots three and four onto the boat, and make sure the crew doesn't dally, alright?"

"Yes, ma'am," they both said simultaneously. Sumi grinned, looking down at her breakfast so she wouldn't laugh. Two burly workmen scared off by a little lady — she really would belong in the women's group.

"Good," Yalkai said, shoving a piece of bread in her mouth. For a moment, though, she softened, turning back toward the man on Sumi's side of the table. "Your wife doing better, Eptos?" she asked.

"Yes," he said, nodding quickly. "Um…thank you for…doctor. Better now." He nodded again.

Yalkai smiled, seeming like a different person, her face shining.

"Good," she said, "she needs proper rest with the baby on the way. Take some extra olives home once we're back, alright? You too, Merin, don't think I've forgotten about Serika."

They went back to their food as other workers started to storm into the mess hall. Soon, there was an army of men in thick leathers stuffing themselves with fish. Not all of them were as shy as the first two, and one or two actually spoke pretty decent Berillai. Just as she was about to finish her breakfast, Erso and Parimu finally appeared.

Parimu had shaven again, while Erso looked like he'd just rolled out of his blankets. She'd gotten used to him constantly shaping himself a fresh outfit, but he was actually more handsome like this. The stubble on his face cut across his chin in a dashing way, and his hair looked oddly perfect falling across his face. Not to mention his arms, the sleeves without a suit coat just—

She took a hasty sip of her tea, her neck burning. Maybe she'd gotten a bit carried away there… She stole one last glance at Erso, and he met her eyes, winking as he walked over to Arkesht.

"You've really come up in the world, old friend," he said, slapping Arkesht on the back. "If I recall, you and I used to eat out of trash cans."

He stepped over to the table, where, true to Arkesht's warnings, there was very little food left, little piles of anchovies and olives with a half a plate of eggs.

"I see you left me the Ekosinaran scraps, eh?" Erso asked, grimacing as he held up a spoonful of olives.

"That's a delicacy, you blimey *serik*," Arkesht said, knocking the spoon out of Erso's hand. He leaned over, digging around under the table until he emerged with a plate of pretzels.

"Found these for you at the baker's yesterday," Arkesht said, dropping them on the table. "Figured you'd need something for your sensitive stomach."

"Forget everything I said!" Erso yelled, trying to grab Arkesht in a bear hug. "You're like one of those saints you lot pray to!"

"Alright, alright," Arkesht said, pushing him away as he laughed. "Just eat the damn things, so I don't have to look at 'em anymore, will ya?"

He turned to the rest of his crew where everyone else had swallowed their food in record time.

"And you lot!" he yelled. "Get that barge loaded before the rats wake up!"

The room burst into action, two dozen burly men all fighting to get through one tiny door. They started singing in Narala as they went, the room seeming to shake with their voices.

"*Aroulan gatan yoroooo,*" they sang, surprisingly in harmony. Sumi closed her eyes, finally reaching out for Essomuai. It wouldn't be rude to eavesdrop on public singing, right?

"*My life to the rats, 'twas saved by the cats,*" the men sang. "*The wind will blow, to make it so, come find me in the mooooorning!*"

She shuddered to think how many rats there must be to get their own song… Still, it was lovely. She hadn't ever seen the factory workers in Berill sing like that. Maybe there was a lesson in that…

"Well," Erso said, plopping down with a plate of pretzels and a mug of tea, "that was anticlimactic. I was hoping to get some saucy stories out of those sailors."

Parimu sat down next to him with a more…Ekosinaran plate, though Erso had at least shared a couple of pretzels with him.

"I think you'll get your chance," she said, rolling her eyes, "it's a long canal. At least you finally got some sleep."

"Sure did," he said, offering her one of his pretzels. She waved him off, already stuffed to the gills. "It's blessedly dark in this warehouse, and I may have found Arkesht's secret stash of wine."

"Well, you better drink your tea, then," she said. "It's too sunny in this country for a hangover."

"No problem," Erso said, waving a hand at her as he bit into a pretzel, "that's what hats are for."

Suddenly, the crew pulled the warehouse doors open. The sun was already reflecting off the water, and a dazzling bar of light shot directly into the mess hall. Erso winced, putting a hand in front of his eyes.

"Okay," he said, groaning, "I'm gonna need a really big hat." He drained his tea, standing up. "No use putting off the headsman, eh?"

"This is gonna be fun to watch," she said, chuckling.

Parimu had silently devoured his breakfast, so he stood too, taking his plate over to the large metal tub where the other workers had dropped theirs. Erso knocked around the cabinets of the kitchenette until he found a little sackcloth where he dumped the rest of his pretzels. Then, they came out into the warehouse, finding it completely transformed.

Multiple rows of boxes were gone, already loaded up, the crew carrying everything onto a long, low-slung barge. It had to be some fifty feet long, though it was extremely narrow — presumably for navigating the crowded canal. There was a raised part at the back with a wheel and a flag the same color as the men's shirts. Yalkai stood up there barking orders as the men organized the cargo, Arkesht hauling boxes with the others.

It was quite a spectacle to watch, though the best part by far was the cats. They'd arrayed themselves in a wide arc around the doors, watching the men work. There were almost too many to count, with seemingly every possible breed. When the crew arrived at a new row of boxes, the cats were already there, perched on top. Instead of a rough shove, though, the men would scratch their heads, cooing as they slipped them a sardine. Only then would the cats jump off the boxes, moving on to the next row. It was incredible they got anything done!

Sumi shook her head, chuckling as she went to roll up her blankets. It made her miss Amis even more, though it did give her a few ideas… If he ever got bored in the garden, she could find him some work at a warehouse. Not that he would do any actual work, but the treats would suit him. As she knelt down to gather her things, the dream finally came back to her mind, as if touching the coarse blankets had pushed her back into the dream world.

What *was* Essomuai trying to tell her? Vilodai had been their goddess, and she had saved them from the Isles of Dawn…though that had kicked off another eight hundred years of war and destruction. But without Vilodai, the Berillai would still be trapped, and she likely wouldn't have even been born. There was so much to this, so much hidden behind the veil. But how did you embrace that history and still find a way to undo the broken parts?

She finished packing her things and stood, slinging everything over her shoulder. *Poor Eto,* she thought, looking at the leather saddlebag. They'd been forced to leave the horses at the inn. They should be well taken care of — at least fed properly with Erso's extra coin until they were sold — but she still wished she'd been able to say goodbye. Eto had been a lovely horse, and it felt wrong to abandon an animal whose name you knew.

Maybe that was her answer… Essomuai was the goddess who knew all things, after all, even the name of a horse. And that meant Essomuai *was* history, one long song about everything that had ever happened. So maybe it was the only way she knew how to call her, to explain why she needed Sumi's help. Like Nela had said in her letter, 'only by knowing them can we shape them'…

I'm listening, Essomuai, she thought. *No matter what, I'm listening.* She'd keep her heart open and hope she knew what to do once she heard the whole song.

———

The ship's bell began to clang, and she hurried onto the dock, finding the entire crew gathered around the barge. Arkesht was standing on the gangplank, just above the others, a large blue bag in his hand. He held the bag up, the others reaching out a hand to touch it, muttering to themselves. She opened herself to the songs just in time to hear what he said to the others.

"It's time," he said, raising the bag above his head. He opened it up, putting his hand in and pulling out a giant handful of what looked like dandelion fluff.

"Mother Itorunai," he said, releasing it on the breeze, "you know the paths we chart and where we come to rest. May your sacred breath keep us aloft so long as you are willing and fill our lungs with life."

By the time he was done, scattering the entire bag by the handful, it looked like it was snowing, dandelion seeds swirling in clouds over the canal. The men kept their heads down for another moment, muttering prayers under their breath. She closed her eyes too, putting her hands together, feeling Essomuai wash over her.

"Alright, men!" Arkesht finally called out. "Fate will find you, whether you like it or not, so let's get on the bloody boat!"

The crew burst into action again, lifting what little gear remained on the dock as they swarmed the boat under Yalkai's watchful gaze. When they were all gone, Arkesht looked at her, raising his eyebrows.

"So?" he asked in Berillai, stepping over. "What'd ya think?"

"It was beautiful," she said, nodding. "But I guess I'm confused. Do you…worship Itorunai?"

He laughed, slapping his belly.

"Worship is a strong word," he said. "We don't light anything on fire like you Berillai. But I suppose we do in a way, though, only like you'd worship a shark, begging it not to eat you."

"Obsessed with fate, these ones," Erso said, leaning against a piling on the dock. "They think Itorunai can tell the future — makes 'em bloody awful to gamble with."

"Like you're any better with your little hallways," Arkesht said, chuckling. "But he's basically right. Now, don't get me wrong," he added, tilting his head in the direction of Anushai, "I'm *xorafetri*, just like you, so I don't dislike your golden god in the north. But Essomuai was always an import. We Ekosinarans, we've always trusted the wind."

"You really think she can hear you?" she asked. "Not that I doubt you, of course." She was the dreamy buffoon who spoke to goddesses, after all…

Arkesht looked at her for a moment before he smiled.

"I believe you," he said, chuckling. He shook his head at Erso. "Not like this one, but yeah, I do, and I think the Anushai think so too." He rubbed his fingers together. "What are those little goats you lot chase around the mountains with the black and white stones?"

"Durnijories?" she asked, remembering the name from Nela's stories.

"That's the one!" he said, pointing at her. "Anyway, that's Itorunai too. She made the animals, yeah? And it seems the Anushai are just as keen to learn their future as anybody else."

"The sacred breath," she muttered to herself, nodding. "I guess so. Well, thank you for showing us," she said, "it really was beautiful — Erso notwithstanding."

"I'm glad," Arkesht said, "let's just hope it works. This one's bad luck, and the ship could use a good run." Laughing, he moved toward the gangplank. Erso tried to look indignant, but he was quietly chuckling.

"Come on," Arkesht said, waving for them to follow. "If you stay on the docks, I'm leaving you with the cats."

17

An apprentice slipped into the treasury yesterday and actually touched the Sekoren Stone. Somehow, it gave her a second vision of Umilai's vessel. The girl has never seen a boat in her life, and somehow she was able to guide the carpenters through new blueprints. Lady Esorana has confirmed that it seems to match the one first seen by the Angel of the Sea.

-Sea Scroll #146
Estimated Date 315 PN

—:—

Parimu looked down at the water from the edge of the barge, the canal slipping by as they made their way to Sykala. He grimaced, taking another drag on his pipe to mask the smell. The water was a bright shade of green — and not a natural one. It no doubt came from all the tanneries dotting the countryside. Relimora was said to have ten cows for every person, but the Ekosinarans had always made the leather. They were good quality too, but at the moment, though, the smoke filling the sky from the tanneries seemed like a steep price to pay.

That was the way of industry everywhere, he supposed. Still, he wished the world would slow down and think about what they were hurtling toward with all of it. How many leather coats did a man really need? Back in Emillon, you had one good coat, and you mended it until you simply couldn't anymore. The men who zipped around the barge following Arkesht's orders — or Yalkai's, rather — didn't seem bothered by the smell. In fact, they seemed pretty happy for men working so hard. Even though they were just one link in a long chain of buyers and sellers, the crew felt like a family, liking something more than their industry and toil.

Maybe he could have been on a crew like this in another life... Jalicyne had always liked ordering him around when they were children. His mother had joked once that the only reason he joined the navy was because he'd gotten used to taking orders as a boy. If she had lived, maybe he would have been a merchant instead of a police officer, and how different things would have been...

But wouldn't that make him a different man altogether? As much as he hated himself for what he'd become, protecting Sumi made it all seem worth it. Besides, at his age, it was too late to think of living his life all over. Still, if he were lucky, perhaps he'd get a chance to build a life again. Maybe he could be like Arkesht on his boat, a man with a purpose, a trade he could use to live a better life.

He sighed, looking out at the hills in the distance. The canal seemed to wind its way through whatever part of the country was flattest, the land just beyond rising through the haze, olive groves dotting their slopes. Even though half his life had been spent in ignorance of the world, at least he was really seeing it now. Of course, a part of him had liked the narrow view of the world he'd gotten in the navy, so orderly, hidden by the rules of a port and ship. But to really know the world, you had to get right up next to it. You had to stare at its beauty, even if you could only see it through smoke.

But could he really be part of such a place, so beautiful and complicated? Or had he always stood back from the world because he wasn't enough for a real life? Sumi said that Essomuai knew all things — loved all things — but was there really anything worth redeeming in the nooks and crannies of his heart? He knew what he was now, he knew the truth, but it came with the crushing realization of what he'd done. He would serve Sumi until the end, but after, he'd have to find out if he could put a window where a wall had been.

He turned from the water, looking for her. Somehow, Sumi always found a way to reassure him, to make him feel like his life still counted for something. How did she do that? She looked at him like he belonged, like he was back in Emillon, where everyone knew his name. He was still just a man, however flawed, but that was suddenly enough. He wasn't a police officer or a laughingstock, or even a navy officer. He was just Relsenair Parimu, and even his shape apparently had a song.

He finally spotted her, standing alone about three-quarters of the way down the boat, staring intently at a stack of leathers. Was she looking at all the patterns? It seemed the Relimorans had every possible kind of cattle in their herds — shaggy, red, spotted. She didn't notice him approach, but she didn't jump when he said her name, either, looking up and blinking as if she'd been asleep. He didn't want to bother her, of course, but she never seemed to mind. And he had promised Erso they'd keep her with them, reminding her of the real world when they could.

"Hello," she said, finally smiling as her confusion faded. She looked back down at the hides, her lips pursing again. "Sorry, I was distracted by these songs. They're some of the strangest I've heard yet."

He nodded, running his hands along the leather. He tried to listen to it, but he still couldn't seem to hear the songs. He was able to hear keyholes now, obviously, and with Sumi's, he could just pick out a sliver of that strange music he'd heard when they merged in Anushai. Were the songs like that, or was that just in his head, a memory of what he'd heard?

"What does it sound like?" he finally asked.

"It's a long song," she said, tapping her chin. "Now that they're leather, they're a lot like the songs of things, but with a certain sadness to it. I'm afraid to listen too closely, but there's parts of the song about being a cow, almost as if the hides still remember. Or maybe it's Essomuai that remembers?"

She looked back to the leather, gently placing a hand on it.

"I'd been thinking all these songs were the memories of things themselves, but now… Maybe it's all just Essomuai. She *would* feel sad if a cow had to die, even if she can still find the joy in being leather. The legends say there's a bit of Essomuai in everything — she's Wellonai's blood, after all. So it just got me thinking, I guess. Sorry to ramble," she added, smiling again.

"Not at all," he said, shaking his head. "It's honestly fascinating." He loved hearing about Essomuai. It helped remind him there was something bigger than himself, someone ordering his steps, and this time a goddess, no less.

"Are we getting close to Sykala?" she asked, looking back at the water. "It's a bit embarrassing, but I have no idea how much time passed."

"I think just another hour or two," he said. "I heard a few of the ship hands talking earlier." He pointed to a stretch of hills on the horizon where a particularly large mountain stood out. "I think once we cross those hills and take the next bend to the south, we'll be able to see the city."

"Oh, good," she said, "I didn't want to miss it." She pointed over to the bow, where Erso was sitting, smoking his pipe. "Let's go up front for the last bit. I feel in the way over here anyway."

"Good idea," Parimu agreed. You'd think there wasn't that much to do on a boat that had no sails, but the workmen were constantly darting around. Between adjusting the cargo and checking the depth gauges every two minutes for Arkesht, it was easy to feel in the way. They walked up to the front where the boat narrowed at the bow, the thick wooden gunwale opening up onto a wide prow where Erso sat, leaning onto a railing with his feet above the water. He turned toward them as they approached, nodding with his pipe in his mouth.

"Like bloody bees, these blokes, eh?" he asked.

Parimu shot a glance back where the blue-clad workers were making another sweep, tightening ropes and calling out measurements.

"Seems like a lot of work for a barge," he said, nodding. "Does make me wonder why they need depth gauges in a canal, though."

Erso puffed out another cloud of smoke, leaning back against the railing, looking down into the water.

"Kesht was complaining about that," Erso said. "I guess nobody's dredged it in a while, sand builds up in spots. Anyway, sounds like everything else in this bloody kingdom. Nobody can agree which city is supposed to pay for the thing, and the southerners would rather be done with it and get a new train line."

He looked down in the water too, shaking his head. It was hard to believe they'd let something like a canal go to waste. The canal looked deep from the surface, the water dark against the side of the boat despite its greenish hue. It was supposed to be a hundred years old, and now it was closing up over some petty squabble? How long had it taken to dig the whole thing without machines?

"What a shame," Sumi said, joining Erso on the prow. "It's dirty, but it's beautiful too."

"Way of the world, my friends," Erso said. "Like they say in Amoriai, 'if you don't like the teapot, put a hole in the spout.'"

"Is that a real saying?" Sumi asked, cocking an eyebrow at him.

"Can't remember," Erso said, shrugging. "Spending too much time with you barbarians." He reached into his pocket, offering up his smoking pouch. "Anyway, can't solve all the world's problems. Might as well smoke a pipe and let the boat float, you know?"

"Can't argue with that, I suppose," Parimu said, nodding. He took the bag and filled his own pipe before sitting on the opposite side of the prow. If a giant canal could be neglected, it seemed anything could be abandoned. It didn't bode well for a small man like him, but at least he was with friends — if he deserved to call them that — and he had a full pipe in the sun. For now, that'd just have to be enough.

———

Two hours later, Sumi was still sitting by the bow with Erso and Parimu, Sykala approaching on the horizon. The time had gone by quickly, chatting with the others, the pipe smoke and the breeze just enough to push away the stink of the canal. As Parimu had suggested, the city had appeared just after the last mountain. Arkesht had sent a crew member over with some sandwiches since there apparently wouldn't be much time to eat in the city as they switched from the barge to the wagons. Judging by the frantic movements of the crew, though, they probably also hoped to keep them out of the way.

As they got closer to the city, the entire boat was being reorganized yet again. She didn't know much about boats beyond what Grandpa had told her, but balancing the weight seemed to be important. The leather had started pretty well spread out, but now that they were getting closer, the crew was re-stacking everything on the right side of the boat. Maybe it would help them pull it onto the dock? The boat still seemed stable, though it was starting to lean just a bit, the workers standing on the opposite side to balance it out.

She turned back to the water, taking another bite of her sandwich. It was salted beef on a crusty olive bread. Parimu was eating his primly, carefully picking it up with both hands, while Erso just nibbled at his. It was probably too workaday for his refined palate, but hers was already more than halfway gone. She was just a simple working girl, after all, but it seemed like every meal she had on the Continent was just about the most wonderful thing she'd ever tasted.

"I'm eating yours if you're gonna fuss over it," she said to Erso, raising her eyebrows. He scoffed, quickly picking up his sandwich and taking a big bite.

"I'll eat it," he said with his mouth full. "Just never been one for olives — bit slimy if you ask me."

"Maybe they remind you too much of yourself?" she asked with as much fake innocence as she could. He rolled his eyes, giving her the perfect opportunity to pop one of the olives out of his bread and toss it into her mouth.

"How about you, Relsenair?" she asked. "How do you like the Ekosinaran food so far?"

"Oh, I'll eat anything," he said, smiling. "Old navy habit, I guess. If it was made on land, there's no way it could be worse than something stuffed in a barrel for six months."

"Sounds like my grandfather," she said, nodding. "I don't think he even looked at the plate before he started eating."

"My pa was like that too," Erso said, chuckling. "Couldn't get ma to eat less than caviar — star that she was — but pa used to drive his own wagons as a merchant, said he'd eaten day-old fellerhurn once."

He glanced at Parimu, biting his lip, but the other man didn't seem to notice the slight. Erso hadn't ever called him a fellerhurn to his face, of course, but the memory was probably hard to shake. At least they seemed to be making progress on their…quasi-friendship.

She smiled at Erso, sliding along the prow to face the city. She wanted a look at the skyline before they were in the thick of things and the view was lost to the chaos of the docks. It was still strange to think that the two cities had been separate kingdoms for so long — they both spoke Narala, after all — but now that she was looking at Sykala, you could tell immediately how different it was. It looked like something out of the Relimoran desert, the walls and buildings made of thick beige sandstone like a sandcastle. The roofs all seemed to gleam with the same red tile too, no doubt quarried from the dusty lands on the border of the Void.

Every place they had stopped on the Continent had been so completely…itself, each one with a totally different character. She was so used to thinking about cities as monoliths — things that were incredibly beautiful but mostly set in stone. But they weren't just mountains that had been built up by chance… They were living relics of their ancestors — built by hands, shovels, and unfortunately, the occasional sword.

The songs in each city were different too. She probably would have struggled to explain it to the others, but the songs had an…undertone that seemed to connect them, like the strata of a rock collecting the same minerals over time. Living things all shared common melodies, of course, but within a place, there was something there, something just barely heard. She wouldn't have realized it if they hadn't passed through Ageleat, but the songs there had been almost…mysterious, as if the people's time spent at sea had influenced their songs, the hidden depths of the ocean looming in their minds. What story would the songs in Sykala tell?

Fortunately, she didn't have to wait long to find out. As her eyes traced the canal, she spotted a giant hole in the wall where the canal went straight through. It looked wide enough for four boats abreast, disappearing into the shadow of the tunnel. Their boat suddenly slowed, stopping beside a little hut where a man was waving signal flags. They waited there for a moment as other barges zipped in and out of the city until the canal officer waved a green flag in the air.

They began to pick up speed again, and soon after, they were crossing under the wall. Sumi tilted her head back and closed her eyes, letting the song of the city wash over her. The walls had been there a long time, much longer than the canal, and the stones all hummed in harmony, eager to tell their story. They remembered how olive groves had covered the entire peninsula, the city slowly appearing by the water as the population grew, digging up the stones and putting them together. She smiled, opening her eyes.

"Can you hear them?" Parimu asked, squinting up at the smooth stone.

"Yeah," Erso asked, "what are they saying?" He reached out from the edge of the prow, letting his hand run along the smooth wall of the tunnel. It was so perfectly constructed, if she hadn't listened to the song, she never would have known the tunnel had been carved into the wall instead of being built that way.

"Mostly talking about olives," she said with a grin. "Oh, and keeping nefarious characters out of their city."

"Hey," Erso said, raising his hands in surrender, "just passing through."

They all laughed, though she did feel a twinge of guilt. She could tell the difference now when Erso was joking because he was happy and joking because he was worried about her. In those moments, she could feel Beysal in him, and the summer after Erso's parents died when they were just trying to survive. *I care about you,* the jokes seemed to say, *you don't have to talk about it, but I'm right here. I don't know what to say either.* She was supposed to be their leader — however much it chafed her to admit it — but right now, she just felt like their dotty old aunt they'd been forced to escort to the market.

Not a moment later, the tunnel ended, and the canal widened, suddenly dropping them into a frenzy of boats sliding in and out of their moorings, porters scurrying in every direction. Arkesht rang his bell, pulling the barge alongside a set of docks that matched the ones they'd left behind in Ageleat. As soon as the bell rang out, a battalion of dockworkers — all wearing the same sky blue — popped their heads over the edge of the canal and started waving. Then gangplanks were hoisted across, and workers began to dash back and forth, carrying lighter things over their shoulders while heavier things were attached to a winch crane.

Once again, they had no choice but to stand back and watch. It felt wrong to watch someone work without helping, though it was fascinating. While the barge had come down with mostly leather, a huge variety of things were being loaded back on to return to Ageleat. It seemed that Arkesht's larger warehouses were here, near the roads. There were olives, of course, but there were also cords of a strange, spindly desert wood, huge jugs of oil, and crates of grapes that had to be from Alara.

When they were finally done, Arkesht and his wife spoke to a man for a while, who nodded before heading up to the helm of the barge. Then, they stepped over, their own luggage in hand.

"Alright, you lot," Arkesht said, "I think we're ready to be off." He nodded over his shoulder at the man who had taken the wheel. "Niosal will run the barge while we're gone, but we'd better get in the wagons and shove off; it's best to be well on the road before sunset."

She nodded, following the others as they shuffled behind Arkesht. As soon as her feet left the gangplank, the ship's bell was ringing, already leaving for Ageleat. She looked back at it one last time, tempted to wave goodbye. It was yet another temporary home they had to leave behind. She followed the others, moving quickly over the dock as they took one more step into the unknown.

18

The Northern Bank shall have no more than four Berillai galleons in concurrent patrol. This rule shall not apply west of Saran Deep, where the shores of the Isles of Dawn shall be the exclusive territory of the Berillai for both civilian and naval craft.

-Excerpts from the Treaty of Trilathdrei
Third Page, Fifth Paragraph

—:—

Commissioner Kollenail sat in his office in Berill, turned toward the window where he could watch the ships sailing in and out of the bay. He tried to keep his mind clear, spinning the large silver ring on his left hand. It was the only sign of his office he was allowed to wear, and it had been passed down from Commissioner to Commissioner as long as the Thorns had existed. It was an old habit, to spin it idly like this, but one that was meant to bring him calm. Today, though, it seemed a thin veneer, his foot starting to tap again, the nervous rhythm cracking any clarity he had built up in his mind.

"Bah!" he shouted, pushing himself out of his chair as he began to pace. His predecessor, Tursent, had always advised him to have a 'strategy day.' Generally speaking, it was good advice. When you were constantly dealing with the monotonous drivel of day-to-day tasks, it was nearly impossible to keep your mind firmly on the bigger picture. So, he always kept one afternoon completely clear on his schedule each week. Only, on a day like today, the whole exercise seemed futile. How was he supposed to think about strategy when the biggest bloody piece on the board was still in his opponents' hands?!

He turned, crossing the room quickly and wrenching the door open.

"Serkis!" he barked at his secretary. "Anything?"

To his credit, the man didn't jump. He was almost disturbingly calm, especially when the stakes were high. Serkis calmly swiveled around in his chair, blinking behind his wire-frame glasses.

"No, sir," he said. "I'll be in the moment they have something."

"Fine, good," Kollenail said curtly as he went back into his office. He kept himself from slamming the door, if only just, before walking back to the window. He tried to look at the water again but found himself drawn to the imperfections in the windows instead. Like the rest of the building, they were crude, industrial things. The panes of glass were sooted over in places from the train station smoke, and the brick wall holding the timber window frames was already cracking apart.

He really shouldn't complain — it was the humility of his pretend position that allowed him such freedom to pursue his real goals, after all. It wasn't as if he wanted the gold thread and silks of his "betters." Furniture and clothes were not power, even if the others liked to pretend it was. And yet, when he was hamstrung like this, waiting for information, he wished his station was higher, that his orders had reach beyond the cloak and dagger.

Still, at least if he couldn't have the best office, he could have the best location. Far more important than the view was his proximity to the train station. It added to the soot on the windows, of course, but it gave him ready access to the telegraph wires. The wires followed the train lines, crisscrossing the Continent with the truest source of power in the world — information. And if the wires took a little detour into the basement of his office before they went to the police and the foreign office? Well, that was more than reasonable compensation for everything he did for the kingdom.

That's why he just needed this one bloody telegram to come through! The Ekosinar foreign office was in the process of writing their report on that damned incident in Ageleat, and he was being forced to wait to hear what their determination was. Some officer Monderin had turned out to be. He'd at least had the decency to send a telegram that he'd failed, but then the coward had gone ahead and disappeared before he could properly clean up his own mess...

Somehow, three Shapewalkers had scared off him and his men, killing two in the process. Monderin had given no detail on that, but even worse, he hadn't even stayed long enough to clean up the bodies, and now the Ekosinarans were involved, teetering on the brink of a royal inquest. It wasn't as if they'd never had a stray corpse show up on foreign soil before... But the timing — and the politics — out east couldn't be worse.

Just like the rest of the bloody country, allegiances in the Berillai foreign office there were split clean down the middle — so much so that they may as well start hanging those bloody blue and green flags on their doors! Half the office was aligned with Pont'dulairn and half with the Queen. Kollenail had spies, of course, but not nearly enough influence to make sure their report on the incident didn't go the wrong way. They could smooth things over well enough with the Ekosinaran king, old fool that he was, but what the foreign office would tell Welaya — and when they would tell her — left him completely exposed.

He couldn't very well fix his lies to the Queen until he had that report in hand. And depending on how much was in it, things could begin moving far more quickly than he wanted them to. Not to mention Pont'dulairn's bill, which could very well take the navy right out from under them if Welaya kept bungling everything…

He clenched his fists, leaning against the window as he tried to occupy his mind. Eventually, he lost track of time until suddenly, a knock came on the door.

"Sir," Serkis said behind him, "I think we have it."

Kollenail turned from the window, rubbing his hands together. The truth was like clay — it cracked if you didn't prepare it to be molded. He didn't have enough time this afternoon, but he was an artist, and it was time to begin.

Welaya sat in her throne room, staring into the roaring fire as she clutched her teacup in a vice grip. The throne was some thirty feet from the fireplace, but it wasn't there for warmth — not hers anyway. Supplicants were forced to kneel on a rug in front of that fire, the flames roaring even in summer to remind them of the crown's eternal light. Still, it was a crude gesture, and one that felt especially empty with enemies on every side. Besides, a fire could be doused, could it not? And what of her? The crown would carry on, but would her legacy?

She drank the last of her tea, setting it on the table beside her, where it was immediately refilled by her head butler.

"Brew it stronger next time, Roderne," she said.

"Your Majesty," he said in reply, bowing low before disappearing again to wait in the shadows.

It was probably a bit odd to take tea in the throne room, but that was why Roderne attended her alone today. He of all people would understand. These days, the crown — which had never weighed lightly — seemed fit to crush her. But this new habit of hers seemed to help, at least a bit. Even if it couldn't chase away her worries entirely, the tea banished the fog of sleepless nights, and the throne reminded her of who she was — or, at least, who she ought to be...

Her father had sat on this same throne along with every monarch before him, all the way back to Laeryia. What had they done when they felt doubts this great? Her father had never said, had never given so much as an inkling that he felt anything but confidence. He had likely thought there to be a great lesson in that, though not a very practical one. Every fool on the street knew the Berillai demanded strength from their rulers, but a stiff upper lip seemed to do little now to quiet the storms raging outside her walls.

Unfortunately, thoughts such as these only made her worry more for her precious little Lissande. She may only be three, but she'd had the luck — if you could really call it that — of being the firstborn, which meant Berill would have another queen. It was time to begin her education, but what was she meant to teach the girl if she couldn't even figure out what her father had been trying to teach her?

Even worse, if the crown weighed heavily on any head, it weighed doubly so on a woman. Even though she was the twelfth queen in a long line, some of her ministers still stared at her as if she were the first. Forget that every woman had presided over far greater victories than their male counterparts, they seemed to think her just another false Kesselia, strolling into camp with her knife out.

What more could they possibly want from her? Her father had begun many promising projects, true, but she had finished them. The final stations on the train lines had gone in under her watch, and trade had nearly tripled since she'd taken the throne, the treasury bursting with coin. Having to deal with Pont'dulairn was one thing — the man seemed specially created by Umilai to vex her — but the questioning looks she got from her own ministers were disgraceful, not to mention the admirals... The moment she tried to move a ship on the board herself, you'd think she'd grown horns!

And now she had this before her... She turned back to the tea tray, picking up the report she'd received from the foreign office. There were many odd things about it, although the strangest by far was it being delivered to her directly. Formal reports like these almost always came through middlemen, and she hadn't heard a peep from Kollenail yet — a rare occurrence indeed. The report spoke of an incident in Ekosinar, and one that seemed to involve Shapewalkers. Yet, instead of sounding the alarm about the vile creatures, it seemed almost written to shame the Berillai officers that had been hunting them...

The whole thing sniffed of Pont'dulairn, of course. The man's cursed bill to strip her of war powers had basically soared through the chamber, after all. At least Elikora had slipped away in time to warn her, her crown stay arriving by the time the bondsman had tallied the votes. Still, a stay on the bill would only buy her another two months, and all Pont'dulairn needed was three more votes to make twenty-five and overrule her. Elikora and Coerendul gave plenty of assurances, of course, but those were basically worthless with the salvo of bribes Pont'dulairn would be firing at their coalition. In the end, the only thing that mattered was strength.

For her, it only made the foreign office report more vital. She *had* to find those Shapewalkers. Every day they were loose was another slap in the face, another chance for Pont'dulairn to make her look weak. Unfortunately, clues had been scarce — like hoofprints in the forest — and this could be the last sign she ever got of her quarry. The report almost glossed over the most important part, droning on about the 'disrespect shown to the Ekosinaran crown.' Still, there *were* witnesses, and they described some kind of supernatural fight in the alleyways of the city, leaving two men dead and the Shapewalkers free.

She crumpled the report in her hand. These Shapewalkers had cost her too much — her own Director of Reality disappearing, dead or worse, and now Ekosinar. She was no fool — she understood the eastern kingdoms were hanging by a string, waffling between the northern savages and Berillai steel — but the foreign office seemed to think letting wanted criminals run free was the way to win them over. It was absurd! They needed to be firm. It was the train lines and the navy that had brought Ekosinar this far, not pampering the ego of some scarecrow king who was happy to harbor that monstrous filth in his city!

Just then, one of the doors behind her opened, and she heard footsteps approaching. Whoever it was whispered for a moment to Roderne, allowing the head butler to approach himself. He came up beside the throne, bowing formally again.

"Your Majesty," he said, "Commissioner Kollenail just arrived at the back gate with an important report to share. Perhaps you would be more comfortable in your sitting room?"

So, the worm finally decided to crawl out of the apple. He'd have a good bit of explaining to do as to why she was only just hearing about this bloody report. Still, she composed herself, nodding to Roderne. Thank goodness she could rely on her butler. She was tired enough to invite Kollenail into the throne room, but, of course, he lacked the station to petition her there.

"Thank you, Roderne," she said, forcing a smile to her face for him. She rose, allowing him to lead the way toward her sitting room. As they left the throne room, they picked up her personal guards, the four of them winding through the palace in formation. When they finally reached their destination, Roderne paused, bowing with his hand on the door handle.

"Perhaps more tea, Your Majesty?" he asked.

"And some biscuits, if you would," she said, inclining her head. "I'm feeling a bit peckish."

"Of course, Your Majesty," he said. With that, he stood tall, swinging the door open.

"Her Royal Majesty, Queen Welaya, the First of House Berill," he announced. She always liked to hear Roderne announce her. In all these years, the man had never deviated from the exact tempo and cadence he always used. He was like a train, the gears perfectly shifting to the rhythm of some strange engine.

She stepped through the door, just barely able to suppress her scowl as she realized that Kollenail had already taken a seat. He stood hastily as she entered the room, giving a perfunctory bow. He was getting far too comfortable, and in her private sitting room, of all places!

"Perhaps just one cup of tea," she said to Roderne. He would understand — whenever he returned with the tea tray, Kollenail was to be shooed away. Not that he ever stayed long... She crossed the room, taking her normal chair facing the window — at least he hadn't had the nerve to sit there! — ever-so-gently inclining her head.

"Please," she said, turning her palm back toward the chair Kollenail had already been sitting in. He promptly sat, reaching into his coat for a few pages of telegraph paper. He'd sent a message the day before that *something* had happened in Ekosinar, but now she'd bloody heard about it on her own!

"We've finally received the full report from Ekosinar," he said, smoothing out the papers. He opened his mouth to go on, but she interjected.

"I know," she said, "I've just had the same report from the foreign office."

He looked genuinely surprised, his eyes flickering between her and the papers.

"Yes, well," he said hurriedly, "I'll be brief about what you already know, then. The Ekosinaran crown is thinking of opening an inquest. It's rather delicate, but we've offered our full cooperation. What wasn't in the foreign office report, however, is that the Shapewalkers slipped out of the kingdom on the eastern road today, heading for Relimora."

"Is that so?" she asked, feeling a flush of heat on her neck. He thought he could come in here with just another clue? He ought to be flogged for his failure! "And how did your men come to ascertain this information? If they knew the Shapewalkers' whereabouts, why would they not apprehend them?"

"I will find out, Your Majesty," he said, nodding his head and scratching some notes on his pages. "I presume the agent in question lacked the resources to apprehend them himself, but I made sure all exits out of the kingdom were carefully watched. Casting a wide net, however, does require distributing our manpower more…evenly. For now, I suggest we take the necessary steps to stabilize the situation with the Ekosinaran—"

"You will do no such thing," she said, her voice turning to ice. "It is *they* who should be stabilizing the situation with *us*. They can open whatever inquest they like when this is done, but for now, they will help me apprehend these creatures, or they can go the way of the Anushai. You will immediately telegraph Ageleat and tell them to prepare for a naval attache to assist with the search. And while you're about it, send for Heller; I need to see the admirals immediately."

Clearly forgetting himself yet again, Kollenail began to babble almost as soon as she closed her mouth, not quite interrupting her but almost.

"And what should I tell Heller?" he asked. "Surely, there's no need to involve the navy. We already have ships lining up along the western gap, and coming any deeper into the Erril Basin will risk—"

"That is *my* business," she said. For the second time, he had to stop speaking immediately, the muscles on his jaw bulging with the effort. "They are my ships," she continued, "and I will move them where I please. Remember, Kollenail, I put that ring on your finger, and I can take it off again. For now, please leave me; there's much to do."

"Your Majesty," he said stiffly, standing and bowing far more formally than when she'd first arrived. He left the room, and she finally let out a long breath. There was something he wasn't telling her. First the report from the foreign office, and then him showing up in her study, all ready with some plan to smooth things over. He'd never seemed particularly interested in Shapewalkers, but she'd thought he at least agreed with her on Ekosinar…

She propped her fingers under her chin, staring into the fire. Surely he'd agree that the navy was better under herself than Pont'dulairn, no? If that came to pass, he'd have less influence, which seemed to be the only thing the little rat actually cared about.

She stayed that way until she finally heard the wheels of the tea cart approaching, arriving not a moment too soon. The game appeared to be getting more dangerous, and even if she'd already had a dozen cups of tea, she'd likely need more to see her through. But one way or another, she'd see those monsters hung, even if she had to tie the bloody rope herself.

———

Kollenail finally reached his carriage where Serkis was waiting for him outside the Peerage.

"Sir?" Serkis asked as he wrenched open the door. He rapped on the roof to tell the driver to return to headquarters before fully ducking inside.

"Went about as poorly as it could have," he said, grinding his teeth. He pulled the telegraph papers back out of his pocket, throwing them against the opposite seat. Serkis, who was sitting on that side, calmly collected them, unruffled as always, simply adding the papers to his own.

"She still wants the Shapewalkers, then?" he asked.

"That's all she bloody thinks about," Kollenail said, shaking his head. "We have two months on this crown stay, but she's apparently happy to sacrifice two hundred years of work for a damned peasant. She clearly wants to move more ships — told me to summon the admirals — but that'll only spook Ekosinar. Bloody gods above! We all know war will come someday, but you don't light the bloody powder keg when you're standing next to it!"

"Is it time for the…alternative?" Serkis asked.

Kollenail forced himself to take a deep breath, closing his eyes. It would be so easy to say yes, to let the blade fall. But it wasn't time for that, not yet.

"No," he finally forced himself to say. "I need to speak to Heller myself, but hopefully we can arrange the ships in a way that keeps her happy without scaring the sheep. Maybe even a replacement Shapewalker for her to hang, and we'll have to make a show of searching Ekosinar, provided we don't ruffle too many feathers. Anyway, prepare two telegrams for me — one for Heller and the other for Fisk."

Serkis started scratching out his notes while he leaned against the window. Perhaps it was time — or getting close to it anyway. He was determined not to strike out in anger, though. Removing her now would only push more peers into the reform camp. Still…it felt like the precipice was near, far nearer than ever before. The only strange thing was how excited he felt at the thought of jumping off.

19

How I wish I could speak the holy words of Umilai! I myself have never been graced with one of the visions, though I've read the records. How could a single word put a whole world into your mind? Every night I pray the first word I was taught from the ledger: Kelanoramisan — how many secrets are hidden in that word alone?

-Sea Scroll #177
Estimated Date 250 PN

—:—

Sumi followed the others, climbing to the street and leaving the boat behind. She could see workers from a dozen different crews, hastily loading draft carts in a dizzying mix of shirt colors. Arkesht's men, however, simply carried things across the street to where he had another warehouse. As they walked toward it, Yalkai fell in beside her.

"It'll be nice having you on the caravan" Yalkai said, grinning as she watched her out of the corner of her eye. "It's pretty rare to get female company in this line of work."

Sumi nodded gratefully, looking around at the scrum of workers around them. It must get hard, though Yalkai seemed to have no trouble managing the men.

"I'm sure you've had it hard enough roughing it with those two in the woods these past few weeks, though, eh?" she asked, nodding toward Erso and Parimu.

"Oh," she said, cocking her head. "I guess I hadn't thought about it. It wasn't too bad, really."

"Well," Yalkai said with a knowing smile, "it's not a palace, but I like to think I've gotten the caravans at least a little more comfortable over the years. Just come to me if you need anything, especially if you get your monthly."

She blinked, nearly stumbling on the cobblestones. She certainly hadn't thought of that! She'd been lucky enough to have it just before they left Anushai, but between Essomuai and the songs, she'd just plumb forgot. Now, though, she tried to summon the calendar, rapidly counting in her mind.

"It's alright," Yalkai said, laughing as she patted her shoulder, "you're in the east now, girl. Goodness, but I forget how prim you Berillai are."

Yalkai shook her head, still chuckling as she disappeared into the warehouse to organize the crews. Well, she *was* out east now. But when had she started being embarrassed by her period, anyway? Was it really a Berillai thing? Nela certainly hadn't taught her to think that way, so it must have been the girls at school…

She'd gotten her first monthly not too long after Grandpa had died, only making that year more stressful. Thank Essomuai she hadn't gotten it at school! Still, when she'd run to find Nela, they'd done that strange little ritual. After helping her wash the blood off her knickers, Nela had marched her into the garden, having her carefully pour the rust-colored water over one of her prized roses. Then, she'd clipped one of the buds off the plant, telling her to sleep with it under her pillow. They'd only done it the one time, but it definitely didn't seem like a Berillai custom.

"You body is *life*, child," Nela had said. "Be glad to be grower."

She had mostly been in a rush to get in and out of the garden before the neighbors saw, but now that she was older, she could see how beautiful the tradition was. Essomuai was the grower of life, after all, the blood of Wellonai. And if a woman could grow life from her very body, that seemed to be just about the most glorious thing in the world. Thousands of women had been brave enough to come before her, and she needed to start taking pride in that.

She walked into the warehouse looking for Erso and Parimu when she paused, staring at the wagons. There were eight in all, and they were strange, insect-looking things with long flat backs and a dozen wheels on each side. They were open to the air with only a simple cloth for keeping off the sun. All the wagons were already hitched to a full team of horses, and workers scurried about the rest of the fleet, loading things up.

She found the others stowing their own luggage on a wagon in the back, which was already stuffed with leathers, explaining why they'd been allowed to loiter around it. There were two benches behind the horses, and Erso stashed her bag beneath one of them before climbing down.

"These are odd, no?" she asked, poking at one of the strange wheels. The wood seemed sturdy but felt like it would bend if you pushed hard enough.

"They're Relimoran," Parimu said, chiming in, "made to go through the desert. The axles help get them over the dunes, and the wheels are flexible in case they need to be dug out."

She and Erso both turned to him, their eyebrows identically cocked.

"Don't ask me why I know that," he added hastily, scratching the back of his head. "But at any rate, they'll move just as quick as a normal wagon on stone, it's just the desert that trips up the normal kind."

"Well, I'll be," Erso said, clapping Parimu on the back. "And here I thought you only cared about boats."

She smiled at him before turning back to the wagon. She ran her eyes over their luggage again but didn't see the tents anywhere.

"What's the…uh…sleeping situation on these things?" she asked, peering at the heaps of leather.

"Under the stars," Erso said, swinging his hands wide like a rainbow as he wiggled his fingers.

"Oh," she said, biting her lip. So maybe she wasn't completely ready to be like her ancestors…

"You sleep in these, I think," Erso said, pointing to a row of rolled-up blankets in a side compartment. At least they looked thick and wooly. "It's dry out there, so you usually just curl up underneath."

"Sounds kind of nice," Parimu said, kneeling down and looking under the wagon. "I always loved the stars on the crow's nest at night."

Maybe he was right; she did love the star song, after all… Besides, Essomuai was in the dirt too, right? Erso hopped up on the back of the wagon, unfurling one of the blankets to show her. It had a swirling pattern like the scarves in Amoriai, only about a foot thicker. It was hard to imagine with all the sunshine, but she had heard once that deserts got cold at night.

"They do look nice," she said, nodding. "But are you sure they're up to your standards, Mr. Milak'erat?"

"Who, me?" he said, pointing at his chest with a look of surprise.

Just then, a loud clanging came from the center of the warehouse, and they came around the wagon, finding Arkesht standing on a crate, ringing a large cowbell. The loading apparently done, blue-clad workers were lining up all around while Yalkai zipped between the wagons muttering to herself, a long checklist in hand.

"Pollaesyik!" Arkesht called out in Narala. She opened herself to the songs, just catching the next part of his announcement.

"Yal and I are joining you this trip, so we're going with the usual assignments except for Jorin and Likoj — you can ride with Seronn and Kep. We're gonna try to make Three Ring Hill by sundown, so keep an eye on your horses and stay sharp; bandit reports are up."

He paused as Yalkai stepped up beside him, nodding firmly as she folded up her list.

"Alright, gents, we're loaded."

He made as if to ring the bell again but paused, meeting Sumi's eyes.

"Oh, and don't forget to be welcoming to our guests, they're paying good coin for your courtesy!" There were a few laughs at that, but mostly, the crew members turned and smiled at her as Arkesht rang the bells again. "Load up and ship out!"

The workers split up, going in seemingly every direction. Some headed back out the doors toward the barge while others disappeared into the warehouse stacks. The rest went to the wagons in pairs, quickly checking harnesses and wheels. The two men who finally approached their wagon were the ones she'd sat with at breakfast — Eptos and Merin. They both smiled, greeting them in thickly accented Berillai before starting their own checks on the wagon.

"You know," Parimu said, his eyes running down the length of the fleet, "I think I'll hop on another wagon. Don't want it getting crowded on here."

"You sure?" she asked, her hand instinctively grabbing his shoulder. "You don't have to leave for our sake. I'm sick of Erso anyway."

She struggled not to grin as she heard the usual "Oy!" from Erso, but Parimu shook his head, smiling.

"No, no," he said, "it's alright. It might be good for us to spread ourselves out, get to know more of the crew."

"Okay," she said, "but make sure you find us at dinner."

"I heard that, you know," Erso said, putting his arm around her as Parimu headed back into the scrum.

"I know," she said, "that's why I said it."

"Figures," he said, chuckling, "I've created a monster."

He let his arm fall, pinching her hip, sending a jolt of electricity up her spine.

"Guess I'd better meet our drivers," he added, winking at her as he walked to the front of the wagon.

Her face couldn't seem to decide how to feel, a wide smile appearing, followed by a furious flush. Was this what real love felt like — a stumbling blend of laughter and desire? She'd never imagined being loved by anyone in the first place, but now that she was learning to heckle him, the echoes of Nela and Grandpa made Erso feel even more like family. It was simultaneously like coming home and meeting a stranger at the same time.

She followed him around the side of the wagon, where Eptos was standing by the front bench, checking the horse harnesses. He turned to her, smiling.

"We...almost finish. You...sit?" he asked, pointing to the second bench. She hadn't wanted to eavesdrop on them back at breakfast, but she didn't want them to feel forced into speaking Berillai the whole trip either... Without thinking, she opened herself to Essomuai, trusting Narala would come out of her mouth as Eptos's song rushed in.

"That would be lovely," she said, "thank you for having us."

His eyes nearly popped out of his head for a moment before his smile widened.

"I didn't realize you spoke Narala," he said.

"Sometimes," she said, grinning. She cocked her head at Erso. "He doesn't, though, so feel free to call him a clown."

"Hey, I know that word at least," Erso said. He must have spoken Berillai, but the words apparently still came into her ears just fine.

"Eh, Merin," Eptos said, calling back to his partner, "the girl speaks the gods' tongue!"

"Oh, yeah?" Merin asked, coming around the front of the horses. "You should've said so at breakfast! This is gonna be a treat; it's usually so boring on the road."

"Please, please," Eptos said, gesturing again to the seat behind him, "make yourself comfortable, we'll be leaving shortly."

"Thank you," she said, climbing up. She turned back to Erso, patting the bench next to her. He cocked an eyebrow at her but climbed up all the same.

"Well," he said, "you figured that trick out, eh?"

"I guess so," she said. "I just open my mouth and speak. I still can't tell it's any different from Berillai, but it's only weird if you think about it too much."

"*That*," he said, chuckling, "is the story of my life. Other than calling me a clown, can you at least figure out if these blokes smoke pipes? I gotta do some bonding of my own if they're gonna be carting us around."

She nodded, turning back to Eptos. She'd just have to keep talking while she was open to the songs and hope Essomuai did the rest, not that she could stay open to the songs all the time and keep her wits about her...

"Hey, Eptos," she said, "do you two smoke pipes? Erso wants someone to share his leaves with."

He turned around, the same broad smile on his face.

"If you find a wagon man who doesn't smoke a pipe, I'll give you a thousand crowns." He turned to Erso, nodding his thanks. "You're from Amoriai, yeah? Bet you smoke that good polis leaf?"

She couldn't tell anything different — all of it still sounded like Berillai — but Erso actually responded. Did that mean Eptos had switched to Amoriai?

"Of course," Erso said, grinning, "only trains ought to belch black smoke, you know?"

"Here, here," Eptos said, nodding. "We usually smoke tobacco mixed with olive leaf — keeps us from getting sick on the road — but nothing's smoother than polis."

"You're gonna get this one in trouble," Merin said, climbing onto the driver's bench. "His wife's been trying to get him to quit for years."

"Oh, that's right," Sumi said, leaning forward. "Yalkai said your wife is pregnant, right? I'm sorry you have to be on the road right now."

"Don't worry about him," Merin said, laughing. "He's got six more at home already."

Eptos scratched the back of his head. "Keril always wanted a big family. Just hope business stays good so Arkesht can hire them when they're grown."

The cowbell began to ring again, and Eptos turned back toward the front, grabbing the reins.

"Time to head out," Merin said, nodding. "We'll have to focus on the traffic for a bit, but you two just enjoy the view, alright?"

The wagons pulled out one by one, weaving into a long line that went out the bay doors on the other side of the warehouse. Finally, their turn came, and Eptos flicked the reins, coaxing their horses to follow the others. After crossing the length of the warehouse, they came out of the shade of the building and back into the sunny afternoon, finally giving them a good look at Sykala. Their column was turning left onto a wide boulevard, a lushly planted median in the middle separating thirty to forty feet of cobblestones on either side. It was easily twice as wide as anything in Berill, but it seemed necessary with the dozens of other wagon teams already crowding the streets.

As their party fully emerged onto the street, they continued in single file alongside the greenway. There were no lines on the streets or anything, but there seemed to be a clear division all the same — carts and pedestrians on the right and wagon teams on the left. Traffic went up and down the boulevard in both directions in the same pattern, and Eptos waved his hat at a few of the other wagon teams they passed going the other way.

Sumi took off her hat and leaned back, trying to catch the sun on her face as they rolled through the city. Just like the walls, the inside of the city felt like being inside a sandcastle. There were still plenty of other warehouses built with the same sturdy brick as Arkesht's, but the majority of the buildings had those smooth sandstone sides and peaked red tile roofs. It would have been nice to stay a while — at least have a walk around like they had in Ageleat — but after that run-in with the Thorns… Well, it was probably good to clear out for a while.

The people seemed just as thoroughly Ekosinaran as they had in Ageleat — wide-brimmed hats and leathers crowding around every street corner. And their commerce seemed just as bustling. The boulevard they were on seemed to be one of a handful of thick arteries crisscrossing the city, but all the others might as well have been alleyways, jammed full of vendors and knots of people buying produce and whatever else came off the caravans.

After a few more minutes, they reached the southern rim of the city wall, where it opened up onto the bay. The whole thing was like a backwards C as the wall ran right up to the shore. It hadn't been as obvious on the canal side, but there were dozens of watchtowers along this length of the wall, the specks of guards appearing along the parapets. It was hard to tell what they'd be guarding against with the whole shoreline being part of Ekosinar, but maybe they were looking out for the wrong color flag…

After another minute, the boulevard curved along the wall to the east, and they reached a huge intersection where they were waved into another giant hole in the sandstone wall. She listened to the wall's song again as they passed underneath, a half-minute of darkness before emerging back into the sun. Her eyes widened, the contrast almost too much to take in. While the city had been one unending scrum, outside, there was…nothing — no olive groves or hills on this side, just a yellow grassland that seemed to stretch into infinity, broken only by the road they were on and the one snaking east to Relimora.

Erso had been quietly filling everyone's pipes the whole way through the city, and as soon as they breached the wall, he passed them back out, all three men turning the wagon into a blue smokestack.

"Well," Erso said, sighing out in satisfaction, "sure smells like freedom out here."

"I hope so," she said, nodding. She would need a break from the songs soon, but before she did, she turned to the south, feeling for Essomuai. Somewhere out there, she could feel the goddess, her song pulsing beneath the others. It was still calling to her, beckoning her to seek its answers, to sing in harmony. The wagon rolled on toward it, bringing her one step closer to her goal and everything that would follow after.

20

The Umi'ceurae is nearing completion, and it is time to build the altar. We are sending for the following stones for immediate release from the Council of Houses: the Sekoren, the Gurani, the Erenosana, the Italkorae, and the Sesoniak. May the joining of the stones provide a beacon for our people of Umilai's guiding light.

-Sea Scroll #291
Estimated Date 5 PN

—:—

After several long hours on a hard wagon bench, they finally approached their destination for the night, the sun burning red as it tilted toward the horizon. Parimu shielded his eyes as he watched it set, looking for the point on the horizon where the glowing orb would come to rest on Berill. He'd never felt so far from home. Even in the navy, he'd always known the exact date he'd return to port. And yet, he'd never felt so hopeful either — hopeful he might finally find the answers he needed to make going home worthwhile.

He turned back to his drivers, the two men slowly guiding their wagon train toward Three Ring Hill. He'd gotten lucky, somehow finding the two crew members that spoke the best Berillai. Lorend and Karunil were brothers, though they looked nothing alike — one tall and thin, while the other was built like a circus strongman. They'd been happy to take him aboard, but more importantly, they'd been more than generous in answering his endless questions. There was something about the crew he wanted to understand, some secret that felt just out of grasp.

"So, what about the profit-sharing?" he asked. "How do you figure out your shares?"

"Well," Lorend said, "s'long as my fool brother gets half what I do, I don't worry too much about the shares."

"Yeah, well, good thing they pay you in fleas, *kishton mera*," Karunil growled, getting up as if he meant to put his brother in a headlock. Somehow, though, the much skinnier man held him off without letting go of the reins.

"Excuse my brother," Lorend said, still grinning as he turned around to face Parimu. "It's honestly pretty simple — warehouse guild sets the rates. Couldn't tell you the first thing about how the math works with all the bloody men on the crew, but it changes based on how long you stick around."

As if on cue, Lorend turned back to the horses, Karunil taking his place.

"I got the head for numbers," Karunil said, "so maybe I can explain. We call the shares *ravidak* — 'stick' in Berillai."

"Like a stick on a tree?" Parimu asked.

"*Exactly*," Karunil said, pointing at him. "At the end of each circle — that's three months — they pile up the coin and take out the costs. Whatever's left goes forty Arkesht, forty us, and twenty back into the business. Our forty is split by how many sticks we got. You get one stick for joining, one for every five years you stay, and you can pick up extras working the lift crane and such."

"Seems sensible," Parimu said, scratching his chin. "Why are they called the...*ravidak*, was it?"

Karunil chuckled. "Probably because they're actual *ravidak*," he said. He whacked his older brother on the shoulder. "You got more; show him."

With one hand, Lorend went into his leather jacket, pulling out three stout-looking sticks. He fanned them out, showing them off over his shoulder. They were dark in color and finely lacquered but did look like ordinary sticks, albeit with colorful painted tips. There was a white one, a green one, and an orange one.

"You can hold 'em if you'd like," Lorend said, waving them at Parimu. He hesitantly took them, holding them in both hands as he ran a finger along an edge, finding it perfectly smooth, though a bit of grain from the wood still showed.

"White's for joining up and green's for the five years," Karunil said as Parimu handed back the sticks. "I got those too — Lorend only joined a couple years before me — but the orange one's for being a guild voter. Not worth the share if you ask me, though, the fool's always stuck in meetings while I'm at the pub."

"Ah, okay," he said, nodding. "But *why* the actual sticks?"

"Ekosinarans *love* tradition — live for it, actually," Lorend said, "but this is one of the oldest, older than the canal or the wagon crews. Comes from the original sailors' guild. Anyway, back in the day, captains used to keep all the profits, even if they weren't on the boat. Some of 'em would manage whole fleets, born with the bloody golden leaf, if you catch my meaning. Anyway, they would take awful risks with our lives, forcing men out during storms, runs to Mesopyn without enough food, rubbish like that. There were an awful lot of mutinies back then, and a good amount of ships never came back — decided to be pirates or died or whatever."

Parimu blinked at that. He'd never seen a mutiny, but the thought had sometimes kept him up at night, especially when his crews didn't like him very much. He'd always wondered, would they ever just stop following orders? It wasn't much of an issue in the Royal Navy, of course, but whenever things got tense, the possibility had still seemed to linger in the air.

"Then one famous captain came along," Lorend continued, "*Keptan Dikoiyan*. Treated his crews like bloody human beings. Never sent out a boat if he or one of his first mates weren't going themselves. They'd go out for months, run whole seasons before coming back, and never a single mutiny. Anyway, legend has it he had an estate on Perous with a giant olive tree, and you could see the yellow flowers in the springtime for miles down the coast. They'd have a massive feast, and at the end, you could take a stick from one of the branches of his olive tree. Every year you stayed, you'd get a bigger cut, all based on the sticks."

"Not bad, right?" Karunil asked, seeing Parimu's face. "My brother's usually a knucklehead, but he tells that story right, at least."

"Makes sense for a boat with the mutinies and all that," Parimu said, "but why keep the sticks on the wagon crews?"

"Part of every guild in the kingdom now," Karunil said, nodding proudly. "Can't run a proper Ekosinaran business without a guild — other than the bloody trains, that is…" His face darkened for a moment before a grin returned. "Anyway, makes things run real smooth. Arkesht is one of the best men I know — even gives us a bonus on *Fengaran* — but not every shop is run by an Arkesht, you know? Without rules, life would just be…*itorkunar* — like rolling dice. Besides, guild shops do better business — sets the right mood for the customers, gives us enough coin to buy some leathers — keeps it all humming.'"

It seemed too simple, but maybe it wasn't — like Sumi. She had completely changed his life, and all it had taken was her seeing him for what he really was. Maybe the sticks were about being seen too? By making them feel like a family, these men were free to act like one. And maybe if Berill saw its factory workers as something other than beasts of burden, they'd feel like a family too. Maybe…someone would have nursed Jalicyne back to health instead of waiting for her to die so they could rent her room. The details in life could be complicated, but the heart usually wasn't.

Finally, they came over a short rise, and the full enormity of Three Ring Hill came into view. It looked like a giant tortoise had laid down on the dusty plain and gone to sleep, the dirt and grass finally covering its shell. He was about to ask where the name came from when they came around the left side of the hill, the tortoise ending up being only one of three separate hills clumped together. They created a sort of protected triangle where a half dozen other wagon teams were already setting up for the night.

He looked up at the clear blue sky. How hadn't he noticed the smoke? The other caravans were circled up already, each one with a roaring bonfire in the center surrounded by workmen in their own colors. Now that he knew what to look for, he could also make out a handful of men at the top of each hill, a mix of the various colors with their own fires to match. Karunil caught him looking up at the hills and nodded.

"Great place, right?" he asked. "Wagon men been staying here since the bloody *trepolek*. Protected on three sides, easy to spot bandits — it's paradise compared to the plains."

"Not to mention a hundred wagon brutes to fight off," Lorend added, laughing.

Their team pulled off the road, approaching the leftmost side of the triangle. The sun was already well behind the hills, shrouding the campsite in shadow. Men from the other wagon teams noticed them, some of them waving their hats as they walked over. They formed their circle, leading the other wagons in a wide loop. Then, almost as soon as the last wagon came to a stop, the entire crew burst into a frenzy.

Men were dashing everywhere, pulling an impossible number of barrels from the wagons as they set up the campsite. As promised, there were no tents for sleeping, but they still set up a canopy, piling water and food barrels underneath. Their efficiency certainly seemed to prove the guilds worked. Even in the Royal Navy — arguably the most disciplined group on Wellonai — he'd only ever seen men move this quickly in a storm. Even the threat of the Queen's justice seemed to be no match to what these men had built.

Before long, men from the other wagons made it across the field, and the campsite became a blur of handshakes and hugs. Even before the campfire was lit, there were some two dozen clouds of smoke floating off of pipes. He chuckled to himself and jumped off the wagon. Hopefully, he could find something useful to do before all the work was done. There were probably times these men fought like family too, but tonight, they all moved as one, and oddly, it felt like home.

———

After dinner, as the fires burned low, Sumi followed Erso through the camp toward the looming shadow of the nearest hill. A few of the men had already wandered off to bed beneath the wagons, though they'd stayed by the fire for a while, surrounded by stories and pipe smoke. But as the stories grew fewer and farther between, they'd slunk off, looking for a little privacy, the little moments with Erso made all the more precious now that they were surrounded by two dozen burly wagon men.

Besides, after stuffing themselves at dinner, it felt good to stretch a bit. Maybe they'd spent too much time eating beans, but Arkesht's crew seemed to eat like kings. It was still simple fare — dark rice and salted cod — but they'd pulled it off the wagon by the barrel and made everything in gigantic pots that looked like they could feed an army. Unfortunately, some of the men noticed how many bowls she'd put away and started calling her *Skafi*. It hadn't translated through the songs — maybe because it was a name? — but it sounded suspiciously like the '*skafiti #3*' branded on the back of their wagon…

They finally reached the slope and began to climb, Erso taking the lead as they picked their way through the scrubby bushes dotting the hill. They wound around toward the south until they were well away from camp, facing the great expanse of nothingness on the Ekosinaran plains. They hadn't brought a lantern or anything, but it was surprisingly bright beneath the stars.

She struggled to take them all in, her eyes darting between the mass of constellations. She opened herself to the songs, eager for the familiar melody of the stars, but as she listened closer, each cluster seemed to hum its own verse… Why hadn't she noticed that in the forest? Maybe the trees had blocked them somehow, but they were just stars, right? Even if people picked out random shapes from the sky, what could be different about each little dot of light?

She was about to mention it to Erso when he stopped, sitting on a log. He patted the place beside him, so she sat too, forcing herself to take a deep breath as she closed off the songs. She'd gotten a few breaks on the wagon, but it felt like she'd held her mind open all day, especially after a long dinner chatting in Narala.

He put his hand over hers where it was resting on the log, leaning in for a kiss. She tried to breathe him in, thinking of nothing else until he pulled back, offering his shoulder for her to lay her head on. They stayed that way for a while, listening to the wind until she heard a rustle in the bushes behind them. She jumped, whipping her head around as Erso put his arm around her. The men had promised there wasn't anything poisonous out here — that sort of thing wasn't until the Relimoran desert — but they did say the lizards could grow to be the size of dogs...

"What are you so worried about?" Erso asked, patting her head. "If you see a lizard, just turn into a bigger one. Or maybe you could sing to them?"

"Oh, shush," she said, nestling her head deeper into his shoulder. "I'll just fly back to camp and let it eat you."

"That's a shame," he said, stroking his chin with his free hand. "The lizards are probably hungry, and little *Skafi* would make a much better snack."

She squirmed, trying to smack him, but he held on tight, laughing as she struggled until they finally ended up in another kiss. Heat washed through her body until she forgot all about the reptiles roaming in the dark. Finally, Erso pulled away, but he stayed turned toward her, running his thumb over her cheek.

"Bloody gods, you're beautiful," he said, sucking in a breath. *"Ed'hazin meran."*

She raised an eyebrow at that, which only made him laugh.

"Sorry," he said, "I'm starting to take your language thing for granted — it means 'lucky me.'"

Fortunately, her eyebrow was already arched because she was forced to follow it with an eye roll.

"Not that I think you're lying," she finally said, staring at the sky, "but...why exactly do you think I'm beautiful?"

"Fair question," he said, unhooking his arm and leaning forward on his knees as he rubbed his hands together. She'd started noticing him doing that when he was thinking. Where had he picked that up? She was tempted to listen to his song again, to see if it was something his father had done, but with him, it could just as easily be a nervous habit, his hands wishing for a pipe to hold.

"Honestly, I do kind of hate that word," he finally said. "It feels so...simple for describing something so *infinite*, you know?" He shot a glance at her, grinning. "Maybe you can ask your goddess for a proper word to describe someone so heavenly."

She moved to kick him off the stump, but he put his hands up quickly in surrender.

"Only joking!" he said. "Seriously, though, I have always hated thinking of beauty as something you can put in a box, you know? Like those wretched fashion magazines they litter all over the Continent — this kind of nose, that kind of hat. As if you could let someone else tell you what beauty is supposed to be."

He shook his head, chuckling.

"Reminds me of my mother, actually. She was a handsome woman, don't get me wrong, but she wasn't popular for her face. Even when she wasn't Shapewalking, she had this…presence on stage. No matter which character she played, you remembered her. I guess for me, you were like that. The moment I saw you, you seemed so…real, so entirely yourself. And when I got to know you — well, there was no question I was gonna love you then."

"That's lovely," she said quietly, almost forgetting to respond she'd been listening so intently. "I don't know if it's true, but with an answer like that, I guess I have no choice but to believe you."

She paused, looking up at the stars again. They were…beautiful? Stunning? Awe-inspiring? He was right. It *was* a bit silly to use the same word on a hat you'd use to describe this…infinity.

"I never needed to be beautiful," she continued, looking back at him. "I actually preferred thinking I wasn't, if I'm honest — anything to separate me from those wretched girls I grew up with. But the way you just explained it, beauty doesn't feel so…confining. I'm okay being beautiful if I'm beautiful to *you*. It's like all the buildings I love back home, they're…a part of me. This doesn't really help me deal with you being the handsomest man I've ever met, but I do feel a little better accepting your compliments."

Erso laughed, scooping her under his arm. He planted a kiss on her cheek, his mustache sending a spark down her spine.

"I'll have to remember that one," he said, still chuckling. "Next time I'm running away from the scene of a crime, I'm gonna yell that over my shoulder — 'You're the handsomest man I've ever met!' Should slow 'em down for a second, at least."

She smacked him gently on the cheek, but it only made him chuckle harder until she couldn't help but laugh herself. She leaned harder into his arms, and they slipped into silence, letting the night wash over them. They sat there for a long time until Erso finally spoke again.

"You know," he said, "I was wondering…if you'd do me a favor. Not to sound jealous or anything, but I was hoping you could do the memory thing on me you did with Parimu? I keep finding myself wishing I could know you like that. Like just now, talking about beauty, I want to see the world through your eyes. And as much as I'm sure I'll regret it…I guess I want you to know everything about me too."

"I'd love that," she said without hesitation. Of course, she'd thought about it too. She supposed she'd just been waiting for him to ask. Parimu had been an accident, and she'd heard a good amount of Erso's life through his songs already. Sharing her own life just felt like an imposition, but if he wanted to see it… There was no one she'd rather share it with.

She sat a bit taller on the log, opening herself to the songs as fully as she possibly could. The music of the hillside flooded into her mind, making it painfully obvious how much she'd been forced to stifle them. Still, it was so beautiful it was almost impossible to think about anything else. Suddenly, the night was no longer frightening, filled only with the love Essomuai had for…everything. She could even sense the lizards now, dozens of them dotting the scrubby hillside, their songs not scary but almost goofy as they chased crickets in the dark.

When she opened her eyes, the entire landscape was transformed. As if someone had lit hundreds of candles, the hill was full of pinpricks of light like a second sky full of stars. Were these like…keyholes for ordinary things? She supposed she'd never opened herself up this much, but she'd never noticed all this light before. Erso was shining the brightest by far, his keyhole more like a fire, the golden glow she'd seen in Anushai completely covering his heart.

He was looking back at her, his eyes searching.

"Are you ready?" he asked quietly.

Of course, he couldn't see this other side of the world, hadn't noticed anything other than her opening her eyes. She nodded, reaching toward the glow of his heart, but she paused. This time, she knew what she was doing. When she touched his keyhole, she'd be picking up his heart and giving hers to him. She didn't feel doubt, exactly…only a sort of awe. Even more than sharing his bed someday, this would be sharing their *souls*. She took one last breath, moving her fingers the last inch to touch his heart, flashing them to that golden place.

Even though she'd known where they were going, it came as a shock to arrive there. A golden…nowhere, their beings seeming to disappear into the deepest parts of Mu'lalat. It was filled with light, completely consuming her as their songs mixed and harmonized together, converging with another melody she now recognized — Essomuai's song, or part of it anyway. The melody, no longer hidden in the mountains, seemed to be right beside her, echoing against her very being.

Slowly, Erso's life began to fill her mind, appearing before her eyes as if she were looking out through her own, filling in every detail that hadn't made it into his melody. She saw the house he grew up in, the garden out back — the entire neighborhood sprouting up around her from before it had become the burned hull of *Su'selo'mae.* She saw Beysal as her own uncle, felt the thrill of being thrown around the garden as they wrestled. She saw her mother on stage, her heart bursting with pride as the audience gave her a standing ovation. Such a beautiful childhood! She felt the makings of Erso's heart growing inside her — his humor, his kindness — each precious piece forming brick by brick.

And then…her heart felt as if it were being torn in two. She felt his fear, running for her life, the heat of the fires on her face. Even knowing the story and having heard the song, nothing could have told her how it felt to hold that scrap of bone in her hands, all that was left of her beautiful mother. She wasn't sure if she even had a body in that golden nowhere, but she still felt tears coming from her eyes, threatening to drown her as they poured out, unceasing.

The rest of his life seemed to gravitate around that terrible point. Joy began to return in fits and starts — the summer afternoons with Beysal, tender kisses shared with A'lufell — but so many nights filled with whiskey, anything to get the stars to shimmer as she tried desperately to forget. But there was no forgetting for them, their life still circling around that day like the world around the sun. No matter how far she ran, no matter how many Shapewalkers she saved, the ice would still be there in her heart, only slightly thawed by those brief days of sun.

But then, she saw herself… She knew those moments already — running into Erso at the trolley station, being saved by him at the jail. Only they weren't her memories now, they were his, and she felt his emotions instead. Curiosity and admiration, things she'd never felt about herself before. And finally — after so many weeks of denying it and dancing around it — there was love. So much love she felt her heart might burst. She had to feel it twice, her own love for Erso and his love for her, her heart stretched to bursting as it tried to hold it all.

Just as suddenly, the visions were gone, and she found herself in a body again. Still in that golden nowhere, but just as with Parimu, she was in Erso's body now and found herself staring back, her eyes wide and filled with tears just as hers surely were. The other Sumi spoke with Erso's voice.

"Sumi," was all he managed to squeeze out before they embraced. They clung tightly to each other, and she could feel the strength of Erso's arms as she wrapped them around her own back. They didn't transform as she had with Parimu. There was no need to be a hawk, nothing to fly away from. All they could do was hold each other and try to hang onto the weight of everything they had seen — the pain, the love, all of it mixing together into the new life they had now.

"I love you," she whispered.

The light began to fade, returning them to their own bodies and the dark quiet of the night. The songs were still, and the hillside no longer shone like the stars. It was back to normal, and yet, everything was different. She took her hand from Erso's heart, and they embraced again, this time in their own bodies. Even in the darkness, the love between them somehow glowed just as brightly as Mu'lalat.

21

Terms of Peace with Berill, 3rd Tudammes 1606 N.E.
Her Mother Empress Kiyelpean on behalf of the Joint Kingdoms and King Pelloyen of Berill, people of different gods acting in good faith, have concluded an armistice on the following conditions:

-Excerpts from the Treaty of Trilathdrei
First Page, First Paragraph

—:—

After rushing through her bedtime ritual, Sumi found herself beneath the wagon, covered in the thick woolen blanket roll the crew had given her. They had stayed on the hillside as long as they could until they couldn't stifle their yawns any longer. They'd crept back to camp, finding most of the men already sleeping, their snores challenging the sounds of the night for dominance. Eptos and Merin had been kind enough to roll their blankets out for them, both of them already fast asleep on the other side of the wagon.

She'd been a ball of nerves climbing into the sleeping roll for a dozen reasons — chief among them the possibility of lizards or worse creeping in to sleep beside her… Erso had chuckled quietly as she shook out her roll, running her hands through all the layers of wool. Even with that settled, though, she still had to think about the prospect of sleeping a foot away from Erso. In the woods, she'd at least had a layer of tent between them. What if she snored too? What if she drooled or made an ugly face in her sleep? But it wasn't like she had much choice… It was either sleep beside him or move further into the cold night where more lizards awaited her.

Finally, she'd settled in, and it wasn't long before Erso seemed to drift off himself, his blankets becoming still. She laid awake, her eyes tracing the lines of the wagon in what little light remained from the fire, blinking more and more heavily. Even if they had another full day of riding in the wagon tomorrow, she wasn't likely to get much rest — she needed to dream again. Her run-in with the Thorns made her want to dream every night if she could, but her time with Erso made her feel it even more urgently.

This man — this wonderful man who had lost so much — was still risking his life for her, and it made her desperate to do more herself. There was still so little she could actually do, but the hillside *had* served as a reminder of how infinite Essomuai was. The night had burst with light, everything full of the goddess. That would have to be the way forward, trusting that light, believing that answers would come.

She closed her eyes and let the songs back in, letting the symphony overtake the quiet of the night. This time, she didn't hold onto herself at all, simply disappearing as she let herself be absorbed into that light. Even when the dream began, Sumi was already gone, and only Essomuai remained.

———

Long after Sumi's breath deepened into sleep, Erso lay awake in his bedroll, staring at the wood above him. He could really use a pipe, though the wagon blokes probably wouldn't much appreciate being smoked out. Why had he been so keen to merge with Sumi? Jealous of bloody Parimu? It was beautiful to see her life, of course — probably the most beautiful thing he was ever gonna see — but it hadn't just been him, had it? She'd been forced to look at his bloody life too.

Not that he was ashamed — okay, maybe a little — but it was like…your grandmother catching you in the pub. Nothing wrong with being in a pub, of course, and it's not like your grandmother is some dowdy old woman who *hates* pubs. She's a perfectly nice lady — bakes you cookies, tells you stories, even swears once in a while. But you're in the pub in the middle of the day, just trying to scratch the itch like anybody else. And she walks by, frowning at the dirty glass, and sees you, her beloved grandson, hamming it up at the bar with a bunch of sailors. She would still bake you cookies, probably wouldn't ever mention the incident, but it was enough to make a man think about his choices.

At least he knew himself, right? Some men stumbled through life, doing horrible things without feeling a drop of shame. Sure, he had to drink enough to forget so he could keep on living, but it was better than the alternative. Still, the difference between knowing what he was and letting Sumi know was as wide as the bloody Erril Sea.

Sumi shifted in her blankets, mumbling in her sleep. Was she having another dream? Just like her to peacefully drift off and have a chat with the gods while his sorry self soaked in the darkness. He leaned over and kissed her cheek before lying back, taking a nip from his flask as he looked at the crack of stars he could see past the edge of the wagon. He refused to abandon her — he'd sooner die. But maybe, one day, he could get her to see him for the beast he really was and get *her* to leave him. If only he could be so lucky.

———

Lord Rummon sat on his throne in House Berill, staring at his sword in the vanishing light. There were plenty of marks on the blade, though it still had a shine to it. He may need a new one eventually, though he'd hate to part with this one after everything they'd been through together. Still, with the help of the priestesses and all their ore, his next sword might last forever like the kind on the Continent they passed from father to son. But this one would have to do for one more season. Winter was coming quickly, and the wind readers had promised a good year for raids.

Even if you couldn't talk to the gods, you'd be a fool not to know what kind of winter it would be. It was only the fifth of Runginom, and already there was frost on the ground, the type of year when the winds would finally let them off the Isles. Not that he understood the patterns, but even Alomus couldn't hold them there forever, apparently. Not that he feared the snow, of course, but he wouldn't freeze with his bloody sheep if he could feel the sea spray on his face. Like father always said, the other houses participated in the raids to flee the cold, but the Berillai did it for sport. And for politics, of course…

At least, that was a game he played far better than father ever had. Still, the other houses letting him lead the winter voyages — however begrudgingly — was just a start. He wanted to be *king*, like the kind they had on the Continent. The alliances and honors of the winter raids all but vanished the moment spring arrived, forcing him to spend his summers spilling blood in the same never-ending dance. House Pont and House Oeskidara were unquestionably his, but that left seven others to control — to crush in his palm if they wouldn't kneel.

After that…he would see the entire Continent kneel before him. The other houses may be content fighting over pebbles on the damned Isles, but he was sick of waiting. It had already been five hundred years since the Angel of the Sea found the first speaking stone, giving them Umilai's promise of a better life.

And yet, the winds had only died down some twenty-five times since then — only four of them in his lifetime — and the others were content, counting their little piles of treasure when they returned. Didn't they dream of it as he did? The Continent, endless green, a paradise without end, ripe for the taking. Why satisfy yourself with mutton when you could pluck grapes from the damn vine?

He would make the fools see — by the pen or the sword, it didn't much matter to him. He gripped his sword and stood from the throne, striding to the black stone platform in the center of the room where a giant blue speaking stone stood on its end. Like all the houses, Berill had collected a fair number over the years, but this was the largest by far.

He had taken it in a raid on House Apalimar two years earlier. Rather than bend the knee — or die — they had fled their castle. They returned eventually with reinforcements, but not before he'd cleared out their treasury and taken the stone. In truth, he didn't care about Apalimar yet — he'd rather take Elikora or Gentoaln first — but the stone held something far more precious — the voice of Umilai. His dream, above all others, was to be anointed by the gods, *chosen* to rule.

He had done everything the priestesses had told him to — prayed the Rites of the Sea, sacrificed a quintile of his flock, even built a statue of Ereilea — and still, the stone had not spoken. Something more was required of him, some further strength to be shown that would prove him worthy. It was only the bold that Umilai rewarded, like the Angel of the Sea prying the first stone from the rock with her bare hands. He would be as bold, and after centuries of the stones not speaking to any man, he *would* hear the god's voice before he was done.

Still, even for the women, for at least three decades now, the stones had only said one thing — *Eporisalkaman*. He didn't understand the language of the gods, but they told him it meant 'strength,' describing the image as a bundle of rods being broken and put back together again. The stones said nothing more. They wouldn't admit it, but the priestesses seemed to fear it would be the last thing the stones *ever* said. It wasn't like the beginning, with detailed instructions sending them across the sea.

And yet, the priestesses still counseled patience. That seemed at odds with a command for strength, though their advice was usually decent. It was Kesselia, after all, who had helped him plan the raid on Apalimar. He employed five of them from the tower now. In addition to the rites and rituals, he had allowed each to manage their own share of the stones, paying the tower good money to let them stay longer than the priestesses normally did on their rotations. Perhaps he would marry one someday too… But for now, he just wanted to keep the set he had, their honesty more valuable than the gold they cost him.

Each woman had already been in service for fifteen years before they reached him and had traveled to almost every house on the Isles. Usually, a tower priestess would never reveal the secrets of another family's stones, but these women… Perhaps they also saw the potential of becoming his bride, but either way, they saw strength in him, and so they stayed, eager to fulfill the demands of their god. He would show them strength, alright, more than they could imagine.

He looked up at the stone, stepping onto the edge of the dais. He didn't touch it, laying his fingertips just on the edge of the platform. What more did Umilai require? He would keep fighting for the power he desired, though he wished the god would answer. Would he be a king, or did the gods not care so long as *someone* was the strongest? If he heard a single whisper from the gods, he knew he could conquer the entire world.

Just then, the doors to his throne room burst open, and some two dozen of his men entered, dragging in the prisoner. They were followed by his priestesses, who silently lined up against the wall. Laeryia held the prisoner's left arm, while his lieutenant, Erakan of House Pont, held the right. The prisoner was Pesolarin, the heir of House Dulairn, though you'd never know that by looking at him. His beard had grown thick over the few short weeks of his imprisonment, and his skin looked ashen. Their eyes met, and the man snarled like a caged animal.

"Release me, coward!" he yelled. "My family will come for me. They don't fear you and your th—"

He was silenced as Laeryia backhanded him. Rummon raised a hand, calling his brother off. He stepped toward them, his sword still in hand.

"A coward, am I, boy?" he asked, chuckling. "If only that were so. Your family *will* come for me, but by the time they arrive, it will be too late for you. House Oeskidara will have penned them in with their ships, and I'll smash their army on my beaches. At least you can rest knowing your pitiful life bought another jewel for my crown. Soon, I'll control your entire island."

The boy's eyes widened, his face losing any color it had retained in the dungeon.

"You wouldn't," he whispered. His eyes darted to one of the windows, likely the first time he'd seen daylight during his imprisonment. "It's nearly winter, and there…there's to be no violence between houses during the voyage. It is the law!"

"There is only one law," Rummon said, turning and looking at the blue stone. "And that law is strength."

He motioned to his men, and they forced the prisoner to kneel as he swung his sword, beheading the heir of House Dulairn. He wiped the sword on his gauntlets, covering them in blood. Every priestess but one — the gorgeous Kesselia — had a look of utter shock on her face. They had grown used to most of his methods, but apparently not this. Perhaps he knew which one he should marry, after all…

Before they could stop him, he returned to the dais, yelling to the heavens, his hands to the sky.

"Umilai! You have asked us for strength! I call on you now to answer me, who will be king?!" He brought his arms down, seizing the stone in bloodied hands. The last thing he heard was the women gasp, and everything went black.

Rummon blinked in the blackness that had replaced his sight. There was an unrelenting…pressure, like when he and his brothers would dive as children, pushing down until your lungs ached, the cold water threatening to pull you away. It was like the thrill of battle when your enemies threatened to snatch your life away. There was little time to have such thoughts, though, because the next moment, there was a *voice*. He felt it more than heard it, the sound seeming to come from within his own mind.

Relomarisenal, the voice shook. It sounded like the language of the gods, which he didn't know, but somehow, now, he understood… An image entered his mind of a crown being placed on a child's head. *Son of sons, son of the king,* it seemed to say. Surely he had dreamt it, but was he such a king?

Yes, he answered in his own mind. The shaking grew more intense, threatening to disintegrate what little remained of his soul. Suddenly, a string of images appeared in his mind, a flurry not brought on by any spoken word. It was almost as if by agreeing with the god, he no longer needed to hear the words for the thoughts to be put in his mind.

He saw a beach, what looked like the coast of the Continent as he had seen on so many raids. But now, it was green, not the colors of winter he knew so well. There was a port, one he had seen before on the western coast. He had never seen men there, but it was a beautiful place, a cove where they sometimes waited out storms. Then, he saw a sword, glittering like silver in the darkness. The darkness faded, and he saw…his own lands, a place far from his castle on the northern coast.

There were caves there, full of black rock, carved by centuries of waves. The darkness returned, the rumbling growing stronger as two more words were spoken.

Perubana'emon Relomarisenal. The first was an image of two people passing something to each other — *to take a gift*. The second was the one from the beginning, *the son of sons, the king*. The crown, a gift from the gods to him? He opened his mouth to ask when the darkness vanished. He was still somehow gripping the stone but had fallen to his knees. The priestesses surrounded him, Kesselia first among them, touching his face as she tried to lift him to his feet.

"Are you alright, my lord?" she asked, holding tightly to his shoulder. He blinked, taking her hand with a bloodied gauntlet. She didn't recoil from the blood that stained her skin, merely squeezing him tighter. *Yes,* he would have to consider her again. If he was to be king, he would need a queen.

He opened his mouth to answer her when the ground began to shake. For a moment, he thought he was being carried back to the realm of the gods when the entire castle seemed to bounce with the force of the rumbling. Cracks appeared on the stone floor, splintering their way up the wall. He caught Kesselia as she fell, gripping her by the waist. The blue stone rattled in its holder, the blood still smeared along its glowing edges. Just as soon as it started, though, the shaking stopped.

"What's happened?" Laeryia asked, approaching the dais, his hand gripped tightly around his sword. He had known, of course, of Rummon's plan, but it was one thing to consider speaking to a god and another to watch the ground shake after the thing was done. The image reappeared in his mind, the black caves on the northern shore. He knew by instinct the gods had a gift for him, and he would find it there.

"The gods have chosen us to be kings," he said, releasing Kesselia as he moved away from the dais. "We ride north to the black caves!"

He strode forward, leaving the others to hurry behind. There was something there, something that would make him king. He had seen a sword and the beautiful green lands he would conquer. He had shown the strength required, and it was time to seize what was his. Not by birth, but by strength and the power of the gods.

22

Why is there no pattern to the stones? Our greatest scholars have spent their entire lives studying where they appear, and it is only chaos — mountaintops, fields, and forests with seemingly no distinction. I have seen the maps of Sister Yuranial, and while she insists she is close to discovering a pattern, to my eyes, it was nothing but a blob, her findings flying randomly around it. It seems we must simply trust the wisdom of Umilai and be content in our human ignorance.

-Sea Scroll #92
Estimated Date 403 PN

—:—

Three days later, Sumi was still in the wagon, her floppy hat blocking the sun as they rolled through the dusty countryside. You'd think it'd be boring, doing nothing, but the days just slipped away. Even when she wasn't open to Essomuai, the wagon seemed to sing its own song, the creaking of the wheels and the jangling of the reins soothing her mind. The others seemed to feel it too, conversation slipping out at a predetermined pace — just a few stories told, seemingly on the hour, before silence reigned again.

Perhaps she was trying to fool herself, acting out a calm she shouldn't feel, but like Grandpa used to say, 'if you act like a king long enough, they might just put a crown on your head.' The first morning after her dream of King Rummon, she'd woken shaken, unconsciously clinging to Erso in her sleep. But the mind could only hold so much fear before it scrambled to find a familiar calm. She may have never seen these dusty

160

plains before, but scenery had always been her favorite balm, and she had it in spades now.

Still, the fear was there, in the back of her mind. Vilodai *was* Umilai. She had given Rummon the silver to make the sea blades, even showing him where Berill could be found. She had responded to him beheading someone and drenching a speaking stone in blood by *rewarding* him. And she was just supposed to waltz into Vilodai's Heart? Each day they pushed further south, and soon, they'd be crossing the train line to the mountains of Alara, and then…

She took a deep breath, squeezing her eyes shut as she repeated her mantra again in her mind: *Essomuai loves you, this isn't a trap. Essomuai loves you, this…is not…a trap.* She nodded, taking in one more deep breath before forcing her mind to focus on the scenery again.

The wagon was even quieter than usual. Maybe that was why she was so in her head? Erso had decided to ride with Arkesht, and Parimu was still with his own wagon up front. Well, she'd been alone for most of her life; she could handle one day on her own, right? She tilted her head back, looking past the wagon's awning at the sky.

She'd had no idea there could be so much…blue. The sky back home did often seem like it could go on forever, but there was always some other drama happening — the mountains, storms coming off the water. This was just *sky* for miles and miles, and more often than not, it was cloudless, the deepest blue she'd ever seen.

Since leaving Three Ring Hill, the land had only grown flatter, which was strange, considering how famously hilly Alara was supposed to be. But according to Eptos, they'd entered 'the goddess cleft.' When she asked what that meant, the man had paled like a ghost, forcing a laughing Merin to answer.

"Ignore him," Merin had said. "Even with all those kids, the man's still a prude. The cleft is like…cleavage," he said, running a finger down the middle of his chest. "Only the mother's breast — the 'goddess' — can give life. You have Ageleat in the north," he said, wiggling the fingers on his left hand, "and Alara in the south." He wiggled the others before clapping his hands together. "In the middle, you have nothing. No breast means no life — only dust."

She'd giggled, mostly at how bashful Eptos was, though she personally liked the metaphor. She was after just such a life-giving goddess, after all. Still, sacred cleavage or not, this place *was* desolate. They hadn't seen a single town or village, and most of their nights had been spent sheltering in creek beds, anything to get a bit of cover by the road. For her, there was still a symphony in the plains — bushes, rocks, and tiny critters singing from the thickets — keeping her from feeling so alone in all that nothingness.

The next hour passed in much the same way. Besides staring at the view, she spent some time reading and even tried sketching a bit in her notebook — poor excuse for an artist that she was — in an attempt to capture the beauty of the plains. She was leaning over her lap, clutching her pencil when the others began to mutter in Narala. She opened herself to the songs, just catching the end.

"...think they own the bloody place," Merin was saying, "even out here."

She was about to ask what they were talking about when she saw a break in the horizon ahead of them, a dark square shape lifting out of the plains.

"What is that?" she asked.

"Finally reached a station," Eptos said, pointing to the west. She craned her neck, catching the glint of metal as the lonely stretch of train tracks came into view. Berill owned the trains, of course, but would they own all the stations too?

"Are there...Berillai officers there?" she asked, trying not to gulp.

Eptos met her eyes, waving a hand with a smile.

"There are," he said, "but you should be fine. Just a bunch of bumpkins waitin' to take our money. I don't think they send the sharpest ones to the middle of nowhere if you catch my drift."

She nodded, squinting toward the horizon as she tried to make out...well, anything through the dust. She'd spent so much time worrying about Vilodai, she'd almost forgotten there were plenty of her own countrymen willing to kill her, no magic required! She could just make out the dark shadows of people moving about, but it was impossible to tell anything about them.

"There's no way to avoid the station?" she asked.

"Not with this much cargo," Merin said. "They lined the stations up with all the major roads. Even if we could bushwhack on the way there, they'd wanna see how many customs stamps we had on our way back."

She took a deep breath, trying to find that fleeting calm again. Everything would be fine; it had to be. Like Eptos said, this was the middle of nowhere. The Thorns knew they were on the run, of course, but they had no way to know where they were headed, no reason to suspect they'd be heading south. But when she didn't say anything, Merin turned, giving her the same look Eptos had. Apparently unsatisfied by the little smile she gave him back, Merin turned more fully on the bench, gently taking her by the shoulder.

"Why don't you pop in the back and give yourself a…makeover? They won't think twice about another Ekosinaran sitting back here, eh?"

She blinked in surprise. Arkesht had said his crew was okay with Shapewalkers, but she still hadn't thought their situation was common knowledge. Of course, they'd have to have some kind of reason to join a caravan to the middle of nowhere… Still, it felt strangely heartwarming to have her Shapewalking simply be.

"Thank you," she said, flashing him a much wider smile as she slipped into the back.

She crouched down between the stacks of leather, her mind zipping through forms, though none of her usual ones seemed like the right fit. Seriai was Berillai too, obviously, and Nela, despite being Anushai, seemed too old to ride on a caravan. The best thing would be to match the crew, but who could she use from Ekosinar?

As she ran her mind over everything she'd seen in Ageleat, somehow, she found her memory full of songs. Each image filled her mind with music as if it were right in front of her again. Maybe that shouldn't have come as such a surprise, worshipping a goddess of memory… But until now, she'd only thought of the songs as something there one moment and gone the next. Still, that seemed to infinitely increase her choice of disguises, like moving the needle on a phonograph to any song she chose.

As she listened, the snippets of songs around her in the present rushed in too, competing for space in her mind. One of them grabbed at her, and she opened her eyes, realizing it was Eptos. His melody seemed to circle around a lovely woman — an extremely *pregnant* woman — who had to be his wife waiting for him back home. She could hear snippets of her song, too, her name — Serolan — bubbling up inside her. There was a sort of…tugging from Essomuai, Serolan's song growing almost giddy as it swirled around the baby growing inside of her.

Well, alright then, she thought. Nothing would be easier than stepping through a door Essomuai was already excited about. She took a deep breath, putting all her focus on the song within the song, the glow rushing to surround her.

She blinked her eyes open, finding herself transformed. She looked at her hair, silky and flaxen, picking up a strand and rubbing it through her fingers. It was so soft! But as she looked down, her eyes widened as she took in her giant belly. She'd known Serolan was pregnant, obviously, but for some reason, she still hadn't expected herself to be… Hesitantly, she reached down, running her hand over its beautiful curve as she felt a kick, nearly jumping clear out the back of the wagon.

She chuckled nervously, struggling to her feet. That kick sprouted about a billion questions in her mind, but there wasn't much time to ponder the mysteries of Essomuai before they reached the station — not to mention how little use there had ever been in wrapping her mind around an infinite god. She shook her head, waddling back to her bench. Eptos was still focused on driving the horses, but Merin looked back, his eyes nearly popping out of his head. As he regained his bearings, he finally started to chuckle, hitting Eptos on the arm.

"Hey, Ep," he said, "don't pit your olives or nothin', but you're gonna recognize Sumi here."

Eptos moved the reins to one hand, raising an eyebrow at Merin as he swiveled around in his seat. As soon as he set eyes on Sumi, though, his jaw dropped open, starting as he recognized her. He reached out with his free hand as if hypnotized, stretching his fingers toward her swelling belly. Sumi smiled encouragingly — it was his baby, after all — but he stopped about a foot shy of touching her.

"Sorry," he said, shaking his head as he finally cracked a shy smile. "I forget how real you *xorafetri* look. Arkesht never shows us his shapes."

So that's what they called Shapewalkers in Narala… It was always odd when Essomuai chose not to translate something, but that must mean the name had some significant meaning, like *mu'amashdar* in Amoriai.

"It's alright," she said, "you can still touch my belly if you want."

She left out the fact that she really *was* his wife — at least as far as Essomuai worked. That probably wouldn't help him much… Eptos just laughed, turning back toward the horses.

"That's alright," he said, "I miss her too much to start now. Besides, our turn is almost up."

She looked up, surprised to find they were already pulling into the station. It wasn't much larger than a small house, though they'd still fashioned it like a barracks. The walls were of thick quarried stone, and the sea snake of House Berill was waving from a flag on the roof. Out here, in this beautiful countryside, the building felt nothing like home — it felt like a threat. Of course, everyone else on the caravan had learned to fear her people long ago, and for her, it was only luck that had kept her from feeling it before now…

She took her seat on the wagon bench, clenching her fists. This was what she had to change. Images of King Rummon floated up from her dream — his sword in hand, the blood-covered stone. Even worse, though, his dream had largely come true. His armies now stood on foreign lands, their swords demanding customs from people that were not their own. And yet…

Essomuai had shown her Elomikarus first, the Berillai being banished from their true home, a place that, in truth, wasn't that far to the west. In some ways, Vilodai had been justified in returning her people to the Continent. But she'd succeeded *eight hundred years* ago, and still, the violence continued. No one should have to be afraid in their own country, a foreign flag hanging from their train stops. She'd have to survive facing Vilodai first, but…she had to change this, she just had to.

The wagons pulled off the road onto a long strip of paving stones. There was a matching one on the other side where another caravan was stopped on their way north. Navy-clad guards moved slowly in pairs, circling wagons and climbing in and out, inspecting the cargo and interviewing the passengers. It was…quite the operation. The train tracks were just ahead, cutting behind the outpost. There was no train at the moment, but dozens of other inspectors were standing there, perhaps waiting for one to come through.

As she watched the guards crawling over the caravans, her pulse started to throb in her throat. She had to stay calm. The guards had no reason to be suspicious, right? Even if the Thorns had broadcast their descriptions this far out, they'd be expecting three Berillai together, not a pregnant woman with her husband.

She craned her neck, trying to get a look at the others, but she couldn't see a thing past the other wagons. Still, even if Parimu hadn't changed his form, just one Berillai sitting separately shouldn't be enough to match their description. Everyone just needed to stay calm and act naturally, herself included… She took a deep breath, forcing her eyes to stop darting around.

The guards finally approached the caravan, a half-dozen of them moving up to the first wagon. One pair looked to be interviewing the drivers while the rest crawled around the merchandise. She closed her eyes, stretching her awareness as far as she could as she listened for Erso and Parimu in the muddle of songs. Finally, she found Erso, the familiar deep sound like a tuba. Only…its tempo had picked up, fear and agitation infecting its rhythm. She gulped, suddenly remembering he'd taken his musket with him. He was too brave for his good sometimes, and he may very well decide to fight dozens of guards if he thought she was in danger…

There had to be a way to tell him she was alright. Her mind raced, fumbling through everything she'd ever learned about Shapewalking. There was that lesson they'd done in Amoriai, sending auras to each other, but they'd been touching then, somehow making the link through Mu'lalat. But that was before she had Essomuai… What was Mu'lalat really but a way to understand the light connecting them all?

Essomuai, she prayed, *please help me tell Erso that I'm alright. Please, please.*

Suddenly, a word came into her mind — *ressarelanumai.* That was…the goddess tongue, like she'd heard in her dreams twice now. It put an image into her mind of a mother swaddling a baby — calm, peace, it seemed to mean.

Keeping her eyes squeezed shut, she spoke the word in her mind over and over, calling to Erso with all her might, speaking it to his song. For a moment, she thought nothing had happened, but then, his song slowed, calm washing through it until he was back to normal. She couldn't see him, though the guards were moving down the line again. And whether it was the magic or luck, it was better than doing nothing.

She closed her eyes again, listening for Parimu's song. At first, she was worried she wouldn't find it until she heard another strangely familiar song. It was rhythmic, like the pounding of iron against an anvil… Parimu's father! So he'd disguised himself too. She listened closer, finally hearing his own song underneath, hidden but still present. She breathed a sigh of relief. The guards were already well past him at the front of the caravan, but she still spoke the word to his song before slumping against the bench, breathing a sigh of relief.

Sheyol, she prayed, thanking Essomuai, *sheyol, sheyol.* Everything would be alright.

The guards continued their search — mostly digging through the leather — though the interviews were going by more quickly than before. It was awfully invasive… If they paid the customs — which they shouldn't even have to in their own country — shouldn't they be allowed to leave? What did they expect to find in all those stacks?

Finally, they made their way to her wagon at the end, four men marching past to search the back before the questioning even began. She didn't have anything to hide, but it was still a struggle to sit there, acting calm while she worried they'd tear apart her letters. She glanced at the officers who remained, their eyes shaded by their caps, though they were frowning underneath closely cropped mustaches. One moved his eyes over a ledger while the other stared hard at Eptos.

"Anything we should know about on this wagon?" he asked in Berillai.

"No," Eptos said, sounding out the words as carefully as he could. "Nothing."

"Alright," the guard said, glancing toward the back, "we'll know soon enough."

He turned to Sumi, narrowing his eyes.

"You his wife?" he asked, though it didn't come out much like a question.

She panicked, a lump forming in her throat. She couldn't very well answer in perfect Berillai, but open to the songs, she was just as scared she'd accidentally speak in Narala. She swallowed hard, adopting her best Nela impression.

"I…wife," she said, nodding.

"Hard road for a pregnant woman, no?" he asked, cocking an eyebrow at her.

"Yes, *preg-nant*," she said, smiling. "Stay…husband."

The man stared at her for another second, but then, thankfully, he laughed.

"We should all be so lucky," he said. "Right, Kerald?" he asked the man with the clipboard, nudging him with his elbow.

The man grunted in reply, writing something on his ledger before moving to the back to join the others.

"Alright," the first guard said, nodding at them, "carry on. Keep your eyes open out there, lots of bandits on this road."

After a few more excruciating minutes, a whistle blew, a guard at the front waving their caravan back onto the road.

______

She waited a good hour — the station long disappeared from the horizon — before she waddled into the back to change her form. As she emerged, she found Erso and Parimu walking toward her, the wagons rumbling slowly past as they ambled to the back of the line. When they saw her, Erso started clapping.

"There she is, the world's greatest Shapewalker!" he called out. "Take a bow for us!"

She cocked an eyebrow at him but gave him a little curtsy, fanning out her dress. They hauled themselves up onto the wagon, cramming onto the tiny bench. Erso was all smiles, though he seemed…tense still. Maybe the train station had been more stressful for him than she'd realized?

"What's all this about, then?" she asked.

"Your message, of course," Erso said, Parimu nodding eagerly beside him.

"Oh, good," she said. "I honestly wasn't sure if you'd be able to hear it, but I wanted you to know I was alright."

"Oh, we heard it," Erso said.

"It was the darnedest thing," Parimu agreed, shaking his head. "I saw a picture of you in my mind, touching my shoulder. And suddenly I felt…calm."

"I've only ever heard of a few people who can send words," Erso said, "and that's still only when they're touching the person. How'd you manage it?"

"I'm not really sure," she said, shaking her head. "I guess I…spoke to your song? I used one of those goddess words, so I guess the image still came through in a way."

"It's an odd feeling," Erso said. "That's what it's like in your dreams?"

"Sometimes," she said, nodding, "if a goddess speaks to someone, anyway. I don't quite understand it myself, but it puts the idea right into your head."

"I guess I'd better watch out," Erso said, chuckling. "One day I'll be at the pub, and bam! You're speaking right into my brain, telling me to get home at once. At least we might actually have a shot at surviving this whole thing, seeing as you're all powerful and all."

"I don't know about that," she said, rolling her eyes. "Essomuai does all the work."

"Sure, sure," Erso said, patting her on the back as he dug out his pipe. "Humble, too," he added to Parimu. "If she won't revel in her success, I will. How about a smoke?"

"I have to agree," Parimu said, handing over his pipe as he grinned.

"Oh, right!" she said, remembering his song. "What about you, Relsenair? I felt you turn into your father; the guards didn't give you any trouble?"

"Nope," he said, patting the breast pocket of his jacket. "I still have those factory orders from the Queen. I guess they bought it, just had to make sure I wasn't wearing my usual face."

"What's all this?" Merin asked, turning around.

"We're celebrating getting past the guards," she said, grinning. "Free smokes on Erso, so you better grab some before he gets stingy."

Apparently, they'd spoken in Amoriai because Erso shot her a look as he lit his pipe.

"You heard the lady, gents," he said. "Go ahead and pass me the pipes. Like the saying goes, if you're gonna drink when you're crying, you better drink when you're glad."

She smiled, turning to the horizon as a cloud of blue smoke drifted past her. In the distance, she could just make out the beginnings of the Alaran mountains. There was no telling what waited for them beyond that, but she had the songs, and she would follow them to the end.

23

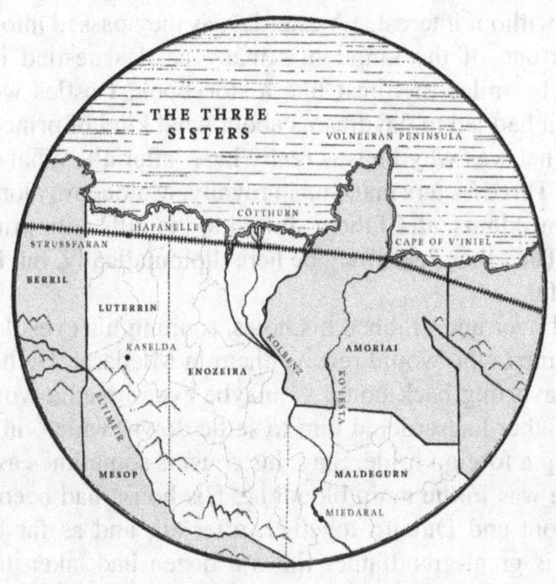

For centuries, we have followed the seven moon pattern of Umilai to serve the Houses. And yet, we now find ourselves in a time of change. Henceforth, the rotation of the sisters shall be chosen by Houses Berill and Pont, a doubling of their monthly support of the tower in return.

-Sea Scroll #274
Estimated Date 14 PN

—:—

Twenty-seven Years Ago

Kemarin Pont'dulairn lay in his cabin on the riverboat, one arm draped over his eyes. He should probably be above deck, representing the family and all, but he'd had enough of this bloody traveling. His father's trains still only went as far as the borders of Enozeira — the line to Cötthurn was only about halfway done — so the rest of their journey had been a tiresome blur of carriages and boats. There were some peers on the expedition, but without Father there to scold him, he had feigned a headache and retreated to his room.

Mostly, he was sick of waiting, ready to reach Miedaral and begin the work Father had set out for him. Not that the time on the boat was completely without interest... Yesterday, as they passed into Maldegurn, they'd seen one of the kingdom's many castles nestled in the hills, surrounded by miles of forest like a storybook. Castles were fine, of course, but it had led to daydreams about what kind of princesses might be inside. That was why he was really here, after all. What they lacked in clout, the Three Sisters made up in royalty. Maldegurn alone had some fourteen princedoms, all of them stuffed to the gills with princesses and duchesses. The other Peers may be here diplomatically, but he was here to find a wife.

He rolled over and grabbed his notes, running his eyes down the list of royal women who would receive them in Miedaral. He had done his fair bit of cavorting back home — maybe even loved a woman or two — but his father had ordered him to settle down, which, in his family, meant taking a foreign bride. Sure, his cousins sometimes avoided their duty, but he was in the main bloodline. His house had been formed by marrying Pont and Dulairn together, after all, and as far back as the founding, his great-grandfather times a dozen had taken the defeated Mesop princess as his wife.

That, more than anything else, was the key to their strength. Berill was the most powerful kingdom on Wellonai, of course, but it was *his* family moving it forward, making progress precisely because they refused the prejudice so common in the others. Building train lines, signing treaties instead of waging wars — all of that required vision. One day, he may even be made King of the Three Sisters once trade smoothed the way for him, but it all had to begin here.

The boat sounded its whistle, and he sprang for the tiny round window in his berth, fogging up the glass as he stared through it. So perhaps he was here for more than duty... After all, like Mother said, it was unbecoming of a man to find no excitement in the prospect of marriage.

Besides, everything they said about Miedaral made it sound like another fairytale — neatly cobblestoned streets winding toward a castle flanked by the Ko'lesta, its waterfalls glittering like sapphires.

Perhaps that last bit was more tale than truth... The water slipping past the boat looked to be the same ruddy color of every other river on the Continent. Still, he *was* excited to find a wife. The Maldegurnian princesses were famous for their beauty, of course, but he was here for more than a pretty bauble or a horse trade. His marriage would be the very root of his soul, unlocking a world of possibility if he chose the right woman. And the choice was entirely his, Father's only stipulation being that he return engaged. For someone of rank, that may as well be a storybook ending. His wife would be here, somewhere, and it was *his* heart that would seek her out.

As soon as they docked, porters had dashed in from all directions like so many ants, carrying valises and crates. After a dizzying burst of unloading and loading again, he finally found himself on a coach heading up to the palace. The white carriages sent from the palace only sat four, so they were left with a small armada rolling up the hill, every eye in the town glued to them. That was the point, of course. Every person in Miedaral would know they were here, and within the week, every other house in the region would know who the Berillai favored.

Like every other princedom in the Three Sisters, the palace had been built on what seemed to be the highest point for miles, the river valley spreading wide on either side of the town before giving way to the endless forest. Unlike the Berillai, Sisters folk seemed to care only for the high ground, the sweeping castles often built on little more than an acre of flat land nestled among the limestone cliffs. Still, they'd learned their business well. The princedoms had wars like the Berillai had dinner, but even if a neighboring prince managed to take your village, he'd lose a good deal of men if he wanted the castle to go with it.

After passing through the village, they reached just such a fortified hill, climbing a cobblestone drive to the top where their caravan wrapped around a large fountain. Unlike some of the other glorified forts, though, the Miedaral palace was immense. They had leveled off the entire hilltop with wide, grassy grounds on either side, the turrets soaring in the air.

As if on cue, an army of palace servants in olive green livery burst from the doors of the palace, flanking the stairwells and bowing in unison. As they rose, a butler stepped forward, facing them from the top of the steps.

"A warm welcome," he said in Berillai, "to our most distinguished guests. If you would kindly follow me into the grand hall, your hosts have prepared a traditional greeting for you."

After the tepid welcome they'd had in the other princedoms, he could hardly imagine what a *traditional* Miedaral one would look like, but most of the peers simply shrugged, wandering toward the doorway. He made sure he was at the tail end. Being the last to enter a room often gave a unique perspective, both of what was to come and what happened in the room you left behind. As if on cue, the moment he stepped away from the carriage, the army of servants descended on the luggage, quickly and methodically coordinating with the Berillai valets as to what went where.

He paused for a moment on the stairs, enjoying the spectacle. Other men didn't seem to care how such things happened, but he had always been fascinated by the efficiency of servants. Their masters may want a new shirt for dinner just minutes from now, but the valets would still somehow have everything unpacked by then. Royals always wanted something, but it was working men who got it done. That was exactly why his family had to succeed, so commerce — and not blood — could become the law of the land.

He followed the others into the hall, a giant stone room with arrow slits for windows and an imposing iron chandelier. Ahead of them, on a wide double staircase that seemed to lead to a ballroom, were the royals of Miedaral. There were some thirty in all, princes and duchesses and everything in between, arranged in a tableau with the women on the right stairwell and the men on the left. In the center was an older couple who must be Lord and Lady Tauschfeig, the king and queen of Miedaral, though, even in his head, he couldn't seem to capitalize the words...

"Gentlemen," Lord Tauschfeig said, sweeping his arms wide, "a most humble welcome to my home. We are so pleased you've decided to join us. We wanted to welcome you in the traditional way of this kingdom — with song."

With a wave of his hand, the men broke out into song, their voices surrounding them as they crashed against the stone walls. They sang in Trierlien, and like everything else in their bloody 'culture,' the song seemed to be about hunting. Hopefully, they wouldn't spend all their time sporting... Every other princedom they passed through had kept them in the field day and night, surrounded by horses and dogs when he'd only come for the women.

He turned toward the other side of the hall, where the more beautiful half of the receiving party still stood watching as the men sang. They were like a cornucopia of somehow varying perfection, like a prism dividing the light. Each of them — all distant cousins, he'd been told — had the same flax-colored hair, like the mountains of grain they'd passed on the barges from Amoriai. They were all cherub-faced, with dimples gracing every cheek, though the vagaries of character still hid amongst a variety of eyebrows and noses. Their heads rose and dipped at different heights, and even the way they stood belied a personality that would hopefully offer some clue as to their prospects.

His eyes scanned down the row, a smile glued to his face. One or two nodded at him when they made eye contact, but none stood out, either. Perhaps none of them— Three-quarters of the way down the row, one woman stood stock-still, no smile on her face. Unlike the others, who had all trellised their hair beyond recognition, hers was in a thick braid. She held her head high, almost defiantly. Their eyes met for a moment, and she neither smiled nor nodded, simply staring back at him, looking through him. Now *that* was intriguing…

Finally, it was the women's turn to sing, their mouths opening in unison. The song was no less of a bore — something about meadowlarks — but he no longer seemed to mind. He stared with no concept of time, watching that woman until the song ended. Suddenly, he was being pulled along, the diplomats corralling everyone to the dining room and an imprisonment of tea and crumpets. The women began filing through the broad double doors, the men shaking hands and clapping each other on the back. He followed in a daze, his eyes carefully watching the unsmiling woman until she disappeared.

Finally, after two long hours of stilted conversation and bitter mountain tea, the party broke up until dinner. The others went to their private chambers to freshen up, but Kemarin found himself wandering the palace, hoping he could track down the strange, unsmiling woman. He hadn't asked directly — he was no novice, after all — but he had at least gotten her name: Elisal Swurdinel. And knowing that… Well, suffice it to say, her story had stood out in Father's briefing book, and it more than explained her dour expression.

She was — or rather, had been — a princess in Rachelar, a middling princedom in the southeast. At any rate, the year before, her father had been murdered by a handful of his liege lords. Even for a backwater, it was quite the scandal. Even worse, with no bloody central command in the Three Sisters, there hadn't been enough willing military resources to take the princedom back. These were Elisal's cousins, so she had moved into the palace in Miedaral, but the bastards who killed her father were still busy feasting in her home, doing plenty of trade to pay for it all.

Most would think her spoiled goods with a grisly story like that, but not him — there was a great deal of value in being down on your luck. If anything, it bred ingenuity. Take Princess Dialasera, for example, only marrying into his family after her people were eviscerated in the Mesop Wars. In spite of everything, she'd had such a keen mind that the family was still benefiting from the savvy moves she'd made before her death. So, in his mind, it only made Elisal more interesting. She may still have a claim to the Maldegurnian throne, however complicated, but more importantly, she might have the grit he'd need to rule the world.

He turned down another identical marble hallway, trying to find the library where Elisal should be.

"Always with the books," Prince Kerand had said.

His brother had agreed, nodding somberly as he nearly whispered, "Like a ghost, she is."

They must be ashamed, unable to avenge her poor father. But more than that, she probably scared them, showing them how precarious their own position was. If someone staged a coup in this palace, would they survive? They were seeking an alliance with the Berillai, after all. Their navy could be up the river in four days and have the palace leveled the next if the cannons were aimed in the right direction.

After a bit more wandering — and directions from a maid — he finally found the large lion statue that marked the library, although simply calling it a 'lion statue' seemed like an understatement. The statue was enormous, featuring a lion curled up on the ground, its jaws firmly around the neck of a flailing deer, its eyes wide in terror. Perhaps this was where the princes met with their enemies…

The library door was like every other, but as soon as he pushed it open, he found a most enchanting place. Three of the walls were covered in books, stacked high enough to have a sliding ladder, while the other wall was covered in windows, the room glowing in the afternoon light. Elisal sat in the furthest chair from the door, her nose in a book, though she looked up as he stepped inside. She gave him a sharp look, returning to her reading without a word.

Unfortunately, that sort of thing only made him more interested. He strolled toward her, running his fingers along the shelves. He picked a volume at random, something with a red cover, and took it to the chair next to hers. He sat down, opening it to a random page.

Hirschel reselntt dendal weald. Sie museln dan, ihrelli gutelk farenz. Ah, right, of course, the books here would be in Trierlien… He spoke a fair amount, enough to trade surely, but perhaps not enough to read. At any rate, the book seemed to be about hunting, which was abominably boring. It was absurd that men sat in the woods waiting for deer when their empires could rise or fall at the sweep of a hand.

"Well, my selection is dreadful," he announced, snapping the book shut and turning toward Elisal. "What are you reading?"

She snorted, perhaps somewhat derisively…looking up with her eyebrows arched. She turned back to her book, but thankfully, she spoke. Her accent had the loveliest tinge to it, just as matter-of-fact and forceful as he'd hoped.

"It is a treatise on a princedom to the south," she said. "I believe you'd find it boring, *Sohnleist*."

That last, at least, he knew to be Trierlien for 'prince.' They probably wouldn't have a proper word for the son of a Peer…

"I think you'd be surprised by what I find interesting," he said, grinning. This little exchange probably wouldn't seem like much to someone else, but he already knew he had her. Disdain was the most easily subverted emotion, even more than rage. He wasn't positive she would love him — that was far too alchemical a process to guess without playing the fool — but she would be his ally, eventually…

She shut her book, letting out a deep sigh.

"I think you will find," she said curtly, "that I am no longer surprised by anything. For ten years, you Berillai have come in droves. You run around the palaces, fill our lodges and shoot our deer. Then, you leave, a few of our women in tow, and you don't come back until it's time to pillage us again. You know nothing of our customs, little of our language, and even less about our lands."

"Yes, quite," he said, leaning back with his hands laced behind his head, staring at the intricate ceiling. "I won't vouch for my countrymen — a bunch of fools, the whole lot of them — but I think you'd find my interests to be less…provincial. For example, I'd wager a guess that the southern princedom *you're* reading about is Rachelar. And based on how new that folio you're holding looks, I'd guess it's an analysis of the bastard that killed your father."

He didn't dare look at her — that would only ruin the game — but from the corner of his eye, he saw her mouth fall open for the briefest moment before she clamped it shut. She sucked in a breath, turning more fully in her seat.

"I don't know who you think you are," she said, her accent thickening with anger, "but you have no right to tell me about—"

"Easy," he said, gently touching her arm. She tensed for a moment, like a skittish animal, before she finally relaxed. "I didn't mean to offend," he went on quickly. "I only mean to show you that I care more about what happens in these kingdoms than my fellows."

This next part was the most important, the threading of the needle that would determine her trust for the rest of their relationship. What she needed to understand was that their interests *could* align. She needed an ally with some backbone, and he needed a local with sharp eyes, someone who saw behind all the princely drivel.

"I mean to rule this place someday," he said quietly. It was a naked truth, but it was the only kind a woman like her would accept. "Call me a despot if you like, though I don't plan to do it by the sword. Still, I'll need friends like you, friends whose eyes aren't clouded by all the foolishness the other Berillai are playing at."

"And why would I ever help the likes of you?" she asked, setting her jaw.

"Because your people have failed you," he said. "Those men killed your father, and your cousins did nothing. They're terrified, holding onto their tiny pieces while they've lost sight of the board. I mean what I say about ruling this place. I don't give a damn about a crown, but the world *will* change. Small men will bow to a different god, the god of steel and commerce. And I promise you, when my train line is finished and I come for this kingdom, I'll personally give you the head of every man who dared touch your father's throne."

Her eyes darted across his face, still cold, but she finally seemed to truly consider him as more than a slug that had gotten beneath her boot. He stared back at her, not even daring to breathe for the one moment that would decide it all.

"Perhaps," she said quietly, "you are more interesting than I'd thought. A fool, but an interesting one."

With that, she stood, putting the book on her homeland next to him meaningfully before she walked from the library. He sat back and smiled. It was beginning, and that was all he needed. Too many men wanted to begin at the ending, rushing ahead as they failed to realize most of the game was won in the first move. The rest simply followed after. He took up the treatise she had left. He was a man of his word, after all, and he likely had a lot of names to memorize if he was to mete out her revenge.

24

—whose border shall not stretch further east than the fork of the Eltimeir River to both the north and south until the Erril Sea and the Mesop forfeiture at Coerendul. All nations of the Erril Basin shall forthwith be free to sign their own treaties, no longer subject to the confines of their kinship with the Northern Empire.

-Excerpts from the Treaty of Trilathdrei
First Page, First Paragraph

—:—

Two days later, Sumi was staring up at the mountains of Alara, the sheer rock sprouting in every direction as the road snaked between the cliffs. Even once the mountains had appeared on the horizon, it had been another whole day across the plains and another following the pass. Today, though, they would finally reach the river and — assuming Arkesht really could find them a boat — start sailing toward Vilodai's Heart.

"You're gonna love Atanas," Erso said from beside her. "Not that we'll be staying long, but the view is amazing."

"Is there anywhere you haven't been?" she asked, turning toward him with a grin.

"Bloody hell, I hope so," he said, shaking his head. "There's gotta be somewhere my face isn't on wanted posters..."

"Sure, sure," she said, pushing his arm.

He still seemed...off somehow, the stress clinging to him since the train station. She was loath to press him on it — she couldn't even

imagine what she'd worry about if she'd been through what he had —
but at least he was joking more today.

"Atanas really is stunning, though," he went on. "The river ends in
this giant lake surrounded by mountains. Whole world seems to pass
through there — sometimes feels like more of a dock than a city — but
the view is really something."

"Interesting…" she said, unconsciously looking to the south as if she
could see the city through the rock. "If it's such a hub, why isn't it the
capital?"

"Too low, I guess," Erso said, shrugging. "Alarans love their
highlands, keeps 'em from rolling around in the garbage with rats like
me."

"*This* is too low?" she asked, gesturing at the rock surrounding them.

"I mean, these mountains are big, sure," Erso said. "But Atanas is
technically still part of the lowlands. The rest of the kingdom sits on one
big slope, and it just keeps climbing until we reach your goddess."

"Wow," she said under her breath, imagining the map in her mind.
"Do you think we'll actually be able to find a boat to take us all the way
there?"

"Should be," he said, "how much gold you got left?"

She didn't have to think to answer. With the river approaching, she'd
started counting their money almost compulsively, as if the number
would change while she wasn't looking.

"Seventy crowns," she said, "and a handful of Anushai."

"That should be more than enough," he said. "I was talking to Arkesht
about it last night. Says there's tons of boats that go south to run down
the Eltimeir, just gotta pay 'em enough to make one hell of a detour, but
that shouldn't be too hard. I swear, though, if we get on one more
contraption, I think I'll break my personal record for modes of transport
on a single trip."

"What's your previous record?" she asked, arching an eyebrow.

"Rode a cow once," he said with a shrug.

"No, you didn't!" she said, laughing as she pushed him again.

"I swear," he said, trying to fend her off as he grinned. "Down in
Mesop, bloke said he couldn't spare a horse."

Merin turned around from the driver's bench, a grin on his face.
Finally used to the dance, she opened herself to the songs just in time
for him to speak.

"You better watch this one in Alara," he said, pointing at Erso. "You
get drunk a lot faster in the highlands."

"I'll keep that in mind," she said, "though I think he could get drunk in a swamp."

"I won't dignify that with a response," Erso said. "Though, in defense of swamps everywhere, they are wonderful places for drinking."

She cocked an eyebrow at that, but Erso folded his arms, keeping the secrets of the swamp to himself.

"I'm gonna miss you two," she said to Merin. "Who's going to make fun of him with me?"

"We'll miss you too, dear," Merin said. "But I don't think you'll have any trouble finding a replacement with him around." He winked at Erso, turning back around.

"Yeah, yeah," he said. "Just hand over your pipes before I forget what an easygoing bloke I am. This'll be your last chance for polis before you lot are stuck smoking bloody olive leaves again."

———

Finally, they reached the end of the road, the hard stone of the pass giving way to smooth paving bricks. The road ended on a bluff overlooking a wide valley, the city spreading out beneath them. It was…incredible. The river wound from the south, emptying into a giant lake that pushed up against the edge of the mountains. The city stretched along the shore, climbing onto every inch of flat land, its massive docks crowded with boats where the river met the lake.

"Wow," Sumi whispered, her eyes struggling to take it all in as the wagons wound their way toward the docks.

"What'd I tell ya?" Erso asked.

She nodded absently, staring at the buildings. They were like something built by a giant child, huge piles of stacked blocks all trying to fit on the little strip of land.

"It's beautiful," she said, "I can't believe this isn't the capital."

"Well," Erso said, "if they decided things on beauty, I'd be king. But just wait 'til you see Puyuln, they call it the 'cloud city.' It doesn't have a lake or anything, but it gives Atanas a run for its money."

As they turned onto the main road, they were suddenly surrounded by traffic, hundreds of wagons scrambling between the city and the docks. It was probably nothing compared to an evening rush in Berill, but after so many days in the wilderness, it came as a complete shock. Eptos barely seemed to notice, though, weaving their wagon into the fray behind the others. Without thinking, she opened herself to their songs, getting lost in the mix of people and places, the whole Continent suddenly distilled in the small stretch of road.

When they reached the docks, their caravan pulled up along a long embankment fronting the river. The crew began to descend from their benches, the familiar stretching and jostling spreading through the group.

"Well," Eptos said, turning around, "I guess we'd better get your bags, eh?"

"I guess so," she said, smiling sadly as she followed the others to the back of the wagon. They hadn't been together all that long, but these men had molded her life to their rhythm, and leaving them felt like being rudely woken from a dream. Unfortunately, even with all the stacks of leathers and olives, it only took a moment before she and Erso had their bags in hand.

"Well," Merin said, scratching the back of his head, "I guess this is it."

Sumi nodded. "Would you mind…if I gave you both hugs?"

Merin laughed. "I think that violates the caravan tough guy code, but I wouldn't miss my chance."

Eptos blushed but nodded. She embraced Merin first, squeezing his stiff leather jacket as the scent of caravan — smoke, sweat, and dust — filled her nose for the last time. Erso stepped up after her, clasping arms with Merin. They may be too stuck in their manly nonsense to hug, but she still caught him passing Merin an extra bag of polis leaves.

"I'll miss you, Eptos," she said, moving over and hugging him next. "I wish I'd met your wife, but tell her hi for me, alright?"

"Oh, I'll do more than that," he said, patting her shoulders as he pulled away. "You're giving us hope, you are. Just take care of yourself out there."

She cocked her head.

"Hope?" she asked.

He nodded firmly.

"We may not be like you with the…well, you know. But Parimu's been telling everybody about how you're trying to change things, and I figure, if you help the *xorafetri*, you'll help the blokes like us too. So just…don't give up, alright?"

She hardly deserved praise like that. Would she be able to change things? She may be able to speak to Essomuai, but she'd hardly make it ten feet without the others. Still, he felt so sincere. She couldn't let him down.

"I will," she said, nodding. "Thanks for getting us here safely, Eptos. I'll never forget it."

"Yeah, alright," he said, scratching the back of his head like Merin had as he smiled. "You better be off. Boss hates us lollin' about with cargo in a port."

"Okay," she said, laughing. But as she turned, she had to force herself to suck in a deep breath, trying not to cry. She came around the end of the wagon, finding Arkesht already waiting there.

"Well, my lady," he said, making a little bow, "how about we get you a ship, eh?"

"That'd be lovely," she said.

She turned for a moment, running her eyes over the rest of the caravan. Parimu was coming toward them with his own bag in hand, the rest of the crew already scurrying about under Yalkai's orders. With Erso and Parimu in tow, they walked past the other wagons, heading toward the stairs that led to the docks. The men all stopped in turn, raising a hand or calling out their goodbyes before stooping back to the piles of leather. At the second-to-last wagon, they finally passed Yalkai herself, her arms folded and her foot tapping. Still, she turned as they passed, raising a hand.

"Goodbye," she called out. "Good luck!"

"Thank you," Sumi called back, "for everything!"

She was tempted to stop for a hug, but Yalkai didn't seem the type. Still, it felt strange to just leave people behind like this. How did you get used to so many goodbyes? The crew already felt like friends, and seeing as she'd never had that many… She shook her head. She would just have to see them again. She couldn't let facing Vilodai make her feel like this was the end.

She glanced at Erso ahead of her, joking with Arkesht as he pointed at the docks. He never seemed to have any trouble moving on — he'd easily lived in a dozen places a year before they met. He hadn't been able to leave her in the end, but was that right for him? If they survived, could she really ask him to stay in one place? Would he even enjoy that kind of life?

Here she was, trying to cling to a wagon crew she'd just met like all the beautiful things she stared at back home, never willing to let a single building or tree escape. That was probably part of why Essomuai had chosen her, of course. She needed someone who would listen, who would remember her people's pain. And she *would* remember. Only…how could she ever ask Erso to carry that burden with her?

She didn't have much more time to think on it, their little group suddenly surrounded by ships as they stepped down onto the docks. Arkesht moved quickly between them, pointing at large crests painted on their hulls as he tried to find the captains he knew. They all seemed to be of the same type, long and skinny like the barges in Ekosinar, but with high sides and thick metal hulls. The decks all had tall cabins in the middle, and funnels were belching smoke into the crisp mountain air. At least the crests made it possible to tell them apart... Each one had a brightly colored painting as tall as she was — animals, flowers, and knights, all bursting out of shield-shaped crests.

About halfway down the first stretch of dock, they stopped beside a dark green boat with a raccoon painted on it. The gangplank was down, but they didn't climb it. Instead, Arkesht reached out, yanking on a bell attached to the side.

"Serkot!" he called out. Was that 'hello' in...Alaran maybe? She shook her head. When had she left the songs behind? It was getting harder to remember when she drifted in and out these days, especially after her time on the wagon, casually letting them in every time a crew member spoke... She reopened herself, the many songs of the docks rushing back in just as a sailor poked his head over the side of the hull.

"Yes?" the man asked, lifting his eyebrows, a large earthen jar in his arms.

"Your captain on?" Arkesht asked. "I'm Arkesht, blue sevens. Looking to send some friends up the river."

"Sure," he said, "I'll go get her."

A moment later, a stout woman appeared at the edge of the ship, her eyes popping open when she saw Arkesht.

"Cerranis!" she shouted, coming down the gangplank and clasping arms with Arkesht. "How are ya, you old bastard?"

"Fine, fine," he said, nodding with a big smile on his face.

"You need to move some leathers or something?" she asked.

"A few," he said, "probably gonna offload at least half here before we go for wine in the East Hills. But I was actually hoping you could take a few friends south for me? Paying friends, mind."

The captain seemed to notice them for the first time, running her eyes over them and their luggage.

"Could probably fit a few more," she said, turning back to Arkesht. "Where they going, Puyuln?"

"Bit further, I'm afraid," Arkesht said. "Southern mountains."

The captain actually guffawed, covering her mouth as she laughed.

"Sorry," she said, catching her breath. "Just caught me by surprise. There's nothing down there, and it's an extra five hundred miles. Bloody cloud king's beard, why would anyone wanna go down there?"

She didn't address any of them with her questions, though, of course, she probably didn't think they understood Alaran...

"This one's a botanist," Arkesht said, pointing a thumb at her. "Lookin' for some kind of plant, I guess. But they're good guests, everybody loved 'em on the wagons."

"Sorry, my friend," the captain said, shaking her head. "You know I love doing business with you, but I don't think I can swing it. Gotta get this vinegar to Mesopyn by Erikon at the latest."

"No problem," Arkesht said, leaning in and clasping the captain's arm again. "Just go see Yalkai if you want a couple olive crates for the trip, eh?"

"I will," she said, nodding. She looked them over again, nodding when her eyes met Sumi's. Then she was heading back up the gangplank, muttering something to herself about plants that didn't sound much like a compliment.

"Well, not this one," Arkesht said with a shrug. "It'll be tough, but we'll find somebody. There's a Mesop fort south of the fork at Kerat, so worst case, we'll still get you a good bit more south than you are now. Let's try again."

They continued down the dock, finding more of Arkesht's friends the further they went. They stopped at dozens of boats with crests of hares, nightshades, and twirling ivy. Every captain seemed genuinely happy to see Arkesht — which wasn't a surprise, of course — but they only got more refusals. No one else laughed, thankfully, but they got plenty of strange looks. Maybe they should have thought of something more believable than being a botanist...

After snaking their way through all of the docks on the north side of the river, they crossed over a high bridge to the other side. She tugged on Erso's sleeve, whispering to him.

"You think maybe nobody'll want to take us?"

"Could be you, looking all suspicious," he said, glancing at her. "I'm sure I'll be able to hitch a ride, though."

She raised a hand to smack him when he threw up his arms in surrender.

"Only kidding!" he cried out, grinning. He swept his arms over the rest of the docks, the ones on the south side of the river stretching even further down the lakeshore. "There's hundreds of boats here. Don't worry, somebody'll want our coin."

"We still have enough left for new horses," Parimu offered. "We'll get there one way or another."

"You're right," she said, picturing the map in her mind. "It's not that much further than Anushai to Ageleat was, right?"

"About the same distance," Erso said, scratching his chin. "Gotta watch out for tigers, though."

Sumi whipped her head toward him.

"They have tigers down there?" she asked, biting her lip. They were just giant cats, right? Just like Amis. Although, if she remembered correctly, they also had wicked teeth and claws...

"Supposedly," Erso said, shrugging. "I've never gone far enough to find out. Of course, they'd probably eat you first, sweet as you are."

She rolled her eyes, turning to Parimu, who was instead nodding as if the topic were sensible.

"Tigers are nothing to worry about," he said. "I've never gone that far south either, of course, but we had plenty of practice with bears on shore days in the navy. Just have to keep a nice smokey fire going all night. Besides, the horses would smell a predator like that a mile off."

"You lot are a bunch of doubters," Arkesht said, shooting them a stern look, "have some bloody faith! We got a dozen docks left, I'll work my magic yet."

They walked all the way to the end, turning left onto an outer dock that sat on the lakeshore. The first boat there was flying an odd pink flag with an even odder sigil — a badger with its teeth bared, about to chomp down on a mouse.

"See?" Arkesht said, shaking his finger in the air. "Knew this bastard would be here. If anybody'll take you to the middle of nowhere for some coin, it's Verasa."

He quickly rang the bell, rubbing his hands together as they waited for a crew member to come. After a minute, a short, stout man with a grey walrus mustache stuck his head over the side. He scoffed when he saw Arkesht, immediately coming down the gangplank.

"Well, I'll be damned," he said in Berillai. She might not have realized, being open to the songs, but his accent had carried through. She couldn't quite place it, but he was decidedly not Berillai. He marched down the gangplank until he reached the end, where he stood with his fists on his hips.

"Come to sell me more of those lousy olives?" he asked.

"No, no," Arkesht said, smiling. "Got something better for you — paying passengers, heading to the southern mountains."

"Ha!" he yelled, barking more than laughing. She felt her neck get hot, bracing for the shame, but instead of telling them how foolish they were, Verasa simply narrowed his eyes. "You said paying, eh?"

"Of course," Arkesht said, "they paid me to get 'em here from Ageleat, Berillai sovereigns, too."

The man scratched his chin, nodding as he sized them up.

"Only got a bunch of Relimoran clay on board, so it won't go bad or anything — not like those stinking untreated leathers you sold me two years ago."

He laughed, which Arkesht echoed, apparently fine with his description of his goods.

"Why you going down there?" he asked, suddenly looking right at Sumi.

"We're, uh…looking for plants," she said. "I'm a, uh…botanist?"

"Well, that's a bloody lie," he said, "but that's fine. How much you paying?"

"Oh," she said, biting her lip. What was she supposed to do, just name her price? They only had so much money…

"How about thirty sovereigns?" she asked.

"Hmm," he said, tapping his fingers together. "You probably won't cost me the contract on the clay, but the bloke who bought it wants it in Berill by the end of the month."

"Berill?" she asked, her eyes lighting up. "We're heading there after the mountains if you can take us the whole way."

"I'll do it for fifty," he said simply. "It'll cost us three days to get down there and two back to the fork. So I can only give you…one day in the mountains. That work for your *plants*?"

She gulped — that was two-thirds of their money! But if they could get all the way home… She had no idea if one day was enough or not for what she had to do, but even if he left them, at least they'd be at Vilodai's Heart. Luckily, Arkesht spoke up.

"Now, these are friends," he said, pointing a finger at the captain. "For fifty, it's gotta be separate bunks and hot meals, alright? And if you leave 'em early in those bloody mountains, I'll make sure you're pulled off the guild list."

"Works for me," the captain said, turning back to Sumi. He flashed her a sly grin, holding out a hand. "We got a deal, m'lady?" he asked.

"Deal," she said, taking his hand.

"Good, good," he said. "Let's just do half now and half in Berill, eh?"

"Um…sure," she said, reaching for her wallet.

"You can pay on the boat," he said, raising a hand to stop her. "It never does to wave money around the docks."

He nodded at the others before taking Arkesht's hand.

"This better be easier than olives, my friend," he said.

"Oh, much easier," Arkesht said. "These three are good people, like family. You get 'em there safe, and I'll give you a free crate of leathers next time."

"We'll see about that," Verasa said, laughing. "Alright, you lot, let's get you on board."

Without a second glance, he turned on his heel and marched up the gangplank. She looked at the others.

"Well," Erso said, shrugging, "we got a boat. Guess we better get on with it, eh?"

"Yeah, I'd get on if I were you," Arkesht said, chuckling. "Verasa doesn't like to be late, and he'll hold you to that one day in the mountains too. You'll be safe with him, though. Write to me when you can, yeah?"

She nodded, smiling.

"We will. And thank you, Arkesht. For everything."

"My pleasure," he said, stepping in for a hug without her needing to ask. "Erso," he said, nodding as he pulled away. "Good to see you again, mate. I'll sleep a lot better knowing you don't got a favor on me anymore."

"Me too," Erso said, laughing as he clapped him on the shoulder. Parimu stepped up, giving him a formal bow before shaking his hand.

"Thank you for having me on," Parimu said.

"Pleasure was all ours," Arkesht said with a grin. "You're a pretty easy rider, Mr. Parimu. Don't think I've ever seen a paying guest do so many dishes."

"Until next time," Erso said, touching the brim of his hat as he stepped onto the gangplank. "Not many people are unlucky enough to see me twice, but let's hope you get a third, eh?"

"Yeah, yeah," Arkesht said, turning back toward the caravan, letting go as easily as Erso did. As she reached the gangplank, he turned back just once, shouting over his shoulder, "Just don't come back before you marry the girl, you damned weasel!"

Erso raised his hat in the air, disappearing over the edge of the boat. She tried to watch Arkesht leave, but soon he was lost in the traffic of the docks. As she came aboard with Parimu, Verasa was nowhere to be seen, but a younger man was standing by Erso, waiting for them.

"Hello," he said with a nod. "I'm Üvatel, Verasa's first mate. He wanted me to show you to your berths."

"Great," she said, "thank you."

"Don't thank me yet," he said, chuckling as he turned away, motioning for them to follow.

"Warm welcome," Erso whispered.

They walked past the looming central cabin where they finally caught sight of Verasa, shouting at a man holding the boat's wheel. They came around the back of the cabin where a large afterdeck opened up before wide metal stairs that ran down into the belly of the boat. There were more crew members back there, some fiddling with ropes as others carried large jars down the stairs.

"Alright," the first mate said, pointing at the deck directly beneath him. "The hold is right beneath us, so try to stay out of the cargo. Mess hall is beneath the wheel room; meals are at seven, two, and seven. Feel free to come up here and pass time on the deck. The men aren't too talkative — mostly contractors — but they're harmless. Just try to stay away from the ropes. Any questions?"

It seemed distinctly unlike the familial crew Arkesht ran, but it was straightforward enough. And at least they'd be on their way to the mountains…

"No," she said, shaking her head quickly, "no questions."

"Good," Üvatel said, nodding. "I'll get you to your berths, and you can give me the first half of the payment. We'll be getting on the river soon."

He turned sharply again, heading down the metal stairs.

"Well," Sumi said, looking at the others, "here's to the next adventure, eh?"

"Oh, yes," Erso said, chuckling. "This will most definitely be adventurous."

They followed into the hold, just paying guests heading to their berths. A goddess may be waiting for them, but for now, they were nothing more than cargo on a boat. But at least they were on their way.

25

Henceforth, no Shapewalker shall legally enter the territory of Berill for any purpose. All consular attachés shall be required to make an oath upon silver to their true form before meeting with any of the signatories herein.

-Excerpts from the Treaty of Trilathdrei
First Page, Second Paragraph

—:—

The boat pushed its way upriver, the engine belching smoke that drifted over the back of the barge where Erso sat with Parimu. They were still winding their way through Alara, the river the only remotely smooth thing in the hilly country. In the distance, he could just make out the edge of Puyuln, the capital sitting on the edge of a giant cliff. Buildings spilled down the hills on either side, the famous wineries taking up every other inch of green space in the area.

The wineries… Now that was enough to make your mouth water. He was still jealous of the night Sumi and E'loseir had snuck off and cracked that bottle of cloud wine. If only they had time to bloody stop! Verasa said they'd only have an hour for a cargo swap, but maybe there was some way he could bribe the greedy little bastard? If only he could convince—

"And then what do I do?" Parimu asked, jerking Erso back to attention.

"Er, sorry, mate," he said, pulling his pipe out of his mouth. "Got a little dreamy there looking at the wineries."

Parimu poked an eye open, sucking in a sharp breath as he noticed the

city. Well, at least the view could distract him from the poor teaching…
He was supposed to be helping Parimu break the block on his
Shapewalking, but the man was still struggling something awful, passing
long minutes between each instruction, sitting like a statue with his eyes
closed. With the city on the horizon, he'd more or less forgotten he was
teaching in the first place…

"I've never been," Parimu said, still looking at the jagged lines of the
city's cliffs. "It really is the cloud city, isn't it?"

A wide puffy cloud had floated through the valley and was crossing
over the city, the tips of the buildings shrouded in mist.

"Sure is," he said, nodding. "Never gets too hot up there, either.
Makes me wish I could bottle those clouds and take 'em with me.
Though, I guess that's what the cloud wine is for."

Parimu looked at him with questioning eyes. No, the man probably
hadn't ever had cloud wine before… Not a self-indulgent one, Relsenair
Parimu. He supposed there was a lesson in that — he certainly never
missed a chance to indulge. Although…maybe that was the root of the
problem with his Shapewalking? Running the halls required a
certain…gusto, a zest for life that demanded satisfaction. Parimu
couldn't seem to let go, holding the world so tight to his chest he might
crack it.

"You know," he said, "maybe we take a pause, chat for a bit? My
uncle — bloke who taught me and Sumi — prefers talking over
practicing anyway." He pulled off his hat, running a hand through his
hair. "So…what do you think it is holdin' you back? I see you struggling
when you close your eyes; your face looks like somebody's twisting
your arm."

Parimu clenched his fists, staring down at the deck.

"Don't get me wrong," Erso added quickly, "there's no shame in it —
we've all been there at some point. I just think we ought to talk about
what's holding you back. Shapewalking is about letting go, and until
you're ready to do that, I don't think jumping in the pool will do you
much good, you know?"

Parimu took a deep breath, nodding as he looked back out at the city.

"You're right," he finally said. "It's just all these…regrets. Of course,
I did hundreds of awful things before I realized what I was. But even
before that, there's just so much I wish I could have done differently. I
don't know if I'm just getting old, but it feels like a dozen more regrets
pile up every year." He looked back at Erso, actually grinning for once.
"I suppose you wouldn't know about that yet, still young and dashing
and all that."

Erso cocked an eyebrow at that but said nothing. Unfortunately, his regrets came by the dozen too, and they didn't seem to come with an age requirement.

"Anyway," Parimu went on, "every time I close my eyes to get in the pool, I see something from my past — some awful thing I've done or failed to do. And it just…sucks me in, reminding me why I don't deserve any of this. I mean, I spent half my damn life using these powers to hunt my own kind."

Erso nodded, letting out a sigh. He was no fellerhurn, but he knew what it was like to close your eyes and see ghosts staring back at you. As much as it galled him to admit it, they were more similar than he'd have ever guessed. This was by far the toughest case he'd ever had to take on as a teacher, but surprisingly, he really did want to help the man. Like him or not — and he *was* growing on him, believe it or not — Parimu's loyalty to Sumi was beyond question. So the best thing he could do was make sure this man would be ready to protect her when the time came.

Unfortunately for them both, though, teaching a lesson this serious probably called for some personal honesty, which was obviously not his strong suit… He reached into his pocket and pulled out the tiny tin flask he kept there. It was completely unadorned, not his usual style, but this one was pa's. He had inherited it through Beysal, seeing as though not much of their house remained after the fire. But he had always kept it with him, filled with whiskey more often than not, the same Amoriai brand Beysal and pa used to drink in the evenings.

He took a nip of it and held it out for Parimu, his eyebrows raised. To his surprise, the other man took it, taking a decent pull. Parimu coughed but then let out a contented sigh. 'Fire first and roses after,' as pa used to say — at least, that was how bloody decent whiskey was made back home.

"I understand how regret can hold you back," Erso said, looking down at the water. "I couldn't shape for a month after my parents died. No matter what I tried, I couldn't stop seeing my mother's face when I went to the pool. I tried to push her from my mind, but it only made it worse. She ended up behind every door in the hall. She came in my dreams too, every single night. If I hadn't known her better, I'd have thought she was haunting me from Mu'na'sokar."

"I'm sorry," Parimu forced out, though he sounded like he really meant it. "I…can't even begin to imagine."

"Well," he said, "I got through it, and so will you. But lucky for me, my uncle's a smart guy, and I just ended up taking his bloody advice like

I always do. He told me to talk to her, all the time, whenever I was alone. I'd close my eyes, find her wherever she was in the halls, and have a conversation. I'd imagine what she said back, mumbling that part back to myself."

He chuckled, taking another nip from the flask.

"Probably looked like a fool, to be honest, but it really did help. I stopped pushing her away, so she didn't have to force herself in front of me. I think our regrets needle us because they're afraid we'll forget, you know? As if whipping ourselves is the only way to prevent it happening again. But talking to her, I could let go just a little. She'll always be there in my mind — my *mu'seris* as we say back home — but it doesn't stop me anymore."

Parimu looked out at the river, nodding as he listened, his jaw clenched. The man might not think this story had anything to do with him — their regrets must seem awfully different from the outside. Still, he'd had enough regret to know it all worked the same. You were carrying around your pain but didn't think you deserved to feel it, so it held you down like an anchor.

He offered Parimu the whiskey again, which he took, looking grateful even as he coughed again. Erso took another nip himself before speaking.

"I know you probably don't think you deserve it, but you need to find peace. These things you've done, they're a part of you now, whether you like it or not, and you have to look right at 'em. Whatever we've done or failed to do, it's brought us to this moment, with this woman, and she needs us. I guess that's what Essomuai's all about, right? She still wants our songs, broken as we are. Like my uncle says, Essomuai could spend a lifetime as a flower or a cockroach, and she'd love 'em both the same."

Parimu turned, their eyes meeting.

"Thank you," he said. "For everything — being willing to train me, for being so honest. I don't deserve it, but I'll do my best to do right by you both."

"I know you will," Erso said. "This may not sound like a compliment, but I thought I'd hate you, and I don't — and I can't even hear your song. But Sumi's right about you; just hold onto that."

He stood from the wooden railing, hesitating for a moment before taking the man's shoulder.

"I'm gonna go to the front of the ship now, but I want you to try what I said. Think about the people you've failed, the people you've hurt, the people you miss. Just talk to 'em. You'll be carrying them the rest of your life, but the load doesn't have to be so heavy."

Parimu nodded again, and he turned to go. Even over the wind and the rush of the water, he thought he could hear the man begin to talk, looking his past in the eye. What about him? Could he still take his own advice? He saw Sumi ahead, standing at the front of the ship as she stared up at the city. He'd gotten good enough at facing his past to keep living, but that felt like a long way off from deserving Sumi.

She turned and saw him — bloody song probably giving him away — and waved him over. He forced a smile onto his face. He *would* serve her; he could still do that much. But if he would ever be good enough to be more to her, it might take a hell of a lot of talking to ghosts.

26

So too are no two stones alike, neither in shape nor size. Yet another sister studies this phenomenon, though with equally mixed success. I truly hope by the time the next scroll is unfurled we'll have an answer, though it is my duty as the Steward to give an honest assessment of the research as it stands.

-Sea Scroll #92
Estimated Date 403 PN

—:—

An hour later, they'd finally wormed their way through the river traffic to the other side of the city, docking at the port on Puyuln's southern edge. While the northern side ended in a sheer cliff, the south was one long, gentle hill, climbing higher and higher to where the dark stone of the old city wall stretched up into the sky.

Apparently, the docks were paid for by the hour because the moment they docked, Verasa had started shouting about the crew costing him money with their dillydallying. Erso was itching to have a look around, of course, but it was probably for the best. As soon as he stepped on land, he knew he'd be sniffing out the first bottle of cloud wine he could find. At least he could pass the time with the others, he and Sumi having walked over to find Parimu again at the back of the boat.

"I think I need to go into town," Sumi said.

"What?" he and Parimu asked simultaneously.

"I think I need a map," she said. "You heard those captains in Atanas — they practically choked when they heard where we wanted to go,

193

nothing down there but jungle… I can follow the songs to an extent, but I think we'll need something better. Puyuln is the last big city we're going to pass through, and if anyone makes maps of the south, it'll be the Alarans, right?"

"Not a bad point," he said, nodding. He tried to picture the vast nothingness supposedly waiting for them down south. In his mind's eye, it just looked like more of the woods they'd already passed through, but of course, it'd be even bigger than that — not to mention being filled with mulakerris and tigers… Sumi's magic notwithstanding, it wasn't exactly the kind of place you wanted to wander about.

"I do think we should be careful," Parimu said, glancing around the docks.

"Right," Erso agreed. "It was easy enough getting on a boat in Atanas, but you have to assume the Thorns have more people in a big city like this. Only way I can figure they tracked us in Ageleat was watching for three people together. Only one of us should go."

"I think it should be me," Sumi said. "I need to make sure we get a map I can use."

"Well," he began to say just as Parimu opened his mouth to speak too. Erso chuckled, shaking his head. "What me and the detective are trying to say is that you're too important to risk. Then again, we are also mere simple servants, brutish and blunt in our operations. Is there any way you can describe to me the map you so desire, my fair mistress?"

He earned a hell of an eye roll for that one, but a moment later, Sumi was staring up at the city again, tapping her chin.

"What about a joint transformation?" she asked quietly. "Like you and Beysal did with the elephant, but you know, more subtle?"

"Huh," he said, cocking his head. An image came to mind of joining with Sumi in a bright flash of light. "Do you think you can manage subtle? What with all the…you know." He waved his hands in the air, some approximation of 'all-powerful goddess that has completely overturned my comprehension of magic.'

"I think so," she said, nodding. "What we did was more Essomuai than me, anyway. If we just do a normal transformation while we're connected, it should work. I can still transform on my own without the songs, after all."

"It is nice to think you wouldn't have to be alone," Parimu said. "As long as we're discreet, of course." He pointed to a thick knot of trees just outside the dock gates. "How about over there?"

Sumi looked at Erso, eyebrows raised.

"Are you up for it, my brutish servant?"

"You know me," he said, shrugging, "I'll try anything once. Twice if you ask nicely."

Sumi smiled, dragging them off the boat toward the trees. There was a wide boulevard that ran past the port and up the hill with thick clumps of buildings on either side. It was hard to believe this little patch of forest had been left alone, though it probably fit with the Alarans' overall devotion to greenery, what with the wineries encircling the city and all. As they reached the trees, Parimu stood guard at the edge while he followed Sumi through the thick underbrush until they found a little hollow in the center.

"Alright," she said, hands on her hips. "I think I have someone in mind for our disguise. Do you wanna let go and have me tug you along?"

"Easy enough," he said, extending an arm for them to link like he did with Beysal, but she batted his hand away.

"Oh, please," she said, stepping closer and grabbing him in a hug. That was bold for her! Not that he was complaining... He relaxed, sighing out as he slipped into the embrace. He pictured his pool, imagining himself easing into the water, eager to be carried away on Sumi's currents. He started his own transformation, just enough to open the door to hers. A glow filled the space, and he felt himself growing lighter until they were joined.

He blinked his eyes open, surprised to find himself inside a person's head. He'd only ever done animals with Beysal, somehow always ending up in the rear... But this was something else entirely. He looked down, finding himself in a dress, but he couldn't focus on that for long as a massive wave of sound crashed down on him, like a thousand birds singing at once.

What on Wellonai is that? he thought.

Erso? Sumi's voice said in his mind.

Sumi? he asked back. *Is that you...in my head? Do you hear all that noise?*

She disappeared for a moment, the sounds quieting to a dull hum.

Sorry, she thought to him, *those are the songs.*

This is what you listen to all the time? he thought. *No wonder you get lost in it...*

He tried to focus on them, to see if he could understand them the way she did, but it was still just noise to him.

Well, I didn't expect this. How are we holding this form?

I don't really know, she thought. *I guess we're both letting go enough? It's not like we don't trust each other...*

I guess so, he thought. He must just be too used to Beysal bullying his way into the lead… Still, he suddenly felt exposed, his mind as open as his past was in the songs. What was even the difference between these thoughts and the ones she heard?

They'd kept their eyes closed as they talked to each other inside their head, but he suddenly heard footsteps crunching toward them through the leaves. They forced their eyes open, finding Parimu in front of them, though their eyes felt too wide, like a bug.

"Are you both…in there?" Parimu asked, peering at them. "And who are you?"

"Don't rightly know," Erso said in an unfamiliar woman's voice.

"My mother," Sumi said immediately after. It was strange to feel his mouth moving as Sumi's mind spoke the words, but it was even stranger they could keep the whole thing going…

"Ah," Parimu said, nodding. "I vaguely remember her from your memories now that you mention it… I can see the resemblance, though, she was a handsome woman."

He felt his neck getting hot at the compliment just like Sumi would. How strange! He shook his head. Their head? This had to be the oddest thing yet, goddesses aside. Parimu took out his watch, flicking his eyes over to the ship.

"You two better get going," he said. "I'll go back in case we need to hold the captain, but you only have about three-quarters of an hour."

"Right," Erso said as they both nodded, their head bobbing extra low. *Um…onward!* Erso thought.

They began to walk, but like everything else they'd done, they tried to do it at the same time. It felt like they had too many knees, lifting their legs much too high and sticking their feet too far out before putting them down.

"You may want to sort that," Parimu said wryly, glancing toward the street. "You look like you're trying to burgle a house."

Right, Erso thought to Sumi, *it must be bad if the detective's making jokes. How 'bout you steer the horse, eh?*

Don't call my mother a horse, she thought.

They began to walk normally, one mind moving the legs with no trouble. He completely let go, as he did with Beysal, though it was a good deal more fun watching through human eyes, even if it was a bit uncanny… They waved goodbye to Parimu and were off, picking their way through the trees and back onto the main road.

So, where do you find a map in a place like this? Sumi asked. *You've been here before, right?*

Few times, yeah, he thought, *though not for map shopping.* He moved their hand, pointing down the first street they came to. *Hell of a winery down that way, tint their cloud wine with blueberries, it's just—*

No wine, Sumi thought. *And don't point, we'll look daft!*

I feel pretty daft with you in my head, he thought, chuckling to himself. *What about up there?*

He didn't point that time, using just enough force to flick their eyes toward a booksellers. *Books, maps, same idea, right?*

Good a place to start as any, she agreed, turning their feet toward the shop. It was a cozy little place with a squat tiled roof and wide windows. Oddly, as they approached, he felt a warm sunny feeling filling his mind, like he wanted to hug the building or something. Was this how it felt to see things as Sumi? Sacred halls, no wonder she was such a good person. If his world were this beautiful, he'd be a quarter less debauched, at least!

As they reached the entrance, he caught their reflection in the glass. Her mother really was handsome. She looked a lot like Sumi, if maybe a touch less Berillai. Odd to think he'd ever prefer someone being *more* Berillai, but thankfully, he still preferred Sumi by far. It wouldn't do to fancy your mother-in-law, even if the poor woman was already more than twenty years gone…

They pulled open the door, which had a little chime hanging off it that tinkled as they walked in. There were six or seven rows of books and a large desk in the back. At the sound of the chime, an old man came out from a back room.

This is all you if he speaks Ezimk, Erso thought.

Why did I bring you again? she thought, their mind filling with laughter. He'd really need to be less of an effective teacher with the old verbal jousting…

"Zedairez," the old man said as they walked over. Just then, the songs grew louder again, blocking out everything else. They disappeared just as quickly, but as they faded back to a buzz, the shopkeeper seemed to be speaking in perfect Berillai.

"How can I help, ma'am?" he asked. They ought to take offense at that — Sumi's mother couldn't be more than a few years older than himself, though he only felt a soothing calm from Sumi's half of their mind. *Typical.*

"We…I mean, uh…*I*…am looking for maps," Sumi said. "Do you have any of the south?"

"South of…Alara?" the man asked, raising an eyebrow. "I don't think so. There's not really much down there."

Still, he walked them over to a table where he had a bunch of maps stacked in leather folios. He flipped through a few of them, eventually shrugging.

"Like I said, not much here. Are you going down there?" He eyed them again, Sumi biting their lip.

"No, no," Sumi said, "more of a research project. I'm interested in the mountains."

"Oh," the man said, nodding as if finally satisfied. "Are you Anushai, by chance? I know some of your old legends take place down there, but I don't carry much of that sort of thing. I do have a friend who runs an antique shop in the inner city; he might have something for you."

He held up a finger, dashing behind his desk where he pulled out a piece of paper, hastily scribbling a map. He handed it to them, smiling.

"He's a good friend, tell him Preyu sent you."

"I will, thank you," Sumi said, smiling back warmly. They didn't seem to be in any pain, though it felt like his lips had stretched too far. He felt like he wanted to massage their cheeks, the muscles tight from such an inappropriate amount of happiness. Was that how she got that perfect smile? And what had he been doing his whole life, grinning?

They went back out to the street and looked up at the high walls of the city. The map seemed to follow the hill they were on before curling around the inside of the wall to where the antique shop was marked with an X.

Seems a bit far, she thought. *Do you think we have enough time?*

He took their hand, unconsciously reaching for his pocket watch, but, of course, it wasn't there.

Not sure, he thought back. *Couldn't have been more than a few minutes in there, though. Probably at least a half-hour left?*

Sumi turned them around, looking back toward the boat. They'd made it at least halfway up the hill, so it probably made just as much sense to keep going as to turn back.

Alright, she thought, *let's just be quick, alright?*

They started up the hill, their legs burning as Sumi pushed them forward.

Couldn't have picked somebody with longer legs? he thought. *Not that I'm complaining.*

Shush, she thought. *It was the first thing I thought of. Besides, I've always wanted to try being her.*

No, you're right, it's nice, he thought. *I want to meet all your family at some point, even if it's only through Mu'lalat.*

Just wait 'til we get in our first fight, she thought. *I'll bring Grandpa out to scare you straight.*

He couldn't help but force a gulp down their throat at that.

This probably won't surprise you, he thought, *us both being orphans and all, but I'm not too keen on authority figures.*

Sure, sure, Sumi thought. *They won't be real, mind you, but I can still write to Beysal if you really get out of line.*

I'll be good, I swear, he thought, raising their hands in surrender. An older woman passing them on the street stared at them as Sumi yanked their hands back down.

Quit it with all the gesturing!

She turned their focus back to walking, curling up the left side of the hill where they met the city wall at the cliff's edge. There was a huge arch in the wall there that let them into the inner city, though there were no longer any gates on it. They passed through, where Sumi paused, staring up at the city around them.

It felt like being in a chasm, huge swaths of stone reaching up on either side as the street narrowed, just wide enough for two carriages to pass each other. The buildings were stacked nearly on top of each other as they climbed the hill, the castle on the other side of the city nearly blending in with every other slate-covered roof. Narrow streets branched out from the main avenue like fingers, bending in random directions around the buildings.

This place is like a fairy tale, Sumi thought, pulling out their little map, which pointed them down the first street on their right along the inside of the wall.

It sort of is, he thought back. *No train line, no trouble for Shapewalkers, all the wine you can drink — that's paradise if you ask me.*

They followed the street about halfway down the wall, where they finally spotted the antique shop. It was a tiny cabin-looking building stuck onto a much larger one that looked like a cathedral. The cabin had red roof tiles, and the sides were whitewashed, easily making it the brightest thing on the street. More importantly, there was a sign that read *'Cherkan nad Antichen.'*

They went through a gate and opened the door, stepping into a jumble of seemingly every antique that had ever existed. It was sort of like the bookstore in its layout, assuming the other store had exploded first. There was the semblance of shelves, but they were stacked with mountains of odds and ends, many spilling onto the floor where new piles had formed. There were some books along the walls, though they'd been stacked on top of each other horizontally to make more shelves with globes, vases, and even a skull — that was hopefully not human? — stacked on top.

Sumi wove their way through the various piles, finally reaching the back of the shop where a desk seemed to grow out of the inventory, an older man sitting behind a mostly square-shaped pile. He looked even older than his friend down the hill and had a white walrus mustache. He was looking through a ledger with an open bottle of wine next to him on the desk. It wasn't cloud wine by the looks of the bottle, but even the cheap stuff in Puyuln could send you to the heavenly halls. The Alarans really did have living figured out…

Now, remember, he thought to Sumi, *we're just one person.*

Shut up, she thought, forcing a grin onto their face.

"Excuse me," she said, making the man look up. He blinked behind thick glasses, and their mind suddenly filled with a warm, familiar feeling. Did he…remind Sumi of someone?

"Yes?" he asked.

"Your friend Preyu sent us," she said gently. "He said you might be able to help us find a map?"

"Ah," the man said, nodding, "Preyu, eh? How is the old badger? He doesn't walk up the hill to see me anymore, claims he's too old, but I'm the one going on a hundred!"

It seemed like an exaggeration, though it was hard to tell from the man's face. Still, that kind of longevity didn't hurt his own argument for having a daily bottle of wine…

"Um…he seems well," Sumi said, nodding. "We're looking for an older map, so he thought your shop might do the trick."

"Oh yes, we have the finest antiques!" he said, patting his ledger as if it could possibly hold any information about the snowstorm of merchandise behind them. The man, presumably Cherkan, pushed himself up from his chair, looking a good bit more spry than a hundred.

"Maps, maps, maps," he muttered, shuffling around the desk and into the piles. They followed slowly behind, making a sort of figure-eight as they wound their way through the store. Finally, Cherkan paused at a cubby in a corner. It was like a wine rack, a lattice of wood making little diamond shapes, only instead of bottles, there were rolls of paper.

"Here we are," he said, his breathing heavy. He hiccoughed before clearing his throat and knocking on the thick wood of the cubby. "These are all the maps. What kind did you say you needed?"

"Of the south," she said, "Vilodai's Heart."

"Ah," Cherkan said, "no wonder Preyu sent you to me. That is an odd map…"

"That's what I'm gathering," Erso said with their mouth before he could stop himself. She knit their eyebrows as if shooting him a sharp look, though it mostly just left them frowning at a bookshelf.

"What was that?" Cherkan asked, turning back around and blinking.

"Oh, nothing," Sumi said, smiling warmly as she filled their mind with what could only be described as a warning. Cherkan shrugged, going back to the cubbies.

"No," Cherkan kept saying as he ran his fingers from row to row. "No, not there, either."

Erso couldn't do much to control where their eyes looked, but he let his own mind wander as Sumi watched the shopkeeper patiently. He felt like he was drifting in a dark space behind their eyes, a strange light coming from somewhere to his side. It was hard to tell if he was in his own mind or *theirs,* but he finally snapped back to attention as Cherkan seemed to find something.

"Aha!" the old man shouted, sliding out a short roll of paper. "I knew it was here somewhere. You see, in my day, there was a famous dowager, Lady Kressival — Alaran royalty. You probably wouldn't know her, young as you are." He paused, eyeing them for a moment. "Plus, it seems you're foreign."

Quite the detective, this one, Erso thought. *Tell him to unroll the map. Shush,* she thought back, *or I'll kick you out.*

"Anyway," Cherkan continued, "Lady Kressival had quite the adventurer for a husband. He died young — occupational risk, of course — but he made quite a few maps on his journeys. I went to her manor in Eorosik when she died — quite a scandal with the estate sale they had to have to save the house — but I found a desk full of these maps, and this one stood out."

He finally unrolled the parchment, revealing a rough map done in thickly brushed ink. With all the mountains, it was almost like someone had gotten into a competition to see how many times they could write the letter 'M,' but Sumi was clearly impressed.

"These are the southern mountains?" she asked, their eyes widening as they looked up at the shopkeeper.

"Surely seem to be, no?" Cherkan asked. He pointed to a bit of scribbled writing in the bottom corner. That could very well be what cursive looked like in Ezimk, though next to the mountains on the map, it just looked like the artist had tried to add in some grass.

"This says *Surtesk Viyodash*," Cherkan said. "Basically our name for the big mountain, what you called Vilodai's Heart, I think." He offered the map up to them, and Sumi took it with both hands, staring down at it with their eyes still wide.

"This is amazing," she said, their eyes running over every corner of the map. "How much would something like this cost?"

"Depends," the old man said, his eyes suddenly becoming quite a bit sharper, "what kind of coin do you have? I do a bit of trade abroad, and I could give you a discount for the right denomination if you save me the money changer's fee."

Try the Anushai? Erso thought. *Won't be easy to spend where we're going.*

"Would you take Anushai?" she asked.

"I surely could," the man said, nodding. "Two julens should do."

Their jaw dropped open.

Two julens?! Sumi thought. *I felt bad when you spent three keyeols on those flowers. That's nearly…thirty times that.*

It's your money now, madam, Erso thought back, chuckling, *I just do what I'm told.*

Not helpful, Sumi thought. *Ugh, I hate haggling.*

"Is…uh…the price really so high?" she asked the shopkeeper as a hot flush ran up their neck.

"Well, this is a very *rare* artifact," Cherkan said, "I'm sure a collector such as yourself can appreciate the difficulty of acquiring such pieces."

"Surely," Sumi said. "It's just that I have a long journey ahead of me. What about…uh…one julen and three yeonams?" she asked. "I'm afraid that's the best I can do."

Is that really the best you can do? Erso asked, trying to hold back his laughter. *How's this old man supposed to pay for all that wine?*

Well, I don't want us to have nothing left! she shot back. *Besides, how long was this map sitting here before we came along?*

"I think that would work," Cherkan said, holding out his hand.

"Thank you," Sumi said, breathing a sigh of relief as she shook his hand. The man's hand was equal parts bony and slimy, like a wet eel, but at least the deal was done.

"Follow me to my ledger," Cherkan said, "and we can get this wrapped up."

The next few minutes were a delight to behold, Sumi nervously pulling the coins out of their purse while Cherkan watched. He wrote up a bill of sale and had her sign the ledger, but then they were free, finally back out on the street with the map rolled up neatly in Sumi's bag.

You were most definitely not helpful in there, she thought. *Why did I bring you again?*

For protection or something? he asked. *Or was it my roguish charm?* Heat began to rise in their cheeks, but at least she couldn't slap him without slapping herself… *Alright, alright, I'm sorry,* he thought quickly. *It's just too cute when you squirm like that.*

You'll look cute when I push you in the river, she thought, though she thankfully chuckled right after. *Anyway, do you think that was too much money?*

Nah, Erso thought. *We don't need it that badly. Besides, our purse is ninety percent Berillai sovereigns, right?*

True, she thought, *though who knows how long we'll need to make it last?*

I'm sure it'll be fine, he thought. *Money's like a fish — eat it when you catch it or it'll stink up the place.*

Is that a real saying? she asked.

He was about to answer when a smell drifted over on the breeze and into their nose. It smelled quite a bit like the turned fish from his saying, actually, but before he could wrinkle their nose, Sumi got their mouth watering.

Ugh, what is that? he asked. She turned them in a circle, spotting a vendor that had wheeled a cart onto the street while they were in the shop.

Squid! she thought, walking quickly toward it.

I refuse to let you spend good money to put that in our body, he thought.

I thought it was my money? she thought back. Apparently unperturbed by spending when there were disgusting sea creatures to purchase, she quickly figured out the price and paid in Anushai again, walking away with two thick-looking squid skewers in hand.

You could wait, you know, Erso thought. *It'll only be a moment to pop back down the hill.*

No time, she thought back before shoving one of the skewers toward their face. He tried to clamp their mouth shut, but he basically just helped her take the first bite, the squid's head rolling into their mouth. He didn't want to fight so hard that they lost the transformation, but he did what he could, forcing her to swallow the squid head like a pill. Pleasure somehow still filled their mind, though their stomach at least did a somersault, torn between the warring factions in their brain. He was trying to squirm as she forced the rest of the first skewer into their mouth, when he suddenly felt another odd sensation near their stomach.

Do you...uh...need the privy? he thought, finally realizing what it was.

Oh dear, Sumi thought. *Um...yes. Oh gods above, I hadn't thought about that! Why didn't I notice sooner?*

He tried to get a look at the street as Sumi made their eyes dart around, their hands starting to sweat around the skewers.

Nothing to worry about, he thought. *I'm sure we can find a tea shop or something.*

Absolutely not! she thought. *I'm not doing that with you in here!*

Come on, he thought, chuckling, *it'll be fun. Besides, you owe me for the squid.*

Never! she thought. *I'd rather go in that ghastly privy on the ship before doing it with you in my head. Time to head back!*

She looked longingly for a moment at what was left of their squid but shook their head, tossing it in a rubbish bin as they jogged back down the street.

Surprisingly fast, your mother, Erso thought as they made their way back through the city gates. *Legs just a hair longer than yours, eh? Probably has a bigger bladder, too.*

I haven't forgotten about pushing you in the river, she thought, picking up the pace. The steep hill lengthened their strides, and before he knew it, they were back down in the copse of trees by the river, flashing back into their own forms. He patted down the sleeves of his coat, making sure everything was in order while Sumi sifted through her bag. She gave the map a once-over and jangled her purse.

"That was really something," Erso said, grinning.

"As much as I hate to admit it," she said, "it was sort of fun." She winked, turning quickly back toward the river — and the privy. As they reached the street, Parimu dashed toward them.

"Boat's leaving!" he yelled, waving for them to follow. "Told Captain Verasa to wait a minute, but he's not happy."

"Maybe he can hold the boat just one more minute for you," Erso said to Sumi, "keep the privy from bouncing around and all."

"Not a word," she said, pointing a finger in his face. She turned, catching up to Parimu while he strolled behind, laughing the whole way.

27

—:—

That night, Sumi lay awake in the boat, wedged into her little bunk above the mass of crates in the hold. She stared at the little map in the darkness, the moonlight from the porthole next to her just enough to see by. Her eyes traced the curves of the mountains. As unreal as those swooping black lines seemed on this old map, she had to believe they'd find what they were seeking there. She leaned back onto her pillow, opening herself to the songs as she stared out the window. The river slipped by outside as the boat chugged forward, the fields and the hills beyond all singing quiet lullabies.

Essomuai, she prayed in her mind, *teya sheyalm. I need you.* She wanted to stay present — needed to stay present — for the others, but she needed this magic so badly too. Without it, she was just some silly girl, running off to the mountains without a plan. This was the only thing keeping her hope alive — that the goddess would be on the other end, waiting to help her make sense of it all. Because even if she could face Vilodai, would she really emerge from the mountains strong enough to change Berill?

She thought of the Anushai and the incredible sigils they'd made in the sky. She'd seen glimpses of them in Elomikarus's memories, their shapes forever burned in his mind — banners the size of mountains, snakes that seemed to eat the sky. Her ancestors hadn't just changed the course of the battle that day, they'd changed the world forever. How would she ever do as much? Even if they had an unlimited supply of Shapewalkers, was it even possible to connect them like that? It'd just been her and Erso in their body earlier, and they'd still bumbled about like they had three legs.

Still, she smiled. What they'd done was incredible, at least to her. Not that she had these strange powers from Essomuai, but that the two of them could share a body without falling apart. Even with everything seeming to weigh on Erso lately, that seemed a truer testament to their love than anything they could ever say to each other.

She closed her eyes, listening to the songs again. Across the riverbank, there were thousands of crickets singing, Essomuai somehow carrying their songs through the water and the glass, past the din of the engine. This was life itself, singing for no other purpose than to fill the night with beauty. If she could sing even half as loud, the world had to hear her. *Let me be enough,* she prayed to Essomuai. She took a deep breath, preparing herself to dream, hoping more answers would come.

———

Sumi found herself in a dream, pacing along a wide strip of marble. As her own mind slipped away, she felt an immense pressure — so many things to worry about, so many heavy burdens. But of course, he was stressed! He was Lelman Geomongiar, the bloody Emperor of Anushai, and his problems were the stuff of life and death. He paced along the throne room, a single blessed moment of peace without his advisors breathing over his shoulder.

As he passed the middle of the room, he stopped, staring at the golden disc in the middle of the floor. It was a small thing, really, only a few feet across, and yet, it was the heart of his problem. The war was finally over for good. Elomikarus was dead, his children and followers sent across the sea forever. But now, how was he to remake his own kingdom? The people did not forget easily, and there were all too many secrets to hide.

Take this golden disc. The Elders had seen communing with Essomuai as so important that they built the disc into the bloody floor of the palace. But the goddess was a liability, a wet nurse with none of the strength needed to build an empire. But how was he to banish her from the people's minds without allowing them to lose the heart of what it meant to be Anushai? His plan had been masterful, surely, but there were still a thousand tiny details that could spell his undoing.

He still couldn't believe his luck with the Elders. He'd been terrified to deal with them, powerful as they were, but they had all just…left. Tudal, the first Empress and Mother of Earth House, had just woken up one day and abdicated. The city had grown too large, and she wanted to live in the countryside. It seemed they all preferred the days when they were just children by the river, listening to Essomuai sing. The others had left soon after, giving them this tiny window of opportunity. They had done the impossible, summoning Itorunai and destroying Elomikarus. Still, in doing so, they had effectively abandoned their own god.

But what was he to do?! Essomuai demanded softness from them, and softness meant death. He had seen the battlefields in the south — dead littering the field as crows feasted on the remains. Did they really think Elomikarus would stew in his shame forever? The Elders had sat by, passively humming their little songs while the world burned, and it had almost cost them the kingdom. It was only by luck that Elomikarus had lost his courage that day, and luck didn't last forever. So they had broken the pact with Vilodai, abandoning one peace in favor of another. He just had to make sure that this one lasted.

It wasn't as if they hadn't planned this well — if anything, their plan had been almost too perfect. Essomuai had handed them this chance, trapping herself and Vilodai in those damned mountains. She may be the blood of all things, but her heart was in the south, and it would take an incredible amount of focus to attune her now. More importantly, Vilodai was as good as buried in gold, the Voice forever barred from summoning another Elomikarus. The hard part wasn't stepping into this bold future they'd crafted for themselves, it was what to keep from the old. Oddly enough, the *values* of Essomuai still rang true — a little naïve, perhaps — but he did want this kingdom to stand for peace, a home for all people. But how to remind the people of that without reminding them *too* much?

The fountain had to stay, that much was obvious. Even this disc could stay once the new palace was built. The real change had to come from the heart of the people. They had to be convinced Essomuai was just…an *idea*. That was done easily enough with the commoners — they had no idea where the Shapewalkers started and Essomuai ended. All the humans wanted when they fled north was food and a warm bed. Still, that left him with over a quarter of the city. The soldiers who could sing wouldn't easily forget the sigils they'd created that day, though they, too, would age out eventually. What he needed most were the heads of the houses. If they wanted this to become the truth, they needed to lead with it.

He glanced over at the corner of his throne room where Itorunai's crystal tower sat. There were only a half dozen people who knew what it really was, and it would be buried with him in his crypt when he finally died — along with anything else that couldn't be allowed to stay in the kingdom. As for himself… The Elders had always said the dead returned to Essomuai. Would she forgive him for doing what he thought was right? What more could any ruler promise?

Still, damned or not, it was his burden, and he'd known he could carry it the moment they sailed for Esjeneyam. Even if he'd bought peace with his soul, it would hold as long as Itorunai kept her word. He wasn't as well-versed in the language of the gods as the Elders, but he had known well enough to form the pact. Itorunai had promised him endless wind and an impossible cold for Elomikarus's children. Wherever that hidden land was, it would hold them, giving the rest of the Continent a chance to live.

He took a deep breath, walking back toward the entrance hall. He would need to summon Huwalgiar to finalize the ceremony at the fountain. He chuckled — this had better work. If he failed, he'd have three goddesses competing to crush him like a bug. Still, he would carry on. There were still many steps to take on this path, and as long as he could walk, he would take them.

28

Upon the stone, write the sacred name. And around the cliff, facing the sea, build a cairn of animal bone. None must be hunted, only carefully collected from the forest, given the utmost respect.

-Sea Scroll #37
Estimated Date 655 PN

—:—

The days on the boat slipped away, like the water running past the hull, nothing holding them back as they blurred together. After Puyuln, there were still a few towns dotting the horizon, but eventually, as the captain had warned, there was simply nothing. There was only the boat, rising inexorably along with the foothills, which, even at their elevation, became taller and taller as the air grew thin and crisp.

Sumi stood on the railing watching the sailors move about. They really were friendly enough — besides Verasa — so long as you stayed away from their ropes and things. She'd found this place on the deck to be the best for her to stand in, the back left — or was it port…aft? — far away from anything even remotely vital or mechanical. She usually stood looking at the view, but something kept pulling her eyes back to the sailors.

One man passed her — Tulerin, he said his name was? — muttering to himself as he fumbled with a little silver tube on a chain around his neck. It was about the length of her thumb, though no thicker than a twig, with scrollwork along the sides. Ever since Puyuln, it felt like she'd seen at least one sailor doing the same thing every time she looked up. They

209

seemed to do it more in the evening when the sun was low as it was now, but it seemed to be increasing. She hadn't known nearly enough about Ekosinaran tradition on the wagon crew, but she knew even less about Alara. Would it be rude to ask? After Tulerin rolled the tube through his hands, he tucked it back under his shirt, never breaking his stride.

Just then, Erso came from below deck. He and Parimu had been working on something, though they didn't say what. He stopped at the top of the stairs, scanning the deck. When their eyes met, he seemed surprised to find her watching him. But where else would she be? She'd hoped things would get back to normal after Puyuln, but he only seemed more distant. Not that it was easy to tell, smooth talker that he was, but something was still off, like a wobbly leg on a chair you didn't notice until you sat down.

He strolled over to her, slipping between the crew members like a fish between rocks, nodding at a few as he passed. He joined her at the railing, facing toward the water.

"These blokes seem off to you?" he asked from the side of his mouth.

She turned, raising an eyebrow.

"Yes," she said, frowning. "But how can you already tell? I've been watching them for hours trying to figure it out."

"You, my dear, are a kind soul, and you probably just thought them delightfully eccentric. I assume everyone I meet would like to stab me — keeps me alert."

She rolled her eyes, turning back toward the deck as she tapped her chin.

"They're playing with those silver things a lot," she added in a whisper.

"*Sheweign,*" Erso said, nodding. "They're for luck."

"It's an Alaran thing?" she asked.

"Yeah, means 'life reed' or something. It's like…a flute, I guess? Get 'em when you're born, but they only play one note. Alarans swear they're all different, but how many bloody notes could there be, you know? Anyway, fondling them isn't any big deal; when they're really nervous, they'll start blowing on 'em."

"I know you'll say something smart about Berillai worshipping sheep or whatever, but…what's the point?"

"That's pretty good," he said, chuckling as he turned around. "Don't tell Parimu that one, I'll try to get him with it at dinner. But yes, it *is* a better tradition than lighting things on fire on the beach. Anyway, has something to do with fate — these blokes are as superstitious as the bloody Ekosinarans. They say the whistle speaks for the gods, tells you

how long you're gonna live and all that. So if I were a gambling man —
which, of course, I am — I'd say they blow 'em when they're nervous
to prove they're still alive."

The sacred breath, she thought, remembering the dandelion fluff in
Ageleat. She opened her mouth to respond, but the dinner bell started to
clang below deck.

They followed the men toward the kitchen, all of them pouring down
the stairs like a sad school of fish, a pack of tired — and apparently
superstitious — men ready for their dinner. Just like every night, Captain
Verasa stood by a giant pot in the galley kitchen, stingily ladling out
some sort of gruel to each man before they took their places at the long
table. She and Erso hung near the back, letting the crew eat first as
Parimu joined them in line.

"So, Verasa," Erso asked as they got to the front, "what's in the,
er…slop today?"

"Very funny," Verasa said, dropping a heap of grey sludge into Erso's
bowl with a thud. "It's rice. Eat it or don't eat it, I don't care."

There were a few quiet chuckles from the crew behind them, Erso's
real audience seeming to get the joke.

"Delightful," Erso said, accepting the bowl with a nod. "I'd hate to
see what you serve the passengers who don't pay their weight in gold."

"No such thing," Verasa said, dropping an eerily identical ladleful
into Sumi's dish. "You don't pay, you get dropped in the river."

"Thank you," Sumi said, smiling, receiving a grunt in return. They
took their spot at the end of the table, everyone eating in silence until
Verasa stormed toward his cabin with his own — substantially more full
— bowl, slamming the kitchen door on his way out. As soon as his
footsteps stopped ringing on the metal gangway, the others broke out in
a dozen hushed conversations.

"So," Erso said to Parimu, grimacing as he took a bite of the stew,
"any luck?"

"Some," Parimu said, smiling shyly. "Appreciate the help."

"What's this?" she asked, raising an eyebrow.

"Just a bit of training," Erso said, ducking his head as he took a nip
from his flask. He grimaced, shaking his head before tucking back into
his stew. She gave him a withering look, but he only shrugged.

"Better whiskey than whatever dusty pepper's in this sludge," he said.

They fell into their own conversation, talking about the scenery
mostly when one whisper, in particular, seemed to push into her ears. It
was in Alaran, apparently, the songs still in her mind.

"—going to the end of the bloody earth," Tulerin said. "It's bad luck to go where nobody else does, like your sails blowing the wrong way."

She met Erso's eyes, inclining her head toward the conversation. She opened herself to his song, knowing somehow that her whisper would come out in Amoriai.

"Men don't seem happy," she said. "Think it'll be trouble?"

Apparently used enough to her songs to not bat an eye at her Amoriai, Erso glanced toward them and shrugged.

"Sailors like to complain," he said. "And we *are* going pretty far. Going upriver like this, we're probably clearing about eighty miles a day, believe it or not. They're bound to ask questions, but I'll keep an ear open while we dice tonight, alright? Anything too dark from the men, and we'll fly the rest of the way."

She nodded, catching a worried look from Parimu.

"Anything I should worry about?" he asked, looking between them.

"Nah," Erso said, "just sleep with your shoes on if you know what I mean."

Parimu simply nodded, looking back down into his gruel without a second thought. Oh, to have a soldier's mentality! She went back to her meal as well, the mess hall slowly unraveling into the clinking of spoons, the boat still chugging deeper and deeper into the unknown.

29

All rivers north of the Great Fork shall provide free passage to any vessel, provided they fly under the flag of their home country at all times. Taxes levied upon goods shall not differ from those traveling by land and shall not be paid more than once provided they are conveyed with the proper forms and receipt of duties paid.

-Excerpts from the Treaty of Trilathdrei
Third Page, Third Paragraph

—:—

Three days later, long after night fell on the river, Sumi found herself above deck again, looking out at the southern mountains where they loomed in the darkness. They were drawing closer to the end, and just as Erso promised, the land had simply never stopped rising after Puyuln, the river now surrounded by peaks. The air had only grown colder, a thick dew appearing on the porthole each morning, the water rushing past a crystalline blue in the cold.

For the last day, their ship had been the only one on the river, and now, they were the only source of light beyond the moon and the stars, a single pinprick in the deep night. According to Verasa's maps, they would reach the end of the river by morning, her own map showing a thick knot of waterfalls that would send them the rest of the way on foot. Even without the map, though, she could tell how close they were, Essomuai's song growing louder in her mind, its rhythm seeming to pulse against her core.

She could just make out the trees that covered the mountains, tall and

213

sinewy with trunks that ran up hundreds of feet before the first branch, their canopies rocking in the wind. She couldn't see much beyond that, though she could still tell the forest was full of creatures. Even without the songs, hoots, screeches, and bellows filled the night, the voices of things she'd likely never seen before.

"Kuwaaaaa," came one long, mournful call from somewhere in the east. *"Kuwaaaaa,"* answered another from across the river. She closed her eyes, focusing on the sound as the cries echoed off the water. One of the sailors had called it the 'cry of the ghosts,' though Erso had said they were Mulakerri, the Shapewalking birds. The sailors seemed to keep a wary eye on the forest whenever they passed, some of them whispering about lost souls.

Where had they come from, and why did they cry like that? According to the stories, Itorunai had made the animals, but then, how had they learned to Shapewalk? Was it this place where Itorunai's breath ran up against the voice of Vilodai? Or perhaps it was the fountain, the strength of Essomuai's song teaching them to shape.

"Thought I'd find you up here," Erso said from behind her. She didn't turn around, hoping he'd embrace her from behind, but he kept his distance, his hands in his pockets as he leaned against the railing.

"Why do the mulakerri cry like that?" she asked.

"I'm not sure," he said, shaking his head. "Barely ever see 'em in Amoriai anymore. Though a buddy of mine, bloke named Ju'lal, thinks they only cry when a Shapewalker is near, like they sense the keyholes or something. He was in the woods once — south of where we took you — and he saw one in a tree. Said it was perfectly quiet until it looked right at him, making that same cry before it flew off as a hawk."

"Wow," she breathed, staring into the darkness. Every shadow seemed as if it could hold one, some phantasm waiting to wander the night. She shook her head, turning back to Erso.

"Done gambling already?" she asked. They'd been dicing and playing cards even later into the night the past few days, though he usually wandered by on his way to bed to check on her.

"Yeah," he said. "Big day tomorrow. Besides," he added, scratching his chin, "I was doing a fair bit of losing tonight."

"I'll do my best to ignore that last bit," she said, rolling her eyes. "Still, you're right about the other part. This is what we've been waiting for, whatever's up there." Her eyes wandered toward the south, in the direction of the mountains.

"Listen," he said quietly, his hand suddenly squeezing her shoulder for one brief moment. "I know I don't have the best track record with being flighty — and I promise I'm not trying to run — but…we don't have to go up there tomorrow. Just remember you have a choice. Even if you stop now, you'd still be the most amazing person I've ever met. Goddesses are great and all, but don't get chewed up and spit out for their games, alright?"

He sucked in a breath, shoving his hands back in his pockets as he turned to face the river.

She grew completely still, a pressure building in her throat. She believed him. Whatever he was going through, he'd proven he would stay. But she was beginning to recognize that strain in his voice too, knew how much it took for him to say something so serious. She was risking their lives, and she owed it to them to take the risks seriously, but she couldn't run away either, not without losing everything she'd built in herself.

"Thank you," she finally said, forcing herself to start with the most obvious words. "I know you won't run." She locked eyes with him, giving him a small smile. "And I understand why you're nervous. You're right to be." She looked to the south again, the point in the darkness where the songs began. "I'm nervous too. Just looking at these mountains, everything I've seen in my dreams, I can only imagine how powerful Vilodai is. But I have to go."

Somehow, as always seemed to be the case around Erso, the words began to come more easily, like the first time they'd spoken in that tavern in Berill. Whatever was going on between them, the truth never seemed to hide around him.

"It's funny," she continued, "I feel like I'm at this…crossroads in time. On the one hand, all these thousands of years of history remind me just how little I matter, but on the other, Essomuai still remembers. We could run off, live whatever life we wanted, but it wouldn't change that connection. The women on the Isles, even Elomikarus, all of our lives are links in this chain, even when we don't know it. For whatever reason, I can see it now, and Essomuai is calling to me, asking me to carry that chain to somewhere better, somewhere her people won't hurt so much. I still don't know if I can, but I have to try, even if it's only one more step. She's waiting for me, for all of us, and we have to go."

Erso turned, meeting her eyes. She stared back, unmoving, the glare of the ship's running lights glinting off those dark pools. His song played just at the edge of her consciousness, the memories she'd seen filtering up again. Of course, he would ask if it was time to run. All that time his parents had spent arguing in Amoriai, going back and forth about whether or not to flee — they would feel like precious moments wasted to him, their last chance to escape alive. He meant what he said about staying to the end, but how could he love someone again without trying to save them?

"Alright," he said, nodding. "We go."

He actually hugged her, pulling her into a tight embrace, clutching the back of her head.

"Whatever's up there, we face it together," he said from her neck, his warm breath tingling down her spine.

"We will," she said, squeezing him back. "We will."

___

The next morning, Erso found himself up early, pacing the deck as the boat fought against the rising current of the river. Lately, he'd been sleeping better than in those bloody tents. The sun took much longer to filter through the portholes, and the late-night gambling didn't hurt either... Still, this morning, he'd been wide awake before dawn. Or maybe he'd never really fallen asleep in the first place? It was hard to tell between all the tossing and turning, the difference between dreams and thoughts blurred beyond distinction.

"Oh, well," he said to himself, taking another long drag on his pipe. The morning was beautiful, at least, with the sun creeping over the looming green mountains. Besides, if you were going to face possible death, it was probably better to do it on no sleep, muddle the senses a bit. King Verasa was already up, along with the third of the crew that worked nights, the small man barking inaudibly from the cabin as always. Suddenly, the captain turned from the wheel, storming through the round metal door of the wheelhouse.

"You!" he yelled, pointing at Erso.

"Uh...me?" he asked, pointing a thumb at his chest.

"Yes, you," Verasa said. "We'll be at the falls in three hours, so make sure your botanist is awake. This current is hell on my engine, so you better be back here by the time we go downriver. I meant what I said about leaving you behind, understand?"

"Yes, sir," he said, making a sharp little mock salute off the brim of his hat. Verasa turned red as if he were about to pop, but all he did was nod curtly before storming down the stairs into the belly of the ship. It probably wouldn't do to get Sumi actually left behind, but she also hadn't brought him along because of his affinity for taking orders. That was more Parimu's department...

He was about to return to his pacing when he heard more steps on the stairs. Parimu appeared, the man looking neat as ever in his suit, though it was a wonder he could keep things looking so proper without shaping his clothes. He himself was, of course, far too lazy to brush a suit and shine shoes, though the end result was sharp enough. Parimu paused at the head of the stairs, his eyes quickly scanning the deck. Erso raised a hand, and Parimu nodded gratefully, stepping over as he pulled his own pipe out.

"Big day," Parimu said, packing his pipe. "Thought I'd have a smoke to calm the nerves."

"I think I'll have several," Erso said, nodding.

Parimu finally got his pipe lit, and the two men stood in silence for a while, plumes of blue and grey smoke twirling together in the air until they were snatched up by the billowing smoke from the ship's engine. Parimu was actually wearing his sword already, which looked slightly odd next to his suit, but at least the man was prepared — not that a sword could do much to a goddess… Still, it suited him, and it brought up memories of their fight in Anushai — a fight Erso would have almost certainly lost if Sumi hadn't stepped in.

"Say, Parimu," he said over the stem of his pipe, "would you ever consider teaching me a bit more of the sword? I can get by, but… Well, after that tussle with you, I wouldn't mind getting better."

Parimu blinked in surprise, his eyes shooting down to the sword on his hip and back again.

"Right," Parimu said, wringing his hands together, "sorry again about that."

For a second, he thought he'd have to keep the man from jumping off the boat, but then, thankfully, he grinned.

"To be honest," he continued, "I wasn't so sure which one of us had that fight. Still, I'd be happy to teach you what I know. We tend to lead with the cannons in the navy, but we did our share of sword drills."

He paused, looking around the deck as if he'd magically find a bunch of practice swords rolling about. He didn't exactly mean he wanted to practice this second, but this may be the last chance before they all died in the mountains…

"I'm fine using my cane," Erso offered. "Probably not worth shaping it in front of all these blokes, but it's firm and about the right length."

"Alright," Parimu said, nodding. "I can use my sword with the scabbard on. Probably good for me to practice with some weight anyway."

They both took a few more puffs on their pipes before knocking them out into the water and stepping into the wide space of the stern.

"To be honest," Parimu said, "there isn't that much I can teach you.

You fight with passion, and you can't teach that."

He glanced over his shoulder toward the belly of the ship where Sumi slept.

"Obviously, I know now why you fought that way... But out of curiosity, who taught you the sword?"

A face flashed through Erso's mind, a man with a dry laugh and an eyepatch. *Novash.* Those were memories he'd buried nearly as deeply as those of his parents, from the first time he left home. He was getting better at remembering his family, but some things were better off forgotten. He shook his head.

"Just an old friend," he said. "He was pretty good with a blade, but I'm not sure where he picked it up."

"Interesting," Parimu said, nodding. "Well, I've seen you fight twice now, and you can hold your own against trained men. Especially on that rooftop in Amoriai. Part of that is passion, but it comes from your speed too. You have a good head for knowing where your advantage is. When it was just you and I, your speed turned into a liability. I think we could work on controlling the pace of a fight after that first attack."

Erso looked down at his right arm, still feeling the phantom sting of all those silver cuts. It had been an absolute bear to get those to heal in the woods. Parimu was right, though... He'd always relied on aggression, swamping his opponent before they could properly react. It hadn't failed him yet, he supposed — outside of Parimu — but he'd always had enough smarts to know when to run, too. When it came to protecting Sumi, though, running wasn't necessarily an option anymore.

"That's good advice," he said, nodding. "What do you suggest?"

"We can work on your defensive parries," Parimu said. He held his sword by both ends, showing it to Erso. "You'll get a bit more protection from the curve of a cutlass, but it'll be the same idea with your cane. Anyway, the goal will be to hold the fight to a central point, working away my thrusts to score hits on my arm and slow things down. Sound good?"

He nodded, getting into his sword stance. They began to practice, going through every exercise Parimu remembered from the navy. It felt good to spar, letting the world fall away as he focused all his energy on the end of Parimu's sword. More importantly, he began to see what Parimu meant — controlling the pace of the fight with his parries, turning the sword and measuring his usual speed. He wasn't sure how much time passed, but sweat began to form on his brow. When they finally took a break, there was a little crowd of sailors standing by the stairs, watching.

"We wanna see who wins!" one of them called out in Amoriai, the others hooting and clapping.

Erso laughed, taking a little bow. He pulled off his jacket, grateful to finally be rid of the mountain chill for a moment. He draped it over the railing, and as he turned back around, Sumi was there, walking over with a smile on her face.

"You aren't actually going to start fighting each other again, are you?" she asked, crossing her arms.

"No, no," he said, waving her off. "Though, if we do have to fight again, I just want to make sure I win, right, Parimu?"

"Exactly," the other man said, chuckling. "Though mostly, I just want to make sure he survives any tigers we come across."

Sumi turned, looking up at the giant green mountain that had appeared on the horizon.

"Well," she said, "by the end of the day, we might have bigger things to worry about than tigers."

"Right," Erso said, no longer feeling much like laughing.

Heavy footsteps came banging up the stairway, a clear sign of Verasa approaching. The crew burst into a frenzy, all of them trying to escape the stairwell and look occupied, though it didn't seem to do them much good.

"You lazy barrel of rats!" Verasa roared, his voice eerily loud for a man his size. "Breakfast is on in the mess, so you got three options: get eating, get working, or dunk yourself in the damn river!"

The men began ducking their heads and scrambling below deck, off to eat more pitiful food. The past two days had been beans, which made sense given how Verasa liked squeezing pennies 'til they screamed. It wasn't much better than what they ate in the woods, but at least he didn't have to cook it. They were about to follow the crew down for breakfast when Verasa rounded on them.

"And you lot!" he said, thumping across the deck where he stopped, pointing upriver. "Your bloody mountain is up ahead, so don't sit around gabbing all day, alright?"

He glared at Erso as if challenging him to salute again. Luckily, Sumi, ever the ambassador, stepped in with a good deal more manners than the old goat deserved.

"Thank you, Captain," she said, bowing slightly. "We'll be back on time, I promise."

"You better be," Verasa said, "or pay up front so I can leave with the coin."

He stomped off toward the wheelhouse, the three of them slipping toward the mess hall. Something deadly could be waiting for them up in those mountains, but before death, it seemed there'd always be another bloody plate of beans.

30

Sworn truly and freely in the name of whichever god you so fear, the people of Umilai and Essomuai hereby sign to these terms on the 3rd Day of Tudammes (the 5th Day of Ruvarinan) to cease all hostilities in the name of a durable peace and a growing prosperity.

-Excerpts from the Treaty of Trilathdrei
Fifth Page, Final Paragraph

—:—

Parimu followed the others over the gangplank, a burlap sack over his shoulder and his sword at his side. The ship's cook had been nice enough to give them a bit of extra food from the kitchen, though they weren't carrying much else. They weren't bringing tents, which seemed a bit optimistic, but then again, Captain Verasa probably wouldn't have let them off the boat if they'd seemed too prepared to not return with their coin. The captain stood by the gunwale watching — along with the rest of the crew — though it wasn't long before the man was barking orders again. There likely wouldn't be much to do while they were in the woods, but he knew well enough from the navy the dangers of idle hands on a ship.

Sumi was in the lead, her antique map unfolded in her hands as she led them toward the tree line. The ship had stopped beside a sandy shoal some hundred yards downstream from the first waterfall. He looked over his shoulder, still able to see the top of the falls above the trees. It was probably to be expected — being in the home of the gods and all — but the falls were shockingly beautiful. They came from somewhere beyond

221

the mountains, the water pushing its way out from the middle of the peaks, the crystal clear water roaring as it crashed down in steps. Sumi had called them 'Vilodai's tears,' but to think water could have such raw power this far from the sea…

He shook his head, focusing on keeping up. They moved quickly across the clearing toward the forest, the same soaring trees they'd seen along the river clinging to any bit of space they could find as they climbed the steep green slopes. Once they were out of sight from the crew, Sumi stopped beside one of the spindly trees, holding up the map against the trunk.

"So, this map isn't the most detailed, obviously," she said with a nervous grin, "but I can tell the songs are loudest directly east, in the direction the water's coming from."

She took a finger, tracing a line around the nearest mountain.

"It looks like this pass will lead us up and around to this gap here between the peaks."

He leaned in, squinting at where she pointed. There did seem to be a sort of gap between the mountains, though judging by the crude elevation lines, the place was no valley — easily still a thousand feet higher than where they were now. Ahead of them, there was a sort of pass between the stone walls that seemed to match, wrapping around the mountain as it ran to the east. Erso looked between the map and the surrounding woods, shrugging his musket more firmly onto his shoulder.

"You don't happen to have any tiger dens marked on there, do you?"

"Quite a few, actually," she said. "I figured we could have you turn into a chicken and run past them as a distraction."

Parimu started to chuckle, but Erso simply stood tall, glowing as he turned into a large rooster. He took off up the ravine, leaving them behind as his bright red comb flashed against the forest floor.

"Well," Sumi said, rolling her eyes, "I guess we're off to a good start."

She folded the map, nodding before they followed up the ravine.

He stayed in the rear, his eyes swiveling around the woods as Sumi set a brisk pace up the hill. They fell into a rhythm, Erso rejoining them as a human as they marched in silence. It was a lot like marching in the navy, actually, his breathing the only thing that interrupted the birdsong from the canopy, his mind free to wander. Eventually, he thought of Jalicyne, her face always coming to him when his mind was quiet.

Still, Erso's advice really was helping. When he thought of her now, he didn't find himself recoiling with regret. He simply imagined her climbing beside him, her favorite goat leather boots making easy work of the ravine. At first, it had been strange pretending she was responding, but with a bit of practice, he didn't have to try so hard anymore.

He wasn't always as honest with himself as he could be, but it still set him free a little bit, preparing him for the moments when the truth really came. The first time he'd spoken to her, he'd apologized for not being there when she died, and she'd simply forgiven him. But the fifth or sixth time, when he told her he loved her, he finally had the courage to face what her true response would have been.

"I didn't love you back," she'd said, "not like that, though I'll always love you like a brother, Rels. I wouldn't be who I am without our days in the woods. I'm sorry I didn't wait for you to come back — to tell you that to your face — but I had bigger dreams in the city. The way things were with my mother…I just had to go. Still, I'm glad you think of me still, just as I think of you."

Funny to think of that bringing him some measure of peace, but somehow, it really did. He supposed he had known it all along, but it made him feel better knowing he hadn't abandoned her going off to the navy. Maybe things could have been different, and maybe they couldn't, but he was still glad he had spent so much time thinking of her. It had changed him in ways he could never regret. Now, he simply hoped that from wherever she was watching — whether from Erso's hallways or the bottom of the sea — she would watch over them.

"You'll look out for us, won't you, Jalicyne?" he asked.

She still focused on the path ahead of her, holding up her skirt as she moved over the leaves, but she turned, grinning.

"Of course, I will, you big oaf," she said. "Your mother would never forgive me if I let a tiger get you."

"Of course not," he said, chuckling to himself. "Thank you, old friend."

———

Sumi sat on a stump at the edge of the trail, catching her breath. If you could call the ravine a trail… They'd been climbing for a few hours, but with how steep the hills were, it felt like they'd barely moved at all. She was supposed to be the best walker in the group, but she suspected the others had called for a break because of how winded she was. Maybe it was the lack of sleep, but her cheeks felt flushed, and the front of her blouse was already damp with sweat despite the cold mountain air. She shut her eyes, listening to Essomuai's song as it echoed off the mountains.

"You look like a beet," Erso said, tapping her on the shoulder with the butt of their canteen. "How about a bit more water?"

She opened her eyes, shooting him a look as she took a long drink.

Even coming from Verasa's old rain buckets, it seemed to taste better than anything she'd drunk in her whole life.

"You really know how to flatter a girl," she said, tossing the canteen back to him — only slightly aiming for his head.

He caught it with a grin, offering her a hand up from the stump.

"Hey," he said, "you're the one who said you didn't want to be treated like a princess."

"Fair," she said, "but I was hoping for something more than a barmaid."

"Stablemaid?" he offered. She pushed him off the path before heading toward Parimu. He was a ways ahead, having wandered to the next rise in elevation to scout out the next stretch of the path.

"How's it look?" she asked, coming up beside him. "Impenetrable?"

He smiled, shaking his head.

"Not for you, I suspect," he said. He pointed to the next ridgeline, where things seemed to flatten out in a sort of valley before the final mountain. "It's still a good ways off, but that looks like the spot on your map," he said. "Might even be the source of the falls if my guess is right."

She followed his finger, nodding. If the land was flat there, maybe the Anushai had left behind some kind of shelter — though what would still be standing after so many years was anyone's guess.

"Well," she said, "I guess we'll know soon enough. Off to our impending doom?"

Parimu shrugged and smiled, motioning for her to lead the way as Erso caught up.

"Did somebody say doom?" he asked, passing them to the front of the line. "That's my specialty."

She followed him up the ravine, at least slightly less fatigued than before, though it wasn't long before she fell back into a sort of hiking trance. She kept her mind on the songs, unable to keep them out with nothing else in her mind but putting one foot in front of the other. Even when they reached a short rock ledge that Erso had to help her up, she was hardly paying attention. She took his hand, about to haul herself up when the ground began to shake.

Her hand slipped from Erso's, and she fell backward, hitting the ground as she tumbled head over heels. Erso was there in a moment, kneeling beside her as he covered her head, the mountain dancing around them. The trees shook, and one or two seemed to pop, the sound of splitting wood shooting from the forest like a cannon. She lifted her head, finding Parimu scrambling toward them, crouching beside them beneath the ridge.

"Look out for falling rocks!" he shouted over the din. With a great groan, part of the cliff a dozen yards downhill gave way, cracking as a huge clump of rock fell, crashing into the ravine before it rolled off into the trees. And then, just as soon as it began, the shaking stopped. The forest was completely silent for a moment before the birdsong finally came back as if the world itself had been stunned.

"What in the bloody halls was that?" Erso asked, lifting Sumi to her feet.

"Vilodai," she said without hesitation, her eyes turning toward the highest peak.

"Well, that's swell," Erso said, forcing out a chuckle, "knew there'd be something worse up here than tigers. Guess that explains the boulders blocking the path, though, eh?"

"Must be," Parimu said, still carefully watching the cliffs.

"At least it means we're close," she said. "Let's try to reach the top before the next one comes."

The others nodded, and they fell into line, scrambling back up the rock ledge as they continued up the ravine.

It took another two hours of climbing — this time with no breaks for fear of another quake — before the incline started to level off. Then, they walked through one last thicket of bushes, finally emerging into a valley nestled between the mountains. The largest peak was still thousands of feet higher, but the mountain they'd climbed around bled into it, wrapping the bowl-shaped valley in a tight embrace.

"Wow," Erso said, moving to the side as he pointed.

She looked down from the peak, stopping short as her mouth fell open. In front of them spread a wide field of wheat, arranged in neat rows, the golden fronds waving in the wind. And beyond that, there was…a village? She'd expected an abandoned temple or maybe some old stones, but not…this. There were a few dozen buildings, all of them in good repair. But more importantly, the wheat was far too organized to be wild, and if that were the case…

She turned toward Erso and Parimu, but they both just stared back at her. What about her dream of the Anushai emperor, hadn't he abandoned this place? Could it be populated by Alarans who had simply traveled too far south? The valley walls did cut the wind, and there was plenty of water and sun. But how were you supposed to run a farm next to a vengeful god that shook the earth?

"You didn't see anything about this place in your dreams, did you?" Erso asked, working the lock on his musket as he eyed the chamber.

She shook her head.

"Never anything like this," she said. "But…Essomuai would have warned me, right? Let's keep the weapons away for now, but be ready to leave in a hurry."

Both men nodded, and they stepped into the field, keeping to a narrow path that cut through the wheat. There was no one in the field, though the sun was already close to touching the peak of the western mountain. She kept herself just slightly open to Essomuai, enough to change quickly without losing her focus. At the edge of her consciousness, she could make out Erso and Parimu's songs, their rhythms like violins tuned too tight.

As they crossed the field, the buildings came more into view. They seemed to be made from stacked mountain stone with rough-cut glassless windows. As her eyes passed over the nearest building, something moved, a flash of color passing the window. Had someone seen them? At least no one had sounded the alarm…

As it turned out, no alarm was needed. When they finally reached the end of the field, they climbed up a short berm where they found the entire village waiting for them. There were some three dozen people arranged in neat rows with a short, elderly woman at their head leaning on a gem-laden cane. Some of the men in the back had bows, but they were still slung over their shoulders. The old woman was stooped with age, but she still raised the cane high above her head, calling out in a loud voice.

"*Huwen geolmannes etorisala,*" she said.

Sumi blinked. That hadn't been translated by the songs, but she could still understand it somehow. Strangely, it was like a cross between the high form of Anushai and the language of the gods — though it didn't put any pictures into her mind. It seemed to be a greeting, something like '*welcome, treasured friends.*' So there were still Anushai here? They certainly looked it, not to mention the keyholes shining off of every one of them.

"Thank you," Sumi said, bowing. She spoke from the heart without worrying how the words would come out on the other end, the villagers' songs rushing into her ears. "We have come a long way, called here by our mother, Essomuai. We do not wish to disturb your beautiful village, but we are looking for the Fountain and were hoping you could guide us."

The old woman looked startled for a moment, but she quickly recovered, her face smooth as she considered them for a long moment. Finally, she bowed in return.

"You are most welcome here, Daughter of Essomuai," the woman said. "We had begun to doubt if you would ever come. It has been many lifetimes since the Houses sent an emissary, and I fear our time grows short. The hateful one grows restless, and the Fountain may not hold. My name is Serunal, and I am Eldest here. From which child of Essomuai do you hail?"

Did she mean which house she was from? But if they still associated with the houses, did that mean Geomongiar had left them here on purpose? It would make sense, of course. You couldn't just leave the fountain unguarded, even if you were going to abandon the pact. But time growing short, the earth shaking... Perhaps things were more precarious than she'd thought. Not wanting to appear too unsure, she quickly gestured to her emerald pendant.

"I am a daughter of Saldal," she said, "and we thank you for your welcome."

"Please," Serunal said, sweeping a hand behind her, "join us. Rest in our village, and we will guide you to the cave."

With that, the woman turned, passing through the rows of villagers who turned and followed her.

"Didn't catch a lick of that, obviously," Erso said. "But I guess I'm game to follow if they aren't planning to kill us."

She looked at Parimu, and he shrugged, nodding.

"Alright then," she said, starting off after the villagers. They had formed two lines behind Serunal, leading them down a neatly organized dirt-packed street. They marched with their backs straight, though many of them glanced back at her, looking away the moment their eyes met. Eventually, they reached what looked to be the center of the village, where a wide building sat, taller than the others, with stained glass in its windows.

They marched straight through wide double doors in the front, stepping into a kind of dining hall. Six long tables stretched the length of the room, with a head table raised up in the front. It was rustic, like the rest of the village, but it also gave off the feeling of refinement for hosting important guests. Old iron chandeliers hung from the ceiling — albeit without any candles — and a blazing fire roared in a neatly tiled hearth along the left wall.

The villagers began to sit, quickly moving throughout the room as if their places were assigned. Oddly, they used all of the tables, sitting in pockets of five or six. A few of the younger villagers still scurried about, hanging giant teapots from hooks over the fire while Serunal climbed to the head table.

"Honored guests," she said, bowing, "please join me."

Sumi bowed as graciously as she could before leading the way up the center aisle, every eye in the room glued to them. Serunal pushed them into chairs on either side of her as the tea was served, the youths pouring a greenish liquid into short cups carved from dark mountain stone. With a nod from Serunal, the whole room began to slurp their tea, so Sumi hastily grabbed her cup. Like the porcelain Nela had always used, it had no handle, so she carefully took it with two fingers, raising it to her nose. It had a lovely smell, like flowers, and as she slurped it, it tasted almost sweet.

Once the tea was served, more villagers came through doors to either side of the head table bearing trays, covering the tables in baskets of hot bread and crocks of butter. The villagers began to tuck in, whispering among themselves, though they all kept looking toward the head table, their eyes seeming to drift unconsciously toward them before darting back. Serunal pushed them to take some bread, eating in silence for a while. Finally, as the dining hall fell into the calm buzz of conversation, the older woman scooted closer, speaking in a low voice.

"Excuse my impertinence, my Lady," she said, "but why is your retinue so small? I was surprised you arrived with so few — and foreigners besides. Have you come to shore up the fountain? We've kept up the rituals, but I fear we need more gold, and it seems you haven't brought any. Only I enter the caves, of course, as the law requires, but with my age, I haven't made the descent in some ten years. Still, last I saw the fountain… Well, surely you've felt the quakes. I'm not sure how long the sacred mother can hold with only part of her body in the cavern."

She seemed to regret saying so much, even with her voice lowered, pausing as she scanned the room as if checking for eavesdroppers.

"You can understand my not wanting to worry the others, my Lady. But I *am* worried."

Sumi nodded, staring into her tea. So, Geomongiar *had* abandoned these people along with Essomuai. But how could she break that to them? They'd stayed some two thousand years already, spending generations watching the fountain. She took a deep breath. No matter how uncomfortable it was, these people deserved the truth. That could even be why Essomuai had called her here. Once they knew the treaty with Vilodai had been abandoned, maybe they'd be free to leave.

"I'm sorry," Sumi said, "I came on my own. I'm not…an emissary, though I *am* here to answer Essomuai's call. She…wouldn't have brought me here without you in mind as well."

"Ah," Serunal said, nodding as she stared off into space. "So it is true. After all this time."

Sumi bit her lip, watching the older woman. She felt a surge of emotion from the songs, a sadness from Essomuai, and…love. Without thinking, she took Serunal's hand.

"She cares for you still," she said. "She hasn't forgotten."

Serunal looked up, placing her other hand over Sumi's as she smiled sadly.

"No, I suppose not," she said, squeezing Sumi's hand. Serunal nodded to herself slowly. "If you've come, then perhaps our prayers *have* been answered. We need only for one that can hear the mother. I suppose it need not be an Elder."

"You can't…hear her?" Sumi asked.

Serunal stared at her, pulling her hands back as if burned.

"I would never dare listen to the sacred mother, my Lady," she said, her voice rising. She glanced again at the room, where the conversations had paused. She shook her head, looking back before she whispered, "We feel her, of course, and some of the children hum the songs before they learn their place. But…the vow is *sacred*, my lady. Better to leave for the city like the forgotten than to break it. This is why we waited for an Elder, why I supposed you…"

She had thought of the songs as sacred in a way, but not as something forbidden…

"I suppose I am an Elder in a way," she said quickly. "My grandmother was the last princess of House Saldalgiar."

"Last?" Serunal asked, her eyebrows raised.

"Er…well, no, I—" Sumi began, not knowing how to add that tiny piece of bad news on top of everything else.

"Never mind," Serunal said thankfully, waving a hand. "Our grass acolytes will be pleased to hear it. You see, the last house to visit us before the weeping was Earth, and there has been quite a bit of contention as to who would come next."

She motioned with one hand at the tables surrounding them, calling out in the echoing voice she'd first greeted them with.

"Saldalgiar! Present yourselves to your sister!"

Five of the villagers stood from one side of one of the long tables. They each raised an arm, pulling back their sleeves to reveal a tattoo of the Grass House sigil, though a seemingly much older version of it. She bowed her head graciously before the Grass House members sat back down, laughing as they returned to their bread.

"Our numbers are no longer so great," Serunal added quietly. "The children are out playing in the forest, but even counting them, we have lost many over the years."

"What became of the others?" she asked, her heart skipping a beat. Had Vilodai…cut their numbers somehow?

"It happened slowly," Serunal said, shaking her head, "over generations. Some simply give up hope, assuming the Houses have abandoned us, which…I suppose you prove is true — not that the forgotten would ever be permitted to return to tell us." She took a deep breath, setting her jaw. "Still, this place is our oath, it is everything to us. We are the children who stayed. We are here to watch, to protect, lest another man seek to wield the power of the wrathful one."

She paused, meeting Sumi's eyes.

"If the sacred mother has brought you, perhaps you can fix the fountain in a way that we cannot. I suppose it's far past time she took things into her own hands. I will show you to the cave, but please, allow me to present the others."

Serunal moved on from Grass House, each group standing as she went through the paltry roll call. The largest number were from Earth — some eight in all. If the legends were true, it would make sense. Their house *had* supplied all the oxen to carry the gold up the mountain. And perhaps it was true…everything else she'd seen so far had been truer than she ever could have imagined.

"Well," Serunal said when she was finally done, pushing herself out of her chair, "I suppose we best not delay."

"No," Sumi said, standing, the songs pounding in her mind. "I think it's time."

31

We are finally free of the shackles of Alomus, though it pains me greatly to leave this place where we have built so much and labored so greatly. Still, we will do as our god commands and forsake everything we have known. I am filled with joy at our freedom, but a piece of my heart will always be at the tower.

-Sea Scroll #300
Estimated Date 0 PN

—:—

At a sharp wave from Serunal, the room burst into action, most of the villagers dashing from the dining hall. A few stayed behind to gather the tea things, but by the time they reached the street, the entire village was lined up again, somehow having changed into formal-looking robes in their house colors. Two men on either end had wide drums strapped to their chests while a handful of others held thick golden discs. Someone had apparently even run to collect the children from the forest, a gaggle of kids in tiny robes standing beside the adults.

They stood firm in their rows, though they seemed almost giddy, glancing at each other as they smiled. What would it feel like to practice a ceremony for generations, never knowing when an elder would come to see it? It would probably be like Umilai actually stepping out of the sea on Alomidiar. Serunal stepped forward, a woman handing her a shawl with a large Essomuai flower on it. She pulled it over her back, turning to face Sumi as she spoke in a loud voice again.

"We have an Elder among us," she said, "oh, children of Essomuai.

231

The Elders are closest to our mother, having set us upon this sacred task. For generations, we have guarded this place, and for ages more, we will stand until the sacred mother has no need of us. Lead the way now with honor, and take our sister to the cavern of our peace."

The villagers bowed low at the waist before turning on their heels in formation. The drummers beat out a rhythm as they marched from the village — *boom-clack-clack, boom-clack-clack* — striking the leather drumhead and the wooden sides in turn. As the procession passed them, Serunal motioned for them to follow, falling in behind the others. She hardly felt the part of an elder in her ragged traveling clothes, but it seemed she'd have to do.

They wound through the village until they left the buildings behind, marching into another large field on the eastern side. This one held corn, a sea of green stalks waving in the breeze. Above them, the mountain loomed, its black stone like Vilodai herself staring down at them. No one spoke as they walked, though the villagers began to hum to the beat of the drums. It sounded almost like Essomuai's song. Could they have somehow transcribed the forbidden notes and passed them down?

"Is this her song?" Sumi asked.

"Yes," Serunal said gravely. "It is our piece of the sacred mother, what we have vowed to sing and remember. That and…the last word she gave us through the elders, the word the children still hear when they are young — *set'oreimanilan*."

This time, the language of the goddesses filled her mind with images. She saw a woman sitting by the side of a stream, plants growing around her, flowering in all sorts of colors. As always, she somehow understood its meaning — to thrive, to live fully.

"Some have understood this differently over the years," Serunal continued. "It is part of why we are so few. Some have taken it to mean we are allowed to leave this place once the Elders…failed to return. Some thought it should mean we should continue to honor the treaty, as it is the best way to preserve life. I suppose, given the love our mother has for us, she meant for us to choose ourselves. Still…how could we abandon her? After all, it is only her sacrifice that traps the wrathful one."

Sumi nodded sadly, looking up toward the peaks. It did hurt to think of Essomuai trapped here, sealing Vilodai's power. But how much was Vilodai being held back, really? She thought of her dream on the Isles, the blue stones cracking through the earth to reach the Berillai. Perhaps whatever hold Essomuai had on her was still there, despite the broken treaty, forcing her to speak through the stones. Still, it did sound like Essomuai, allowing the villagers to choose for themselves. They were her children, and whether they stayed or went, she would want them to sing.

They finally reached the base of the mountain, the path narrowing as it left the fields to wind between rocky crags, a sheer stone cliff rising above it. There was a wide tree covering the path where it disappeared into the rock. Despite its shade, the ground beneath the tree rippled with golden light. Hundreds of tiny gold medallions hung on its branches, spinning in the breeze as they caught the sun. The villagers split along the middle, forming ranks along either side of the tree, the procession apparently gone as far as it would go. Each person put a hand over their heart, facing forward as they continued to hum.

The ground began to shake again as if Vilodai had sensed their approach. This close to the mountain, the tremors almost seemed to have a rhythm to them as well, though not exactly like the songs. It felt more like…a voice, like a thousand mouths speaking at once. It was deep as if the stones themselves were speaking, the entire mountain vibrating like a tuning fork. There was immense power in it, the rage of a goddess waiting for her below.

Serunal walked down the middle of the villagers, turning as she reached the base of the tree.

"We can go no further, Daughter of Essomuai," she said, spreading her hands wide. "As we have vowed, we will protect this place, and we will guard the entrance for your return."

"You mean you're not coming?" Sumi asked, her eyes widening. Serunal had mentioned her age keeping her from the cave, but she'd thought with an elder to help her make the descent…

"We trust the fountain to your wisdom," Serunal said, inclining her head as the villagers bowed on either side. "When a bearer of the sigil comes, even the first among us dare not enter the sacred place."

She opened her mouth to speak but shut it again. These people had given everything to guard this place. Even if there were words to convince them, what right did she have to ask them to abandon their vows? There was no turning back. She'd have to face this alone, even if the goddess burnt her to ash…

"Thank you," she managed to say, bowing in return.

Serunal turned toward the tree, reaching into its trunk where she pulled out a golden bracelet. She motioned for Sumi to approach, fastening it around her wrist.

"Wear this," Serunal said. "It holds the strength of our people, so even if we do not join you, you will not walk alone."

She nodded, her eyes wandering toward the end of the path where she could now make out a wide, dark opening at the base of the mountain.

"Serunal," she whispered, "I'm not sure what will happen in there. You know by now that the treaty is…broken. If I don't return, please take your people and leave this place. You've kept your vow, and Essomuai would want you to be free."

The older woman met her eyes, squeezing her hand.

"Fear not," she said, "the sacred mother is with us. Gold can be tested by fire but never melted away."

"Very well," Sumi said, smiling sadly. "Then I'll just have to see you soon."

She turned, walking quickly back to where Erso and Parimu were waiting.

"I think I have to leave you here," she said. "No one but an elder can enter."

They both frowned, eyeing the villagers as if trying to figure out how many they could fight before being overwhelmed.

"Sumi," Erso hissed, looking back at her, "we can't let you go alone. These people can chew rocks for all I care. If you need me, I'm coming."

"It's alright," she said, gripping his arm. "I think…I have to do this alone."

He looked deep into her eyes, searching her for something, but finally, he nodded.

"Alright," he said, "but I'm standing right here until you're back, I don't care how long it takes."

"I know," she said, smiling. She smiled at Parimu, squeezing his arm too before she turned, walking through the line of villagers. Their humming filled her ears, and she opened herself to the song beneath their song, taking in more of Essomuai than she ever had. Every song in the world seemed to rush in after it — the sky, the sun, the mountains, the world bursting with life. She paused for just one last second, looking at the beauty of the sunny valley in case she never saw the world above again. This was her protection, her golden light in the darkness. She turned, stepping between the rocks, the inky blackness of the cave pulling her toward whatever awaited her below.

32

*The third sister waited long beneath her bondage, her rage simmering
like a hot coal. How long could we have truly expected her to wait? Or
perhaps more truthfully, how long could any eternal Mind lay dormant?
It is only in our naïveté that we forgot this truth — stars know only
burning, and galaxies only collapse. My friends, it is only the watchful
who nurture the seed of life.*

-Excerpts from the Letters of Si'is Nîn

—:—

At first, the cave was completely dark, and Sumi cursed herself for not
thinking to bring a lantern. Serunal hadn't mentioned it, though, so
maybe there would be light further down? Or maybe they thought she
was more powerful than she was… Somehow, she found the courage to
continue, making her way with one hand along the wall. The mountain
was still shaking, but strangely, the ground beneath her seemed calm,
the tunnel somehow insulated from the vibrations.

She walked until the sunlight was gone, and then she walked some
more, the tunnel marching steadily downward. Her eyes darted about the
darkness, her mouth subconsciously whispering Essomuai's prayer
when she suddenly noticed a light. At first, she almost thought it was her
imagination, the tiny pinprick of light appearing like a star in the night.
She crept toward it, finally revealing a glowing blue speaking stone,
rough and jagged as it pushed through the ceiling like the ones in her
dreams.

She stared at it for a long time, the light like water after being lost in

235

the desert, even if it came from Vilodai. As she stood there, she found herself unconsciously trying to feel its song. It…didn't have one. There was a sort of vibration coming from it, though, as if it were echoing the shaking of the mountain. It felt like its voice was trying to speak to her if only she knew the words. She shivered, forcing herself to continue down the tunnel.

Once she passed the first vein of speaking stone, the darkness never returned, at least not fully. The gemstones were sporadic at first, but eventually, they were everywhere, their glow filling the tunnel with a blue haze. The air began to feel thick like a hot summer day, the mountain air giving way to something…more. She began to sweat but pushed on, time slipping away until she heard the sound of water. She hurried ahead, where she found a widening in the tunnel.

The walls were suddenly smooth, forming a sort of dome as the ceiling opened up. The fountain was nowhere in sight, though, so maybe it was a kind of…resting point? Looking to her right, she found the source of the water — a wide underground pool some ten feet across. Water trickled down from the ceiling in a little stream, collecting in the pool before it overflowed, disappearing into a dark cleft along the wall.

In the center of the water were nine large stones. Black and perfectly smooth, they sat just above the water as if they had grown up out of it. They were oval-shaped with a hole in their center where gems of every different color glittered. The voices of the stone seemed stronger here, their whispers clamoring for her attention. Memories flooded in from her dreams — the earth erupting around enemy armies, the power to shift the land on a whim. She shuddered to think of the destruction even as a temptation raised its head — she could remember what that power *felt* like, and it was absolute. If she took one of these stones, she could conquer the world, impose peace on those who would kill her kind…

She shook her head, clenching her fists as she forced herself to look away. These stones could never be used again. Conquering was no peace. Elomikarus to the Anushai, the Anushai to the Berillai, it was *violence* that had created this world, and only peace could end it — true peace. But those whispers… She could see now how easy the decision had been for Elomikarus, how tantalizing it would be to change the world at a touch when you felt so small.

She forced herself to continue down the tunnel, walking quickly away from the pool and its bright glow as she descended deeper. She walked for what could have been miles until she saw a light again, brightly shimmering in the distance. As she reached it, she found the ground leveling out, revealing an immense cavern so large she couldn't even see a ceiling in the darkness. Like the undergrowth of a strange stone forest, there were hundreds of speaking stones, waist-high and spilling from the ground in all directions.

She looked out across the rocky field of blue until she caught sight of a different color, a golden glow… *The Fountain of Essomuai.* It was just like the one she'd seen in Anushai, at once familiar and mystical, glowing in the darkness with its own light. It sat on a large golden disc, surrounded by the mirrors embodying the world: the snake, the tree, and in the back, the mirror of Essomuai, the beautiful woman standing taller than the rest. In the center was the prism, an impossible-seeming enclosure made of golden glass, and within it, the fountain itself, the pool-shaped altar where her ancestors had danced the forms.

Her eyes wide, she stepped into the cavern, the ground trembling again as the whole mountain thrummed with Vilodai's power. Still, it was like being in the center of a storm, her feet sure even as the vibrations seemed to enter her, pushing into her bones, her skin tingling with them. She ignored everything else and simply walked, following a tiny path between the speaking stones, her eyes glued to that golden light.

She reached the platform, pausing for a moment at the edge. Even more than the temple in Anushai, this *was* Essomuai, the body of her goddess, the most sacred place she would ever step. She took a deep breath, stepping onto the golden disc. The moment she did, the shaking seemed to stop, shrinking to no more than a whisper as Essomuai's song suddenly burst into her mind. She sucked in a breath, feeling the goddess wrap around her. Even after having heard it for so long, it was incredible, each part growing deeper as it unfurled into infinity.

"I'm here," she said, "I've finally come."

She stepped toward the prism. It was at least twice as tall as she was, far larger than the replica in Sky House, the fountain wide enough to hold ten Shapewalkers around it at least. The prism seemed solid, like a gemstone, but as she climbed the steps built into the base, she found a door built into the glass. She grabbed the handle, suddenly feeling the vibrations of the cavern again as they worked their way through the glass. She let go, staring at her hand as it tingled. How could Essomuai stand it? So much pressure, and for so many centuries…

She stepped through the door and shut it behind her, the stillness returning as she approached the fountain. There was water in the basin, absolutely still despite the shaking and glowing with a golden light. She looked up, finding the goddess's face directly across from her. She was just as stunning as in the palace in Anushai, smiling serenely despite how long she'd waited for someone to come. Sumi unconsciously smiled back, leaning against the rim as she looked into the water.

How was she supposed to use it exactly? She couldn't join hands as the elders had, and she didn't know the steps they'd used to dance the forms. All she had was the water. But if Essomuai was in that water… She took a deep breath, plunging both hands into the basin. The water was warm, though not like a bath, almost as if it had been set to the exact temperature of her hands. It also had a sort of buoyancy to it, like ocean water, though she didn't dare taste it.

The songs seemed to grow even louder, her body as close to Essomuai as she could possibly be. But how was she meant to *use* it? Maybe…it was like Shapewalking. She pictured her own pool, the one from her mind, and she imagined stepping into it, opening herself to Essomuai as if she were taking on a new shape. She felt herself floating as if the water were all around her. There was a brilliant flash, filling her mind with golden light, and she was gone.

As the burst of light faded, Sumi found herself in total darkness. It was almost as if she had no form, the water and the altar inexplicably vanished. Still, there was a kind of….*presence* pressing in on her, reminding her she still existed, like the golden light of Essomuai if it had an exact opposite. She began to feel something at the edge of her mind like a sandstorm of thoughts, memories, and impressions, all pressing for her attention.

As she listened, words seemed to flicker across the void in the goddess tongue, disappearing just as she began to understand them. Was this…Vilodai surrounding her? Terrified, she reached out for Essomuai. She still felt the other goddess, but she was distant, reaching her through a hazy mist. It was like when Parimu shot her with the silver arrow, only thicker and more oppressive. Suddenly, a memory came to her from her dreams, of King Rummon on the Isles. He had seen this same darkness when he touched the speaking stone. This was why she'd been summoned, why her people had built the fountain. This altar was a way to speak to Vilodai.

Before she could lose her nerve, she spoke as loudly as she could, unsure if she even had a mouth in this place as the words filled her mind.

Vilodai, she thought, *I have come. Please speak.*

The void began to shake, the same vibration from the cavern surrounding her, a hundred times stronger now as it filled her being. The memories flitting by the edge of her consciousness began to enter her mind, every scene familiar from Essomuai's dreams. Elomikarus, her people being banished, the winter on the Isles of Dawn, all of it seen again from the outside. Suddenly, there was a voice like an earthquake itself. The voice of Vilodai.

Eshernulam, the goddess said, speaking directly into her mind, more vibration than word. It was the goddess tongue, images almost forming at the edge of her consciousness, though they too seemed to be snatched away by the pressure of the void. Still, she found she understood, the meaning left behind in the wake of the vibration — *a peace that was promised.* Just as soon as that word disappeared, though, there was another. *Kelomayara,* the voice vibrated. *A treaty broken.*

Suddenly, Essomuai was there, pressing against the void, her song pushing through the darkness and the shaking of the mountain. *Dilaremusae,* Essomuai said in her mind, her voice somehow distinct from Vilodai's, as golden as her light, like flax and honey, the voice of someone she had always known. This time, she saw an image of women dancing around a fire. *Dance the dance that is,* it seemed to say. The dance… The same one her ancestors had danced to show Vilodai the shapes of the world, the dance that had first formed the peace.

She still didn't know exactly what it meant, but she let herself go, letting Essomuai pull her along through the veil of Vilodai's power. Thousands of images sprang up in her mind, memories of everything that had formed the world, the notes of the song suddenly given life. Golden light began to fill her mind again, pushing back against the boundary between herself and Vilodai. The light grew brighter, and she began to change, becoming a sweeping field of flowers, a tiny golden island in a sea of blackness. Somehow, she knew this place, this moment, Essomuai's memories feeding into her own. This was…the beginning, before Itorunai had made the animals, when Essomuai's flowers had first covered the world.

Essomuai's memories took on a life of their own as if she were a palette and the goddess a painter, new shapes appearing as time flowed freely, her memories converging on the golden field. Suddenly, beneath her, there were seeds in the ground, and saplings began to push up through the grass, growing into the towering trees of Vilodai's Heart, their branches swaying in an unseen wind. Birds began to flit through the air, landing on the branches as they chirped in harmony with the song. She was with the birds, and she *was* the birds, her own being somehow stretching into every form, her light mixing with Essomuai's as they created their tiny world.

Animals began to wander through the field, deer eating leaves from the branches and bees buzzing through the flowers, tickling her as they brushed against the petals. The song seemed to quicken with every note, the endless time Essomuai had spent in the beginning giving way to the chaos of the world. As the aeons slipped away, the memories seemed to condense, the air warping as the world changed. Suddenly, there were two humans in the field, a man and a woman walking toward each other. She couldn't make out their faces, their forms a swell of golden light, but they met in the middle, embracing as they were suddenly surrounded by children, the brief moments of a human life colliding together.

Vilodai began to rumble more violently than before, the void of darkness pushing at the boundaries of their transformation.

Searnulunraes, Vilodai said, echoing against her mind. The word had a circularity to it as if it dipped back in on itself and began again. Something about…*seeing before what has been shown.* In the stories, her ancestors had moved Vilodai to tears with their dancing, showing her a world she had never been allowed to see. But now, she seemed angered by it, the memories probably serving as little more than a reminder of the betrayal of the Anushai.

Suddenly, the field of flowers flashed away, and Sumi found herself reappearing as a rocky shore. She was both the beach and the water, her waves crashing in upon herself. As the light faded, she realized there were people there, walking up to the water with baskets in their arms. She knew this place, the black stone of the Isles stretching far in either direction. The people dropped their baskets as they played in the water, an earnest joy pulsing from Essomuai as they danced in the waves. Was she…trying to show Vilodai what she'd missed during her children's exile? It was a joyful moment, yes, but Vilodai only shook harder, the light bending against the darkness.

Peskotemuyanal, Vilodai shook, an image floating up of lava beneath stone, capped under the weight of rock. *Trapped,* Sumi thought in the human tongue, the word seeming to seethe with heat. Suddenly it all clicked — Geomongiar's plan, the villagers above, the speaking stones. The fountain wasn't just to communicate with Vilodai — it really had been used to trap her here. Everything Vilodai had done — the Isles, King Rummon, Umilai's Heart — all of it had been to free her people, to seek revenge for what had been done to her.

She reached out for Essomuai, holding those thoughts in her heart. As she touched the other goddess, she felt an immense sadness in return. Of course, Essomuai understood betrayal. Even as she tried to reach her sister with her beautiful visions, her people had abandoned her too. Even though she was in all things, the Anushai had left this giant piece of her heart in the cavern and never returned. Now, both sisters were forced to watch life and death spill out across the Continent, endless wars begun in their names being carried out in their absence.

As she touched Essomuai, it was like she could see the whole cycle before her, memories of pain and misery repeating as they looped back on themselves. Elomikarus, the Anushai — it didn't matter where it had begun, the hate they'd created was feeding on itself, and it would burn the world to ash if it wasn't stopped. It had taken Erso's parents, carved up the Continent, and taught the Berillai to fear magic. Even now, when they no longer spoke to Vilodai or even remembered her true name, the goddesses had never forgotten.

As if sensing their thoughts, Vilodai suddenly bubbled up with sadness, the emotion nearly overwhelming her as it churned beneath the rage. How was she supposed to hold back such a storm? She was just one person, a pitiful offering before all that pain. And even if Essomuai needed her to work the fountain, what could they offer Vilodai? She didn't need to see the lives she had lost, the children who'd suffered in exile. She needed to see her children's joy, the promise of what true peace would look like when they lived together. The goddess needed…someone like her.

Somehow, Sumi began to sing, finding her own body in that void as she sang the songs with her own lungs, her own lips. The notes poured from her, and as she sang, her body began to thrum with two powers, the songs and the earth somehow meeting within her. Her own memories began to lift from the song, passing through her mind, the blood and earth in her joining. The light flashed again, two figures appearing in a field of gold. They were familiar, the shapes of a man and a woman, only the woman had a glowing orb at her center. A…keyhole? Sumi reached out with her awareness and caught hold of the woman's face, finding Nela standing there, her face wreathed in gold.

The images began to move quickly, a single life sprinting by in the eyes of a goddess. Soon, the couple had a baby, and shortly after, the baby was grown. Their daughter, Sumi's mother, had no light in her center, but there was still a golden aura to her. A new man arrived, sweeping her in an embrace, and then, finally, a baby appeared with her own glowing orb for a heart. The baby began to grow, and suddenly her own form appeared as she knew herself to be, the streets of Berill rising up in gold as she stood smiling at the city.

Vilodai's shaking began to change, the vibration of the darkness evening out as a question pushed against her mind. *Serushalenomay?* There was an image of women in a line, each one younger than the last as they rested their arms on the women before them. *Daughter?* it seemed to ask.

"Yes," Sumi said, speaking in her mind. "I am yours and Essomuai's. Help me find peace, help me change them. *Eshernulam.*"

Eshernulam, Vilodai thought. *Eshernulam.*

The shaking shifted until it too seemed to vibrate in tune with her own song, her body feeling lighter in the void, like floating. The curtain of Vilodai's power seemed to back away, releasing its power until it was a vessel no different from the cavern. Then, there was only Essomuai, golden light enveloping her like a warm embrace.

Daughter, she heard again, but in Essomuai's voice. The golden light moved again, and Sumi's whole life flashed before her eyes just as Parimu's and Erso's had, the pain and joy all passing through the golden gauze of Essomuai's eyes. She wanted to laugh and cry at the same time, the light growing brighter until she was suddenly herself again, standing in the fountain with her hands in the water.

She raised her hands, blinking as her eyes adjusted to the light of the speaking stones. *Daughter,* she heard again in both of their voices. The cave was quiet now, but she could still hear Essomuai's song, and beneath it, the vibration of Vilodai's voice, still in her heart somehow, awakened from where it had slumbered.

She opened the door and walked out of the fountain, finding the mountain completely still. The blue stones seemed to fade for a moment, and suddenly, a brilliant blue light glittered on the ground in front of her. She knelt, finding an iridescent stone sitting on the floor of the cavern. Had that been there when she entered the fountain? It was like the stones from the pool up above, only much smaller, the size of a river stone with a brilliant sapphire in its center. Hesitating, she reached out and touched it, Vilodai's voice filling her mind.

Wellonashirah, the voice said in her mind. *We go together.*

"I can't," Sumi whispered, thinking of the weapons above, the horrible power of the stones that could break the earth.

Eshernulam, Vilodai's voice said, the stone beginning to vibrate, seeming to harmonize with Sumi's own song again, her skin prickling at the familiar echo of herself. *Wellonashirah,* Vilodai spoke again, *together.*

Somehow she knew this stone was different. Perhaps any stone could be a weapon with Vilodai's power, but the others had no sapphires in their center. There was an impression in her mind of an eye, the stone allowing Vilodai to see the world. This was much more than another speaking stone. If she took it, Vilodai would be free in some small way, finally released from the cavern, no longer trapped in her rage and misery.

Sumi nodded, standing with the stone in her hand. She reached into her pocket, where she had a leather band for tying her hair. She wrapped the stone in a simple knot and hung it from her neck, placing it next to her golden pendant. She listened in her mind, still hearing them both even though she'd left the fountain, the faint thrum of Vilodai gliding beneath the songs.

She opened her eyes and began to climb from the cavern, the tunnel no longer seeming so dark. She was the same, and yet, she had completely changed. She had no more plan than she had in the morning, no more clue of how to bring peace back to the world. But she had seen something true, something that couldn't be denied, a glimmer of possibility that spelled a hope she'd never thought possible. *Eshernulam,* a peace for all people. There was pain, and there was loss, but behind it all was a beautiful music, a strange harmony stretching over an ancient river of time. The stones of two gods — two sisters — hung around her neck, and she was their daughter, however humble, carrying them back toward the light.

—:—

They will emerge, like the sun from darkness, and they will shape the world as if the stone had turned to clay. The surging of their river shall rend the earth, preparing the steel for the unknown flame. Six sparks and a blazing fire, like stars in the ancient sea, united, the Voice and the Mind.

-Final Stanza
Chant of the Kerinin

THE END OF BOOK THREE

Dear reader,

Thank you so much for reading my story! It means the world to me that you decided to explore Wellonai with me, and I truly believe your commitment to reading has the power to change the world. If you would be kind enough to leave me an honest review, that would be incredibly helpful. As an indie author, knowing what you loved (or hated!) will help others find (or avoid!) this book.

If you'd like to follow me on Instagram, I'm at @jhtomen and love to hear from readers there, too. I admittedly don't post that often (working on new books for you!) but I will occasionally post cute pics of cats or talk about book launches. Thank you for everything you are and everything you do. May you always find hope and light in your own shape.

JH Tomen

www.ingramcontent.com/pod-product-compliance
Lightning Source LLC
Chambersburg PA
CBHW010742310726
48971CB00010B/2911